MAIGRET'S BOYHOOD FRIEND

AND

MAIGRET AND
THE WINE MERCHANT

When Maigret receives a visit from Léon Florentin he does not expect its purpose to be a serious one, for Léon had been the joker of the class at their old school, and although he had only seen him once since they had both left, Maigret remembers him well. But serious it really is, and Léon Florentin is not laughing now: his mistress is dead, and he wants Maigret to investigate the whole sordid affair. As things turn out, both the old schoolfriends are due for a surprise. . . .

* * *

The second story concerns Oscar Chabut, a prosperous wine merchant, who is shot dead after leaving a fashionable bordello. When Maigret questions Chabut's widow and his mistress, they both reveal, graphically, that he had been a man of voracious appetites, and that, basically unsure of himself, sexual conquest had to him meant power and self-esteem. Hints of blackmail, anonymous telephone calls and a mysterious stranger who persistently dogs Maigret's footsteps, all complicate a difficult case. Maigret is uncertain where to begin, because a man such as Chabut, who had had so many women, undoubtedly had at the same time created as many potential enemies. . . .

Also by
GEORGES SIMENON

★

MAIGRET RIGHT AND WRONG
(*Maigret in Montmartre* and *Maigret's Mistake*)
MAIGRET AND THE YOUNG GIRL
MAIGRET AND THE BURGLAR'S WIFE
MAIGRET'S REVOLVER
MY FRIEND MAIGRET
MAIGRET GOES TO SCHOOL
MAIGRET'S LITTLE JOKE
MAIGRET AND THE OLD LADY
MAIGRET'S FIRST CASE
MAIGRET HAS SCRUPLES
MAIGRET AND THE RELUCTANT WITNESSES
MADAME MAIGRET'S FRIEND
MAIGRET TAKES A ROOM
MAIGRET IN COURT
MAIGRET AFRAID
MAIGRET IN SOCIETY
MAIGRET'S FAILURE
MAIGRET'S MEMOIRS
MAIGRET AND THE LAZY BURGLAR
MAIGRET'S SPECIAL MURDER
MAIGRET AND THE SATURDAY CALLER
MAIGRET LOSES HIS TEMPER
MAIGRET SETS A TRAP
MAIGRET ON THE DEFENSIVE
MAIGRET AND THE HEADLESS CORPSE
THE PATIENCE OF MAIGRET
MAIGRET AND THE NAHOUR CASE
MAIGRET'S PICKPOCKET
MAIGRET HAS DOUBTS
MAIGRET TAKES THE WATERS
MAIGRET AND THE MINISTER
MAIGRET HESITATES

MAIGRET'S BOYHOOD FRIEND

and

MAIGRET AND THE WINE MERCHANT

★

GEORGES SIMENON

THE
COMPANION BOOK CLUB
LONDON

This edition, published in 1972 by
The Hamlyn Publishing Group Ltd,
is issued by arrangement with
Hamish Hamilton Ltd.

THE COMPANION BOOK CLUB

The Club is not a library ; all books are the property of members. There is no entrance fee or any payment beyond the low Club price of each book. Details of membership will gladly be sent on request.

Write to:

The Companion Book Club,
Borough Green, Sevenoaks, Kent

*Made and printed in Great Britain
for the Companion Book Club
by Odhams (Watford) Ltd.*
SBN/600871487
6.72/248

CONTENTS

*

MAIGRET'S BOYHOOD FRIEND

page 7

MAIGRET AND
THE WINE MERCHANT

page 153

MAIGRET'S
BOYHOOD FRIEND

*

*Translated from
the French by*
EILEEN ELLENBOGEN

CHAPTER ONE

THE FLY CIRCLED three times round his head before alighting on the top left-hand corner of the report that he was annotating.

With pencil poised, Maigret eyed it with amused curiosity. The fly had repeated this manœuvre over and over again in the past half-hour. At any rate, Maigret presumed that it was the same fly. It seemed to be the only one in the office.

Each time, it circled once or twice in a patch of sunlight, then buzzed round the Chief Superintendent's head, and finally came to rest on the papers on his desk. And there it stayed for a while, lazily rubbing its legs together, and looking at him with an air of defiance.

Was it really looking at him? And if so, what did it take this huge hill of flesh to be, for that was how he must appear to it.

He was at pains not to frighten it away. He sat motionless, with pencil still poised above his papers, until, quite suddenly, the fly took off and vanished through the open window.

It was the middle of June. From time to time, a gentle breeze stirred the air in the office, where Maigret, in shirt-sleeves, sat contentedly smoking his pipe. He had set aside this afternoon to read through his inspectors' reports, and was doing so with exemplary patience.

Nine or ten times, the fly had returned to alight on his papers, always on the same spot. It was almost as though it had established a kind of relationship with him.

It was an odd coincidence. The sunshine, the little gusts of cooler air blowing through the window, the intriguing antics of the fly, all served to remind him of his school days, when a fly on his desk had often engaged a larger share of his interest than the master who was taking the class.

There was a discreet knock at the door. It was old Joseph,

9

the messenger, bearing an engraved visiting card, which read: *Léon Florentin, Antique Dealer*.

'How old would you say he was?'

'About your age.'

'Tall and thin?'

'That's right. Very tall and thin, with a regular mop of grey hair.'

Yes, that was the man all right. Florentin, who had been at school with him, at the Lycée Banville in Moulins, the clown of the form.

'Send him in.'

He had forgotten the fly, which, feeling slighted perhaps, seemed to have gone for good. There was a brief, embarrassed silence as the two men looked at one another. This was only their second meeting since their school days in Moulins. The first had been a chance encounter in the street about twenty years ago. Florentin, very well groomed, had been accompanied by an attractive and elegant Parisian woman.

'This is my old school friend, Maigret. He's a police officer.' Then, to Maigret:

'Allow me to introduce my wife, Monique.'

Then, as now, the sun was shining. They had really had nothing to say to one another.

'How are things? Still happy in your work?'

'Yes. And you?'

'Mustn't grumble.'

'Are you living in Paris?'

'Yes. Sixty-two Boulevard Haussmann. But I travel a good deal on business. I'm only just back from Istanbul. We must get together some time, the two of us, and you and Madame Maigret ... I take it you're married?'

The encounter had been something of an embarrassment to both of them. The couple's pale green, open sports car had been parked near by, and they had got into it and driven off, leaving Maigret to continue on his way.

The Florentin now facing Maigret across his desk was more seedy than the dashing figure he had seemed to be in the Place de la Madeleine. He was wearing a rather shabby grey suit, and his manner was a good deal less self-assured.

'It was good of you to see me without an appointment. How are you?'

After the first formal greeting, Florentin, a little uneasily, reverted to the 'tu' of their boyhood. Maigret, somewhat grudgingly, did so too.

'And you . . .? Do sit down. How's your wife?'

For a moment Florentin's pale grey eyes were blank, as though he could not remember.

'Do you mean Monique? The little redhead? It's true we lived together for a time. She was a good sort, but we were never married.'

'You're not married, then?'

'What would be the point?'

Florentin made a face. His sharp, well-defined features were so flexible that they might have been made of india-rubber. His knack of twisting them into an infinite variety of comical grimaces had been a source of endless amusement to his schoolmates and exasperation to his teachers.

Maigret could not muster the courage to ask what he had come for. He was watching him covertly, finding it hard to believe that it had all been so long ago.

'I say, I like your office. I must admit I never expected to see good furniture in Police Headquarters!'

'So you're an antique dealer now?'

'In a manner of speaking . . . I buy old furniture and do it up. I rent a small workshop in the Boulevard Rochechouart. You know how it is, almost everyone is an antique dealer, nowadays.'

'Doing all right, are you?'

'I can't grumble. Everything is fine, at least it was until the sky fell about my ears this afternoon.'

He was so used to playing the clown that, almost mechanically, his features took on an expression of comical dismay. All the same, his face was grey, and his eyes troubled.

'That's what I came to see you about. I said to myself: he's the only one who'll understand.'

He took a packet of cigarettes from his pocket, and lit one. His long, bony fingers were trembling slightly. Maigret thought he caught a faint whiff of spirits.

'To tell you the truth, I'm a good deal bothered. . . .'

'Go on.'

'That's just the trouble. It's hard to explain. I have a friend, a woman. For four years now. . . .'

'You and she have been living together?'

'Yes and no. . . . No. . . . Not exactly. . . . She lives in the Rue Notre-Dame-de-Lorette, near the Place Saint-Georges.'

His stammering hesitancy and shifting glances astonished Maigret. Florentin had been noted for his easy self-assurance. Maigret had always envied him a little on this account, and also because his father had owned the smartest confectioner's shop in the town, facing the cathedral, and Florentin had had a walnut cake named after him. In time, it had become something of a regional speciality.

Florentin had never been short of money. However much he played up in class, he was never punished. It was as though he enjoyed a special immunity. And, when school was over, he used to go out with girls.

'Go on.'

'Her name is Josée. . . . Well, actually her real name is Joséphine Papet, but she prefers to be called Josée. . . . I prefer it myself. She's thirty-four, but you'd never think it. . . .'

As he talked, Florentin's mobile face never ceased to change and crease and twitch. It was almost as though he had a nervous tic.

'It's so hard to explain, my dear fellow.'

He got up and went over to the window, a tall, sharply-etched figure against the sunlight.

'It's hot in here,' he sighed, mopping his forehead.

The fly had not returned to its place on the corner of the report on the Chief Superintendent's desk. Cars and buses could be heard rumbling across the Pont Saint-Michel, and, from time to time, a tug, sounding its siren before lowering its funnel to pass under the bridge.

In Maigret's room, as in every office in Police Headquarters, not to mention all the other government departments, there was a black marble clock. The hands stood at twenty past five.

'I'm not the only one. . . .' stammered Florentin at last.

'The only what?'

'I'm not Josée's only friend. That's what makes it so hard to explain. She's a marvellous girl . . . the very best. . . . I was everything to her, lover, friend and confidant. . . .'

Maigret, struggling to contain his impatience, relit his pipe. His old friend returned from the window, and resumed his seat opposite him.

After a silence that threatened to become unbearable, the Chief Superintendent ventured a little gentle prompting:

'And she had a good many other friends?'

'Let me think. . . . There was Paré . . . one. And Courcel . . . two. Then there was Victor . . . three. And a youngster known as *Le Rouquin*—I never saw him . . . that's four.'

'Four lovers who visited her regularly?'

'Some once a week, the others twice.'

'Did any of them know about the others?'

'Of course not!'

'In other words, each of them was under the delusion that he was keeping her?'

Florentin, nervously tapping the ash of his cigarette on to the carpet, seemed to find this way of putting it embarrassing.

'I told you it was difficult to explain.'

'And where, in all this, do you come in?'

'I'm her friend. . . . I go there when she's alone.'

'Do you sleep at the Rue Notre-Dame-de-Lorette?'

'Every night except Thursdays.'

Maigret, trying not to sound sardonic, asked:

'Because that's someone else's night?'

'Yes, Courcel's . . . she's known him ten years. He lives in Rouen, but he has business premises in the Boulevard Voltaire. It would take too long to explain. I daresay you despise me for it.'

'I've never despised anyone in my life.'

'I realize it's a delicate situation, and that most people would frown on it. . . . But you have my solemn word for it, Josée and I love each other.' Abruptly, he added: 'Or rather, I should say, loved each other.'

Though careful to avoid showing it, Maigret was shaken by this use of the past tense.

'Are you saying that you've broken with her?'

13

'No.'

'Is she dead?'

'Yes.'

'When did she die?'

'This afternoon. . . .'

And Florentin, looking him straight in the face, said, in a tragic manner which Maigret could not help feeling was somewhat theatrical:

'I swear it wasn't me. . . . You know me. . . . It's because you know me, and I know you, that I've come to you.'

True, they had known each other at twelve, at fifteen, at seventeen, but they had long since parted and gone their separate ways.

'How did she die?'

'She was shot.'

'By whom?'

'I don't know.'

'Where did it happen?'

'In her flat . . . her bedroom. . . .'

'Where were you at the time?'

Maigret was finding it more and more awkward to use the informal 'tu'.

'In the cupboard.'

'In her flat, you mean?'

'Yes. . . . It wasn't the first time. . . . Whenever I was there, and the bell rang, I . . . it sounds despicable to you, I daresay . . . but I swear it wasn't like that. . . . I work for my living. I earn. . . .'

'Try and describe exactly what happened.'

'Where shall I begin?'

'At midday, let's say.'

'We had lunch together. She's a marvellous cook. . . . We were sitting over by the window. . . . She was expecting someone, as always on a Wednesday . . . but not before five-thirty to six.'

'Who was it?'

'His name is François Paré. He's a man in his early fifties, head of a Department in the Ministry of Public Works. . . . He's in charge of Waterways. . . . He lives at Versailles.'

14

'Did he never arrive early?'

'No.'

'What happened after lunch?'

'We chatted.'

'How was she dressed?'

'In her dressing-gown. . . . Except when she was going out, she always wore a dressing-gown. . . . It was about half past three when the bell rang and I took refuge in the cupboard. . . . It's a sort of closet really . . . in the bathroom, not the bedroom. . . .'

Maigret was beginning to find all this a little wearing.

'And what then?'

'I'd been in there about a quarter of an hour, when I heard a sound like a shot.'

'That would have been at about a quarter to four?'

'I imagine so.'

'So you rushed into the bedroom?'

'No. . . . I wasn't supposed to be there. . . . Besides, it might not have been a shot, but just a car or a bus backfiring.'

The whole of Maigret's attention was now focused on Florentin. He recalled that, in the old days, most of the tales he told were pure fantasy, almost as though he had been unable to distinguish between lies and truth.

'What were you waiting for?' Without realizing it, Maigret had addressed him as 'vous'.

'Why so formal? . . . Don't you see?'

Florentin looked hurt and disappointed.

'Sorry, no offence meant. What were you waiting for, there in the wardrobe?'

'It isn't a wardrobe, more of a large clothes closet. I was waiting for the man to go.'

'How do you know it was a man? You didn't see him, you say. . . .'

Florentin looked stunned. 'I never thought of that!'

'Was it because Josée had no women friends?'

'As a matter of fact, I don't think she did. . . .'

'Any family?'

'She came from Concarneau originally. I never met any of her family.'

15

'How did you know when the caller had gone?'

'I heard footsteps in the sitting-room, and the door opening and closing.'

'What time was that?'

'About four.'

'So the murderer was there about a quarter of an hour after he killed her?'

'I suppose he must have been.'

'When you went into the bedroom, where did you find her?'

'On the floor, next to the bed.'

'How was she dressed?'

'She was still wearing her yellow dressing-gown.'

'Where was she shot?'

'In the throat.'

'Are you sure she was dead?'

'There couldn't be any doubt about that.'

'What was the state of the room?'

'Much as usual. . . . I didn't notice anything wrong.'

'Any drawers left open . . . papers scattered about?'

'No, I don't think so.'

'You mean you can't be sure?'

'I was too upset. . . .'

'Did you call a doctor?'

'No. Seeing that she was already dead. . . .'

'Did you ring the local police?'

'No. . . . I. . . .'

'You got here at five past five. What had you been doing since four o'clock?'

'To begin with, I was absolutely stunned. . . . I just collapsed into an armchair. . . . I couldn't understand it. . . . I still can't. . . . Then I realized that I was the one they'd be bound to suspect . . . especially as that cow of a concierge can't stand the sight of me.'

'Are you telling me that you sat there for the best part of an hour?'

'No. . . . I don't know how long it was, but eventually I pulled myself together and went into a bistro, the Grand-Saint-Georges, and had three large brandies, one after another.'

'And then?'

'And then I remembered that you were now the Big White Chief of the C.I.D.'

'How did you get here?'

'I took a taxi.'

Maigret was furious, but his expression remained impassive. He went across to the door leading to the Inspectors' Duty Room, opened it, and looked uncertainly from Janvier to Lapointe, who were both at their desks. Finally, addressing Janvier, he said:

'Come in here a minute, will you? I want you to ring Moers at the lab, and ask him to join us in the Rue Notre-Dame-de-Lorette. . . . What number?'

'Seventeen B.'

Each time his glance rested on his old school friend, Maigret's eyes hardened in an expression of impenetrable reserve. As Janvier was telephoning, he glanced at the clock. It was half past five.

'What did you say his name was, the Wednesday visitor?'

'Paré. . . . The civil servant. . . .'

'In the ordinary way, you'd be expecting him to arrive at the flat about now?'

'That's right. . . . He'd be due just about now. . . .'

'Has he a key?'

'None of them have keys.'

'Have you a key?'

'That's quite a different matter. Don't you see, my dear fellow . . . ?'

'I'd rather you didn't address me as your dear fellow.'

'There, you see! Even you. . . .'

'Let's be going.'

He grabbed his hat on the way out, and, as they descended the wide, greyish stone staircase, he refilled his pipe.

'What I want to know is why it took you so long to make up your mind to come and see me. . . . And why didn't you get in touch with the local police? . . . Had she any money of her own?'

'I imagine so. . . . Three or four years ago, she bought a house as an investment, in the Rue du Mont-Cenis, overlooking Montmartre.'

'Did she keep any money in the flat?'

'She may have done. . . . I can't say. . . . What I do know is that she distrusted banks.'

They got into one of the row of little black cars parked in the forecourt, with Janvier at the wheel.

'Are you saying that, all the time you were living with her, you never found out where she kept her savings?'

'It's the truth.'

He was hard put to it to stop himself from bursting out: 'Stop playing the clown, can't you!'

Was it pity that he felt for him?

'How many rooms are there in the flat?'

'Sitting-room, dining-room, bedroom, bathroom, and small kitchen.'

'Not to mention the clothes closet.'

'And the clothes closet.'

Weaving his way through the traffic, Janvier tried to pick up the threads from these snatches of overheard conversation.

'I swear to you, Maigret. . . .'

It was something to be thankful for, that he did not address him as 'Jules'. Fortunately, it had been customary at the lycée for the boys to call one another by their surnames!

As the three men went past the glass-walled lodge, Maigret saw the net curtain over the door twitch, and caught a glimpse of the concierge. She was, in every sense, a huge woman, massively built and enormously fat. Her face was large, round and expressionless, and, staring at them, she resembled a larger-than-life statue or oil-painting.

The lift was cramped, and Maigret, crushed up against Florentin, found himself almost eyeball to eyeball with his old school friend. He felt terribly uncomfortable. What thoughts were passing through the mind of the confectioner's son from Moulins? He was making an effort to appear natural, even to smile, but was succeeding only in screwing up his face into a ludicrous grimace. Was he frightened, was that it?

Was he the murderer of Joséphine Papet? What had he been up to during the hour that had elapsed before his arrival at the Quai des Orfèvres?

On the third floor, they crossed the lobby, and Florentin took a bunch of keys out of his pocket, as though it were the most natural thing in the world. The door of the flat opened on to a tiny entrance hall, and Florentin led them straight into the sitting-room. Maigret felt as though he had been transported back fifty years or more.

The elaborately draped curtains were of old rose silk, held back by heavy plaited silk cords. A faded, flowered carpet covered the parquet floor. There was a great deal of plush and brocade upholstery, a number of table-runners, and, on all the fake Louis XVI chairs, antimacassars of lace or embroidery.

Near the window stood a velvet-covered couch, piled high with crumpled cushions of every colour, as though someone had very recently been sitting there. On a pedestal table near by, there was a gilt table-lamp with a pink shade.

This, no doubt, had been Josée's favourite seat. There was a record-player within easy reach, a box of chocolates, and a handy pile of magazines and romantic novels. The television set stood facing the couch, in the opposite corner of the room.

The walls were papered in a pattern of tiny flowers, and here and there were landscape paintings crowded with fussy detail.

Florentin, who was watching Maigret closely, confirmed his impression:

'That's where she nearly always sat.'

'What about you?'

The antique dealer pointed to a shabby leather armchair, that looked entirely out of place in such a setting.

'That's mine. I brought it here for my own use.'

The dining-room was no less conventionally old-fashioned, and conveyed the same impression of overcrowded stuffiness. There were heavy, draped velvet curtains over both windows, and dark green potted plants on the ledges.

The door to the bedroom was open. As Florentin seemed reluctant to go in, Maigret pushed past him. The body was stretched out on the carpet, not six feet from the door.

As so often happens, in such cases, the hole in the woman's throat seemed much larger than might have been expected

19

from a bullet wound. She had bled a great deal, but her face expressed nothing but pure astonishment.

As far as one could judge, she must have been a plump, kindly little woman, the sort normally associated with good home cooking, nourishing stews, and lovingly bottled preserves.

Maigret's glance travelled round the room, as though searching for something that appeared to be missing.

'There was no weapon as far as I could see. . . .' His friend was quick to guess what he was looking for. 'Unless she's lying on it, which doesn't seem very likely.'

The telephone was in the sitting-room. Maigret was anxious to get the necessary formalities over and done with as quickly as possible.

'You'd better ring the Divisional Superintendent first, Janvier. Tell him to bring a doctor. . . . After that, let the Public Prosecutor's office know. . . .'

Moers and his staff of experts would be arriving any minute now. Maigret would have liked a few quiet minutes to himself. He went into the bathroom, and noted that all the towels were pink. There was a great deal of pink all over the flat. He opened the door of the clothes closet, which was a kind of short passage, leading nowhere. Here was more pink, a sugar-pink negligée and a summer dress of a deeper pink. Indeed, all the clothes hanging there were of pastel colours, mostly almond green and powder blue.

'There doesn't seem to be anything of yours here.'

'It would have made things a bit awkward,' murmured Florentin, more than a little put out. 'There were the others, you see. . . . Ostensibly, she was living alone. . . .'

Naturally! There was an old-fashioned flavour about this too: a succession of elderly 'protectors', who came once or twice a week, each unaware of the existence of the others, and fondly cherishing the illusion that he was 'keeping' her.

But had she really succeeded in keeping all of them in ignorance?

Returning to the bedroom, Maigret began poking about in various drawers. He found bills, underclothes, and a jewel box containing a few cheap trinkets.

It was six o'clock.

'The Wednesday caller ought to be here by now,' he remarked.

'He could have been and gone. If he rang and got no answer, he wouldn't have hung about, would he?'

Janvier came in from the sitting-room.

'The Superintendent is on his way, and the Deputy Public Prosecutor will be arriving shortly with the Examining Magistrate.'

In any enquiry, this was always the stage that Maigret most detested, with half a dozen of them sitting about staring at one another, while the police doctor knelt by the corpse, making his examination.

It was anyway a pure formality. The doctor could do no more than certify death. For the details, they would have to await the autopsy. As for the Deputy Public Prosecutor, he merely held a watching brief for the Government.

The Examining Magistrate was looking at Maigret as though seeking his opinion, whereas, of course, Maigret had, so far, not formed any opinion. As for the Divisional Superintendent, he was all impatience to get back to his office.

'Keep me in the picture,' murmured the Examining Magistrate. He was a man of about forty, and must only recently have come to Paris.

His name was Page. He had worked his way up from an obscure provincial post, through most of the major provincial cities, to his present appointment in the capital.

Moers and his men were waiting in the sitting-room, where one of them was examining all likely surfaces for fingerprints.

When he had seen the official party off the premises, Maigret said to Moers: 'It's all yours. You'd better get on with photographing the body before the hearse arrives.'

Seeing that Florentin was minded to follow him out, he said:

'No, you stay here. Janvier, I'll leave you to interview the neighbours on this floor, and, if necessary, those on the floor above. You never know, they may have heard something.'

The Chief Superintendent, ignoring the lift, went down by the stairs. The house was old, but very well cared for. The

crimson carpet was secured by brass stair-rods. All the door-
knobs were highly polished, and beside the door of one of the
flats was a gleaming brass plate, inscribed: 'Mademoiselle Vial.
Corsets and foundation garments made to measure.'

The giantess of a concierge was still standing behind the
glass door of the lodge, holding back the net curtain with the
bloated fingers of her huge hand. As Maigret put his hand
on the door-knob, she moved back a pace, as though pushed,
and he went in.

She looked at him with such a total lack of interest that he
might have been an object rather than a person; nor did his
official badge, when he produced it, evoke the slightest response.

'I take it you haven't heard?'

She did not reply, but her eyes seemed to ask, 'Haven't
heard what?'

The lodge was spotlessly clean, with a round table in the
middle, on which stood a cage with two canaries in it. The
kitchen could be seen through a door at the far end.

'Mademoiselle Papet is dead.'

This at least did elicit some response. She did have a
tongue, it seemed, though her voice was toneless, as blank as
her face. But maybe she was not as indifferent as she appeared.
Was not that very blankness possibly evidence of hostility?
It was as though she looked out upon humanity through her
wall of glass, hating all she saw.

'Is that what all the coming and going is about? There must
be ten or a dozen people up there still, I should think.'

'What's your name?'

'I can't see what business it is of yours.'

'As I shall have to put a number of questions to you, I shall
need your name to include in my report.'

'Madame Blanc.'

'Widow?'

'No.'

'Does your husband live here with you?'

'No.'

'Did he desert you?'

'Nineteen years ago.'

In the end, she condescended to sit down, in a huge armchair that must have been specially made for her. **Maigret,** too, sat down.

'Did you see anyone go up to Mademoiselle Papet's flat between half past five and six?'

'Yes, at twenty to six.'

'Who was it?'

'The Wednesday regular, of course. I don't know their names. He's tall, going bald, and always wears a dark suit.'

'Was he up there long?'

'No.'

'Did he say anything when he came down?'

'He asked me if her ladyship had gone out.'

He had to draw the information out of her, a very little at a time.

'What did you say?'

'That I hadn't seen her.'

'Did he seem surprised?'

'Yes.'

It was exhausting, especially with that blank, fixed stare to contend with. Her eyes were as motionless as her gross body.

'Did you see him earlier in the day?'

'No.'

'Did you see anyone go up round about half past three? Were you here then?'

'I was here, but no one went up.'

'Did you see anyone come down, round about four o'clock?'

'Not till twenty past four.'

'Who was that?'

'That fellow.'

'Whom do you mean by "that fellow"?'

'The one who was with you. . . . I can't bring myself to call him by his name.'

'Joséphine Papet's real lover, you mean?'

That did bring a smile to her lips, a smile at once ironic and embittered.

'Did he speak to you?'

'I wouldn't even go so far as to open the door for him.'

'Are you quite sure no one else went up or came down between half past three and four?'

23

Having already said so, she was not prepared to go to the trouble of repeating herself.

'Do you know your tenant's other friends?'

'Friends! Is that what you call them?'

'Visitors, then. How many of them are there?'

Her lips moved, as though in prayer. At last she said:

'Four, not counting that fellow.'

'Did any of them ever meet? Was there ever any trouble?'

'Not that I know of.'

'Are you in here all day, every day?'

'Except in the morning, when I go out to do my shopping, or when I'm cleaning the stairs.'

'Did you, personally, have any visitors today?'

'I never have any visitors.'

'Did Mademoiselle Papet go out much?'

'Usually at about eleven in the morning, just round the corner to do her shopping. Occasionally, she went to the cinema of an evening, with *him*.'

'What about Sunday?'

'Sometimes they went out in the car.'

'Whose car?'

'Hers, of course.'

'Did she drive?'

'No, he did.'

'Do you know where the car is now?'

'In a garage in the Rue la Bruyère.'

She did not ask him what had caused her tenant's death. She was as devoid of curiosity as of energy. Maigret looked at her with growing wonder.

'Mademoiselle Papet was murdered.'

'Well, it was only to be expected, wasn't it?'

'Why do you say that?'

'Well, with all those men . . .'

'She was shot almost at point-blank range.'

She nodded, but said nothing.

'Did she never confide in you?'

'She was no friend of mine.'

'In other words, you couldn't stand her?'

'I wouldn't go so far as that.'

24

It was becoming oppressive. Maigret mopped his brow, and made his escape. It was a great relief to be outside in the open air. The hearse from the Forensic Laboratory had just arrived. He would only be in the way while the men were bringing down the body on a stretcher. He decided to go across the road to the Grand-Saint-Georges, and have a half-pint of beer at the bar.

The murder of Joséphine Papet had not caused the faintest stir in the neighbourhood, not even in the house where she had lived for so many years.

He watched the hearse drive away. As he went back into the house, he saw the concierge standing watching him exactly as before. He went up in the lift, and rang the doorbell. Janvier let him in.

'Have you seen the neighbours?'

'Those that were at home. There are three flats to every floor, two overlooking the street and one the yard at the back. Mademoiselle Papet's nearest neighbour is a Madame Sauveur, an elderly woman, very pleasant, very well groomed. She was in the whole afternoon, knitting and listening to the radio.

'She heard a sound that might have been a muffled shot about mid-afternoon, but she thought it was a car or bus backfiring.'

'Didn't she hear anyone going in or leaving?'

'I checked that. You can't hear the door opening or shutting from her flat. It's an oldish building, and the walls are thick.'

'What about upstairs?'

'There's a couple with two children. They've been away in the country or at the sea for the past week. . . . The flat at the back belongs to a retired railway official. . . . He has his grandson living with him. . . . He didn't hear a thing.'

Florentin was standing at the open window.

The Chief Superintendent asked him:

'Was that window open earlier this afternoon?'

'I think so. . . . Yes.'

'What about the bedroom window?'

'No, I'm sure it wasn't.'

'How can you be so positive?'

25

'Because Josée was always most particular about keeping it shut when she had a visitor.'

Across from the bedroom window could be seen a spacious dressmaker's workroom, with a dress form covered in coarse canvas, mounted on a black plinth, and four or five teenage girls sewing.

Florentin, though making a visible effort to keep smiling, seemed uneasy. That fixed, forced smile reminded Maigret of the old days at the Lycée Banville, when, as often happened, Florentin was caught out mimicking a master behind his back.

'You won't allow us to forget we are descended from the apes, I see, Master Florentin,' the weedy little fair-haired man who taught them Latin used to say.

Moers and his men were going through the flat with a fine-tooth comb. Nothing, not so much as a speck of dust, escaped them. In spite of the open window, Maigret was feeling the heat. This case was not at all to his liking. There was something distasteful about it. Besides, he felt that he had been placed in a false position, and was finding it impossible wholly to banish the past from his mind.

He had completely lost touch with all his old school friends, and now here was one turning up out of the blue, in a predicament that was delicate, to say the least.

'Have you seen our piece of monumental masonry?'

Maigret looked puzzled.

'The concierge. That's what I call her. I shudder to think what she calls me.'

' "That fellow".'

'So I'm "that fellow", am I? What else did she say about me?'

'You're sure you've told me everything, exactly as it occurred?'

'Why should I lie to you?'

'You were always a liar. You lied for the fun of it.'

'That was forty years ago!'

'You don't strike me as having changed all that much.'

'If I had had anything to hide, would I have deliberately sought you out?'

'What else could you have done?'

26

'I could have made a run for it. . . . I could have gone back to my flat in the Boulevard Rochechouart.'

'To wait there until I came the following morning to arrest you?'

'I could have left the country.'

'Have you any money?'

Florentin flushed crimson, and Maigret felt a twinge of pity for him. As a young boy he had been a kind of licensed jester, with his long clownish face, his jokes and his grimaces.

But, in an elderly man, the old mannerisms were no longer entertaining. Indeed, they were painful to watch.

'You surely don't imagine that I killed her?'

'Why not?'

'But you know me. . . .'

'The last time I set eyes on you was twenty years ago, in the Place de la Madeleine, and that, if you remember, was our first meeting since we were schoolboys in Moulins.'

'Do I look like a murderer?'

'A man may be a blameless citizen one minute and a murderer the next. Up to the moment of his victim's death, he is a man like any other.'

'Why should I have killed her? We were the greatest of friends.'

'Just friends?'

'Of course not, but I'm rather past the age for a grand passion.'

'What about her?'

'I believe she loved me.'

'Was she jealous?'

'I never gave her cause to be. . . . You still haven't told me what that old witch downstairs has been saying.'

Janvier was intrigued by the situation, which was unusual, to say the least. He was watching the Chief Superintendent closely, curious to see how he would handle it. Maigret was plainly hesitant and uneasy. For one thing, he seemed unable to make up his mind whether to address Florentin as 'tu' or 'vous'.

'She didn't see anyone go upstairs.'

'She's lying. . . . Or else the man must have slipped past the lodge while she was in the kitchen. . . .'

'She denies that she ever left the lodge.'

'But that's impossible! The man who killed her must have come from somewhere. . . . Unless . . .'

'Unless what?'

'Unless he was in the house already.'

'One of the tenants?'

Florentin seized upon this suggestion eagerly.

'Why not? I'm not the only man in the building.'

'Was Josée friendly with any of the other tenants?'

'How should I know? I wasn't here all the time. I have my own business to attend to. I work for my living. . . .'

This statement had the unmistakable ring of falsehood. Florentin, who had spent his whole life acting some part or other, now saw himself in the role of breadwinner.

'Janvier, I'll leave you to comb the building from top to bottom. Call at all the flats. Talk to everyone you can. I'm going back to the Quai. . . .'

'What about the car?'

Maigret had never been able to bring himself to learn to drive.

'I'll take a taxi.'

And, turning to Florentin, he said:

'You come with me.'

'You're not arresting me, surely?'

'No.'

'What are you up to then? What do you want me for?'

'Just for a chat.'

CHAPTER TWO

MAIGRET's original intention had been to take Florentin back with him to the Quai des Orfèvres, but as he was about to give the address to the taxi-driver, he changed his mind.

'What number Boulevard Rochechouart?' he asked Florentin.

'Fifty-five B. Why?'

'Fifty-five B, Boulevard Rochechouart,' Maigret said to the taxi-driver.

It was no distance. The driver, annoyed at having been engaged for so short a journey, grumbled under his breath.

Sandwiched between a picture framer and a tobacconist-cum-bar was a narrow cobbled alley leading to two glass-fronted workshops, outside one of which stood a handcart. Inside the other, a painter was at work on a view of the Sacré-Cœur, which was no doubt intended for the tourist trade. Judging from the way in which he was dashing it off, he must have produced them by the dozen. He had long hair, and a pepper-and-salt beard, and wore a floppy bow tie of the kind favoured by pseudo-artists at the turn of the century.

Florentin got out his bunch of keys and unlocked the door of the work-hop on the right. Maigret followed him inside, burning with resentment.

For Florentin had somehow contrived to tarnish his boyhood memories. At the very moment when he had turned up at the Quai des Orfèvres, Maigret had been watching the fly that had settled so obstinately on the top left-hand corner of the report he was studying, and reliving his school days in Moulins.

What, he had wondered, had become of the other boys in his form? He had completely lost touch with all of them. Crochet, whose father had been a notary, had presumably taken over his practice by now. Orban, plump and good-natured, had, no doubt, achieved his ambition and qualified as a doctor. As for the others, they had probably settled in various towns all over France, or gone to live abroad.

Why, among them all, did it have to be Florentin to cross his path, and in such very disagreeable circumstances, at that?

He had a vivid recollection of the confectioner's shop, though he had seldom been in it. For some of the other boys, those with money to spare, it had been a meeting-place, where they ate ices and cakes in an atmosphere redolent of hot spices and sugar, surrounded by marble and gilt-framed mirrors. According to the discerning ladies of the town, a cake was not worth having unless it came from Florentin's.

Returning to the present, he found himself in a dark, dusty room, full of junk, with windows that looked as though they had never been cleaned, and which consequently let in very little light.

'I'm sorry about the mess. . . .'

In the circumstances, for Florentin to call himself an antique dealer was worse than pretentious. God knows where he had got the furniture that was lying about the place, but it was all alike: old, battered, ugly, and quite worthless. The most that could be done with it was to repair the worst damage, and slightly improve its appearance with furniture polish.

'Have you been in this business long?'

'Three years.'

'And before that?'

'I was in exports.'

'What did you export?'

'A little of everything. Chiefly to the emergent countries of Africa.'

'And before that?'

It was a humiliating question. Florentin murmured uncomfortably:

'Oh! well, you know, this and that. . . . I tried my hand at all sorts of things. I had no wish to spend the rest of my days in the shop in Moulins. My sister married a confectioner, and they are running the business now.'

Maigret remembered Florentin's sister, plump as a pigeon behind the snow-white shop counter. Had he not been just a little in love with her? She was fresh-faced and cheerful, like her mother, whom she closely resembled.

'Living in Paris, one has to be up to every trick. I've had my ups and downs. . . .'

Maigret had known so many like him, up one minute, down the next, forever promoting some marvellously profitable scheme, which, in the end, collapsed like a house of cards. Such men were always within a hair's breadth of arrest and imprisonment. Frequently, though they might try to touch you for a loan of a hundred thousand francs to build a seaport in some remote territory, they would gladly settle for a hundred francs, to avoid the indignity of being thrown out of their lodgings.

Florentin had been lucky. He had found Josée. If the workshop was anything to go by, it was evident that he could not be making a living out of selling furniture.

There was a door at the back. It was ajar. Maigret pushed it open, to reveal a narrow, windowless annexe, bare except for an iron bedstead, a washstand and a rickety wardrobe.

'Is this where you sleep?'

'Only on Thursdays.'

Maigret could not now remember who the Thursday caller was, the only one privileged to spend the night in the Rue Notre-Dame-de-Lorette.

'Fernand Courcel,' volunteered Florentin. 'He and Josée were friends long before I came on the scene. . . . He's been coming to see her and taking her out for the past ten years. . . . He can't get away nowadays as much as he used to, but he still manages to find an excuse for spending Thursday nights in Paris. . . .'

Maigret was poking about in corners, opening hideous old cupboards, from which all the polish had been chipped and worn away. He was not at all sure what he was looking for, only that something was bothering him, some detail that had escaped him.

'You did say, didn't you, that Josée had no bank account?'

'Yes. At least, as far as I know.'

'You say she mistrusted banks?'

'That was part of it. . . . But mainly she didn't want anyone to know what she had, because of tax.'

Maigret came upon an old pipe.

'Do you smoke a pipe?'

'Not in her flat. . . . She disliked the smell. . . . Only when I'm here. . . .'

In one rustic-style wardrobe, there were some clothes, a blue suit, some shabby jeans, three or four shirts, espadrilles thick with sawdust, and one solitary pair of outdoor shoes.

The wardrobe of a squalid layabout. Joséphine Papet must have had money. Had she been mean with it, mistrustful of Florentin, who would not have hesitated to squander the lot, down to the last sou?

He had found nothing of interest, and almost regretted having come. After all he had seen, he was beginning to feel sorry for his old school friend. As he was making for the door, he caught sight of something wrapped in newspaper on top of a cupboard. He turned back, took a chair up to the cupboard, climbed on to it, and lifted down a square parcel.

Florentin's forehead was beaded with perspiration.

The Chief Superintendent removed the wrappings to reveal a biscuit tin, with the maker's name stamped on it in red and yellow. He opened it. It was tightly packed with bundles of hundred-franc notes.

'Those are my savings. . . .'

Maigret stared at him blankly, as though he had not heard. He sat down at the work-bench to count the bundles of notes. There were forty-eight.

'Are you fond of biscuits?'

'I like one occasionally.'

'Have you another box like this?'

'Not at the moment. I don't think. . . .'

'There were two, I noticed, of the same make, in the flat in the Rue Notre-Dame-de-Lorette.'

'I daresay that's where I got it. . . .'

He had always been a liar, either because he couldn't help himself, or just for the fun of it. He was for ever romancing, and the more unlikely the tale, the more bare-faced the lies he told. This time, however, there was a great deal at stake.

'Now I see why you didn't get to the Quai des Orfèvres before five.'

'I couldn't make up my mind what to do. . . . I was frightened. . . . I knew suspicion was bound to fall on me.'

'You came here.'

He still persisted in denying it, but his self-confidence was ebbing fast.

'If you won't tell me, the painter next door will.'

'You must listen to me, Maigret.'

His lower lip was trembling. He seemed on the verge of bursting into tears. It was a distressing sight.

'I know I don't always speak the truth. I can't help myself. Don't you remember how I used to have you all in fits of laughter with the tales I made up to amuse you? But you've got to believe me now, I beg of you. I didn't kill Josée, and I truly was hiding in the clothes closet when it all happened.'

He really was a pathetic sight, but then it should not be forgotten that he was also a born actor.

'If I had killed her, would I have come to you, of all people?'

'In that case, why didn't you tell me the truth?'

'I don't know what you mean. What truth?'

He was prevaricating, playing for time.

'At three o'clock this afternoon, this biscuit tin was still in the flat in the Rue Notre-Dame-de-Lorette. Isn't that so?'

'Yes.'

'Well, then?'

'Surely it's not so hard to understand. . . . Josée had completely lost touch with her family. . . . She only had one sister, married to a fruit grower in Morocco. . . . They're rich people. . . . I'm on my beam ends . . . so, when I saw her lying there, dead . . .'

'You took advantage of the situation to slope off with the loot.'

'That's a crude way of putting it, but just look at it from my point of view. After all, I wasn't doing any harm to anyone. . . . And without her, I didn't know what was to become of me.'

Maigret looked fixedly at him, a prey to conflicting emotions.

'Come along.'

He was hot and thirsty. He felt utterly exhausted, and fed up with himself and everyone else.

As they emerged from the little alley, he hesitated for a moment, then propelled his companion into the tobacconist's shop that was also a bar.

He ordered two halves.

'Do you or don't you believe me?'

'We'll talk about it later.'

Maigret drank two half-pints, then set about looking for a taxi. It was the rush hour, and the traffic was at its worst. It took them half an hour to get to the Quai des Orfèvres. The sky was a uniform blue. It was oppressively close. All the café terraces were crowded, and there were men in shirtsleeves everywhere, carrying their jackets.

His office, from which the sun had by now retreated, was comparatively cool.

'Take a seat. . . . Smoke if you feel like it.'

'Thanks. . . . It's a very odd feeling, you know, to find one-self in a situation like this with an old school friend.'

'Don't I know it!' grumbled the Chief Superintendent, refilling his pipe.

'It's different for you.'

'Well . . .'

'You take a pretty low view of me, don't you? To you, I'm just a slob.'

'It's not for me to pass judgment. I'm trying to understand.'

'I loved her.'

'I see.'

'I don't pretend it was a grand passion. We didn't claim to be Romeo and Juliet. . . .'

'I must confess I can't quite see Romeo skulking in a clothes closet. Was that a regular occurrence?'

'No, not more than three or four times. It was most unusual for any of them to call unexpectedly.'

'Did these gentlemen know of your existence?'

'Of course not!'

'Did you never meet any of them?'

'I knew them by sight. I couldn't help wondering what they looked like, so I hung about in the street, waiting for them to come out. I'm being perfectly frank with you, you see. . . .'

'Have you never been tempted to try a little blackmail? They're all married men, I presume, fathers of families, and so on?'

'I swear to you. . . .'

'You're altogether too ready to swear to anything. I wish you wouldn't.'

'Oh! Very well, but how else can I make you believe me?'

'By telling the truth.'

'I never resorted to blackmail.'

'Why not?'

'I was happy with things as they were. I'm not young any more. I've been a rolling stone long enough. All I wanted was a quiet life and a bit of security. It was restful being with Josée, and she took good care of me.'

34

'Whose idea was it to buy a car? Yours?'

'No, we both wanted one. I may have been the first to suggest it. . . .'

'Where used you to go on Sundays?'

'Nowhere in particular . . . anywhere . . . the Chevreuse Valley . . . the Forest of Fontainebleau . . . occasionally, though not so often, we'd have a day by the sea. . . .'

'Did you know where she kept her money?'

'She made no secret of it, as far as I was concerned. She trusted me. For heaven's sake, Maigret, what possible reason could I have had to kill her?'

'Suppose she was tired of you?'

'But she wasn't! Quite the opposite, in fact. The whole point of saving money was so that eventually we could set up house together somewhere in the country. Put yourself in my place. . . .'

Chief Superintendent or not, it was Maigret's turn to make a face.

'Do you possess a revolver?'

'She had one that she always kept in the drawer of her bedside table. It was very old. I found it a couple of years ago in a chest I bought at an auction.'

'Was there any ammunition with it?'

'If you mean, was it loaded, yes, it was.'

'And you kept it at the Rue Notre-Dame-de-Lorette?'

'Josée was rather a nervous type. I thought it would reassure her to have it close at hand in the bedside table drawer.'

'It isn't there now.'

'I know. . . . I looked for it, too.'

'Why?'

'I realize it was stupid of me. . . . I've behaved like an idiot. . . . The trouble with me is that I just blurt everything out. . . . I should have rung the local police, and stayed put until they arrived. . . . I could have told them any old tale . . . that I'd just arrived and found her dead.'

'I asked you a straight question and I want a straight answer. Why were you looking for the revolver?'

'To get rid of it. . . . I would have shoved it down a drain,

35

or thrown it in the river. As it was my gun, I realized it was bound to get me into trouble. And how right I was, seeing that even you . . .'

'So far, I haven't accused you of anything.'

'But the reason I'm here is that you don't believe a word I say. . . . Am I under arrest?'

Maigret looked at him uncertainly. He appeared grave and anxious.

'No. . . .' he said, at last.

He was taking a risk, and he knew it, but he had not the heart to do otherwise.

'Where do you intend to go from here?'

'I'll have to get a bite to eat, I suppose, and after that, I'll just go to bed.'

'Where?'

Florentin hesitated.

'I don't know. . . . I suppose I'd better keep away from the Rue Notre-Dame-de-Lorette. . . .'

Was he really so insensitive as to be in any doubt about it?

'Oh, well, it will just have to be the Boulevard Roche-chouart.'

In the narrow little windowless box at the back of the workshop, where there were not even any sheets on the bed, but only a shabby, old, threadbare, grey blanket.

Maigret got up and went into the Inspectors' Duty Room. Lapointe was on the telephone. He waited until he had finished.

'I've got a man in my office, tall and thin, my age, but rather the worse for wear. He lives at the end of a little alley in the Boulevard Rochechouart, number fifty-five B. . . . I don't know what he'll do when he leaves here, but I don't want you to let him out of your sight. . . .

'See to it that there's someone to relieve you on the night shift. . . .

'And arrange for someone else to take over in the morning.'

'Does it matter if he knows he's being followed?'

'Better not, but it's not all that important. . . . He's as cunning as a wagon-load of monkeys, and he's sure to be on the lookout. . . .'

'I'll see to it, sir. . . . I'd better go and wait for him outside.'

'I shan't keep him more than another minute or two.'

As Maigret pushed open the door, Florentin stepped back several paces, looking thoroughly uncomfortable.

'So you were listening?'

Florentin hesitated, then the corners of his wide mouth twitched in a rather pathetic smile.

'What would you have done in my place?'

'You heard, then?'

'Not everything. . . .'

'I'm having you tailed by one of my inspectors. . . . I warn you that if you make any attempt to shake him off, I'll put out an all-stations call, and you'll find yourself under lock and key.'

'You've no call to speak to me like that, Maigret!'

Much as the Chief Superintendent would have liked to tell him to stop addressing him in that familiar way, he had not the heart to do so.

'Where were you planning to go?'

'When?'

'You knew that there would be an investigation, and that you were bound to be a suspect. It wasn't very sensible of you to hide the money where you did. . . . Presumably you intended to move it somewhere safer as soon as you got the chance. . . . Had you already decided to come to me?'

'No . . . my first thought was to go to the local police.'

'You didn't consider leaving the country before the body was found?'

'It did cross my mind.'

'What stopped you?'

'I realized it would look like an admission of guilt, and I'd be laying myself open to extradition, so, on second thoughts, I decided to go to the local police . . . and then, suddenly, I remembered about you. . . . I'd seen your name in the papers, often. You're the only one in our form to have become almost a celebrity.'

Maigret was still contemplating his old school friend with an air of perplexity, as though he represented an insoluble problem.

'You have the reputation of not being taken in by appearances. It's said that you have a way of keeping at a thing until you get to the bottom of it ... so I was hoping you'd understand. ... I'm beginning to think I was mistaken. ... You believe I'm guilty, and you might as well admit it.'

'I've already told you, I haven't made up my mind one way or the other.'

'I shouldn't have taken the money. I did it on impulse. It didn't even occur to me to take it until I was on my way out.'

'You may go.'

They were both on their feet. Florentin hesitated, as though about to hold out his hand. Perhaps in order to forestall him, Maigret got out his handkerchief and mopped his face.

'Shall I be seeing you tomorrow?'

'Very likely.'

'Good-bye, Maigret.'

'Good-bye.'

He did not stand at the door to watch him go down the stairs, with Lapointe at his heels.

For no very precise reason Maigret was displeased with himself. With himself and everyone else. Up to five o'clock, things had jogged along at an agreeably indolent pace. He had enjoyed his day. Now it was spoilt.

The reports were still there on his desk, demanding his attention. The fly had disappeared, affronted perhaps at his defection.

It was half-past seven. He dialled the number of his flat in the Boulevard Richard-Lenoir.

'Is that you?'

It was what he always said. Absurd, really. As if he didn't recognize his wife's voice by now.

'Won't you be in to dinner?'

He so often wasn't, that she took it for granted that this was what he was ringing to say.

'As a matter of fact, I will. ... What are we having? ... Good. ... Good. ... In about half an hour.'

He went into the Duty Room. Most of the inspectors had gone. He sat at Janvier's desk, and scribbled a message on his pad, for him to ring him at home as soon as he got back.

He was still feeling vaguely uneasy. There were a number of puzzling features about this case, and the fact that Florentin was, in some sense, an old friend didn't make things any easier.

And then there were the others, middle-aged men of some standing, each with a life of his own, regular habits, and a stable family background.

Except for one day a week! Except for ˛ ose few furtive hours in Joséphine Papet's flat.

Tomorrow, the newspapers would be full of the story, and they would all shake in their shoes.

He ought to go up to the attics, to Criminal Records, and find out how Moers was getting on. With a shrug, he stood up and took his hat from its hook.

'Se˛ you tomorrow.'

'Good night, sir.'

He fought his way through the evening crowds as far as the Châtelet, and there joined the queue waiting for his bus.

As soon as he came in, Madame Maigret could see that he had something on his mind, and he read the unspoken question in her glance.

'A wretched business!' he grumbled, as he went out to the bathroom to wash his hands.

He took off his jacket, and loosened his tie a little.

'I was at school with the fellow, and now he's up to his neck in this ghastly mess. And frankly, I can't see anyone having the slightest sympathy for him in his predicament!'

'What is it, a murder?'

'A shooting . . . the woman is dead.'

'What motive? Jealousy?'

'No, not if he did it.'

'Is there any doubt about it?'

'Let's eat.' He sighed, as though he had had more than enough of the subject.

All the windows were open, and the room was bathed in the golden light of the setting sun. There was chicken with tarragon, which Madame Maigret cooked to perfection, garnished with asparagus tips.

She had on a cotton housecoat printed all over with little

flowers. It was one of several that she was fond of wearing at home. He felt tonight that it enhanced the domestic intimacy of their dinner together.

'Will you have to go out again?'

'I don't think so. I left a message for Janvier to ring me.'

Just as he was digging his spoon into his half-melon, the telephone rang.

'Hello, yes. . . . Oh! It's you, Janvier. . . . Are you at the Quai? . . . Anything to report?'

'Very little, sir. . . . First of all, I went into the two shops on the ground floor. . . . You remember, there's a lingerie shop on the left. . . . Chez Éliane. . . . Very fancy stuff . . . the sort of thing you usually only find in Montmartre. . . . Apparently the tourists are crazy about it.

'It's owned by two girls, one dark, one fair, and they seem to spend most of their time watching the comings and goings in the building. They had no difficulty in recognizing Florentin and the dead woman from my description. . . . She was a customer of theirs . . . though she didn't go in for any of the fancy stuff.

'According to them, she was a charming woman, even-tempered, always ready with a smile. Very much the little housewife . . . extremely neat in her person, and very kind-hearted.

'They knew about her and Florentin, and they thought a lot of him, too. He struck them as quite the gentleman . . . a gentleman down on his luck was how they put it.

'They saw Josée go out with the Wednesday visitor one evening, but they didn't think any the worse of her for that. . . .'

'François Paré, do you mean? The Ministry of Public Works man?'

'I presume so. . . . Anyway, that's how they found out about his weekly visits. He always arrived in a black Citroën, punctual almost to the minute, except that he could never find anywhere to park. And, invariably, he came armed with a box of fancy cakes.'

'Do they know about the other men, too?'

'Only the Thursday one. . . . He was the very first. . . .

He's been coming to the Rue Notre-Dame-de-Lorette for years. . . . Some time in the distant past, they think, he actually lived in the flat for several weeks. They call him Fatty . . . he has round, pink cheeks, like a baby, and pale, protuberant eyes.

'Almost every Thursday, he took her out to dinner and the theatre. . . . In the ordinary way, he would have spent tomorrow night in the flat. . . . Quite often, he didn't leave until lunch-time the following day.'

Maigret consulted his notes.

'That would be Fernand Courcel of Rouen. . . . He has an office in Paris, Boulevard Voltaire. . . . What about the others?'

'The didn't mention them, but they're convinced Florentin is the one she was deceiving.'

'And what else?'

'Next, I went into the shoe shop opposite, Chaussures Martin. . . . It's a dark, narrow little place. . . . You can't see into the street, because of the window display, though there is a glass door, if you should happen to be looking out.'

'Go on. . . .'

'The flat on the left on the first floor belongs to a dentist. . . . He doesn't know a thing. . . . Josée went to him for treatment about four years ago . . . a filling . . . she had three appointments. . . . On the right, there's an old couple who are practically housebound. . . . The husband used to work for the Banque de France, I don't know in what capacity. They have one married daughter, who comes to see them every Sunday, with her husband and two children.

'Then there's the flat overlooking the courtyard. . . . It's empty at present. The tenants, a man and wife, have been in Italy for the past month. They're both in the catering trade.

'On the second floor there's the woman who makes corsets. She has two girls working for her. . . . None of them had ever heard of Joséphine Papet.

'Across the way there's a woman with three children, all under five. . . . She's got a voice like a foghorn, and no wonder, considering the row those kids make.

'"It's disgusting," she said, "I've written to the landlord

41

about it. My husband was against it, but I wrote all the same. . . . He's scared stiff of making trouble. . . . Carrying on like that in a respectable house, with children about! It was a different man almost every night. . . . I got to know which was which by the way they rang the bell.

'"The one with the limp always came on Saturdays, straight after lunch. . . . You could tell him by his walk. . . . Besides, he always jabbed at the bell four or five times in quick succession. Poor fool, he probably thought he was the only one."'

'Were you able to find out anything more about him?'

'Only that he's a man of about fifty, and always came by taxi.'

'What about *Le Rouquin*?'

'He's a new boy. . . . He put in his first appearance only a few weeks ago. He's younger than the others, thirty to thirty-five, and it seems he takes the stairs four at a time.'

'Has he a key?'

'No, none of them had except Florentin. . . . According to my informant on the second floor, he's just a high-class pimp.

'"I'd rather have those you see round about the Pigalle any day," she said. "They at least are taking a risk. . . . And anyway, they're not fit for any other sort of work. . . . But he looks as if he's seen better days, and seems to be a man of some education."'

Maigret could not help smiling. He rather regretted not having interviewed the tenants himself.

'There was no answer from the flat opposite, so I went up to the fourth floor, and there I walked straight into the middle of a family row.

'The husband was yelling at the top of his voice: "If you don't tell me where you've been and who with . . ."

'"Surely, I've a perfect right to go out and do my shopping, without having to give you a detailed account of every shop I've been into! What do you expect me to do, get a certificate from the manager wherever I go?"

'"You don't expect me to believe you spent the whole afternoon buying a pair of shoes! Who were you with? Answer me, will you!"

'" I don't know what you are talking about."

'"You must have gone to meet someone. Who was it?"'

'Frankly, I thought I'd better make myself scarce,' commented Janvier.

'There's an old woman living opposite. It's amazing the number of old people there are in that district. She could tell me nothing. She's pretty deaf, and the flat smells of stale food.

'As a last resort, I had a go at the concierge. . . . She just stared at me with those fish-eyes of hers, and I couldn't get a thing out of her. . . .'

'Nor could I, if that's any consolation . . . except that, according to her, no one went up to the flat between three and four o'clock.'

'Is she quite sure?'

'So she says. . . . She also says that she was in the lodge the whole time, and that no one could have gone past without her seeing them. . . . That's her story, and it's my belief she'll stick to it, even on oath.'

'What shall I do next?'

'Go home. I'll see you tomorrow in the office.'

'Good night, sir.'

Maigret, his melon still untasted, scarcely had time to put the receiver down when the telephone rang again. This time it was Lapointe. He seemed excited.

'I've been trying to get through to you for the last quarter of an hour, sir, but it was engaged the whole time. Before that, I tried the Quai. . . . I'm speaking from the tobacconist's on the corner. . . . There have been developments, sir. . . .'

'Go on.'

'Before we were even out of the building he knew he was being tailed. He actually turned round and winked at me as we were going down the stairs. . . .

'Outside I followed about three or four yards behind him. When we got to the Place Dauphine, he seemed to hesitate, and then went towards the Brasserie Dauphine. . . . He looked at me as though he expected me to catch him up, and when I didn't, he came up and spoke to me.

'"Look here, I'm going in for a drink. . . . I don't see any reason why you shouldn't join me, do you?"'

'I had the feeling that he was taking the mickey. He's a bit of a clown, isn't he? I said I didn't drink on duty, so he went in alone. I watched him gulp down three or four brandies, one after the other. . . . I'm not quite sure how many.

'When he came out, having satisfied himself that I was still there, he gave me another wink, and started off towards the Pont-Neuf. The streets were very crowded at that hour, and the cars were jammed nose to tail, with every other driver leaning on his horn. . . .

'We walked in single file as far as the Quai de la Mégisserie, and then, suddenly, he pulled himself up on to the parapet and jumped into the Seine! It all happened so quickly that only those few people nearest to him saw him do it.

'He came up within no more than a couple of yards of a boat made fast to the bank. . . . By that time there was quite a crowd gathered. . . . Then something almost comical happened. . . . The owner of the boat took hold of a long, heavy boathook and held it out to Florentin, who grabbed hold of the hook end, and allowed himself to be hauled in like a fish!

'By the time I had scrambled down the bank and reached the boat, Florentin was on dry land, with a police constable bending over him.

'The whole place was swarming with spectators by then. . . . You'd have thought that something really serious had happened.

'I decided I'd better keep out of it, in case there were any reporters about, who might be curious as to what I was doing there. . . . So I kept watch from a distance. . . . I hope I did the right thing.'

'You did very well. . . . Besides, I can assure you that Florentin was never in any danger. . . . We used to go swimming together in the Allier as boys, and he was far and away the best swimmer in the school. . . . What happened next?'

'The boatman gave him a tot of rum, not realizing that he'd already had three or four brandies . . . and then the police constable marched him off to the station at Les Halles.

'I didn't go in, for reasons I've already explained. . . . I presume they took his name and address, and asked him a few questions. . . . When he came out, I was having a sandwich in the bistro opposite the Police Station, and I don't think he saw me. . . . He looked a sorry sight, I must say, wrapped in an old police blanket they'd lent him. . . .

'He took a taxi back to his place. . . . He changed into dry clothes. . . . I could see him through the workshop window. . . . He caught sight of me as he came out and treated me to another wink, and made a comic face at me for good measure. Then he walked as far as the Place Blanche, where he went into a restaurant.

'He got back here half an hour ago, and bought a paper, and the last I saw of him, he was stretched out on his bed, reading it.'

By the time he had heard the whole story Maigret was looking quite stunned.

'Have you had any dinner?'

'I had a sandwich. I see they sell sandwiches in here, so I shall probably have a couple more before I leave. . . . Torrence will be relieving me at two in the morning.'

'Good luck to you,' said Maigret, with a sigh.

'Shall I ring you again if anything further happens?'

'Yes, no matter how late it is.'

He had almost forgotten about his melon. It was dusk by now. He ate the melon over by the window, while Madame Maigret cleared the table.

One thing was certain. Florentin had had no intention of committing suicide. It is virtually impossible for a strong swimmer to drown in the Seine, least of all in the middle of June, with the Quais swarming with people, and within a few feet of a conveniently moored boat!

Why, then, had his old friend jumped into the water? To create the impression that he was being driven to distraction by the unfounded suspicions of the police?

'How is Lapointe?'

Maigret could not help smiling. He knew very well what his wife was getting at. She would never ask him point blank about his work, but there were times when she was not above angling for information.

'He's in the best of health, which is just as well, because he's

45

got several more hours ahead of him pounding the pavement at the end of a little alley in the Boulevard Rochechouart.'

'All on account of your old school friend?'

'Yes, he's just been making a spectacle of himself by jumping off the Pont-Neuf into the Seine.'

'You mean he tried to commit suicide?'

'No, I'm quite sure he had no such intention.'

What possible reason could Florentin have for drawing attention to himself in that way? Did he just want to get his name in the papers? Surely not, but then, where Florentin was concerned, anything was possible.

'Shall we go out for a breath of air?'

The street lights in the Boulevard Richard-Lenoir were all switched on, although it was not yet dark outside. They were not the only couple taking a quiet stroll, enjoying the cool of the evening after a hot day.

At eleven, they retired to bed. Next morning, the sun was shining, promising another hot day. Already, a faint smell of tar rose from the streets, a smell characteristic of Paris in midsummer, when the road surfaces seem almost to melt in the heat.

Maigret found a huge pile of mail waiting for him in his office, which all had to be dealt with before he could get down to his report. The morning papers mentioned the murder in the Rue Notre-Dame-de-Lorette, but gave no details. Maigret reported to his Departmental Chief with a brief summary of the facts, as far as he knew them.

'Has he confessed?'

'No.'

'Have you any real evidence against him?'

'Only pointers.'

He saw no reason to add that he and Florentin had been at school together. As soon as he got back to his office he sent for Janvier.

'One thing we know for certain, Joséphine Papet had four regular visitors. We have the names of two of them, François Paré and Courcel. I shall see them myself this morning. I'll leave the other two to you. Question as many people as you like, the neighbours, the tradesmen, anyone else you can

46

think of, but I want their names and addresses before the day is out.'

Janvier could not help smiling. Maigret knew as well as he did that it was an almost impossible assignment.

'I'm relying on you.'

'Very good, sir.'

Next, Maigret rang through to the Police Surgeon. Alas, it was no longer his dear old friend Doctor Paul, whose greatest pleasure in life had been to take him out to dinner and regale him, throughout the meal, with a detailed account of his autopsies.

'Have you recovered the bullet, doctor?'

By way of reply, the doctor began reading from the report that he was in the middle of writing. Joséphine Papet had been in the prime of life, and had enjoyed excellent health. All her organs were sound, and it was plain that she had been exceptionally fastidious in her personal habits.

As to the shot, it had been fired at a range of between eighteen inches and three feet.

'The bullet was on a slight upward trajectory when it lodged in the base of the skull.'

Maigret could not help thinking of the tall figure of Florentin. Was it possible that he had fired the shot sitting down?

He put the question to the doctor.

'Could she have been shot by someone sitting down?'

'No, the angle of entry wasn't steep enough for that. A slight upward trajectory, I said. . . . I've sent the bullet to Gastinne-Renette for an expert opinion. . . . If you ask me, I don't believe that bullet was fired from an automatic weapon, but more probably from an old-fashioned cylinder-revolver.'

'Was death instantaneous?'

'Within half a minute at most, I'd say.'

'So nothing could have been done to save her?'

'Absolutely nothing.'

'Thank you, doctor.'

Torrence was back in the Inspectors' Room. He had been relieved by Dieudonné, who was new to the job.

'What's he been up to?'

47

'He got up at half-past seven, shaved, had a cat's lick, and went out in his slippers to the tobacconist's on the corner for breakfast. He had two cups of coffee, and two or three croissants. Afterwards, he went into the phone box. Presumably, he intended to make a call, but, after some hesitation, he came out without doing so.

'He turned round several times to see if I was watching. I don't know what he's like normally, but, at the moment, he seems listless and depressed. . . .

'He went to the newspaper kiosk in the Place Blanche, and bought several papers. Then he just stood there in the street, glancing through a couple of them.

'After that, he went back indoors. . . . Then Dieudonné arrived and took over, and I came back here to report to you.'

'Didn't he speak to anyone?'

'No. . . . Well, not unless you count the painter, who turned up while he was out buying the papers. I don't know where he lives, but he certainly doesn't sleep in his studio. . . . When Florentin got back he called out: "How's tricks?"

'And the painter replied: "Fine". Then he gave me an old-fashioned look. He must be wondering what on earth we're up to, keeping watch in relays at the top of the alley. He was still peering out, when Dieudonné took over from me.'

Maigret took his hat off its hook, and went out into the forecourt. In the ordinary way, he would have taken an inspector with him, and driven off in one of the row of black cars parked in front of the building.

Today, however, he preferred to walk. He crossed the Pont Saint-Michel, making for the Boulevard Saint-Germain. He had never before had occasion to set foot in the Ministry of Public Works.

He looked in bewilderment from one to another of the many staircases, each marked with a different letter of the alphabet.

'Can I help you?'

'I'm looking for the Department of Inland Waterways.'

'Staircase C, top floor.'

There was no lift that he could see. The staircase was as dingy as his own at the Quai des Orfèvres. On each floor the various offices leading off the corridor were signposted with black arrows.

On the third floor, he found the sign he was looking for. He pushed open a door marked: *Enter without knocking*.

It led into a large room, where four men and two girls were working at desks, behind a barrier.

The walls were covered with old, yellowing maps, just as in the classrooms of the lycée in Moulins.

'Can I help you?'

'I'm looking for a Monsieur Paré.'

'What name, please?'

He hesitated. Very likely the Head of the Department of Inland Waterways was a man of impeccable character, and he had no wish to compromise him in the eyes of his staff. On reflection, he decided not to produce his card.

'My name is Maigret.'

The youth, frowning, took a closer look at him, then, with a shrug, turned and disappeared through a door at the back of the room.

He was soon back.

'Monsieur Paré will see you now,' he said, ushering Maigret into an inner room.

Maigret saw, coming forward to greet him, an elderly man of dignified bearing, though somewhat overweight. With formal ceremony he invited Maigret to be seated.

'I was expecting you, Monsieur Maigret.'

There was a morning paper lying on his desk. He lowered himself gently into the chair behind the desk, and laid his arms along the arms of the chair. There was a touch of ritual solemnity in the way he did this.

'I'm sure there is no need for me to tell you that, as far as I'm concerned, this is a very unpleasant situation.'

He was not smiling. He had the air of a man who seldom smiled. He was self-possessed, a little pompous, the sort who would weigh his words carefully before speaking.

49

CHAPTER THREE

THE OFFICE was very much like the one Maigret had occupied before Police Headquarters were modernized. There, on the mantelpiece, was a black marble clock identical with the one in his present office. Maigret wondered if it was as unreliable as his.

The man himself was as impassive as the clock. He was very much the senior civil servant, a combination of self-possession and caution. It must have been a deep affront to his self-esteem to find himself suddenly in the hot seat.

His features were undistinguished. His sparse brown hair was carefully combed to hide an incipient bald patch, and his little toothbrush moustache was too black to be natural. He had well-cared-for white hands, covered with long, fine hairs.

'It was good of you to come yourself, Monsieur Maigret, and spare me the indignity of a summons to Police Headquarters.'

'I'm as anxious as you to avoid unnecessary publicity.'

'I noticed that the morning papers gave little more than the bare facts.'

'Had you known Joséphine Papet long?'

'About three years. . . . It gives me an odd feeling, you know, to hear you use her full name. . . . I've always known her as Josée. . . . As a matter of fact, it wasn't until several months after we met that I learned what her surname was.'

'I understand. . . . How did you meet her?'

'It happened quite by chance. I'm fifty-five, Superintendent. I was fifty-two at the time, and it may surprise you to know I had never before been unfaithful to my wife.

'This, in spite of the fact that, for the past ten years, my wife has been a sick woman. She suffers from a psychiatric disorder, which has strained our relationship a good deal.'

'Have you any children?'

'Three daughters. The eldest is married to a shipowner in La Rochelle. The second is a schoolteacher in a lycée in Tunis. The youngest is married and lives in Paris, in the XVIth Arrondissement. I have five grandchildren in all, the oldest of whom is nearly twelve. As to my wife and myself, we have lived in the same flat in Versailles for thirty years. As you see, most of my life has been wholly uneventful, very much the life you would expect a conscientious civil servant to lead.'

He spoke deliberately, choosing his words with care, as a prudent man should. There was not the faintest hint of self-mockery in his manner, and his face remained expressionless. Had he ever been known to burst out laughing? Maigret doubted it. Even his smile was probably no more than a twitch of the lips.

'You asked me where I met her. . . . Occasionally, when I leave the office, I stop for a drink in a brasserie on the corner of the Boulevard Saint-Germain and the Rue de Solférino. . . . I did so on that day. . . . It was raining. . . . I can still see the rain streaming down the windows.

'I sat in my usual corner, and the waiter, who has known me for years, brought me my glass of port.

'There was a young woman at the next table. She was writing a letter, and having trouble with the café pen. She was using violet ink. There wasn't much left in the bottle, and what there was was reduced almost to a paste.

'She was a respectable-looking young woman, soberly dressed in a good navy-blue suit. . . .

'She called out to the waiter: "Is this the only pen you have?"

'"I'm sorry, madam," he said, "but nowadays most of our customers use their own fountain pens."

'I took mine from my pocket, and held it out to her. It was more or less a reflex action.

'"Allow me," I said.

'She took it with a grateful smile. And that's how it all started. She had almost finished writing her letter. She was drinking tea.

'As she gave me back my pen, she asked: "Do you come here often?"

'"Almost every day," I said.

'"I like these old-fashioned brasseries, where most of the customers are regulars. They have atmosphere."

'"Do you live in this district?"

51

'"No, I have a flat in the Rue Notre-Dame-de-Lorette, but I'm quite often in this part of the world."'

His expression, as he described this first meeting, was as artless as a child's.

'So you see, it was pure chance that we met. She wasn't there the following day, but the day after that she was back, sitting at the same table. She smiled at me.

'There was something about her, her manner, her expression, an air of gentle serenity. One felt one could trust her.

'We exchanged a few words. I told her I lived at Versailles, and I seem to remember that I mentioned my wife and daughters. She came to the door, and watched me get into my car and drive away.

'It may surprise you to know that things went on in this way for a month or more. Some days she wasn't in the brasserie, and I always felt a pang of disappointment when I didn't see her.

'I had come to look upon her as a friend, nothing more. It was just that, with my wife, I always had to weigh every word. She was so apt to take things amiss, and then there would be a scene.

'Before my daughters left home, it was all very different. There were always noisy, cheerful young people about, and, in those days, my wife was energetic and high-spirited. You can't imagine what it's like to go home to a vast, empty flat, and be watched from the minute you're in the door by a pair of eyes, full of anguish and mistrust. . . .'

Maigret, having lit his pipe, held out his tobacco pouch.

'No thanks. I gave up smoking years ago. Please don't imagine I'm making excuses for myself.

'I am on the committee of a charitable organization which meets every Wednesday. One Wednesday I skipped the meeting and went back with Mademoiselle Papet to her flat.

'By then she had told me quite a lot about herself, including the fact that she lived alone on a modest income inherited from her parents. She had repeatedly tried to get some sort of job, she said, but without success.'

'Did she ever talk about her family?'

'Her father, who had been an officer in the regular army,

52

was killed in the war when she was only a child. She lived in the provinces with her widowed mother until she grew up. She had one brother.'

'Did you ever see him?'

'Only once. He was an engineer, and he travelled a good deal. One Wednesday I arrived early, and he happened to be there, and she introduced us.

'He was distinguished-looking, a good deal older than she was. He's no fool. He recently patented a process for eliminating the toxic gases in exhaust fumes.'

'Is he tall and thin, with light grey eyes and an unusually mobile face?'

François Paré looked surprised.

'Do you know him?'

'I've met him. Forgive me for asking, but did you give Josée much money?'

The Head of Inland Waterways flushed and averted his eyes.

'I'm in the fortunate position of being comfortably off, more than comfortably off. I was left two farms in Normandy by a brother of my mother's. I could have retired years ago, except that I shouldn't know what to do with myself if I did.'

'Would it be fair to say that you were supporting her?'

'Not exactly. . . . I saw to it that she didn't have to watch every penny, and perhaps enabled her to enjoy a few small extra comforts. . . .'

'You only saw her once a week, on Wednesdays?'

'It was the only day I had an excuse for spending the evening in town. . . . My wife grows more jealous and possessive with every year that passes.'

'I take it she doesn't go so far as to spy on your movements?'

'No. . . . She hardly ever goes out. . . . She's so thin that she can scarcely stand up. . . . She's seen innumerable doctors, but they all say it's hopeless.'

'Did Mademoiselle Papet lead you to believe that you were her only lover?'

'It's not a word either of us would ever have thought of using . . . although, in the sense that our relations were intimate—I won't deny that—I suppose we were lovers. . . .'

53

'But that wasn't the real bond between us. . . . It was more that we were both lonely people, trying to put a good face on things. . . . I don't quite know how to put it. . . . We talked the same language. . . . We were able to open our hearts to one another. . . . In other words, we were friends.'

'Were you jealous?'

He started, then gave Maigret a hostile look, as though he resented the question.

'I have taken you into my confidence. I've told you that she was the first and only woman in my life, other than my wife. . . . You know that I'm not a young man. . . . I haven't attempted to hide the fact that I set very great store by our relationship. . . . I looked forward with eager impatience to those Wednesdays. You might even say I lived for Wednesday evening. . . . It was our time together that made life endurable for me.'

'In other words, you would have been shattered to learn that she had another lover?'

'Of course. . . . It would have been the end. . . .'

'The end of what?'

'Of everything. . . . Of the happiness I had known for the past three years . . . a modest enough share, in a life-time. . . .'

'You say you only met her brother once?'

'Yes.'

'And you didn't suspect anything?'

'What was there to suspect?'

'Did you ever meet anyone else in the flat?'

He gave a ghost of a smile.

'Just once, a few weeks ago. As I got out of the lift, I saw a youngish man leaving the flat.'

'A man with red hair?'

He stared at Maigret in amazement.

'How did you know? Well, anyway, if you know that, you must also know that he's an insurance agent. I must confess I followed him, and saw him go into a bar in the Rue Fontaine. . . . I got the impression that he was a regular there. . . .

'When I asked Josée about him, she didn't seem in the least embarrassed.

'She just said: "He keeps pestering me to take out a life

54

assurance policy. This is the third time he's called. But what use would such a policy be to me? I have no dependants. . . . I must have his card somewhere. . . .'

'And she began opening drawers and searching through them, and she did, in fact, find a visiting card in the name of Jean-Luc Bodard, of the Continentale, with offices in the Avenue de l'Opéra. It's not one of the larger companies, but it has an excellent reputation. . . . I spoke to the personnel manager, and he confirmed that Jean-Luc Bodard was one of their agents.'

Maigret was puffing reflectively at his pipe. He was playing for time, painfully aware of the distasteful task ahead.

'I take it you went to the flat yesterday?'

'Yes, just as usual. . . . I was a little late. I had to see the Permanent Under-Secretary, and it took longer than I expected. . . . I rang the bell, and was surprised to get no reply. . . . I rang again, and then knocked, but there was still no answer.'

'Did you speak to the concierge?'

'That woman gives me the creeps. . . . I never go near her if I can help it. . . . I didn't go straight home. . . . I dined alone in a restaurant at the Porte de Versailles. . . . Officially, I was supposed to be at my committee meeting. . . .'

'When did you first learn of the murder?'

'This morning, as I was shaving. . . . I was listening to the news on the radio. . . . It was just a bare announcement, no details. . . . I didn't see it in the papers until after I got here. . . . I'm absolutely shattered. . . . I can't understand it. . . .'

'You weren't there, by any chance, between three and four yesterday afternoon?'

He replied with some bitterness:

'I see what you're getting at. . . . I never left the office yesterday afternoon. . . . My staff will confirm that, though, naturally, I should much prefer to have my name kept out of it.'

Poor man! He really was shattered, torn between grief and anxiety. His Indian summer, with all that it had meant to him, had come to a sudden and shocking end, yet he was still very much concerned to preserve his reputation.

'I realized that you were bound to find out about me from either the concierge or Josée's brother, if he's in Paris. . . .'

'There was no brother, Monsieur Paré.'

He frowned, in angry disbelief.

'I'm terribly sorry to have to disillusion you, but you'll have to know the truth some time. The real name of the man who was introduced to you as Léon Papet is Léon Florentin. . . . It's an odd coincidence, but he and I were schoolboys together at the lycée in Moulins.'

'I don't understand.'

'No sooner were you out of Joséphine Papet's flat, than he was letting himself in with his key. . . . Did she ever give you a key?'

'No. . . . I never asked for one. It wouldn't have occurred to me. . . .'

'He practically lived in the flat . . . but when visitors were expected, he made himself scarce.'

'Did you say visitors, in the plural?'

He was very pale, and sat rigid in his chair, as though turned to stone.

'There were four of you, not counting Florentin.'

'What do you mean?'

'I mean that Joséphine Papet was being kept, more or less, by four separate admirers. . . . One of them, she knew long before you met. . . . In fact, many years ago, he practically lived in the flat for a time. . . .'

'Have you seen him?'

'Not yet.'

'Who is he?'

In spite of everything, François Paré still believed that there must be some mistake.

'His name is Fernand Courcel. He and his brother own a ballbearings factory in Rouen, with head offices in Paris, Boulevard Voltaire. . . . He's about your age, and a good deal overweight. . . .'

'I find it hard to believe.'

'His day was Thursday. He was the only one privileged to spend the night in the flat.'

'This isn't a trap, by any chance?'

'How do you mean?'

'I don't know. One hears that the police sometimes resort to devious methods. All you've said seems so utterly incredible to me. . . .'

'There was also a Saturday visitor. . . . I know very little about him, except that he has a limp. . . .'

'What about the fourth man?'

He was putting a brave face on it, but he was gripping the arms of his chair so tightly that his knuckles showed white.

'The insurance agent whom you saw coming out of the flat. He's generally known as *Le Rouquin*, on account of his red hair.'

'He is a genuine insurance agent. I checked up on him myself.'

'Being an insurance agent doesn't stop a man from also being the lover of an attractive woman.'

'I don't understand. . . . You never knew her. . . . If you had, you would have found it just as impossible to believe. . . . I never met anyone like her. She was so sane, so serene, so unassuming. . . . I have three daughters, so I should know something about women. . . . I'd have trusted her with my life, more than any one of my children.'

'I'm sorry to have to disillusion you.'

'I take it you're quite sure of your facts?'

'If you wish, I can arrange for Florentin to tell you himself.'

'I absolutely refuse to meet that man, or, indeed, any of the others. . . . If I understand you, Florentin was what is known as her "steady"?'

'More or less. . . . He's tried his hand at most things in his time, and never succeeded at anything. . . . In spite of which, he has a kind of fascination for women. . . .'

'He's almost as old as I am.'

'Yes, just a couple of years younger. . . . But he has one great advantage over you. . . . He's available at all times of the day and night. . . . Besides, he's never serious about anything. He takes each day as it comes, and lives entirely according to the whim of the moment.'

Paré was a very different case. He bore the burden of a conscience, a sense of guilt. He took life with deadly seriousness. It showed in every line of his face, in his every gesture.

It was almost as though he carried on his own shoulders the whole responsibility of his department, if not of the entire ministry. Maigret found it hard to imagine him in the company of a woman like Josée.

Fortunately for him she had been of an equable disposition. No doubt she had been one of those women who could sit, smiling and nodding for hours at a stretch, while a man, embittered by misfortune, unburdened himself of all his misery.

Maigret was beginning to form a clearer picture of her. She was nothing if not practical, and she knew the value of money. She had bought herself a house in Montmartre, and had had forty-eight thousand francs salted away. Very likely, given time, she would have acquired a second, and possibly even a third house.

There are some women for whom houses are the only hard currency, as though nothing in life has any real substance but bricks and mortar.

'Did you never think that she might come to a tragic end, Monsieur Paré?'

'Never for an instant. . . . She seemed to me the very embodiment of stability and security. . . . Everything about her, her life, her home. . . .'

'Did she tell you where she came from originally?'

'From Poitiers, if I remember rightly.'

A wise precaution, telling each of them a different story.

'Did she strike you as a woman of some education?'

'She had her *baccalauréat*, and had worked for a time as secretary to a lawyer.'

'Did she mention the name of the lawyer?'

'She may have done. . . . I don't remember.'

'Had she never been married?'

'Not to my knowledge.'

'Were you not surprised by her taste in reading?'

'She was sentimental, rather naïve, really. It's not surprising that she enjoyed romantic novels. But she was the first to laugh at her own foibles.'

'I don't want to distress you more than is absolutely necessary . . . but there is one thing I must ask you. . . .

Think back. . . . Try to remember everything you can. . . . You never know . . . the most trivial detail, a few words spoken at random, something that may seem to you of no importance, could provide us with a clue.'

François Paré levered his heavy frame out of the chair. He seemed uncertain whether or not to offer his hand to Maigret.

'I really can't think of anything. . . .'

He hesitated, then, his voice suddenly toneless, asked:

'Did she suffer much, do you know?'

'According to the police surgeon, death was instantaneous.'

Maigret saw his lips move, presumably in silent prayer.

'Thank you. I very much appreciate your discretion in this matter. I'm only sorry we could not have met in happier circumstances.'

'So am I, Monsieur Paré.'

Phew! No sooner was he on the stairs, than Maigret took a deep breath. He felt as though he had just emerged from a tunnel, and was much in need of the fresh air of the daylight world.

Although his interview with the Head of Inland Waterways had not yielded any tangible results, or told him anything which could be immediately useful, it had enabled him to form a clearer picture of the young woman herself.

Had she entrapped all her patrons by means of a letter written with a faulty pen in a brasserie frequented by a prosperous class of customer, or had her meeting with Paré been genuinely accidental?

The first of her lovers, as far as was known, had been Fernand Courcel. She must have been twenty-five at that time. What had she been doing before that? Maigret could not imagine her, with that well-bred air of hers, loitering on the pavements round about the Madeleine or the Champs-Elysées.

Perhaps she really had been secretary to some lawyer or other?

There was a light breeze in the Boulevard Saint-Germain, causing a faint tremor among the leaves of the trees. Maigret savoured the morning air as he walked along. Turning off into a little side street leading to the Quais, he noticed a bistro with a pleasantly old-fashioned air. There was a lorry parked in front of it, from which crates of wine were being unloaded.

He went in and, resting his elbows on the zinc counter, asked:

'Where do you get your wine?'

'From Sancerre. I come from those parts myself, and I get my supplies from my brother-in-law.'

'I'll have a glass.'

It was dry, yet at the same time fruity. The bar counter was made of good old-fashioned zinc, and there was sawdust on the red-tiled floor.

'The same again, please.'

Joséphine, it seemed, had been a purveyor of dreams. What a very odd calling! He had three more men to see, three more of her lovers.

François Paré would not find it easy to replace her. Who else would listen to the outpourings of his sad old heart? Florentin had been driven back to his workshop in Montmartre, to doss down on a miserable bed in a windowless cubby-hole.

Better get on to the next one! He sighed as he went out of the bistro, and made his way towards the Quai des Orfèvres.

Another illusion to be destroyed, more dreams to be shattered!

Having reached the top of the stairs, Maigret, making his way down the long corridor of Police Headquarters, paused automatically to look into the glass-walled waiting-room, always jocularly referred to by the inspectors as 'the aquarium'.

Much to his surprise, he saw, sitting in two of the uncomfortable green velvet armchairs provided, Léon Florentin in company with a stranger, a smallish man, running to fat, with a round face and blue eyes, unmistakably one who appreciated the good things of life.

At present, however, he seemed distressed. Florentin was speaking to him in an undertone, and every now and then, as he listened, he dabbed his eyes with a handkerchief, which was crumpled into a ball in his hand.

Across the room, ignoring them, and absorbed in the racing page of a newspaper, was Inspector Dieudonné.

Maigret passed by unnoticed. As soon as he got to his office, he rang the bell for old Joseph, who appeared almost at once.

'Has anyone been asking for me?'

'Two men, sir.'

'Which of them got here first?'

'This one, sir.'

He handed Florentin's card to Maigret.

'And the other one?'

'He arrived about ten minutes later. . . . He seemed very upset. . . .'

The stranger, it turned out, was Fernand Courcel, of the firm of Courcel Frères, manufacturers of ballbearings in Rouen. The card also gave an address in the Boulevard Voltaire.

'Which will you see first?'

'Bring in Monsieur Courcel.'

He sat down at his desk, with a brief glance through the open window at the glittering sunlight outside.

'Come in. . . . Please sit down.'

The man was smaller and fatter than Maigret had at first supposed, yet there was something attractive about him, an infectious vitality and unforced goodwill.

'You don't know me, of course, Chief Superintendent. . . .'

'If you had not come here this morning, Monsieur Courcel, I should have called on you in your office.'

The blue eyes widened in surprise, but there was no hint of fear in them.

'You know?'

'I know that you and Mademoiselle Papet were very close friends, and that it must have been a terrible shock this morning when you heard the news on the radio or read it in the paper.'

Courcel's face crumpled, as though he were about to burst into tears, but he managed to control himself.

'I'm sorry. . . . I'm absolutely shattered. She was much more than a friend to me. . . . .'

'I know.'

'In that case, there isn't much I can tell you, because I've

61

no idea what could possibly have happened. She was the kindest, the most discreet of women.'

'Do you know the man who was talking to you in the waiting-room?'

It was hardly possible to imagine anyone less like a captain of industry. The owner of the ballbearings factory stared at him in astonishment.

'Didn't you know she had a brother?'

'When did you first meet him?'

'About three years ago . . . soon after he got back from Uruguay.'

'Had he been there long?'

'Haven't you interviewed him?'

'I'd like to hear what he told you.'

'He's an architect. He was out there on a government contract to build a new town.'

'You met him in Joséphine Papet's flat?'

'That's right.'

'Did you, on that occasion, arrive unexpectedly early?'

'To tell you the truth, I don't remember.'

He was taken aback by the question. He frowned, and Maigret noticed that his eyebrows, like his hair, were very fair, almost white. This colouring, combined with his delicate pink-and-white complexion, gave him the appearance of a chubby baby.

'I don't quite see what you're getting at.'

'Did you ever see him again?'

'Three or four times.'

'Always in the Rue Notre-Dame-de-Lorette?'

'No. . . . He came to see me in my office. . . . He had a scheme for developing the coastline between Le-Grau-du-Roi and Palavas as a luxury seaside resort, with hotels, smart villas, bungalows, and so on. . . .'

'And he thought he might interest you in the project?'

'That's right. . . . There was a lot to be said for it, I must admit. . . . I don't doubt that it will be a success. Unfortunately, I have no capital of my own. My brother and I own the business jointly, and I cannot legally act independently of him.'

'So you weren't able to help him at all?'

He flushed, much taken aback by Maigret's manner.

'I lent him a few thousand francs, just to enable him to register the plans.'

'Do you know if the plans were, in fact, registered? Did he send you copies?'

'As I told you, I wasn't interested.'

'Was that the only time he touched you for a loan?'

'I don't care for your way of putting it, but no. . . . He came to see me again last year. . . . It's always the same with any far-reaching project. . . . There are bound to be problems and difficulties. . . . His office in Montpellier. . . .'

'Is that where he lives?'

'Yes, didn't you know?'

They were at cross-purposes the whole time, and Fernand Courcel was beginning to show signs of impatience.

'Look here, why not have him in and ask him yourself?'

'All in good time.'

'You seem to have it in for him, for some reason.'

'Not at all, Monsieur Courcel. . . . In fact, I may as well tell you that he's an old school friend of mine. . . .'

The little man took a gold cigarette case out of his pocket and opened it.

'May I smoke?'

'Please do. . . . How many times did you lend him money?'

He thought for a moment, then said:

'Three times. . . . On the last occasion, he had left his cheque-book at home.'

'What was he saying to you, out there in the waiting-room?'

'Must I answer that?'

'You would be well advised to do so.'

'It's such a painful subject. . . . Oh, well!'

He sighed, stretched out his little legs, and drew deeply on his cigarette.

'He is entirely in the dark as to his sister's finances. . . . So am I, as it happens, but then it's no business of mine. . . . He's invested every penny he owns in this project of his, so, naturally, he's short of ready cash for the time being. . . . He asked me to contribute to the funeral expenses.'

63

Maigret smiled broadly. This really was rich! Courcel was outraged.

'Forgive me . . . but you'll soon see why I can't help smiling. First of all, I'm bound to tell you that the real name of the man you know as Léon Papet is Léon Florentin. His father was a confectioner in Moulins, and he and I were at school together at the Lycée Banville.'

'You mean, he isn't her brother?'

'No, my dear sir, he is not. He is not her brother, nor even her cousin, but that doesn't alter the fact that he was living with her.'

'You mean . . . ?'

He had sprung to his feet, as though stung.

'No!' he exclaimed. 'It's not possible, Josée was incapable. . . .'

He was pacing up and down the room, dropping his ash all over the carpet.

'You must remember, Chief Superintendent, that I have known her for ten years. . . . In the early days, before I was married, we lived together. . . . It was I who found the flat in the Rue Notre-Dame-de-Lorette, and I spent a great deal of time and care decorating and furnishing it to suit her tastes.'

'She was about twenty-five at that time, wasn't she?'

'Yes, and I was thirty-two. My father was still alive then, and my brother Gaston was running the office in Paris. So I was left with a good deal of time on my hands.'

'Where and how did you meet?'

'I knew you'd ask me that, and I realize how it must look to you. . . . I met her in a night-club in Montmartre, the Nouvel Adam. . . . It doesn't exist any more. . . .'

'Did she just take her turn with the other girls?'

'No, she was a hostess, so she didn't have to entertain just anyone . . . only if she was specifically asked for. . . . I found her sitting alone at a table. . . . She was wearing a very simple black dress, and almost no make-up. . . . She looked sad, I thought, and rather shy, so much so that I hesitated for a long time before going up to speak to her.'

'Did you spend the whole evening with her?'

'Naturally. . . . She told me all about her childhood. . . .'

'Where did she say she grew up?'

'La Rochelle. . . . Her father was a fisherman. . . . He was drowned at sea. She had four young brothers and sisters.'

'And her mother? Dead too, I've no doubt. . . .'

Courcel glared at him furiously.

'Do you wish me to go on? If so. . . .'

'Do forgive me . . . but, you see, it's all a pack of lies.'

'You mean she didn't have four brothers and sisters?'

'No, and it wasn't in order to bring them up that she was working in a cabaret in Montmartre. That was her story, wasn't it?'

He returned to his chair and sat, staring at the floor. Then, after some hesitation, he said:

'I find it hard to believe. . . . I was passionately in love with her. . . .'

'And yet you got married.'

'Yes, I married a cousin. . . . I felt the years were slipping by, and I wanted children.'

'You live in Rouen?'

'Most of the week, yes.'

'But not Thursdays. . . .'

'How do you know?'

'On Thursdays you took Josée out to dinner and then to a theatre or cinema, and spent the night in the flat in the Rue Notre-Dame-de-Lorette.'

'That's right. . . . When I married, I intended to break it off, but I found I couldn't.'

'Did your wife know?'

'Of course not!'

'What about your brother?'

'I had to take Gaston into my confidence. . . . Supposedly, I paid a weekly visit to our Marseilles office.'

With quite touching candour, the little man added:

'He says I'm an idiot. . . .'

Maigret just managed to suppress a smile.

'When I think that only in the last few minutes, I almost burst into tears when that man . . .'

'Florentin wasn't the only one. . . .'

'What are you insinuating?'

'I give you my word, Monsieur Courcel, that if she had died in any other way, I would have spared you this. But she was murdered. It is my duty to find the man who killed her, and that can't be done without bringing the truth out into the open.'

'Do you know who shot her?'

'Not yet. . . . There were three men, besides yourself and Florentin, who visited her regularly.'

He shook his head, as though, even now, he could not believe it.

'There were times when I almost made up my mind to marry her. . . . If it hadn't been for Gaston, it's more than likely that. . . .'

'Wednesday was the day of a senior civil servant. . . . He didn't spend the night in the flat.'

'Have you seen him?'

'This morning.'

'Did he admit it?'

'He was perfectly open about his visits, and the nature of his relationship with Josée.'

'How old is he?'

'Fifty-five. . . . Did you ever see a man with a limp, if not in the flat, then perhaps in the lift?'

'No.'

'There was a man with a limp . . . middle-aged. I'll find him soon enough, if one of my men hasn't done so already.'

'Who else?' He sighed, clearly feeling that the sooner he knew the worst, the better.

'A man with red hair, a good deal younger than the rest of you. He's not much over thirty, and he's an insurance agent.'

'I take it you never knew her when she was alive?'

'That is so.'

'If you had, you'd understand how I feel. You'd have thought she was as honest as the day, so frank and open as to be almost childlike. . . . I could have sworn. . . .'

'Were you supporting her?'

'It was a hard job to persuade her to take a penny. . . .

66

She wanted to work in a shop, selling lingerie or something of the sort. . . . But she wasn't strong. . . . She was subject to fits of giddiness. . . . She was always reproaching me for being too generous. . . .'

He was suddenly struck by a thought that had not, up to then, occurred to him.

'What about the others? Did they . . . ?'

'I'm afraid so, Monsieur Courcel. Three of you, at least, were keeping her. I don't know about the redhead yet, but it won't be long before I do. The civil servant whom I saw this morning, at any rate, certainly was. . . .'

'But what did she do with the money? She had such simple tastes. . . .'

'For a start, she bought a house in the Rue de Mont-Cenis. And furthermore, after her death, forty-eight thousand francs in cash were found in the flat. . . . Now, I'm afraid I must ask you to try and take a grip on yourself and think back. . . . I won't ask you where you were between three and four yesterday afternoon. . . .'

'I was in my car on the way from Rouen. I drove through the Saint-Cloud tunnel, and must have come out the other end at about a quarter past three. . . .'

He pulled himself up sharply, and stared at Maigret in blank astonishment.

'You can't mean you suspect me!'

'I don't suspect anyone. It's a purely routine question. . . . What time did you get to your office?'

'I didn't go straight there. . . . I stopped off for a minute or two at a bar in the Rue de Ponthieu, to place a bet on a horse. . . . I go there regularly. . . . It wasn't, in fact, until about a quarter past five that I got to the Boulevard Voltaire. . . . Nominally, my brother and I are partners. . . . I spend a couple of days a week at the factory, and I have an office and a secretary in the Boulevard Voltaire . . . but, in practice, they could perfectly well manage without me.'

'Does your brother not resent having to carry such a large share of the burden?'

'Quite the contrary. The less I do, the happier he is. That way, he's the boss, don't you see?'

'What make is your car, Monsieur Courcel?'

'A Jaguar convertible. . . . I've always had a convertible. My present one is pale blue. . . . Do you want the number?'

'That won't be necessary.'

'When I think that not only Josée but her so-called brother . . . what did you say his name was?'

'Florentin. His father made the best cakes in Moulins.'

He clenched his little fists.

'Don't distress yourself. Unless events take an unexpected turn, your name will be kept out of it. You may rest assured that I will treat all you have said in the strictest confidence. . . . Is your wife of a jealous disposition?'

'I daresay she is, in a mild way. She suspects me of kicking over the traces once in a while, in Marseilles or Paris. . . .'

'Has there ever been anyone, apart from Josée?'

'Occasionally. . . . I suppose, like most other men, I'm intrigued by the unknown.'

He looked about him for his hat, then remembered that he had left it in the waiting-room. Maigret went with him, fearing that he might be tempted to attack Florentin.

Florentin looked at them glumly, obviously in some trepidation as to what Courcel's reaction would be.

When the little captain of industry had gone, Inspector Dieudonné, who had stood up when Maigret came into the waiting-room, asked:

'Shall I report to you now, sir?'

'Has something happened?'

'No. After he'd had breakfast in the bistro on the corner, he went back to his room and stayed there until 9.30, when he left to come here by Métro. He asked to see you. Soon after, the other gentleman arrived. They shook hands and talked. I didn't hear what they said.'

'Thanks. That will be all for today.'

Maigret beckoned to Florentin. 'Come with me.'

He ushered him into his office, shut the door, and gazed at him reflectively for a considerable time. Florentin, meanwhile, kept his eyes resolutely lowered, and his long, bony frame, slumped in a chair, was limp, seeming almost on the point of disintegration.

'You're a worse scoundrel even than I thought.'

'I know.'

'What possessed you to do a thing like that?'

'I'd no idea I should run into him here.'

'What have you come here for?'

He raised his head and gave Maigret an anguished look. It was pitiful.

'Guess how much money I have in my pocket.'

'What's that got to do with it?'

'I assure you, it has everything to do with it. All I have left in the world is a fifty-centime piece. . . . There isn't a shop or restaurant or café in the neighbourhood willing to give me credit. . . .'

This time it was the Chief Superintendent who looked staggered, just as his fat little visitor had done a short while before.

'Have you come here to ask me for money?'

'Who else can I turn to, in my present predicament? I've no doubt you told that pompous ass Paré that I wasn't really Josée's brother.'

'Naturally.'

'So you robbed him of all his illusions, did you? I bet it shook him!'

'Be that as it may, he has a cast-iron alibi. Yesterday, between three and four, he was in his office.'

'And to think that when I saw that little runt coming into the waiting-room, I thought to myself that there was still hope for me!'

'The funeral expenses! Aren't you ashamed of yourself?'

Florentin shrugged.

'When one has had cause to be ashamed as often as I have. . . . Mind you, I guessed he'd tell you about it. . . . But, as I got here first, there was just a chance that you might hear my story before he got his oar in. . . .'

Maigret stood up and went over to the window. He drank in the fresh air as though it were nectar. Florentin watched him in silence.

'What will happen to the forty-eight thousand francs?'

Maigret gave a violent start. It really was almost inconceivable that, at a time like this, Florentin should still be thinking about Josée's money.

'Can't you understand that I'm absolutely destitute? Look, there's no point in trying to deceive you. . . . It's true, I do occasionally sell a piece of furniture for a few hundred francs . . . but the antique business was only a front.'

'I realized that.'

'Well, then, just until I get on my feet. . . .'

'What do you intend to do?'

'If necessary, I'll sign on as a porter in Les Halles.'

'I must warn you that you won't be able to leave Paris.'

'So I'm still under suspicion?'

'Until we get the man who did it. . . . Do you really know nothing of the man with the limp?'

'Even Josée didn't know his surname. . . . She called him Victor. . . . He never mentioned a wife or children. . . . She had no idea what he did for a living. . . . He was prosperous-looking. He wore good suits and hand-made shirts. . . . Oh! and there's one other thing I've just remembered. Once, she told me, when he took out his wallet, she saw his railway season ticket. It was a Paris-Bordeaux ticket. . . .'

Here, at least, was something for his men to work on. Surely, there could not be all that many Paris-Bordeaux season tickets?

'I'm doing my best to be helpful, you see. . . .'

Maigret, taking the hint, got out his own wallet and extracted a hundred-franc note.

'You'd better make it last.'

'Are you keeping a tail on me?'

'Yes.'

He opened the door to the Inspectors' Room.

'Leroy.'

He gave the necessary instructions, and, this time, could see no way of avoiding shaking the hand of his old school friend when it was held out to him.

CHAPTER FOUR

IT WAS THREE O'CLOCK, and Maigret was standing at the open window, hands in his pockets, pipe clenched between his teeth, in an attitude familiar to all who knew him.

The sun was shining and the sky a cloudless blue dome, yet it was raining in diagonal streaks, and the large, widely dispersed raindrops formed black patches on the ground where they fell. The door opened behind him.

'Come in, Lucas,' he said, without looking round.

He had sent him up to the attics of the Palais de Justice to find out from Records whether Florentin had any previous convictions.

"Three convictions, Chief. Nothing very serio s.'

'Fraud?'

'The first conviction—that was twenty-two years ago—was for passing a dud cheque. At that time he was living in a furnished flat in the Avenue de Wagram. He was a fruit importer in those days, and he had an office in the Champs-Elysées. He got a suspended sentence of six months.

'Eight years later, he was convicted on charges of fraud and misappropriation. By then, he had moved to a small hotel in Montparnasse. This time he had to serve his prison sentence. . . .

'Five years ago, another dud cheque. . . . Described as being of no fixed address.'

'Thanks.'

'Is there anything else I can do?'

'You'd better go to the Rue Notre-Dame-de-Lorette, and have a word with the shopkeepers. Janvier has already taken statements from them, but I want you to ask them a specific question. I want to know whether any of them saw a light-blue Jaguar convertible parked outside the building or in a near-by street between three and four yesterday afternoon. You'd better enquire at the local garages as well.'

Left to himself, he stood looking out of the window, frowning. Moers's men had failed to come up with anything of interest. Joséphine Papet's fingerprints were all over the flat, which was only to be expected.

There were, however, no prints on any of the door handles. They had all been carefully wiped off.

Florentin's prints, too, were everywhere, including the clothes closet and the bathroom, but there were none on the drawer of the bedside table, which the murderer must have opened to get at the revolver.

The Chief Superintendent had been struck, from the first, by the scrupulous cleanliness of the flat. Joséphine Papet had neither maid nor daily woman. He could imagine her in the mornings, with a scarf tied round her head and the radio playing softly, going from room to room, dusting and cleaning with meticulous thoroughness.

He was wearing his most surly expression, which meant that he was dissatisfied with himself. The truth was that he had an uneasy conscience.

If he and Florentin had not been schoolboys together in Moulins, would he not, by now, have applied to the Examining Magistrate for a warrant for his arrest?

It was not that he and the confectioner's son had ever been close friends, exact y. Even in their school days, Maigret had had reservations bout him.

Florentin had always been good for a laugh, and had often risked punishment just for the sake of a bit of fun.

But had there not been a touch of defiance, even aggressiveness, in his attitude?

He didn't give a damn for anyone, and would mimic the tics and mannerisms of the teachers with cruel accuracy.

He had had a ready wit, but was quick to take offence if ever one of his quips failed to raise a laugh.

Had he not, even then, been teet ring on the borderline? Had he not begun to see himself as, in some sense, set apart? That was, perhaps, the reason why his witticisms had often jarred.

He had grown to manhood and come to Paris, where he had alternated between periods of semi-respectability and darker phases, during one of which he served a prison sentence.

But he had never admitted defeat. He still had an air about him, a kind of innate elegance, even in a threadbare suit.

He was a born liar, scarcely aware that he was lying. He

72

always had told lies, and never seemed disconcerted when he was found out. It was as though he were saying:

'Well, it was a good story, anyway! Too bad it didn't work.'

No doubt he had, in his time, haunted Fouquet's and other smart bars in the Champs-Elysées, not to mention cabarets and night-clubs. Such places give a man a false sense of well-being.

Fundamentally, Maigret suspected, he was insecure. His clowning was, in reality, just a defence mechanism, a mask, behind which was concealed a sadly inadequate personality.

He was a failure, typical of his kind, and, what was worse and more painful, an ageing failure.

Was it pity that was preventing Maigret from arresting him? Or was it rather that he simply could not believe that anyone as sharp as Florentin would, had he actually been guilty, have left so many clues pointing to himself?

Take the matter of Josée's savings, for instance. He had removed the biscuit tin to his own workshop, wrapped in that day's newspaper. Surely, he could have found a safer hiding-place than the miserable hovel in the Boulevard Rochechouart, where, as he must have known, the police could not fail to search?

Then there was that lapse of time after the shot, when he had stayed hidden in the clothes closet. A whole quarter of an hour!

Was it fear that had kept him there, fear of meeting the murderer face to face?

And why had he chosen to go straight to Maigret, when the obvious course was to report to the local police?

There was certainly a strong enough case to justify Maigret in arresting him. Even the recent appearance on the scene of the young man known as *Le Rouquin* told against him, for here surely was a real threat to Florentin's security, a younger man who might well succeed in ousting him from the cushy billet on which he depended for his very life.

Janvier knocked at the door, came in without waiting for an answer, and collapsed into a chair.

'We've got him, sir, at last!'

'The man with a limp?'

'Yes. . . . I've lost count of the number of phone calls I've

73

made, including half a dozen to Bordeaux. I almost had to go on my knees to the Railways Board, to get them to give me a list of season-ticket holders. . . .'

He stretched out his legs, and lit a cigarette.

'I hope to heaven I've got the right man! I don't know whether I've done the right thing, but I've asked him to come and see you. . . . He'll be here in a quarter of an hour.'

'I'd rather have seen him on his own ground.'

'He live in Bordeaux. When he's in Paris, he has a suite in the Hôtel Scribe. It's almost next door to his office in the Rue Aul r.'

'Who s he?'

'If m information is correct, he's a man of some standing in Bordeaux. He has a house on the river in Les Chartrons, which is where all the old-established families live. As you'd expect, he's a wine grower in a big way, exporting mainly to Germany and the Scandinavian countries.'

'Have you seen him?'

'I've spoken to him on the telephone.'

'Did he seem surprised?'

'He was very snooty at first . . . he asked me if this was some kind of joke. When I assured him that I really was from the C.I.D., he said he couldn't imagine what business the police could possibly have with him, and that we'd better keep out of his hair if we didn't want trouble. . . . So I told him it was to do with what had happened in the Rue Notre-Dame-de-Lorette.'

'How did he take it?'

'There was a long silence, then he said:

' "When does Chief Superintendent Maigret want to see me?" '

'As soon as possible.'

' "I'll come to the Quai des Orfèvres as soon as I've been through my mail." '

'His name is Lamotte,' Janvier added, 'Victor Lamotte. . . . If you like, I'll ring the C.I.D. in Bordeaux while he's with you, and see if there's anything more they can tell me.'

'Good man.'

'You don't seem too happy. . . .'

Maigret shrugged. Wasn't it always so, at this stage of an

74

enquiry, before the case had really begun to take shape? After all, Florentin apart, he had never even heard of any of these people until yesterday.

This morning, he had interviewed a chubby little man who, though quaint, had not struck him as being a person of much character. If Courcel had not had the good fortune to be born the son of an industrialist, what would have become of him? Probably he would have been a commercial traveller, but there was really no telling. He might have ended up like Florentin, part parasite, part crook.

Joseph announced the visitor, and ushered him in. The man, as expected, had a pronounced limp. To Maigret's surprise, he had snow-white hair and a flaccid face. He looked sixty.

'Come in, Monsieur Lamotte. . . . I'm sorry to have put you to the trouble of coming here. . . . I hope you had no difficulty in parking your car in the forecourt?'

'I leave all that to my chauffeur.'

Naturally! He would have a chauffeur and, no doubt, in Bordeaux, a whole retinue of servants.

'I presume you know what I want to see you about?'

'The inspector mentioned the Rue Notre-Dame-de-Lorette. I couldn't quite make out what he was getting at.'

Maigret was seated at his desk, filling his pipe. His visitor sat opposite him, facing the window.

'You knew Joséphine Papet. . . .'

The man hesitated for a considerable time before replying.

'How did you find out?'

'As you are no doubt aware, we have our methods and sources of information. If we had not, the prisons of this country would be standing empty.'

'I don't quite see the relevance of that last remark. You're surely not insinuating . . . ?'

'I'm not insinuating anything. Have you seen a newspaper this morning?'

'Certainly. I read the papers, like anyone else.'

'You must, therefore, be aware that Joséphine Papet, commonly known as Josée, was murdered in her flat yesterday afternoon. Where were you at that time?'

'Not in the Rue Notre-Dame-de-Lorette, at any rate.'

75

'Were you at your office?'

'At what time?'

'Let's say between three and four.'

'I was taking a walk in the Grands Boulevards.'

'Alone?'

'What's so strange about that?'

'Do you often go for solitary walks?'

'Regularly, when I'm in Paris, for an hour in the morning, from ten to eleven or thereabouts, and again for an hour in the afternoon. My doctor will tell you that he has urged me to take regular exercise. Until recently, I was a good deal overweight, and it was putting a strain on my heart.'

'You realize, don't you, that that leaves you without an alibi?'

'Do I need one?'

'As one of Josée's lovers, yes.'

If this was news to him, he showed no sign of it. Looking perfectly composed, he asked:

'Were there many of us?'

There was a tinge of irony in his voice.

'Four, to my knowledge, not counting the man who lived with her.'

'So she had a man living with her, did she?'

'If my information is correct, your day was Saturday. I may say that each of the others had a specific day too.'

'I'm a creature of habit. I lead a very regular life. Every Saturday, after my visit to the Rue Notre-Dame-de-Lorette, I catch the Bordeaux express, which gets me home well before bedtime.'

'Are you married, Monsieur Lamotte?'

'Yes, married, with a family. One of my sons is in the business with me. He's in charge of our warehouse in Bordeaux. . . . Another represents the firm in Bonn, and travels a good deal in the north. . . . My daughter and son-in-law live in London, with their two children.'

'How long have you known Joséphine Papet?'

'Four years or thereabouts.'

'What did she mean to you?'

Condescendingly, not without a hint of contempt, he replied:

'She provided relaxation.'

'In other words, you had no real affection for her?'

'Affection is rather too strong a word.'

'Perhaps I should say liking.'

'She was a pleasant companion, and I believed her to be discreet. So much so that it surprised me that you were able to track me down. . . . May I ask who put you on to me?'

'To begin with, all we knew about you was that you called on Saturdays, and that you had a limp.'

'A riding accident, when I was seventeen. . . .'

'You have a railway season ticket. . . .'

'Ah! I see. . . . Find the limping man with the Paris-Bordeaux season ticket!'

'There's one thing that puzzles me, Monsieur Lamotte. Staying at the Hôtel Scribe as you do, you are surrounded by bars where you could meet any number of attractive women of easy virtue. . . .'

The man from Bordeaux, determined not to be ruffled, answered equably, though not without a touch of condescension. After all, Les Chartrons, where he lived, was the Faubourg Saint-Germain of Bordeaux, the domain of ancient and noble families.

As far as Lamotte was concerned, Maigret was a policeman like any other. Policemen, of course, were necessary to protect the rights and property of honest citizens, but this was the first time he had ever come into direct contact with this class of person.

'What did you say your name was?'

'It's of no importance, but, if you must know, it's Maigret.'

'To begin with, Monsieur Maigret, I am a man of regular habits. I was brought up to believe in certain principles which are, perhaps, scarcely fashionable nowadays. I am not in the habit of frequenting bars. It may seem strange to you, but I have not set foot in a bar or café in Bordeaux since my student days.

'As to receiving a woman of the sort you have in mind in my suite at the Scribe, you surely must see that it would scarcely be the thing, and besides, it's risky. . . .'

'Blackmail, do you mean?. . . '

77

'For a man in my position, there is always the risk. . . .'

'Yet you visited Josée once a week in the Rue Notre-Dame-de-Lorette?'

'A much less precarious arrangement. You must see that, surely?'

Maigret's patience was wearing thin.

'All the same, you must admit you knew precious little about her.'

'What do you expect? Or perhaps you think I should have asked you to make enquiries on my behalf?'

'Where did you first meet her?'

'In the restaurant car.'

'Was she going to Bordeaux?'

'No, she was returning to Paris. . . . We happened to be sitting opposite one another at a table for two. . . . She seemed a very respectable sort of woman. . . . When I passed the breadbasket across to her, I remember, she looked at me as though I had taken a liberty. . . . Later it turned out that we had seats in the same compartment.'

'Had you a mistress at that time?'

'Don't you think that's rather an impertinent question? Anyway, I can't see what it can possibly have to do with your present enquiries.'

'You don't have to answer if you would rather not.'

'I have nothing to hide. . . . I did have a mistress, a former secretary. I had set her up in a flat in the Avenue de la Grande Armée. Just a week before I met Josée, she announced that she was going to be married.'

'In other words, there was a vacancy to be filled. . . .'

'I don't care for your tone, and I'm not sure that I feel inclined to answer any more questions.'

'In that case, I may have to detain you longer than you may find convenient.'

'Is that a threat?'

'Just a warning.'

'I'd be within my rights in refusing to answer questions except in the presence of my lawyer, but it hardly seems worth the trouble. Carry on.'

He was now very much on his dignity.

'How long had you known Josée when you first went to the Rue Notre-Dame-de-Lorette?'

'About three weeks, maybe a month.'

'Did she say she had a job?'

'No.'

'Did she claim to have independent means?'

'A modest allowance from one of her uncles.'

'Did she tell you where she came from, originally?'

'Somewhere near Grenoble.'

Joséphine Papet, it seemed, had been, like Florentin, a compulsive liar. She had invented a different family background for each of her lovers.

'Did you make her a generous allowance?'

'That's a most indelicate question!'

'Nevertheless, I should be glad if you would answer it.'

'I gave her two thousand francs a month in an envelope, or rather, I should say, I left it discreetly on the mantelpiece.'

Maigret smiled. It took him right back to his very early days in the Force, when there were still to be seen, about the Boulevards, elderly gentlemen in patent-leather shoes and white gaiters, ogling the pretty women through their monocles.

Those were the days of furnished mezzanine flats and kept women, women not unlike Joséphine Papet, good-natured, warm-hearted and discreet.

Victor Lamotte had not fallen in love. His life was centred on his family in Bordeaux. He was at home, not in the Rue Notre-Dame-de-Lorette, but in his austere family mansion, from which he ventured forth once or twice a week, to stay at the Hôtel Scribe and attend his office in the Rue Auber.

Nevertheless, he too had felt the need of a refuge, where he could drop the oppressive mask of respectability, and open his heart to a woman. And was not Josée just the woman with whom a man could safely relax, without fear of unpleasant repercussions?

'Did you know any of her other "protectors"?'

'You would hardly expect her to introduce us!'

'There might have been an accidental encounter. You could have come face to face with one of them leaving the flat, say.'

'As it happens, I didn't.'

'Did you ever take her out?'

'No.'

'What about your chauffeur? Did he wait outside?'

He shrugged. Evidently he thought Maigret somewhat naïve.

'I always took a taxi.'

'Did you know she'd bought a house in Montmartre?'

'It's the first I've heard of it.'

He was at no pains to conceal his total lack of interest in her personal affairs.

'What's more, forty-eight thousand francs in notes were found in her flat.'

'I daresay some of it was mine, but, don't worry, I shan't ask for it back.'

'Were you distressed to learn of her death?'

'To be honest with you, no. Millions of people die every day. . . .'

Maigret stood up. He had had enough. If this interview were to go on any longer, he would be hard put to it to conceal his disgust.

'Don't you want a signed statement from me?'

'No.'

'Am I to expect a summons from the Examining Magistrate?'

'I can't answer that, at present.'

'If it should come to a trial . . .'

'It will.'

'Always supposing you get the murderer.'

'We'll get him.'

'I'd better warn you that I shall take steps to keep my name out of it. . . . I have influential friends. . . .'

'I don't doubt it.'

Whereupon the Chief Superintendent stumped over to the door, and held it wide open. As he was going out, Lamotte turned back as though intending to say something by way of leave-taking, but then, apparently thinking better of it, went off without a word.

That was three of them dealt with! There still remained *Le Rouquin*. Maigret was in a foul temper, and felt he must give himself a little time to cool off. He went back to his desk and

sat down. It had stopped raining some time ago. A fly—
perhaps the same one that had haunted him the previous
day—flew in through the window, and settled on the sheet of
paper on which he was idly doodling.

Abruptly, he woke up to the fact that his wandering pencil
had formed a word:

Premeditation.

Unless Florentin had done it, premeditation seemed unlikely.
The killer had come to the flat unarmed. Undoubtedly, he was
a familiar visitor, since he knew that there was a revolver in
the bedside table drawer.

Was it not possible that he had intended all along to make
use of it?

Assuming, for the sake of argument, that Florentin really
had been hiding in the clothes closet, and was telling the
truth, what reason could the intruder have had for hanging
about in the bedroom for a full quarter of an hour, especially
in view of the fact that, as he moved about the room, he
would have had to step back and forth across the body
repeatedly?

Had he been searching for the money? If so, why had he not
found it, since all he would have had to do was force a very
flimsy lock?

Letters? A document of some sort?

Which of them needed money? Not François Paré, the civil
servant, nor tubby little Fernand Courcel. Still less the high
and mighty Victor Lamotte.

Any one of them, on the other hand, might well have
reacted violently to attempted blackmail.

As usual, he was back to Florentin, Florentin, whom the
Examining Magistrate would certainly have ordered Maigret
to arrest, had he been fully informed of the facts.

Maigret was hoping that an opportunity for questioning
Jean-Luc Bodard, known as *Le Rouquin*, would not be long
delayed, but the inspector who had been sent to find him
returned with a disappointing report.

The young insurance agent was out on his rounds, and was
not expected back till the evening.

81

He lived in a small hotel, the Hôtel Beauséjour, in the Boulevard des Batignolles, and took his meals in the restaurant.

Maigret was fretful, as always when he felt something was amiss with the case he was working on. He was uneasy and dissatisfied with himself. He could not bring himself to settle down to the paperwork, cluttering up his desk He got up, went across to the door leading to the Inspectors' Duty Room, and opened it.

'Lapointe,' he called. 'Come along. I need a car.'

It was not until they were driving along the Quai that he said grumpily: 'Rue Notre-Dame-de-Lorette.'

He had the feeling that he had overlooked something important. It was as though the truth had brushed past him, and he had failed to recognize it. He spoke not a word the whole way there, and bit so hard on his pipe that he cracked the ebonite stem.

'Come in when you've parked the car.'

'To the flat?'

'No, the lodge.'

There was something about the huge bulk and stony eyes of the concierge that haunted him. He found her exactly where she had been the previous day, standing at the door, holding back the net curtain. He had to push the door open before she would let go of it and step back.

She did not ask him what he wanted, but just glared at him disapprovingly.

Her skin was very white, unhealthily so. Was she just mentally deficient, a harmless 'natural', such as one used to come across in country districts in the old days?

It was beginning to get on his nerves, seeing her standing there in the lodge, motionless as a pillar.

'Sit down,' he said brusquely.

Unruffled, she shook her head.

'I asked you a number of questions yesterday. I am now going to repeat them, and, this time, I warn you that, unless you tell the truth, you may find yourself in serious trouble.'

She did not stir, but he fancied he detected a flicker of derision in her eyes. It was quite obvious that she was not afraid of him. She was afraid of no one.

'Did anyone go up to the third floor between three and four yesterday?'

'No.'

'Or any of the other floors?'

'One old woman, for the dentist.'

'Do you know François Paré?'

'No.'

'He's a tall man, heavily built, in his fifties, balding, with a black moustache. . . .'

'I may have seen him.'

'He always came on Wednesdays at about half-past five. Did he come yesterday?'

'Yes.'

'At what time?'

'I'm not sure. Before six.'

'Was he upstairs long?'

'He came down straight away.'

'Did he say anything to you?'

'No.'

She answered like an automaton, her face set, her stony eyes fixed unwaveringly on Maigret, as though she suspected him of wanting to trap her. Was she capable of loyalty, of lying to protect someone else? Was she aware of the significance of her testimony?

It was a matter of life and death to Florentin, for if, as she claimed, no one had entered the building, then his whole story was a tissue of lies: the ring at the doorbell, the unexpected visitor, the dash for cover in the clothes closet. There were no two ways about it; if she was telling the truth, Florentin had been the one to fire the shot.

There was a tap on the glass door. Maigret went to let Lapointe in.

'This is one of my assistants,' he explained. 'I repeat, think before you speak, say nothing unless you're sure of your facts.'

Never before in her life had she been called upon to play so important a part, and, no doubt, she was thoroughly enjoying it. For here was the Head of the Criminal Investigation Department almost pleading for her help, something which, surely, she could not have hoped for in her wildest dreams?

83

'You say François Paré came into the building shortly before six. Had you not seen him at all earlier in the day?'

'No.'

'You're quite sure that, if he had been in, you couldn't have missed seeing him?'

'Yes.'

'But there must be times when you're in your kitchen, and can't see the entrance.'

'Not at that hour.'

'Where is the telephone?'

'In the kitchen.'

'Well, then, if it was ringing. . . .'

'It didn't ring.'

'Does the name Courcel mean anything to you?'

'Yes.'

'How do you come to know Monsieur Courcel by name, and not Monsieur Paré?'

'Because he almost lived here at one time. . . . About ten years ago, he often spent the night up there, and he and the Papet woman went out a lot together.'

'Did you find him friendly?'

'He would always pass the time of day.'

'You seem to prefer him to the others.'

'He had better manners.'

'I believe he still spends the night here sometimes, usually on a Thursday?'

'That's no business of mine.'

'Was he here yesterday?'

'No.'

'Would you recognize his car?'

'Yes, it's blue.'

Her voice was flat and toneless. Lapointe seemed very much struck by this.

'Do you know the name of the man with the limp?'

'No.'

'Has he never been into the lodge?'

'No.'

'His name is Lamotte. . . . Did you see him yesterday?'

'No.'

84

'Nor the man with red hair, whose name is Bodard?'

'No, I didn't see him either.'

Maigret would have liked to shake the truth out of her, as one shakes coins out of a money box.

'What you're saying, in other words, is that Léon Florentin was alone up there with Joséphine Papet the whole time?'

'I didn't go up to see.'

It was infuriating.

'You must see that, if you're telling the truth, there's no other explanation.'

'There's nothing I can do about it.'

'You can't stand Florentin, can you?'

'That's my business.'

'One would almost think you were determined to get your own back on him.'

'You can think what you like.'

There was something wrong somewhere. Maigret could feel it. Maybe she really was as stolid as she seemed. Possibly she could not help her monotonous voice. Perhaps she had always been a woman of few words. Even so, there was a jarring note somewhere. Either she was deliberately lying, for some reason best known to herself, or she knew more than she was telling.

Of one thing there was no doubt. She was very much on the defensive, striving to anticipate and prepare for the questions to follow.

'Tell me, Madame Blanc, has anyone been trying to intimidate you?'

'No.'

'If you know Joséphine Papet's murderer, and he has threatened reprisals if you talk . . .'

She shook her head.

'Let me finish. . . . You would do well to ignore his threats. If you talk, we shall arrest him, and you will be safe from him. If not, you are running a grave risk that he may decide, at any time, that you would be better out of the way. . . .'

She looked at him with a faintly mocking expression. What did it mean?

'Few murderers will hesitate to kill a witness who knows

85

too much for their peace of mind. . . . I could tell you of dozens of cases. . . . And there's another thing, unless you take us into your confidence, we can't protect you.'

Maigret's hopes rose.

It was not so much that she was beginning to look almost human, as that he thought he detected a faint tremor, an almost imperceptible softening of her expression, at any rate a hint of indecision.

He held his breath anxiously for a second or two.

'What have you to say to that?' he prompted at last.

'Nothing.'

He had reached the end of his tether.

'Let's go, Lapointe.'

Outside in the street, he said:

'I'm almost certain she knows something. . . . I can't help wondering if she's really as stupid as she looks.'

'Where are we going next?'

He hesitated. The next step should really have been to question the insurance agent. Failing that, he was not sure what he wanted to do. At last he said:

'The Boulevard Rochechouart.'

Florentin's premises were locked up. The painter, who was at his easel in the doorway of the neighbouring workshop, called across to them:

'There's no one there.'

'Has he been out long?'

'He's been gone since this morning, and he didn't come back for lunch. Are you police?'

'Yes.'

'I thought so. . . . Ever since yesterday, there's been someone on the prowl hereabouts, and he's followed wherever he goes. . . . What's he done?'

'We don't know for sure that he's done anything.'

'In other words, he's a suspect?'

'If you like.'

He was the kind of man who wanted nothing better than to have someone to talk to. It must have been lonely for him most of the time.

'Do you know him well?'

'He stops by for a chat occasionally.'

'Does he get many customers?'

The painter gave Maigret a broad grin.

'Customers? For one thing, I can't imagine where they'd come from. . . . Whoever would think of looking for an antique shop, if you can call it that, down a miserable little alley like this?

'Besides, he's hardly ever in. . . . When he does come, it's mostly just to hang up a sign saying "Back soon" or "Closed until Thursday".

'He does, from time to time, spend a night in the cubby-hole, I believe.

'At least I presume he does, because sometimes I see him shaving when I arrive in the morning. . . . I have lodgings in the Rue Lamarck, myself.'

'Did he ever talk about himself?'

The painter worked with rapid brush-strokes. No doubt, he had painted the Sacré-Cœur so often that he could have done it blindfold. Without pausing in his work, he considered Maigret's question.

'He couldn't stand his brother-in-law, that's for sure.'

'Why not?'

'Well, according to him, if his brother-in-law hadn't cheated him, he wouldn't be where he is now. . . . His parents, it seems, had a prosperous business, I can't remember exactly where. . . .'

'In Moulins.'

'You may be right. . . . When the father retired, the daughter's husband took over the business. . . . The agreement was that he should make over a share of the profits to Florentin. . . . However, after the father died, he never got another sou.'

Maigret was thinking of the laughing, rosy-cheeked girl who used to stand behind the white marble counter. It seemed to him, in retrospect, that perhaps his visits to the shop, infrequent though they were, had been chiefly on her account.

'Did he borrow money from you?'

'How did you know? Never very large sums. . . . The fact is, I've never had much to spare. . . . Twenty francs, now and

87

again. . . . Once or twice, but not often, as much as fifty. . . .'

'Did he pay you back?'

'He always said he would pay me back next day, but, actually, it was usually a day or two later. . . . What's he supposed to have done? You're Chief Superintendent Maigret, aren't you? I recognized you at once. I've often seen your picture in the papers. . . .

'If you're taking a personal interest in him, it must be something pretty serious. Murder is it? Do you suspect him of having killed someone?'

'I just don't know.'

'If you want my opinion, I don't think he's capable of murder . . . he's not the sort. . . . Now, if you were to say he'd been . . . well . . . careless over money. . . . But even then, maybe it isn't altogether his fault. . . . He's always full of schemes, you know, and I'm sure he genuinely has faith in them. . . . Some of them aren't half bad either! It's just that he gets carried away, and is apt to fall flat on his face. . . .'

'You don't happen to have a key to his workshop, do you?'

'How did you know?'

'I just thought you might have.'

'Of course, it's only once in a blue moon that a customer turns up, but it has been known to happen. . . . That's why he leaves a key with me. . . . He only has a few bits and pieces to sell, and I know what he wants for them.'

He went indoors, opened a drawer, and returned with a massive key.

'I don't suppose he'll mind.'

'You've no need to worry about that.'

For the second time, Maigret, assisted by Lapointe, searched the workshop and annexe with meticulous care and thoroughness. A sweetish smell pervaded the narrow little annexe where Forentin slept, that of some brand of shaving soap unfamiliar to Maigret.

'What are we looking for, sir?'

Crossly, Maigret replied:

'I've no idea.'

*   *   *

'The Blue Jaguar doesn't seem to have been anywhere near the Rue Notre-Dame-de-Lorette yesterday. The woman who runs the dairy near by knows it well by sight.

' "It's always parked just across the street on Thursdays," she said, then as an afterthought: "That's odd! Today is Thursday, and I haven't seen it. . . . The owner is a little fat man. . . . I hope nothing has happened to him!" '

This was Janvier, making his report.

'I also enquired at the garage in the Rue La Bruyère. . . . I had a look at Joséphine Papet's car while I was at it. . . . It's a Renault, two years old. It's in very good condition, and has only done twenty-four thousand kilometres. . . . Nothing in the boot. . . . A Michelin Guide, a pair of sunglasses and a bottle of aspirin tablets in the glove compartment. . . . I hope we'll have better luck with the insurance agent.'

Janvier, sensing that the Chief Superintendent was still a good deal at sea over the case, assumed a guileless expression, and waited in tactful silence for his comments. In the end, however, he was forced to ask: 'Are you having him up here?'

'He's not expected back at his hotel until this evening. It might be a good idea, if you went round there tonight, say at about eight. . . . You may have a long wait. . . . Anyway, as soon as he gets there, give me a ring at home.'

It was past six. Most people had left. Just as Maigret was reaching for his hat, the telephone rang. It was Inspector Leroy.

'I'm in a restaurant in the Rue Lepic, sir. He's just ordered dinner. I'll take advantage of the opportunity, and have mine here too. We spent the afternoon seeing an idiotic film in a cinema i.. the Place Clichy. As it was a continuous programme, we made a proper meal of it, with me sitting just behind him, and saw it twice round.'

'Did he seem on edge?'

'Not in the least. . . . Every now and then, he turned round and winked at me. . . . If I'd given him the slightest encouragement just now, he'd have invited me to sit at his table.'

'I'll send someone along to the Boulevard Rochechouart shortly, to relieve you.'

'There's no hurry. . . . This isn't exactly a taxing assignment. . . .'

'Janvier, I leave it to you to lay on a relief . . . I don't know who is available. . . . And don't forget to ring me as soon as the redhead gets back to his hotel. . . . It's the Beauséjour. . . . Keep out of sight as far as you can.'

Maigret stopped for a drink at the bar in the Place Dauphine. A depressing day on the whole, and the worst of it had been his meeting with Victor Lamotte.

No, perhaps not the worst, he must not forget his exchange with the concierge.

'Charge it to my account.'

Several of his colleagues were playing *belote* in a corner of the café. He waved to them as he went out. When he got home, he made no attempt to hide his ill-humour. It would have cut no ice with Madame Maigret if he had. She knew him too well.

'When I think how much simpler it would be!' he grumbled, hanging up his hat.

'What?'

'To arrest Florentin. Anyone else, in my place, wouldn't hesitate. If the Examining Magistrate knew just half of what I know, he'd send me off to arrest him here and now.'

'What's stopping you, then? Is it because you used to be friends?'

'Not friends,' he corrected her, 'schoolmates.'

He filled the meerschaum pipe that he never smoked except at home.

'Anyway, that's not the reason. . . .'

He did not seem very sure himself what the true reason was.

'Everything points to him. . . . Almost too much o, if you see what I mean. . . . And I can't stand that concierge.'

She repressed a strong inclination to burst out laughing. To hear him talk, one would have thought that his dislike of the concierge was a major factor in his reluctance to arrest Florentin!

'It's virtually impossible to imagine anyone nowadays leading the kind of life that girl led. . . . As for her gentlemen callers, with their regular visiting hours, it's almost beyond belief!'

He was thoroughly fed up with the lot of them, starting with

Joséphine Papet, who ought to have known better than to let herself be murdered. And Florentin was no better, scattering incriminating evidence right, left and centre. Then there were Paré, with his neurotic wife, and the fat little ballbearings tycoon and, worst of all, the insolent cripple from Bordeaux.

But the most maddening of them all was the concierge. He could not get her out of his head.

'She's lying. . . . I'm certain she's lying, or at least that she's got something to hide. . . . But she'll never be made to talk. . . .'

'You haven't touched your food.'

There was an *omelette aux fines herbes*, succulently moist, but Maigret had not even noticed it. To follow, there was a salad flavoured with garlic *croûtons*, and finally, ripe, juicy peaches.

'You shouldn't take it so much to heart. . . .'

He gave her a preoccupied look. 'How do you mean?'

'It's almost as though you were personally involved, as though it concerned a member of your own family.'

This touched a chord in him, and made him realize how absurdly he had been behaving. He felt suddenly relaxed, and was even able to muster a smile.

'You're right . . . but I can't help it, somehow . . . I can't stand being played for a sucker. . . . And someone in this case is doing just that, and it's burning me up. . . .'

The telephone rang.

'You see!'

It was Janvier, to tell him that the insurance agent had just got back to his hotel.

Next on the agenda: *Le Rouquin*. Maigret was about to put the receiver down, when Janvier added:

'He's got a woman with him.'

CHAPTER FIVE

THE BOULEVARD DES BATIGNOLLES, with its double row of trees, was dark and deserted, but at the end of it could be seen the brilliant illuminations of the Place Clichy.

Janvier, the red glow of his cigarette piercing the darkness, came forward out of the shadows.

'They arrived on foot, arm-in-arm. The man is shortish, especially in the leg—a very lively character. The girl is young and pretty. . . .'

'You'd better be off home to bed, or your wife will have it in for me.'

A familiar smell greeted Maigret in the dim, narrow entrance, for it was in just such a hotel, the Reine Morte in Montparnasse, that he had stayed when he had first come to Paris. He had wondered which dead queen the hotel had been named after. No one had been able to tell him. The proprietor and his wife had come originally from the Auvergne, and had militantly enforced the ban on cooking in the bedrooms.

It was a smell of warm sheets, and of people living in close proximity to one another. A fake marble plaque beside the entrance bore the legend: *Rooms to let. Monthly, weekly or daily terms. All home comforts. Bathrooms.* He might have been back in the Reine Morte, where the proudly advertised bathrooms had numbered one to each floor, so that it was impossible to get near them without queueing.

Seated at a roll-top desk in the office, with the bedroom keys on a board facing her, was a woman with tow-coloured hair, in dressing-gown and slippers. She was making up the accounts for the day.

'Is Monsieur Bodard in?'

Without looking up, she replied, in a somewhat unfriendly tone:

'Fourth floor. Number sixty-eight.'

There was no lift. The stair carpet was threadbare, and the higher he climbed, the more pronounced the smell. Room number 68 was at the end of the corridor. Maigret knocked at the door. There was no reply at first. Then, when he had knocked for the third time, a man's voice called out irritably:

'Who's there?'

'I'd like a word with Monsieur Bodard.'

'What's it about?'

'I should prefer to state my business in private. There's no need for the whole hotel to hear what I have to say.'

'Can't you come back another time?'

'It's rather urgent.'

'Who are you?'

'If you'll just open the door a crack, I'll tell you.'

There was a sound of creaking bed springs. The door opened a little way, and there appeared a tousled head of curly red hair, surmounting the blunted features of a boxer. Maigret could see that the man was naked, though he was doing his best to use the door as a shield. Without a word, Maigret produced his badge.

'Do I have to come with you?' asked Bodard, showing no sign of apprehension or anxiety.

'I want to ask you a few questions.'

'The fact is, I'm not alone. . . . I'm afraid you'll have to wait a few minutes. . . .'

The door slammed shut again. Maigret could hear voices, and the sound of people moving about. He went down the corridor and sat on the stairs to wait. It was a full five minutes before the door of number 68 was opened again.

'You can come in now.'

The sheets on the brass bed were rumpled. Seated at the dressing-table was a dark girl, tidying her hair. Maigret felt as though he had gone back thirty-five years, so strongly did the room recall those of the Reine Morte.

The girl was wearing nothing but a cotton dress and sandals. She seemed out of humour.

'You want me to go, I suppose?'

'I think you'd better,' replied the man with red hair.

'How long will you be?'

Bodard looked enquiringly at Maigret.

'About an hour?'

The Chief Superintendent nodded.

'You'd better wait for me in the brasserie.'

With a malevolent look, she inspected Maigret from head to foot, then grabbed her handbag and went out.

'I'm sorry to have called at such an inconvenient time.'

'I wasn't expecting you so soon. I thought it would take you at least two or three days to track me down.'

He had not bothered to do more than slip on a pair of trousers. He was still naked from the waist up. His shoulders and chest were broad and powerful, with well-developed muscles, which made up for his lack of stature. His feet too were bare, and Maigret noticed that he had unusually short legs.

'Please sit down.'

He himself sat on the edge of the rumpled bed. Maigret took the only armchair. It was exceedingly uncomfortable.

'I presume you've seen the papers?'

'I should think everyone has, by now.'

He seemed a good sort. Apparently, he bore his visitor no ill will for breaking in on his *tête-à-tête*. There was an easy good nature about him. He would always be ready to make the best of things, if the expression of his clear blue eyes was anything to go by. He was not the worrying kind, nor the sort to take a tragic view of life.

'So you really are Chief Superintendent Maigret? I imagined you as much fatter. . . . And I certainly wouldn't have expected anyone so exalted to be going around knocking on people's doors. . . .'

'There are times when it's necessary.'

'I realize, of course, that you've come about poor Josée. . . .'

He lit a cigarette.

'Have you arrested anyone yet?'

Maigret smiled at this reversal of roles. It was he who should have been asking the questions.

'Was it the concierge who put you on to me? What a monstrous creature! She's more like a monument than a woman. She reminds me of one of those marble figures on tombs. She sends a shiver down my spine. . . .'

'How long have you known Joséphine Papet?'

'Let me think. . . . We're in June, aren't we? . . . It was the day after my birthday, so it must have been April the nineteenth. . . .'

'How did you meet her?'

'I called at her flat. I called at all the flats in the building that day. It's my job, if you can call it a job. You know: "I'm an insurance agent and I represent so-and-so"!'

'I know.'

'Each one of us has a round of three or four blocks, and we

94

spend our whole time knocking on doors and trying to drum up business.'

'Can you remember what day of the week it was?'

'A Thursday. . . . I remember because, as I said, the previous day was my birthday, and I had a filthy hangover. . . .'

'Was this in the morning?'

'Yes, about eleven.'

'Was she alone?'

'No, there was a man with her, a bit of a layabout, very tall and thin. He said to the woman:

' "Well, I'd better be going."

'He gave me a good, hard look, and then he left.'

'You sell life assurance, I believe?'

'Accident policies as well, oh! and savings-linked insurance. That's a fairly new gimmick, and it's not going too badly. . . . I haven't been in the job very long. Before that, I was a waiter in a café.'

'What made you change?'

'That's just it, I felt like a change. . . . I used to be a fairground barker. . . . You have to have the gift of the gab for that, even more than in insurance, but insurance is more respectable. . . .'

'Were you able to interest Mademoiselle Papet . . . ?'

'Not in the sense you mean.'

He chuckled.

'How then?'

'Well, to begin with, she was in her dressing-gown, with her hair tied up in a scarf, and the vacuum cleaner was pulled out into the middle of the room. . . . I went into my usual patter, and all the time I was talking I was sizing her up. . . .

'She wasn't all that young, of course, but she was a tidy little armful, and I had the feeling that she quite fancied me. She told me she wasn't interested in a life policy for the very good reason that she had no one to provide for. She had no idea what would become of her money in the end, she said.

'I suggested that she should take out an annuity to mature when she was sixty, or, better still, an accident and illness policy.'

'Did she show any interest?'

'She wouldn't commit herself, one way or the other. So, as usual, I made an all-out play for her. . . . I can't help myself. . . . It's just the way I'm made. . . . Sometimes there's a scene and I get my face slapped, but it's worth a try, even if it only comes off one time in three. . . .'

'Did you bring it off with her?'

'I'll say!'

'How long have you known the young woman who was here just now?'

'Olga? Since yesterday.'

'Where did you meet her?'

'In a self-service store. . . . She's a shop assistant in the Bon Marché. . . . Don't ask me if she's any good. . . . You interrupted before I got a chance to find out. . . .'

'How often did you see Joséphine Papet, after that first time?'

'I wasn't counting. . . . Ten or a dozen times, perhaps.'

'Did she give you a key?'

'No. I rang the bell.'

'Did she fix any special day for your meetings?'

'No, she just told me that she was never there at week-ends. I asked her if the grey-haired man was her husband. She assured me he wasn't. . . .'

'Did you ever see him again?'

'Yes, twice.'

'Did you ever speak to him?'

'I don't think he liked me much. . . . Each time, he just gave me a dirty look, and sloped off.

'I asked Josée who he was. She said:

' "Don't bother your head about him. . . . He's rather pathetic really. He reminds me of a stray dog. . . . That's why I took him in. . . ."

' "All the same, though, you go to bed with him, don't you?" I said.

' "What else can I do? . . . I don't want to hurt his feelings. . . . There are times when I'm almost afraid he'll commit suicide." '

As far as Maigret could judge, Bodard spoke with unfeigned sincerity.

96

'Was he the only man you ever saw in her flat?'

'I never saw any of the others. . . . We had a pre-arranged signal. . . . If she had anyone in the flat when I rang, she would open the door just a crack, I would say that I was selling insurance, and she would say she wasn't interested, and shut the door on me.'

'Did the occasion ever arise?'

'Two or three times.'

'Any particular day of the week?'

'There you have me. . . . Wait a minute though, I've just remembered, one of the times it was a Wednesday.'

'What time of day?'

'Round about four or half-past, I think.'

Wednesday was Paré's day. But the Head of Inland Waterways had told him that he had never got to the Rue Notre-Dame-de-Lorette before half-past five or six.

'Did he see you?'

'I don't think so. She only opened the door a crack.'

Maigret gazed at him intently. He seemed preoccupied.

'What do you know about her?'

'Let me think. . . . Occasionally, she would let fall a hint about this or that. . . . I seem to remember she told me she was born in Dieppe.'

So she had not bothered to lie to the man known as *Le Rouquin*. The Divisional Superintendent had telephoned to Dieppe to enquire about next of kin in connection with the funeral arrangements, and was informed that thirty-four years ago, in Dieppe, a daughter, Joséphine, had been born to Hector Papet, deep-sea fisherman, and Léontine Marchaud, housewife. As far as was known, there was no one left of the family in the town.

Why should she have told the truth to Bodard, when she had lied to all the others, inventing a different tale for each of them?

'She worked for a time in a night-club, until she took up with a man she met there, a very respectable man, an industrialist. He set her up in the flat, and lived with her for several months. . . .'

'Did she tell you where her money came from?'

'More or less. . . . She gave me to understand that she had several rich friends who visited her from time to time.'

'Do you know their names?'

'No. . . . But she would say things like: "The one with the limp is getting to be a bit of a bore. . . . If it wasn't that I'm a little scared of him . . ." '

'Did you get the impression that she really was frightened of him?'

'She was never altogether easy in her mind. That's why she kept a revolver in her bedside table drawer.'

'Did she show it to you?'

'Yes.'

'So she wasn't afraid of you?'

'You must be joking! Why should anyone be afraid of me?'

Why indeed? There was something so very likeable about him. His whole appearance was somehow reassuring, curly red hair, blue, almost violet eyes, stocky body and short legs. He looked younger than his thirty years, and would probably never lose his impish charm.

'Did she give you presents?'

He got up, went over to the chest of drawers, and took out a silver cigarette case.

'She gave me this.'

'What about money?'

'Well, really!'

He was affronted, almost angry.

'I don't mean to be offensive. I'm only doing my job.'

'I hope you put the same question to her tame scarecrow!'

'Florentin, do you mean?'

'I didn't know his name was Florentin. . . . I mean the one who had no objection to being kept by her.'

'Did she talk to you about him?'

'I'll say she did!'

'I was under the impression that she was very fond of him.'

'I daresay she was, to begin with. . . . She liked having someone about the place . . . someone she could talk to . . . who would put up with anything . . . who didn't matter. Most women like to keep a pet, but usually it's a dog or a cat or a canary, if you see what I mean. . . .

98

'Mind you, that character, Florentin, or whatever his name is, went a bit too far.'

'In what way?'

'When she first met him, he gave himself out to be an antique dealer. . . . He was down-and-out, but was expecting to come into a fortune any day. . . . In those days, he really did spend some of his time buying and doing up old furniture. . . . But, as time went by, he got more and more into the habit of doing nothing.

'It was always the same old story: "When I get the two hundred thousand francs owing to me. . . ."'

'And then he'd touch her for fifty francs or so.'

'If she didn't care for him, then why didn't she throw him out?'

'Well, you see, she was really very sentimental. In fact, they don't come that sentimental any more, except in romantic novels. Look! I told you how it all started, didn't I? Well, she wasn't exactly a kid any more, was she? In fact, she'd had a good deal of experience, one way and another. All the same, when it was over, she burst into tears!

'I couldn't make it out. I just sat up in bed and stared at her. Then she said, between sobs:

' "How you must despise me . . . !"

'I mean to say, you come across that sort of thing in old books, but it was the first time I'd ever actually heard a woman talk like that. . . .

'That Florentin fellow had her sized up all right. . . . He knew how to tug at the heartstrings. . . . Whenever things looked like getting sticky, he'd turn on the sentiment like a tap. . . . They used to have the most heartrending scenes . . . sometimes he'd storm out, swearing that he would never come back, that she would never hear of him again, and then she'd go chasing after him to some hovel or other in the Boulevard Rochechouart, where I believe he shacks up. . . .'

There was nothing very surprising to Maigret in this character-sketch of his old school friend. It was just the way Florentin had behaved when threatened with expulsion from the lycée. The story went—and it had not seemed too far-fetched at the time—that he had literally grovelled at the feet

99

of the headmaster, declaring, between sobs, that the disgrace would kill him.

'On another occasion, he took the revolver from the bedside table drawer, and made as if to shoot himself in the temple. . . .

' "I shall never love anyone but you. . . . You're all I have left in the world."

'D'you get the picture? For hours, sometimes even for days, after one of these scenes, he'd have her just where he wanted her. . . . Then, as his self-confidence returned, so did her doubts. . . .

'But if you ask me, the real reason she didn't throw him out was because she dreaded being left on her own, and there was no one to take his place. . . .'

'And then she met you.'

'Yes.'

'And she saw you as a possible successor?'

'I think so. . . . She used to ask me if I still had many girl-friends, and sometimes she'd say: "You do like me a little, don't you?"

'She didn't exactly throw herself at me. . . . It was more subtle than that, just a hint here and there:

' "I suppose I must seem an old woman to you."

'And when I protested, she'd say:

' "Well. I am five years older than you are, and a woman ages more quickly than a man. . . . It won't be long before I'm a mass of wrinkles. . . ."

'Then she'd return to the subject of the antique dealer:

' "You'd think he owned me," she said. "He wants me to marry him." '

Maigret gave a start.

'She told you that, did she?'

'Yes. And she went on to say that he wanted her to invest in a bar or small restaurant somewhere round about the Porte Maillot. . . . She owned a house, you know, and had quite a bit of money saved, too. . . .

'He had it in for me, apparently, and always referred to me contemptuously as Ginger or Shorty.

' "Sooner or later," he used to say, "he'll be leading you by the nose." '

'Tell me truthfully, Bodard, did you go to the Rue Notre-Dame-de-Lorette at any time yesterday afternoon?'

'I see what you're getting at, Chief Superintendent. . . . You want to know if I've got an alibi. . . . Well, I'm sorry to say, I haven't. . . . For a time I gave up seeing other girls, for Josée's sake, though I must admit, it wasn't easy. . . . But yesterday morning, I signed up an old gent of sixty-five for a hefty policy. . . . He was looking anxiously to the future. . . .

'The older they are, the more they worry about the future.

'Well, the sun was shining, and I'd treated myself to the best lunch that money could buy, so I decided to go on the prowl. . . .

'I made for the Grands Boulevards and went into a few bars. . . . It was a bit of a frost to begin with, but then I met up with Olga, that's the girl you saw. . . . She's waiting for me in a brasserie three doors down the street. . . . I ran into her at about seven. . . . Otherwise, I've no alibi. . . .'

With a laugh, he asked: 'Are you going to arrest me?'

'No. . . . But to get back to Florentin, are you saying that, in the past few weeks, his position had become precarious?'

'I'm saying that, if I'd wanted to, I could have stepped into his shoes, but as it happened I had no wish to.'

'Did he know?'

'He sensed that I was a possible rival, I'm sure of that. . . . He's no fool. . . . Besides, Josée must have dropped a hint or two. . . .'

'Surely, in the circumstances, if he'd wanted to get rid of anyone, you would have been the obvious choice?'

'You'd have thought so. . . . He couldn't have known that I'd made up my mind to say no, and that I was already gently easing my way out. . . . I can't stand snivelling women.'

'Do you think he killed her?'

'I've no idea, and, anyway, it's no concern of mine. Besides, I know nothing about the others. . . . Any one of them might have borne her a grudge for one reason or another.'

'Thank you.'

'Don't mention it. . . . I say, old man, I don't feel like getting dressed. . . . Would you mind awfully, on your way out, giving the dolly the green light? Tell her, I'm waiting for her up here.'

Never in his life before had Maigret been asked to undertake such an errand, but the request was made with such engaging artlessness that he had not the heart to refuse.

'Good night.'

'I hope it will be!'

He had no difficulty in finding the brasserie, which was full of regulars, playing cards. It was an old-fashioned place, and the lighting was poor. Seeing Maigret making straight for the only young girl in the room, the waiter smiled knowingly.

'I'm sorry I was so long. . . . He's waiting for you up there. . . .'

She was so taken aback that she could find nothing to say. He left her there, gaping, and had to walk all the way back to the Place Clichy before he could find a taxi.

Maigret's feeling that the Examining Magistrate, Judge Page, had only recently come to Paris, proved to be correct. His office, one of those not yet modernized, was on the top floor of the Palais de Justice. There was an archaic atmosphere about it, reminiscent of the novels of Balzac.

His clerk was working at an unstained deal kitchen table, to the top of which a sheet of brown paper had been fastened with drawing-pins. His own office, which could be seen through the open communicating door, was bare of furniture, though cluttered with files piled up on the floorboards.

Before coming up, the Chief Superintendent had taken the precaution of ringing through, to make sure that the judge was free, and willing to see him.

'Have this chair. . . . It's the best we've got, or perhaps I should say, the least dilapidated. . . . The pair to it collapsed last week under the weight of an eight-stone witness.'

'Do you mind if I smoke?' Maigret asked, lighting up.

'Please do.'

'All our enquiries have so far failed to locate anyone related to Joséphine Papet. She can't be kept indefinitely at the Forensic Laboratory. . . . It may take weeks, or even months, to discover some second or third cousin. . . . Don't you think, in the circumstances, Judge, that the best thing would be to make arrangements for the funeral without further delay?'

'As she was not without means . . .'

'That reminds me, I deposited the forty-eight thousand francs with the Clerk of the Court, because I wasn't too happy about keeping it locked up in my office.

'With your permission, I'll get in touch with a firm of undertakers right away.'

'Was she a Catholic?'

'According to Léon Florentin, who lived with her, she wasn't. At any rate, she never went to Mass.'

'Have the account sent to me. . . . I'm not quite sure what the procedure is. Make a note of it, Dubois.'

'Yes, sir.'

The moment Maigret had been dreading had come. He had not attempted to stave it off. On the contrary, he himself had asked to see the judge.

'You must have been wondering why I haven't let you have an interim report. The truth is that, even now, I'm far from sure I'm on the right track.'

'Do you suspect the man who lived with her? What's his name again?'

'Florentin. . . . All the evidence points to him, and yet I still have the gravest doubts. . . . It all seems too easy, somehow. . . . Besides which, by an odd coincidence, he and I were at school together in Moulins. . . . He's by no means a fool, in fact, I should say that he had all his wits about him, rather more than most. . . .

'Admittedly, he's a failure, but that's because of a flaw in his personality. . . . He resents all authority and is totally incapable of self-discipline. . . . As I see it, he lives in a fantasy world, a kind of imaginary puppet theatre, in which nothing and no one is to be taken seriously.

'He has a police record. . . . Dud cheques. . . . Fraud. . . . He did a year's stretch in prison. . . . But, in spite of it all, I still don't believe him capable of committing murder. . . . Or at any rate, he's incapable of bungling it. . . . If he'd done it, he would have taken very good care to cover his tracks.

'All the same, I'm keeping a round-the-clock watch on him.'

'Does he know?'

'He takes it as a compliment, and makes a point of turning round in the street every so often, to wink at the man on his tail. . . . He always was the clown of the form. . . . You must know the type.'

'There's one in every school.'

'The trouble is that, in a man of fifty, that sort of behaviour is no joke any longer. . . . I've tracked down Joséphine Papet's other lovers. . . . One is a highly placed civil servant with a neurotic wife. . . . The other two also are men of standing and considerable wealth. . . . One lives in Bordeaux, the other in Rouen.

'Needless to say, each of these men imagined himself to be the only one privileged to visit the flat in the Rue Notre-Dame-de-Lorette.'

'Have you undeceived them?'

'I've done more than that. . . . I have arranged, this morning, for each of them to receive a personal summons to a meeting in my office at three o'clock this afternoon.

'I have also summoned the concierge to attend, because I'm quite sure in my own mind that she's hiding something. I hope, by tomorrow, to have definite news for you.'

A quarter of an hour later, Maigret was back in his office, instructing Lucas to make arrangements for the funeral. Then, taking a note out of his wallet, he murmured:

'Here, see that there are some flowers on the coffin.'

The sun had been shining brilliantly for days, and today was no exception, but a high wind had suddenly blown up, causing the trees outside to rock violently, and making it impossible to have the window open.

No doubt all those who had been summoned to the forth-coming meeting were shaking in their shoes. Little did they know that Maigret was even more uneasy than they were. True, it had been something of a relief to unburden himself to the Examining Magistrate, but he was still very much a prey to conflicting emotions.

There were two people constantly in the forefront of his mind. One, needless to say, was Florentin, who, it almost seemed, had piled up evidence against himself out of sheer mischief. The other was that old witch of a concierge, who haunted him like a nightmare. As far as she was concerned, he was taking no chances. Knowing that she was quite capable of ignoring his summons, he was sending an inspector to fetch her.

Realizing that it would be best to put the case out of his mind for the time being, he settled down grudgingly to his neglected paperwork, and soon became so immersed in it, that when next he looked up to see the time, he was surprised to find that it was ten to one.

He decided not to go home for lunch, and rang his wife to tell her so. Then he strolled across to the Brasserie Dauphine, and sat down in his usual corner. Several of his colleagues were there having a drink at the bar, as well as a number of people he knew, from other departments.

The proprietor himself came over to take his order.

'There's *blanquette de veau*. How will that do?'

'Fine.'

'And a carafe of our special rosé?'

He lingered over his meal, soothed by the low murmur of voices, which was punctuated by an occasional burst of laughter. As usual, the proprietor brought him a small glass of Calvados, 'on the house,' with his coffee, and he made it last until it was time to go back to his office.

At a quarter to three, he went into the Inspectors' Duty Room to fetch some chairs, which he set out in a semi-circle facing his desk.

'I don't want any slip up, Janvier. You're to go and fetch her, and then take her into a room by herself, and keep her there until I send for you.'

'I'm not sure I'll be able to fit her into the car all in one piece!' retorted Janvier jocularly.

The first to arrive was Jean-Luc Bodard. He was in high good humour. At the sight of the row of chairs, however, he frowned.

'What's this, a family reunion, or a council of war?'

'A bit of both.'

'You don't mean you're bringing together all . . . ?'

'Just so.'

'Well, it suits me all right, but how do you think the others will take it? You'll get a few old-fashioned looks, I shouldn't wonder.'

And indeed the next comer, ushered in by old Joseph, having looked round the room, turned to Maigret with an expression of unhappy distaste.

'I came in response to your summons, but I wasn't told . . .'

'You're not the only person concerned, I'm afraid, Monsieur Paré. Take a seat, won't you?'

As on the previous day, he was dressed all in black. He held himself stiffly, and was more strung up than he had been in his own office. He kept darting anxious glances at the young man with red hair.

There followed an awkward pause lasting two or three minutes, during which no one spoke a word. François Paré had taken the chair nearest the window, and sat with his black hat balanced on his knees. Jean-Luc Bodard, wearing a loud check sports jacket, was watching the door as though, as far as he was concerned, the others couldn't come soon enough.

The next to arrive was Victor Lamotte, very much on his dignity. Furiously he turned on Maigret:

'What's this? A trap?'

'Please be seated.'

Maigret, ignoring the undercurrents, was playing the gracious host, faintly smiling, imperturbable.

'You've no right to . . .'

'You will have every opportunity of complaining to my superiors in due course, Monsieur Lamotte. Meanwhile, I'd be obliged if you would take a seat.'

Florentin was brought in by an inspector. The set-up was no less of a surprise to him than to the others, but his reaction was a loud guffaw.

'Well, I must say . . . !'

He looked Maigret straight in the eye, and gave him an appreciative wink. He thought he knew every trick in the book, but this was beyond everything!

'Gentlemen,' he said, bowing with mock solemnity to the assembled company.

He sat down next to Lamotte, who at once shifted his chair as far away from him as possible.

The Chief Superintendent looked at the time. The chimes of three o'clock sounded, and a few more minutes went by before Fernand Courcel appeared in the doorway. What he saw was such a shock to him that he spun round, as though minded to take to his heels.

'Come in, Monsieur Courcel. . . . Sit down. . . . We're all here now, I think. . . .'

Young Lapointe was seated at one end of the desk, ready to take down in shorthand anything of interest that might be said.

Maigret sat down, lit his pipe and murmured:

'Please smoke if you wish.'

The only one to do so was the young man with red hair.

Maigret looked with interest from one to another. They were an ill-assorted bunch. In a sense, they fell naturally into two groups. In the first group were Florentin and Bodard, whom Josée had truly loved, and who were now engaged in sizing each other up. They represented, in effect, age and youth, the old and the new.

Did Florentin know that the young man with red hair could have ousted him, had he so wished? If so, he did not appear to bear him any grudge. If anything, he seemed rather to approve of him.

In the second group were the three men who had visited the Rue Notre-Dame-de-Lorette in pursuit of an illusion. Their plight was much the more serious.

This was the first time that they had ever met, and yet not one of them deigned so much as to glance at the others.

'Gentlemen, you can be in no doubt as to why you are assembled here. You have all been good enough to answer my questions separately, and I, in my turn, have given you the true facts of the situation, as far as I knew them.

'There are five of you present, every one of whom has, for a longer or shorter period, known Joséphine Papet intimately.'

He paused for an instant. No one stirred.

'Apart from Florentin and, to a limited extent, Bodard, none of you knew of the existence of the others. That is so, is it not?'

The only response was from Bodard, who nodded. As for Florentin, he looked as though he was enjoying himself hugely.

'The fact is that Joséphine Papet is dead, and that one of you killed her.'

Monsieur Lamotte half-rose from his seat and began:

'I protest . . .'

To judge from his expression, he was near to storming out of the room.

'Kindly keep your protests until later. Sit down. So far, I have accused no one. I merely stated a fact. All but one of you deny having set foot in the flat between three and four on Wednesday afternoon. . . . Not one of you, however, can establish an alibi. . . .'

Paré raised his hand.

'No, Monsieur Paré, yours won't do. I sent one of my men to have another look at your office. There is a second door, leading on to a corridor. You could have gone out that way without anyone seeing you. What's more, if any of your staff had gone into your office and found it empty, they would naturally have assumed that you had been called away by the Permanent Under-Secretary.'

Maigret relit his pipe, which had gone out.

'Obviously, I can hardly expect one of you to stand up and confess his guilt. I am simply telling you what is in my mind. I am convinced not only that the murderer is here in this room, but also that there is present someone who knows who he is, and who, for some reason that escapes me, is keeping that knowledge to himself.'

He looked from one to another of them. Florentin's eyes were turned towards the group in the middle, but it was impossible to tell whether his attention was fixed on anyone in particular.

Victor Lamotte was staring intently down at his shoes. He was very pale, and his face seemed all hollows and shadows.

Courcel, poor man, was trying to smile, but all he could manage was a pathetic little grimace.

Bodard was looking thoughtful. It was clear that he had been much struck by Maigret's last remark, and was trying to sort things out in his own mind.

'Whoever killed Josée must have been well known to her, since she received him in her bedroom. But Josée was not alone in the flat. . . .'

This time, they all looked at one another, and then, with one accord, turned to stare uneasily at Florentin.

'You're quite right. . . . Léon Florentin was there when the doorbell rang, and, as he had been forced to do on other occasions, he took refuge in the clothes closet. . . .'

Maigret's old school friend was making a valiant effort to maintain his air of unconcern.

'Did you hear a man's voice, Florentin?'

He addressed him as 'vous', but, on this occasion, at least, Florentin could scarcely object.

'You couldn't hear much in there, just a murmur of voices.'

'What exactly happened?'

'I'd been there about a quarter of an hour when I heard a shot.'

'Did you rush into the bedroom to see what was the matter?'

'No.'

'Did the murderer leave at once?'

'No.'

'How long was he in the flat after the shot?'

'About a quarter of an hour.'

'Did he take the forty-eight thousand francs from the drawer of the desk?'

'No.'

Maigret saw no necessity to disclose that it was Florentin himself who had made off with the money.

'The murderer must have been looking for something. Every one of you, I presume, must have had occasion to write to Josée, if only to cancel an appointment, or to keep in touch while you were away on holiday.'

Once more, he looked from one to another. They shifted uneasily, crossing or uncrossing their legs.

He was now concentrating his attention on the three solemn-faced men who had most to lose in terms of family, position and reputation.

'What about you, Monsieur Lamotte, did you ever have occasion to write to her?'

'Yes,' he muttered under his breath. He was barely audible.

'The social world in which you move in Bordeaux has changed very little with the times, I fancy. If my information is correct, your wife is a very rich woman in her own right and, according to the scale of values accepted in Les Chartrons, comes from a family even more distinguished than your own. Have you ever been threatened with exposure by anyone?'

'I simply cannot permit . . .'

'And you, Monsieur Paré, did you ever write to her?'

'Yes, as you suggested, when I was on holiday. . . .'

'You are, I believe, in spite of your visits to the Rue Notre-Dame-de-Lorette, very much attached to your wife. . . .'

'She's a sick woman. . . .'

'I know. . . . And I'm sure you would go to great lengths to spare her the anguish . . .'

Paré clenched his teeth. He seemed on the verge of tears.

'And now, Monsieur Courcel, what about you?'

'I may have scribbled a note to her once or twice.'

'Which, I'm sure, would leave no one in any doubt as to the nature of your relations with Joséphine Papet. . . . Your wife is younger than you are, and of a jealous disposition, I daresay. . . .'

'What about me then?' broke in the redhead, making a jest of it.

'You could have had an altogether different reason for wanting to get rid of her.'

'Not jealousy, at any rate,' he protested, and turned to the others as if for moral support.

'Josée could have told you about her savings. You may have known that she didn't deposit her money in a bank, but kept it in the flat. . . .'

'If so, then surely I would have taken it?'

'Not if you were interrupted while you were still searching for it.'

'Do I look as if I'd do a thing like that?'

'Most of the murderers I've met have looked very much like anyone else. . . . As to the letters, you could have taken them with the intention of blackmailing the signatories. . . .

'Because the letters have vanished, all of them, possibly

including some from people we haven't even heard of. You'd expect most women, by the age of thirty-five, to have accumulated quite a volume of correspondence. . . . But there was nothing in Joséphine Papet's desk except bills. Every single one of your letters, gentlemen, has been spirited away, and by one of you. . . .'

They were all so anxious to appear innocent, that none of them succeeded in looking anything but thoroughly guilty.

'I am not inviting the murderer to stand up and confess. I shall simply remain here in the confident hope that, within the next few hours, the man who knows who murdered Josée will come to see me. . . .

'All the same, that may not be necessary. . . . There is still one witness missing, and that witness also knows who the murderer is. . . .'

Maigret turned to Lapointe.

'Fetch Janvier, will you?'

There was a long pause, during which not a sound was heard. The five men held their breath, scarcely daring to move. Suddenly, the room felt very hot. When at last Madame Blanc made her entrance, resembling more than ever a piece of monumental sculpture, the effect was electric.

She was wearing a dress of spinach green, with a red hat perched on the very top of her head, and the handbag she was carrying was almost as big as a suitcase. She stood for a moment, framed in the doorway, her face stony, her expressionless eyes darting from one to another of those present.

When she had taken them all in, she turned her back on them, and it was all Janvier could do to prevent her from leaving. For a moment, it looked as if they might come to blows.

In the end the woman gave way, and came into the room.

'I still have nothing to say,' she announced, glowering malevolently at Maigret.

'I think you know all these gentlemen?'

'I'm not being paid to do your job for you. Let me go.'

'Which of these men did you see going towards the lift or the stairs, between three and four in the afternoon on Wednesday?'

Then a strange thing happened. This stubborn, stony-faced woman was unable to prevent her lips from twitching in a faint ghost of a smile. All of a sudden, she was looking distinctly smug, there was no doubt about it. It was almost as though she had won a victory.

They were all looking at her. Maigret was watching them, hoping to detect signs of special anxiety in one of their faces. But he could not tell which of them was most affected. Victor Lamotte was pale with suppressed fury. Fernand Courcel, in contrast, was very flushed; Maigret had noticed his rising colour for some minutes past. As for François Paré, he was simply overwhelmed with shame and misery.

At last Maigret spoke. 'Do you refuse to answer?'

'I have nothing to say.'

'Make a note of that, Lapointe.'

She shrugged and, still with that enigmatic glint of triumph in her eyes, said contemptuously:

'You can't frighten me.'

CHAPTER SIX

MAIGRET STOOD UP, looked at each of them in turn, and concluded:

'Gentlemen, I'm grateful to you all for coming here. It is my belief that your time has not been wasted, and I have no doubt that I shall be hearing from one of you very shortly.'

He cleared his throat.

'In conclusion, for those who are interested, I am now in a position to inform you that the funeral of Joséphine Papet will take place tomorrow morning. The hearse will set out from the Forensic Laboratory at ten o'clock.'

Victor Lamotte, still fuming, was the first to go. He did not even glance at the others, and, needless to say, took no leave of the Chief Superintendent. No doubt his chauffeur-driven limousine was waiting for him below.

Courcel hesitated a moment, then, with a nod, went out. François Paré, as though he scarcely knew what he was saying, murmured:

'Thank you. . . .'

Le Rouquin was the only one to offer his hand. He bounded up to Maigret, exclaiming appreciatively:

'You certainly don't pull your punches!'

Florentin alone hung back. Maigret said to him:

'You wait here a minute. . . . I shan't be long.'

He left Lapointe, who had not moved from his seat at the end of the desk, to keep an eye on him, and went into the Inspectors' Room next door. Torrence was there, a bulky figure seated at his typewriter, transcribing a report. He typed with two fingers, and applied himself to the task with intense concentration.

'I want the house in the Rue Notre-Dame-de-Lorette watched. . . . See to it at once, will you? I want the names of everyone who goes in or comes out. . . . If any one of the men who have just left my office turns up, he's to be followed inside.'

'Is something worrying you?'

'I'm quite sure the concierge knows more than is good for her. I don't want her to come to any harm.'

'What about Florentin? Same drill?'

'Yes. I'll let you know when I've done with him.'

He went back to his office.

'You can go, Lapointe.'

Florentin was standing at the window, hands in his pockets, looking very much at home. He was wearing his usual expression of ironic detachment.

'I say, you didn't half rattle them! I've never enjoyed myself so much in all my life!'

'Is that so?'

For it had not escaped Maigret that there was something very forced about this display of high spirits.

'The one who really took my breath away was the concierge. . . . Talk about getting blood out of a stone! Do you really think she knows?'

'I hope so, for your sake.'

'What do you mean?'

'She maintains that no one went upstairs between three and four. . . . Unless she changes her mind, I shall have no choice but to arrest you, because if what she says is true, you're the only person who could have done it.'

'What was the point of the confrontation?'

'I was hoping one of them would panic.'

'Aren't you concerned that I might be in danger, too?'

'Did you see the murderer?'

'I've already told you I didn't.'

'Did you recognize his voice?'

'No. I've told you that too.'

'Then what have you got to worry about?'

'I was in the flat. Thanks to you, they all know that now. The murderer can't be sure I didn't see him.'

Casually, Maigret opened a drawer in his desk, and took out the packet of photographs that Moers had sent down to him from Criminal Records. He glanced through them, and handed one to Florentin.

'Take a look at that.'

The confectioner's son from Moulins, assuming an air of bewilderment, examined the photograph carefully. It was of a corner of the bedroom, showing the bed, and the side-table with its drawer half-open.

'What am I supposed to be looking for?'

'Doesn't anything strike you?'

'No.'

'Remember your first statement. . . . The doorbell rang. . . . You bolted into the clothes closet. . . .'

'It's the truth.'

'Very well, let's assume, for the sake of argument, that it is. According to you, Josée and her visitor barely paused in the sitting-room, and went straight on through the dining-room into the bedroom. . . .'

'That's right.'

'Let me finish. Also according to you, they were together in the bedroom for nearly a quarter of an hour before you heard the shot.'

Florentin, frowning, examined the photograph again.

'That photograph was taken very soon after the murder. . . . Nothing in the room had been touched. . . . Look at the bed. . . .'

A little colour rose in Florentin's wasted cheeks.

'Not only has the bed not been turned down, but there isn't so much as a dent or a crease on the counterpane.'

'What are you getting at?'

'I'll tell you! Either the visitor merely wanted to talk to Josée, in which case they would have stayed in the sitting-room, or he came for some other purpose. And since the condition of the bed suggests that it wasn't the usual purpose, perhaps you can tell me what, in actual fact, they were doing in the bedroom?'

'I don't know. . . .'

Maigret could almost see his mind ticking over, as he thought up plausible answers.

'Just now, you mentioned letters. . . .'

'Well?'

'Maybe he came to ask for his letters back. . . .'

'Are you suggesting that Josée would have refused to give them to him? Do you think it likely that she would have tried to blackmail a man who was making her a generous monthly allowance?'

'They could have gone into the bedroom for the usual reason, and then quarrelled. . . .'

'Listen to me, Florentin. . . . I have your statements by heart. . . . I felt from the very beginning that there was something wrong somewhere. . . . Did you take those letters as well as the forty-eight thousand francs?'

'I swear I didn't. . . . If I had, surely you'd have found them, just as you found the money. If I'd had the letters, I'd have hidden them in the same place.'

'Not necessarily. . . . It's true that you were frisked to make sure you hadn't got the revolver, but you weren't searched. I know you're an excellent swimmer, don't forget, and I also know that you took a sudden dive into the Seine.'

'I was fed up with everything. . . . I realized that you suspected me. . . . And besides, I'd just lost the only person in the world who. . . .'

'I'd be obliged if you'd spare me the crocodile tears.'

'When I jumped off that parapet, my only thought was to end it all. . . . It was just a foolish impulse. . . . One of your chaps was on my tail. . . .'

'Just so.'

'What do you mean by that?'

'Suppose that, when you hid the money on top of the wardrobe, you'd momentarily forgotten about the letters, which were still in your pocket? You couldn't take the risk of their being found in your possession. How could you have explained them away?'

'I don't know.'

'You realized that a constant watch would be kept on you from then on. But if you were to jump into the Seine, ostensibly in a fit of despair, you could easily get rid of the incriminating papers. . . . They only needed to be weighted with a pebble or something of the sort, to sink safely to the bottom.'

'I never had the letters.'

'I agree, that's one possibility. If true, it would certainly explain what the murderer was doing in the flat during the quarter of an hour after the shot. But there's another thing that's worrying me. . . .'

'What am I being accused of now?'

'The fingerprints. . . .'

'I daresay mine were all over the flat, but what do you expect?'

'That's just it, there were no fingerprints in the bedroom, neither yours nor anyone else's. Now we know you opened the desk to get at the money. And presumably the murderer opened at least one drawer when he was looking for the letters. . . . At any rate, he can't have spent a quarter of an hour in the room without touching anything.

'Which can only mean that, after he'd gone, all the smooth surfaces, including the door handles, were wiped—by you.'

'I don't understand. . . . I did no such thing. . . . Who's to say that someone didn't sneak in and do it after I'd left? There was plenty of time, while I was on my way to the Boulevard Rochechouart, or coming to see you at the Quai des Orfèvres.'

Maigret did not reply. Noticing that the wind had dropped, he went over and opened the window. There followed a long silence, then Maigret said very quietly:

'When did your notice expire?'

'What notice? What on earth are you talking about?'

'Your notice to quit the flat . . . to part from Josée . . . in other words, to get out. . . .'

'There was never any question. . .'

'Oh, yes, there was, and well you know it . . . you were beginning to show your age and, what's more, you were becoming greedy.'

'I suppose that swine of a redhead told you that?'

'What does it matter?'

'It couldn't be anyone else. He's been oiling himself into her good graces for weeks.'

'He has a job. He works for his living.'

'So do I.'

'Your so-called antique business is only a front. How many pieces of furniture do you sell in a year? Most of the time there's a "Closed" sign on your door.'

'I have to be out and about, buying.'

'No. . . . Joséphine Papet had had about as much as she could take. . . . For want of anything better, she was planning to install Bodard in your place.'

'It's his word against mine.'

'I know you, Florentin. Your word isn't worth *that*. . . .'

'You have got it in for me, haven't you?'

'Why should I "have it in for you", as you put it?'

'You always did, even in Moulins. . . . My parents owned a prosperous business. . . . I always had money to spend. . . . But what was your father? Just a sort of upper servant on the Château de Saint-Fiacre estate. . . .'

Maigret flushed, and clenched his fists. He could have hit him, for, if there was one thing he could not tolerate, it was a slur on his father's name. Maigret senior had, in actual fact, been steward of the estate, with responsibility for twenty or more farms.

'You're despicable, Florentin.'

'You asked for it.'

'The only reason I'm not having you locked up here and now is because I haven't yet got the tangible evidence I need. But it won't be long now, I promise you.'

He strode across to the door of the Inspectors' Room, and flung it open.

'Which of you is in charge of this scoundrel here?'

Loutrie stood up.

'Keep close up behind him, and when he gets home, mount guard at the door. You can arrange a rota among yourselves.'

Florentin, realizing that he had gone too far, looked very much abashed.

'I apologize, Maigret. . . . I lost my head. . . . I didn't know what I was saying. . . . Put yourself in my shoes. . . .'

The Chief Superintendent maintained a grim silence, and kept his eyes averted as Florentin went out. Almost immediately after he had gone, the telephone rang. It was the Examining Magistrate wanting to know the outcome of the confrontation.

'It's too early to say,' explained Maigret. 'It's rather like dragging a pond. I've stirred up a lot of mud, but I can't tell yet what may come up. . . . I've arranged the funeral for ten tomorrow morning.'

A number of newspapermen were hanging about in the corridor. He was unusually short with them.

'Are you on the track of the killer, Chief Superintendent?'

'There's more than one track.'

'And you're not sure which is the right one?'

'Just so.'

'Do you think it's a *crime passionel*?'

It was on the tip of his tongue to say that there was no such thing, because that, more or less, was what he believed. In his experience, a lover scorned or a woman slighted was more often driven to murder by hurt pride than by thwarted passion.

That evening, he and Madame Maigret sat watching television and sipping their little glasses of raspberry liqueur, from the bottle sent to them by his sister-in-law in Alsace.

'What did you think of the film?'

He almost said, 'What film?'

Certainly he had been watching the screen. There had been a lot of movement and bustle and agitation, but if he had been asked to summarize the plot, he could not have done it.

Next morning, with Janvier at the wheel of the car, he arrived at the entrance of the Forensic Laboratory just before ten.

Florentin, looking taller and thinner than ever, was standing on the edge of the pavement with a cigarette dangling from his lips. Beside him was Bonfils, the inspector who had relieved Loutrie.

Florentin gave no sign of having seen the police car draw up. He just stood there with hunched shoulders, utterly dejected, as though he would never again be able to look the world in the face.

The hearse was at the door, and the undertaker's men wheeled the coffin over to it on a hand cart.

Maigret opened the rear door of the car.

'Get in!'

And, turning to Bonfils:

'You can go back to the Quai. . . . I'll look after him.'

'Are we ready?' enquired the undertaker's man.

They set off. In the rear mirror, the Chief Superintendent caught sight of a yellow car, which seemed to be following them. It was a cheap, much battered, little open two-seater. Above the windscreen Jean-Luc Bodard's mop of red hair was clearly visible.

They drove in silence towards Ivry, and almost the entire length of the great sprawling cemetery. The grave was in one of the new extensions, where trees had not yet had time to grow. Lucas had not forgotten to order flowers, as Maigret had asked him, and the young man with red hair had also brought a wreath.

As the coffin was being lowered from the hearse, Florentin buried his face in his hands, his shoulders shaking. Was he really weeping? Not that it meant anything. He had always been able to shed tears to order.

It was to Maigret that the undertaker's man handed the spade, for him to shovel the first sods of earth into the grave. A few minutes later, the two cars were starting up for the journey back.

'The Quai des Orfèvres, sir?'

Maigret nodded. Florentin, in the back of the car, still did not say a word.

When they reached the forecourt of the Quai des Orfèvres, Maigret got out of the car, and said to Janvier:

'You'd better stay with him until Bonfils comes down to take over.'

From the back of the car came an anguished cry:

'I swear to you, Maigret, I didn't kill her!'

Maigret merely shrugged, and walked away slowly, through the glass doors, towards the staircase. He found Bonfils in the Inspectors' Duty Room.

'I've left your customer downstairs. . . . He's all yours.'

'What shall I do if he insists on walking side-by-side with me?'

'That's up to you, only don't lose sight of him.'

To his surprise, when he went into his office, he found Lapointe waiting for him. He looked worried.

'I've got bad news, sir.'

'Not another murder?'

'No. The concierge has vanished.'

'I gave orders that she should be kept under close watch!'

'Loutrie rang through half an hour ago. He was almost in tears. . . .'

He was one of the oldest inspectors in the Force, and knew every trick of the trade.

'How did it happen?'

'Loutrie was mounting guard on the pavement opposite the building, when she came out. She had no hat on, and was carrying a shopping-bag.

'She didn't even look round to see if she was being followed. First, she went into the butcher's, and bought an escalope. . . . They seemed to know her there.

'Still without looking round, she went on down the Rue Saint-Georges, stopping to go into an Italian grocer's shop. While she was in there, Loutrie stayed outside, pacing up and down.

'When, after a quarter of an hour or more, she hadn't reappeared, he began to get worried, and went into the shop. It's very long and narrow, and there's another entrance at the back, opening on to the Square d'Orléans and the Rue Taitbout. Needless to say, the bird had flown.

'After he'd spoken to me, Loutrie went back to resume his watch on the building. As he said, there was no point in trying to search the whole district. . . . Do you think she's done a bunk?'

'I'm quite sure she hasn't.'

Maigret was back at the window, looking out on to the chestnut-trees and listening to the birds twittering in the branches.

'She didn't murder Joséphine Papet, so why on earth should she try to escape? Especially as she took nothing with her except her shopping bag, not even a hat!

'She must have been going to meet someone. . . . I rather suspected she might, after the confrontation yesterday.

'I was convinced from the start that she had seen the murderer, either when he arrived or when he left, or both.

'Suppose that, as he was leaving, he saw her there with her nose pressed against the glass, and those extraordinary eyes of hers, staring at him. . . .'

'I see what you mean!'

'He knew that she was bound to be subjected to questioning. And he, remember, was a regular visitor to Joséphine Papet's flat, and therefore known to the concierge.'

'Do you think he used threats?'

'Threats would cut no ice with a woman of that sort. You saw what she was like yesterday afternoon. . . . On the other hand, I can't see her being able to resist a bribe. . . .'

'If she's already had money out of him, why the disappearing trick?'

'Because of the confrontation.'

'I don't understand.'

'The murderer was here in this room. . . . She saw him. . . . She had only to say the word for him to be arrested. . . . But she preferred to say nothing. It's my belief that she suddenly woke up to the fact that her silence was worth a great deal more than she had been paid. . . .

'So she decided, this morning, to raise her price . . . but she couldn't do much about it with a police inspector at her heels.'

'Get me the hall porter at the Hôtel Scribe.'

As soon as he was through, Maigret grabbed the receiver.

'Hello! Hôtel Scribe? Is that the hall porter? Chief Superintendent Maigret speaking. . . . How are you, Jean? . . .

The children all well? . . . Good. . . . Splendid. . . . I'm interested in one of your regulars, name of Lamotte, Victor Lamotte, yes. I presume his suite is booked by the month? . . . Yes, that's what I thought. . . .

'Put me through to him, will you? . . . What's that? . . . Did you say yesterday? . . . The express to Bordeaux? . . . I thought he always stayed until Saturday night. . . .

'Has anyone been asking for him this morning? You haven't by any chance had an enquiry from a very fat woman, shabbily dressed, carrying a shopping-bag?

'No, I'm perfectly serious. . . . You're quite sure? . . . Oh! well, thanks all the same, Jean.'

He knew the hall porters of all the big hotels in Paris, some ever since they had joined the staff as page-boys.

The Blanc woman had not gone to the Hôtel Scribe, and even if she had done so, she would not have found the winegrower there.

'Get me his office in the Rue Auber.'

He was determined to leave nothing to chance. The offices in the Rue Auber were shut on Saturdays, but there was one member of the staff in the building, catching up on a backlog of work. He had not set eyes on the boss since two o'clock the previous afternoon.

'Try the offices of Courcel Frères, Ballbearings, in the Boulevard Voltaire.'

No reply. Here, on Saturdays, there was not even a caretaker on duty.

'Try his home in Rouen. . . . Don't breathe the word "police". I just want to know if he's in.'

Fernand Courcel occupied the whole of an old house on the Quai de la Bourse, a stone's throw from the Pont Boieldieu.

'May I speak to Monsieur Courcel, please?'

'He's just gone out. This is Madame Courcel speaking. . . .' She had a pleasant, youthful voice.

'Can I take a message?'

'Do you know when he'll be back?'

'He'll be in for lunch. . . . We've got people coming.'

'I take it, he only got back this morning?'

'No, last night. . . . Who is that speaking?'

In view of Maigret's injunction, Lapointe judged it wiser to ring off.

'He's just gone out. . . . He got back last night. . . . He's expected home for lunch. . . . They've got people coming. . . . His wife sounds charming.'

'That only leaves François Paré. . . . Try his number in Versailles. . . .'

Here, too, a woman's voice answered. She sounded tired and fretful.

'Madame Paré speaking.'

'Is your husband available, please?'

'Who is that?'

'A member of his staff,' said Lapointe, telling the first lie that came into his head.

'Is it important?'

'Why do you ask?'

'Because my husband is in bed. . . . When he got back last night, he wasn't feeling well. . . . He had a very restless night, so I thought it best to keep him in bed today. . . . He works too hard for a man of his age. . . .'

The inspector, sensing that she was about to hang up on him, hastily came to the point:

'Has anyone been asking for him this morning?'

'What do you mean?'

'Has anyone called to see him on business?'

'No one at all.'

Without another word, she rang off.

Florentin and *Le Rouquin* had been at the cemetery at the time of Madame Blanc's disappearance, and she had not been in touch with any of the other three suspects.

Madame Maigret, sensing that he had enough on his mind already, decided that he was not to be worried further until he had eaten his lunch. It was not until she had poured out his coffee that she ventured to ask:

'Have you seen the paper?'

'I haven't had time.'

There was a morning paper on an occasional table in the sitting-room. She went to fetch it, and handed it to him.

He read the banner headline:

And below, two somewhat more informative sub-titles:

Mysterious gathering at the Quai des Orfèvres
Chief Superintendent Maigret baffled

He gave a groan, and went off to fetch his pipe before settling down to read the story.

'Yesterday's edition of this paper carried the full story of the murder committed in a flat in the Rue Notre-Dame-de-Lorette.

'The victim was a young, unmarried woman, Joséphine Papet, occupation unknown.

'We ventured to suggest that the killer was probably one of several men who had enjoyed the favours of the murdered girl.

'In spite of the stubborn silence of the Criminal Investigation Department, we are given to understand that a number of persons were summoned to the Quai des Orfèvres yesterday, to attend a meeting which was in the nature of a confrontation. Among those present, we are told, were several men of standing and influence.

'Our attention has been drawn to the fact that one of the suspects, in particular, was in the flat at the time of the murder, and the question arises: Is he the guilty man, or merely a witness to the crime?

'It is a source of some embarrassment to Chief Superintendent Maigret, who is personally in charge of the case, that the man in question, Léon F . . . . . , is an old school friend.

'Can this be the reason why, in spite of the evidence against him, the man is still at large? It seems hard to credit. . . .'

Maigret, grinding his teeth, crushed the paper up into a ball.

'Idiots!' he muttered.

Was it possible that one of his own inspectors had in all innocence committed an indiscretion, led on by the wily gentlemen of the press? He was all too familiar with the methods of newspapermen. They would certainly have left no stone unturned. There was no question but that they must have interviewed the concierge, and it was not unlikely that she had been a good deal more forthcoming with them than with the police.

There was also the bearded painter, Florentin's next-door neighbour in the Boulevard Rochechouart.

'Does it matter so much?'

He shrugged. If the truth were known, the only effect of the article was to make him more than ever reluctant to act precipitately.

Before leaving the Quai, he had received the ballistics report from Gastinne-Renette. This confirmed the opinion of the police surgeon. The bullet was enormous, of twelve-millimetre calibre. There were very few in existence, and it could only have been fired from an obsolete revolver of Belgian make, which would not be obtainable from an ordinary gunsmith.

The writer of the report had commented that it would be impossible to fire such a weapon with any degree of accuracy.

There was no doubt that the murder weapon was the old gun from Josée's bedside table. Where was it now? It would be a waste of time to search for it. It could be anywhere, in the river, in some drain or other, on a rubbish dump, or in a field in the country.

What could have possessed the murderer to remove so compromising an object, instead of leaving it where it was? Possibly, in his haste to get away, he had not had time to remove all trace of fingerprints.

If that were so, then he would not have had time, either, to wipe his fingerprints from the surfaces he had touched in the flat.

Yet the fact remained that all the surfaces in the bedroom, including the door handles, had been wiped clean.

Was it, therefore, to be concluded that Florentin was lying, when he claimed that the murderer had stayed in the flat for a quarter of an hour after the shot had been fired?

Was it not more likely that Florentin himself had wiped away the prints?

Whatever Maigret's line of reasoning, it always led back to Florentin. He was the obvious suspect. But the Chief Superintendent distrusted the obvious.

All the same, he was ashamed of himself for allowing Florentin so much latitude. It almost smacked of favouritism, he felt. Had he not, perhaps, been unconsciously influenced by a sort of loyalty to his own youth?

'It's perfectly ridiculous!' he exclaimed aloud.

'Were you really such friends?'

'I should have said not. . . . I used to find all that clowning rather irritating.'

He did not mention the fact that he used sometimes to go into the shop just to catch a glimpse of Florentin's sister. It almost made him blush, even now.

'See you later.'

She put up her face to be kissed.

'Will you be in to dinner?'

'I hope so.'

He had not noticed that it had started to rain. His wife caught him up on the stairs, and gave him his umbrella.

He boarded a bus on the corner of the Boulevard, and stood on the platform, swaying with the motion of the vehicle, and gazing absently at the people hurrying to and fro along the pavements. What queer cattle human beings were, ready to break into a run at the slightest provocation! Where did they think they were going? What was all the rush for?

'If I'm no further forward by Monday. I'll put him under lock and key,' he promised himself, as a sop to his conscience.

He put up his umbrella, and walked from the Châtelet to the Quai des Orfèvres. The wind was blowing in squally gusts, driving the rain full into his face. This was what he used to refer to as 'wet water' when he was a child.

No sooner was he in his office than there was a knock at the door, and Loutrie came in.

'Bonfils has taken over from me,' he said. 'She's back.'

'What time did she get in?'

'Twenty past twelve. . . . I saw her coming down the street, as cool as you please, carrying her shopping-bag. . . .'

'Was it full?'

'A good deal fuller and heavier than it was this morning. . . . She didn't even deign to look at me as she went past. I think she was trying to needle me. She made straight for the lodge, and took down the sign saying: "Concierge at work on staircase".'

Maigret paced back and forth between the window and the door at least half a dozen times. Then, abruptly, he halted. He had come to a decision.

'Is Lapointe there?'

'Yes.'

'Tell him to wait for me. I won't be a minute.'

He took a key from his drawer, the one that opened the communicating door between his department and the Palais de Justice. He made his way down several long corridors and up a dark staircase to the Examining Magistrate's office. He knocked at the door.

Most of the offices in this part of the building were empty and silent. He was not very hopeful of finding Judge Page still at work on a Saturday afternoon.

'Come in,' said a voice, sounding a long way off.

Maigret found the judge, covered in dust, in the little windowless room adjoining his office, struggling to get things into some sort of order.

'Would you believe it, Maigret, there are documents here, two years old or more, that have never been filed. It will take me months to clear up the mountain of papers left behind by my predecessor.'

'I've come to ask you to sign a search warrant.'

'Just give me time to wash my hands.'

The nearest washbasin was at the far end of the corridor. Maigret warmed to him. A thoroughly decent, conscientious chap.

'Any new developments?'

'I've had trouble with the concierge. That woman knows a great deal, I'm sure of it. . . . Yesterday, when I had them all together, she was the only one who didn't turn a hair. What's more, I believe she's the only one, apart from the murderer himself, who knows who did it.'

'Why won't she talk? Is it just because she looks upon the police as her natural enemies?'

'I don't think that would be enough to keep her quiet, considering the risk. . . . It wouldn't have surprised me if the killer had tried to get rid of her. . . . In fact, with that possibility in mind, I've put a watch on the building. . . .

'It's my belief that she's been paid to keep her mouth firmly shut, though I don't know how much. . . .

'As soon as the crucial importance of her evidence was brought home to her, she must have realized that she hadn't been paid enough. . . .

'So this morning she gave my inspector the slip with all the cunning of a professional. . . . She set the scene first by going into the butcher's, so that my man naturally assumed that she was just doing her ordinary shopping, and then she went into the grocer's. . . . He, of course, suspected nothing, and waited outside for her, for a quarter of an hour, only to discover that the shop had two entrances, and that she'd slipped out by the back way.'

'Do you know where she went?'

'Florentin was with me at the cemetery at Ivry, and so was Jean-Luc Bodard. . . .'

'Did she call on any of the others?'

'Well, she certainly didn't see any of them. Lamotte went back to Bordeaux yesterday on the evening express. . . . Courcel is in Rouen, and was giving a luncheon party. As for Paré, he's in bed ill, and his wife is worrying about him, for a change. . . .'

'Whose name do you want on the search warrant?'

'Madame Blanc . . . the concierge.'

The judge went over to his clerk's table, and took a warrant from the drawer. He filled it in, signed and stamped it.

'I wish you luck.'

'Thanks.'

'Incidentally, don't worry your head about all that stuff in the papers. . . . No one who knows you. . .'

'Most kind of you.'

A few minutes later, he was driving away from the Quai des Orfèvres, with Lapointe at the wheel. The traffic was heavy, and everyone seemed even more in a hurry than usual. It was always the same on a Saturday. In spite of the rain and the wind, they couldn't wait to get out of town, on to the motorways, into the country.

For once in a way, Lapointe had no trouble in parking. There was a convenient space just across the road from the house. The lingerie shop was shut. The shoe shop was still open, but there was no one in it. The proprietor was standing in the doorway, gloomily watching the rain pouring down.

'What are we looking for, sir?'

'Anything we can make use of, but chiefly money.'

For the first time, Maigret found Madame Blanc sitting down inside the lodge. She was wearing a pair of steel-rimmed spectacles on the end of her bulbous nose, and reading the early edition of the afternoon paper.

Maigret went in, followed by Lapointe.

'Have you wiped your feet?'

And as they did not reply, she muttered:

'What do you want this time?'

Maigret handed her the search warrant. She read it through carefully, twice.

'I don't know what it means. What are you going to do?'

'Search.'

'You mean you're going to go through all my things?'

'I do apologize!'

'I'm not sure I oughtn't to get a lawyer.'

'If you do, it will only suggest that you have something to hide. . . . Keep an eye on her, Lapointe, and see that she doesn't touch anything.'

Against one wall of the lodge was a Henri II-style dresser. The top half was a cupboard with glass doors, in which were displayed some tumblers, a water-jug, and a pottery coffee set decorated in a bold flower-pattern.

In the right-hand drawer there were knives, forks and spoons, a corkscrew, and three napkin rings of various shapes and sizes. The cutlery had once been silver-plated, but was now so worn that it looked more like brass.

The left-hand drawer proved more interesting. It was stuffed with papers and photographs. One of the photographs was of a young couple, presumably Monsieur and Madame Blanc, though she was scarcely recognizable. It must have been taken when she was about twenty-five. Although, even at that age, she was plump, no one could have forseen that she would grow into the huge mountain of flesh that she was today. As for Monsieur Blanc, at whom she was actually smiling in the picture, his chief distinguishing feature was a fair moustache.

Neatly folded in an envelope was a list of the tenants, with the rents they paid, and, under a stack of postcards, a post-office savings book.

It went back many years. At the beginning, the sums deposited were small, ten or twenty francs at a time. Later, she had got into the habit of saving fifty francs a month regularly, except for January, when the annual tips from the tenants raised the sum to between a hundred and a hundred and fifty francs.

The total amounted to eight thousand, three hundred and twenty-two francs, and a few centimes.

There were no very recent entries. The last was a fort-night old.

'Much good may it do you!'

Ignoring her, he went on with his search. In the lower half of the dresser, there was a dinner service, and, beside it, a pile of folded check tablecloths.

He lifted the velvet cloth draped over the round table, to see if there was a drawer underneath, but he found none.

To his left there was a television set on a table. He opened the drawer of the table, but found nothing except a few bits of string, and some nails and drawing-pins.

He went into the room at the back, which served a double purpose as kitchen and bedroom. The bed stood in an alcove, concealed by a shabby curtain.

He began with the bedside table and found, in the drawer, a rosary, a prayer book and a sprig of rosemary. For a moment, he could not imagine what the rosemary was doing there, then he remembered the custom of sprinkling aromatic herbs with holy water as a sign of family mourning, and could only suppose that she had kept it in memory of one of her parents.

It was hard to think of that woman as ever having been a wife to anyone, but, undoubtedly, she had once been some-body's child, like everyone else.

He had known others like her, men and women, whom life

had so hardened that they had almost been turned into monsters. For years now, she had been confined, by day and by night, to these two dark, airless rooms, with scarcely more freedom of movement than she would have had in a prison cell.

As for any communication with the outside world, she saw no one except the postman, and the tenants going in and out.

Every morning, regardless of her weight and swollen legs, she had to clean out the lift, and sweep the stairs from top to bottom.

And if, tomorrow or the next day, she should no longer be able to work, what then?

And here he was, harassing her. He felt ashamed of himself. He opened the door of the little refrigerator. Inside was half an escalope, the remains of an omelette, two slices of ham and a few vegetables, no doubt those she had bought that morning.

On the kitchen table stood a half-bottle of wine. It only remained now for him to search the cupboard. Here he found nothing but underclothes and dresses, a corset and a pair of elastic stockings.

It was painful to him now to have to continue the search, but he was unwilling to admit defeat. She was not the woman to be fobbed off with promises. If anyone had bribed her to keep her mouth shut, he must have paid her there and then, in cash.

He went back into the lodge and, on seeing him, her eyes flickered, revealing a twinge of anxiety that she was unable to hide.

It was enough to tell him that there was nothing for him to find in the kitchen. Very slowly, he surveyed the lodge. Where was it that he had failed to look?

He made a sudden dive for the television set, on top of which were stacked a few periodicals. One of these was devoted to radio and television programmes, with accompanying articles and photographs.

No sooner had he picked it up than he knew that he had won.

It fell open of its own accord at the place where she had slipped in three five-hundred franc and seven hundred-franc notes.

Two thousand two hundred francs. The five-hundred franc notes were brand new.

'I'm entitled to my savings, aren't I?'

'I've seen your post-office book, don't forget.'

'What of it? Who says I have to put all my eggs in one basket? I might find myself needing ready money at any time.'

'Two thousand two hundred francs isn't exactly petty cash!'

'That's my business. Just try making trouble for me, and see where it gets you. . . .'

'You're a good deal cleverer than you make yourself out to be, Madame Blanc. . . . I have a shrewd suspicion that you were expecting me today, search warrant and all. If you had deposited the money in the post office, the transaction would have been entered in your book, and I could not have failed to be struck by the unusually large sum, and the date. . . .

'You could have put the money in a drawer or a cupboard, or have sewn it into your mattress, but no—have you by any chance read the works of Edgar Allan Poe?—you chose to slip the notes between the pages of a magazine.'

'I'm not a thief.'

'I'm not suggesting that you are. In fact, I don't believe you asked for this money. It's my opinion that the murderer, seeing you at the door of the lodge as he was going out, came in and offered it to you, before you even knew that a murder had been committed in the building. . . .

'There was no need for him to volunteer any explanation. He only had to ask you to forget you had seen him on that occasion.

'You must have known who he was, otherwise he would have had nothing to fear from you.'

'I have nothing to say.'

'Yesterday, when you saw him in my office, you realized that he was a very frightened man, and that the person he was afraid of was none other than yourself, you being the only one in a position to give him away.

'It didn't take you long to work out that a man, especially if he is rich, probably values his liberty a good deal higher than two thousand two hundred francs. So you decided to seek him out this morning, and see how much more you could get.'

As on the previous day, her lips twitched in a faint ghost of a smile.

'You found no one there. . . . You had forgotten that today was Saturday.'

The expression of the woman's bloated face, at once stubborn and enigmatic, did not change.

'I'm saying nothing. Beat me up if you like. . . .'

'I'd rather not, thank you. We shall meet again. Let's go, Lapointe.'

And the two men went out, and got into the little black car.

CHAPTER SEVEN

SUNDAY was a gloomy day, with a glimmer of pale sunlight filtering through the massed banks of cloud. In spite of this, they followed the crowds streaming out into the country for the day.

When they had first bought the car, it had been their intention to use it only for going to and from their little house in Meung-sur-Loire and for touring on holiday. They had, in fact, been to Meung three or four times, but it was really too far to go there and back in a day. There was no one to look after the house in their absence, which meant that Madame Maigret barely managed to dust around, and prepare a scratch meal, before it was time to leave.

It was about ten in the morning when they set out.

They had agreed that it would be best to keep off the motorways.

Unfortunately, thousands of other Parisians had come to the same conclusion, and the little country roads that ought to have been so delightful were as crowded as the Champs-Elysées.

They were looking for an attractive little inn, with an appetizing bill of fare. They knew from long experience that most of the wayside inns were always full to overflowing, and that those which were not served disgusting food, but this did not deter them from trying again, Sunday after Sunday.

It was the same as with the television set. When they had first bought it, they had vowed that they would only look at programmes that really interested them. At the end of a fortnight, Madame Maigret had taken to laying the table in such a way as to enable them both to face the screen while they were eating.

They did not bicker in the car, as so many married couples do. All the same, Madame Maigret was very tense at the wheel. She had only recently passed her driving test, and was still lacking in self-confidence.

'Why don't you pass them?'

'There's a double white line.'

On this particular Sunday, Maigret scarcely said a word. He sat slumped in his seat, puffing at his pipe, his eyes fixed on the road ahead, glowering. In spirit, he was in the Rue Notre-Dame-de-Lorette, reconstructing the events leading up to the death of Joséphine Papet in as many different ways as he could think of.

He considered each hypothetical reconstruction in turn, having built it up with great attention to detail, even to the extent of inventing appropriate dialogue. Then he tested its validity from every angle. Each time, just when it was beginning to seem impregnable, some flaw would appear, and he was back where he started.

It was like trying to solve a chess problem, with the people involved as the pieces, which could be moved here or there to produce this or that result.

Time and again, he set up the problem, rearranging the pieces in different positions, sometimes removing one or more pieces, sometimes bringing new ones into play.

They stopped for lunch at an inn. The food was no better and no worse than that to be had at any railway station buffet. The only difference was the size of the bill.

They set out for a walk in the woods, but were discouraged by mud underfoot and a steady downpour of rain.

They got home early, to a dinner of cold meat and Russian salad. Maigret was so restless that his wife suggested they should go to the cinema, which they did.

At nine o'clock sharp on Monday morning, he was in his office. The rain had stopped, and the sun, though not very bright, was shining.

The reports of the inspectors who had taken it in turn to keep watch on Florentin were on his desk.

Florentin had spent the Saturday evening in a brasserie in the Boulevard de Clichy. This, it seemed, was not one of his usual haunts, as no one there appeared to recognize him.

He had ordered a half-pint, and taken it over to a table, next to a party of four regulars, who were obviously old friends, and who were immersed in a game of *belote*. He had sat for some time with his elbow on the table and his chin in his hand, following the game in a desultory way.

At about ten, one of the card-players, a weedy little man, who had been chattering away ceaselessly the whole evening, suddenly said:

'I'm sorry, you fellows, but I'll have to be going. . . . Her ladyship will roast me alive if I'm late home, especially as I'm going out fishing tomorrow.'

The others pressed him to stay, but to no avail. When he had gone, they had looked about them for someone to make up the four. One of them had asked Florentin, in a strong southern accent:

'Do you play?'

'I'll join you with pleasure.'

Thereupon he had moved over to the vacant seat at the table and stayed there, playing *belote* until midnight, while poor Dieudonné, whose shift it was, sat gloomily slumped in a corner.

And Florentin, always the gentleman, had stood drinks all round, thus making a substantial dent in the hundred francs that Maigret had given him.

He had gone straight home from the brasserie and, with a final conspiratorial wink at Dieudonné, had retired to bed.

He had slept late, and had not gone into the tobacconist's for his breakfast of croissants dipped in coffee until after ten. Dieudonné, by that time, had been relieved by Lagrume, and Florentin had looked him up and down with interest, as much as to say: 'This is a new one on me!'

Lagrume was the gloomiest of all the inspectors, and not without reason, as he never seemed to be without a cold for more than a couple of months in the year, besides which he was afflicted with flat feet, which gave him endless trouble, and caused him to walk in a most peculiar way.

From the tobacconist's, Florentin had gone into a betting shop, where he had invested in a ticket for the Tote treble, after which he had sauntered off down the Boulevard des Batignolles. He had gone past the Hôtel Beauséjour without so much as a glance. There was no reason to suppose that he knew that *Le Rouquin* lived there.

He had lunched in a restaurant in the Place des Ternes, then, as on the previous Friday, had gone into a cinema.

What was to become of this tall, thin man with the expressive, indiarubber face, when the Chief Superintendent's hundred francs were exhausted?

He had not met a single person he knew. No one at all had tried to get in touch with him. He had gone into a self-service bar for his dinner, and then straight home to bed.

As to the Rue Notre-Dame-de-Lorette, there was nothing of any interest to report from there either. Madame Blanc had emerged from the lodge only to sweep the stairs and put out the dustbins.

Some of the tenants had attended Mass, others had gone out for the day. All in all, it had been a boring and frustrating day for the two inspectors on watch outside in the street, which on a Sunday had been virtually deserted.

Maigret was devoting this Monday morning to re-reading all the reports on the case, in particular those of the police surgeon, the ballistics expert, Moers and Criminal Records.

Janvier, after a discreet knock on the door, came in, looking fresh, cheerful and ready for anything.

'How do you feel, sir?'

'Rotten.'

'Didn't you enjoy your day out?'

'No.'

Janvier could not help smiling. He was well acquainted with this mood, and, as a rule, it was a good sign. It was Maigret's way, when he was working on a case, to soak everything up like a sponge, absorbing into himself people and things, even of the most trivial sort, as well as impressions of which he was perhaps barely conscious.

It was generally when he was close to saturation point that he was at his most disgruntled.

'How did you spend the day?'

'We went to my sister-in-law's, my wife and I and the kids. . . . There was a fair in the market-place, and the children spent a small fortune shooting at clay pigeons.'

Maigret got up and started pacing the room. A buzzer sounded summoning Heads of Departments to the weekly conference for the exchange of information.

'They can perfectly well get along without me,' grumbled Maigret.

He was in no mood to answer the questions that his Chief would undoubtedly ask, nor to give him advance warning of his plans, which were anyway somewhat nebulous. He was still feeling his way.

'If only that frightful woman could be made to talk!'

The huge, phlegmatic concierge was still in the forefront of his mind.

'There are times when I regret the abolition of third-degree methods. I'd like to see just how long she'd hold out.'

He didn't seriously mean it, of course. It was just his way of letting off steam.

'What about you? Have you any ideas?'

Janvier never liked it when Maigret asked him point-blank for his opinion. Somewhat hesitantly, he ventured:

'I think . . .'

'Come on, out with it! You think I'm barking up the wrong tree, is that it?'

'Not at all. It's just that I have a notion that Florentin knows even more than she does. . . . And Florentin is in a much weaker position. . . . He's got nothing to look forward to. . . . If he's able to pick up a few sous here and there by loafing around Montmartre, he'll be lucky.'

Maigret looked at him with interest.

'Go and fetch him.'

As he was leaving, Maigret called him back.

'And you'd better pick up the concierge from the Rue Notre-Dame-de-Lorette at the same time, while you're about it. She'll raise Cain, but take no notice, use force if necessary. . . .'

Janvier smiled. He could not quite see himself coming to

blows with that great battering-ram of a woman, who was at least twice his weight.

Soon after he left, Maigret was on the telephone to the Ministry of Public Works.

'I'd be obliged if you would put me through to Monsieur Paré.'

'Hold on, please.'

'Hello! Is that Monsieur Paré?'

'Monsieur Paré isn't in today. . . . His wife has just rung through. . . . He's not at all well. . . .'

Maigret rang off, and dialled the Versailles number.

'Madame Paré?'

'Who's speaking?'

'Chief Superintendent Maigret. How is your husband?'

'Not at all well. . . . The doctor has just left. . . . He's afraid he may be on the verge of a nervous breakdown.'

'It wouldn't be possible for me to talk to him, would it?'

'The doctor recommends complete rest.'

'Does he seem worried? Has he asked to see the newspapers?'

'No. . . . He's just withdrawn into himself. . . . I can scarcely get a word out of him.'

'Thank you.'

Next he rang the Hôtel Scribe.

'Is that you, Jean? Maigret here. . . . Is Monsieur Victor Lamotte back from Bordeaux yet? . . . So he's left for his office already, has he? . . . Thanks.'

He dialled the number of Lamotte's office in the Rue Auber.

'Chief Superintendent Maigret speaking. Would you put me through to Monsieur Lamotte, please?'

There was a great deal of clicking on the line. Apparently it was necessary to go through a whole hierarchy of subordinates to get to the great man himself.

At long last, a voice said dryly: 'Yes?'

'Maigret here.'

'So I was told.'

'Will you be in your office all morning?'

'I really can't say.'

'I'd be obliged if you'd stay there until you hear from me again.'

'I'd better warn you that, if I'm summoned to your office again, I shall have my lawyer with me this time.'

'You'll be perfectly within your rights.'

Next, Maigret tried the Boulevard Voltaire, but Courcel had not yet arrived.

'He never gets in before eleven, and sometimes he doesn't come in at all on a Monday. Would you care to speak to the assistant manager?'

'No, that's all right.'

Pacing up and down the room with his hands behind his back, and glaring from time to time at the clock, Maigret once again reviewed all the possibilities that he had considered in the car on the previous day.

He eliminated each in turn, until only one was left. This, subject to the tying up of a few loose ends, provided the answer.

Looking more than a little shamefaced, he opened the cupboard in which he always kept a bottle of brandy. It was not intended for his own use, but as a restorative, to be produced in case of need, as when, for instance, someone he was questioning collapsed after making a confession.

He could not claim to be in a state of collapse. It was not he who was going to have to make a confession. All the same, he took a long swig straight out of the bottle.

Having done so, he felt thoroughly ashamed of himself. Once more, he glanced impatiently at the clock. Then, at long last, he heard footsteps in the corridor, and a voice raised in furious anger, which he recognized as that of Madame Blanc.

He crossed to the door, and opened it.

Florentin, though visibly uneasy, attempted, as usual, to laugh it off.

'I'm beginning to look on this place as quite a home from home!'

As for the woman:

'I'm a free citizen, and I demand. . .' she thundered.

'Take her away and lock her up somewhere, Janvier. . . . You'd better stay with her, but take care she doesn't scratch your eyes out.'

And, turning to Florentin:

'Take a seat.'

139

'I'd rather stand.'

'And I'd rather you sat down.'

'Oh! well, if you insist. . . .'

He made a face, just as he used to in the old days, after an altercation with one of the masters, trying to restore his self-esteem by raising a laugh.

Maigret went into the other room to fetch Lapointe. He had been present at most of the earlier interviews, and was familiar with all the details of the case.

Taking his time over it, the Chief Superintendent filled his pipe, lit it, and gingerly pressed down the smouldering tobacco with his thumb.

'I take it, Florentin, that you have nothing to add to your statement?'

'I've told you all I know.'

'No.'

'It's the truth, I swear it.'

'And I know it's a pack of lies, from start to finish.'

'Are you calling me a liar?'

'You always were a liar. Even at school. . . .'

'It was only for a laugh.'

'Agreed. . . . But this is no laughing matter.'

He looked his old school friend straight in the eye, with a very grave expression, in which there was something of contempt and also something of pity. But probably more of pity than contempt.

'What's to become of you?'

Florentin shrugged.

'How should I know?'

'You're fifty-three.'

'Fifty-four. . . . I'm a year older than you are. I had to repeat in the sixth form.'

'You're getting a bit past it. . . . It won't be easy to find another Josée.'

'I shan't even try.'

'Your antique business is a flop. . . . You have no skills, no training, no professional experience. . . . And you're too seedy to work the confidence racket any longer.'

It was cruel but it had to be said.

'You're a miserable wreck, Florentin.'

'Everything always went sour on me. . . . I know I'm a failure, but . . .'

'But you won't admit defeat, will you? You're still hoping . . . what for, for heaven's sake?'

'I don't know.'

'Right. That's settled then. And now the time has come for me to take a weight off your mind.'

There was a long pause, during which Maigret looked searchingly into the face of his old school friend. Then he came out with it:

'I know you didn't kill Josée.'

CHAPTER EIGHT

IT CAME as much less of a surprise to Florentin than to Lapointe. He shot up in his seat, aghast, with his pencil poised in mid-air, and gaped at his chief.

'But that doesn't mean you've got anything to crow about. Your conduct has been far from blameless. . . .'

'But you yourself admit . . .'

'I admit on that one point you've told the truth, which, I must confess, is more than I'd have expected of you. . . .'

'I can explain. . . .'

'I'd rather you didn't keep interrupting. On Wednesday last, probably round about a quarter past three, as you say, someone rang the doorbell of the flat. . . .'

'You see!'

'Oh! Do shut up. . . . As usual, not knowing who it might be, you made a bolt for the bedroom. . . . As you and Josée were not expecting any callers, you listened. . . .

'I take it that one or other of her lovers did occasionally change the time of his visit?'

'In that case, they would always telephone. . . .'

'Didn't they ever turn up unexpectedly?'

'Very rarely.'

'And on those rare occasions, you hid in the clothes closet. On Wednesday, however, you were not in the clothes closet but in the bedroom. . . . You recognized the voice of the caller, and you took fright. . . . Why? Because you realized that it wasn't Josée he had come to see, but you.'

Florentin froze. It was clear that he simply could not make out what process of reasoning had led his old school friend to this conclusion.

'I have proof, you see, that he went up to the flat on Wednesday. . . . Because the gentleman in question, having just committed a murder, panicked and tried to buy the concierge's silence with the sum of two thousand two hundred francs, which was all he had on him at the time. . . .'

'But you yourself have admitted that I'm innocent!'

'Of the murder. . . . But that isn't to say that you weren't indirectly the cause of it. If one can talk in terms of morality where you're concerned, one could say that you were morally responsible.'

'I don't understand.'

'Yes, you do.'

Maigret stood up. He never could sit still for long. Florentin ollowed him with his eyes, as he paced up and down the room.

'Joséphine Papet had fallen in love with someone new. . . .'

'You surely don't mean *Le Rouquin*?'

'Yes.'

'It was just a passing fancy. . . . He'd never have agreed to her terms . . . living with her, skulking in cupboards, keeping out of the way when necessary. . . . He's young . . . he can get all the girls he wants. . . .'

'That doesn't alter the fact that Josée was in love with him, or that she'd had enough of you. . . .'

'How do you know? You're only guessing.'

'She said so herself.'

'Who to? Not to you. You never saw her alive.'

'To Jean-Luc Bodard.'

'And you really believe every word that fellow says?'

'He had no cause to lie to me.'

'What about me, then?'

'You faced the risk of a longish prison sentence . . . probably as much as two years, having regard to your previous convictions.'

142

Florentin took this more calmly. Although he had not realized just how much Maigret had discovered about his past, he had heard enough to be prepared for the worst.

'To get back to the Wednesday caller. . . . The reason you were so badly shaken when you recognized his voice was that, some days or weeks earlier, you had attempted to blackmail one of Josée's lovers.

'Needless to say, you picked on the one who seemed to you the most vulnerable, in other words the one who set the greatest store by his reputation. You raised the subject of his letters. . . .

'How much did you get out of him?'

Florentin hung his head, looking very sorry for himself.

'Nothing.'

'You mean, he wouldn't play?'

'No, but he asked for a few days' grace.'

'How much were you asking for?'

'Fifty thousand. . . . I needed at least that. . . . I wanted to make a clean break, to get right away, and start life afresh elsewhere. . . .'

'So I was right. Josée was trying to ease you out as gently as possible.'

'Maybe she was. . . . She certainly wasn't the same any more. . . .'

'Now you're beginning to talk sense. Keep it up, and I'll do my best to see that you're let off as lightly as possible in the circumstances.'

'Would you really do that for me?'

'What a fool you are!' muttered Maigret in an undertone, not intending Florentin to hear. But he did hear, and flushed crimson to the roots of his hair.

It was no more than the truth. There were literally thousands of people like him living in Paris, subsisting on the border-line of crime by more or less openly exploiting the naïvety or cupidity of their fellow-men.

Such people were always full of grandiose schemes, the realization of which was thwarted only by the lack of a few thousand or a few hundred thousand francs.

Most of them managed, in the end, to cheat some mug out

143

of his money. And then there would follow a brief spell of prosperity, of fast cars and expensive restaurants.

When the money was spent, they were back where they started, and the whole laborious process would begin again. And yet, scarcely one in ten of such people ever saw the inside of a corrective training establishment or a gaol.

Florentin was the exception. All his schemes had come to nothing, and the last had proved the most disastrous of all.

'Now, will you tell the rest of the story, or would you rather I did?'

'I'd rather leave it to you.'

'The visitor asks to see you. He knows you are in the flat, because he's made it his business to find out from the concierge. He is unarmed. He's not of a particularly jealous disposition, and he has no wish to kill anyone. . . .

'All the same, he is in a highly excitable frame of mind. Josée, nervous on your account, denies that you are in the flat, and claims to have no idea where you are.

'He goes into the dining-room, making for the bedroom. You retreat into the bathroom with the intention of hiding in the closet.'

'But I never got that far.'

'Right. . . . He marches you back into the bedroom.'

'Shouting at the top of his voice that I was despicable, beneath contempt,' interposed Florentin, bitterly. 'And with her there, listening.'

'She knows nothing about the blackmail business. . . . She doesn't understand what's going on. . . . You tell her to keep out of it. . . . But, in spite of everything—because you feel it's your last chance—you still cling to the hope of getting that fifty thousand francs.'

'I'm not sure of anything any more. . . . It was all so confused. . . . I don't think any of us quite knew what was happening. . . . There was Josée, pleading with us to calm down. . . . The man was in a furious temper. . . . I'd refused to give him back his letters. When he saw that I meant it, he pulled open the bedside table drawer, and grabbed the revolver. . . .

'Josée began screaming. . . . I admit, I was scared, too. . . .'

'So you took shelter behind her?'

'I swear to you, Maigret, that it was sheer accident that she was hit.

'You could see the man didn't know the first thing about handling firearms. He kept waving the gun about. . . . I was actually on the point of giving him back his blasted letters, when it went off. . . .

'He looked utterly stunned. . . . He made a queer little gurgling noise in his throat, and bolted out of the room.'

'Had he still got the revolver?'

'I presume so. . . . At any rate, when I looked for it, it had gone. . . . As soon as I bent down to look at Josée, I knew she was dead. . . .'

'Why didn't you call the police?'

'I don't know. . . .'

'I do. You were thinking about the forty-eight thousand francs she kept in a biscuit tin, the tin you wrapped in news-paper and took back to your workshop. . . . Incidentally, it was very careless of you to use that day's morning paper.

'As you were leaving, you remembered the letters, and stuffed them in your pocket. . . .

'At last, you had riches within your grasp. . . . For the man whom you had blackmailed by threatening to expose an affair with a woman had now committed a murder. . . .'

'What on earth put that idea into your head?'

'The fact that you removed the fingerprints on the furniture and door handles. It wouldn't have mattered if your prints had been found—even you never attempted to deny that you were in the flat. No, it was the other man's prints that you were anxious to get rid of, because once he was identified and caught, he could be of no further use to you.'

Maigret returned to his chair, sat down heavily, and refilled his pipe.

'You went back to your place, and hid the biscuit tin on top of the wardrobe. . . . For the time being, you forgot about the letters in your pocket. Then, suddenly, you thought of me, your old school friend, who would surely protect you, at least from rough handling. . . . You always were something of a physical coward. . . . Remember? . . . There was that kid

Bambois. . . . As I recall, he only had to threaten to twist your arm to have you shaking in your shoes. . . .'

'Now, you're being cruel.'

'Look who's talking! If you hadn't been such a louse, Josée would be alive today.'

'I'll never forgive myself, as long as I live.'

'That won't bring her back. . . . Anyway, it's entirely between you and your conscience. You came here with every intention of leading me up the garden path, but you'd scarcely opened your mouth before I realized there was something wrong somewhere.

'I had the same feeling in the flat. . . . The whole set-up was phony. It was as though I'd been handed a tangled ball of string, but couldn't find the end that would help me straighten it out.

'Of all the people concerned in this case, the concierge intrigued me most. She's a great deal tougher than you are.'

'She never could stand the sight of me.'

'Any more than you could stand the sight of her. By keeping her mouth shut about the caller, not only did she stand to gain two thousand two hundred francs, but she had you just where she wanted you. As to your dive into the Seine, that was sheer folly. If it hadn't been for that, I might never have thought of the letters. . . .

'It was clear from the start that you had no intention of drowning. No one who could swim as you can would attempt suicide by throwing himself off the Pont-Neuf when it was crawling with people, knowing, moreover, that he would hit the water within a very few feet of a boat moored to the bank.

'You suddenly remembered those letters in your pocket. . . . One of my men was close on your heels. . . . At any moment, you might be searched. . . .'

'I never dreamed you'd guess. . . .'

'It's my job, and I've been at it thirty-five years,' muttered Maigret.

'The secret is never to let oneself be taken in,' he added, and went out to have a word with Lucas.

When he came back into his office, he found all the stuffing knocked out of Florentin. He was just a long, lean husk of a man, with hollowed cheeks and sunken eyes.

'Am I right in thinking that I shall be charged with demanding money with menaces?'

'That depends. . . .'

'On what?'

'On the Examining Magistrate. . . . And, to some extent, on me. . . . Don't forget that, by obliterating the fingerprints, you were obstructing the police, and laying yourself open to a further charge of being an accessory after the fact. . . .'

'You wouldn't do that to me, surely?'

'I'll have a word with the judge. . . .'

'I could probably survive a year or, at most, two in gaol, but if it's a question of being shut up for years, then I'll have to be carried out feet first. . . . I have heart trouble, as it is. . . .'

No doubt he would do his utmost to be allowed to serve his sentence in the infirmary of La Santé Prison. And this man had once been the boy Maigret had known in Moulins, who had kept them all in fits of laughter. He could always be relied on to brighten up a dull lesson, with the whole class egging him on.

And they always had egged him on, knowing how much he delighted in thinking up new practical jokes, and displaying himself in an infinite number of different guises.

The clown . . . there had been that time when he had pretended to drown in the Nièvre. They had spent a quarter of an hour searching for him, and found him, at last, hiding in a clump of reeds to which he had swum under water.

'What are we waiting for?' he asked, suddenly anxious again.

It was certainly a relief to him to have got it over, but he was by no means confident that his old friend might not, even now, have a change of heart.

There was a knock at the door, and old Joseph came in and handed a visiting card to Maigret.

'Show him up. . . . And go and ask Janvier to bring in the woman.'

He would have given anything for a long, cool, glass of beer, or even another nip of brandy.

'Allow me to introduce my lawyer, Maître Bourdon.'

One of the leading lights of the legal profession, a former President of the French Bar, whose name had been put forward for membership of the Academy.

With icy dignity, Victor Lamotte, dragging his foot a little, crossed the room and sat down. He scarcely glanced at Florentin.

'I presume, Chief Superintendent, that you have good and sufficient reasons for insisting on the presence of my client here today? I understand that on Saturday last, also, he was summoned to attend a meeting here, and I should warn you that, on my advice, he reserves his position as to the legality of those proceedings. . . .'

'Won't you sit down, Maître?' said Maigret tersely.

Janvier propelled Madame Blanc into the room. She seemed much agitated. Then she caught sight of the lame man, and froze.

'Come in, Madame Blanc. Please sit down.'

She had been taken completely unaware, or so it seemed.

'Who is that?' she asked, pointing to Maître Bourdon.

'Your friend Monsieur Lamotte's lawyer.'

'Have you arrested him?'

Her protuberant eyes seemed more prominent than ever.

'Not yet, but I intend to do so in a moment. Do you identify him as the man who, on Wednesday last, came down from Mademoiselle Papet's flat, and paid you two thousand two hundred francs to keep your mouth shut?'

She was silent, her lips pressed together in a straight, hard line.

'You were very ill-advised to give her that money, Monsieur Lamotte. So large a sum was bound to put ideas into her head. It didn't escape her that if her silence was worth that much to you before she had even asked for anything, its real value was probably higher. . . .'

'I haven't the least idea what you're talking about.'

The lawyer was frowning.

'Let me explain how I arrived at the conclusion that it was you, rather than any of the other suspects, who were guilty of the murder. . . .

'I have kept Madame Blanc under observation for several days. On Saturday, she managed to shake off the inspector who was following her, by going into a shop and slipping out through the back entrance. . . . Her intention was to see you and demand more money. . . . The matter, you see, was pressing, as she had no means of knowing how long it would be before you were arrested.'

'I certainly didn't see this woman on Saturday.'

'I know. . . . But that's not the point. . . . What matters is that she set out with the intention of seeing you. . . . There were three of you, each with your regular days. François Paré's was Wednesday, Courcel's Thursday night to Friday morning. . . . Jean-Luc Bodard had no set day. . . .

'Most businessmen from the provinces who spend part of the week in Paris return home on Saturday. You did not, because you had an arrangement to spend Saturday afternoons with Mademoiselle Papet. . . .

'The concierge was aware of this, of course, which is why she went to see you that day. . . . She didn't foresee that, as you no longer had anything to keep you in Paris on Saturdays, you would go back to Bordeaux on the Friday night. . . .'

'Ingenious,' remarked the lawyer, 'but a bit flimsy as evidence to put before a jury, don't you think?'

The concierge, silent and motionless, seemed to fill the room with her huge presence.

'I agree, Maître, but I am not relying on that alone. . . . This gentleman here is Léon Florentin. . . . He has made a full confession. . . .'

'I was under the impression that he was the chief suspect.'

Florentin, shoulders hunched, hung his head, feeling that he would never again be able to look anyone in the face.

'He is not the murderer,' retorted Maigret, 'but the intended victim.'

'I don't understand.'

But Lamotte understood. He started violently in his chair.

'It was at him that the gun was levelled in a threatening gesture, designed to secure the return of certain compromising letters. . . . Monsieur Lamotte, however, is a very bad shot, and, what's more, the weapon was unreliable. . . .'

The lawyer turned enquiringly to his client:

'Is this true?'

He had not been prepared for this turn of events. Lamotte did not answer, but instead glowered savagely at Florentin.

'It may help your case, Maître, to know that I am not convinced that your client fired the shot intentionally. He is a man accustomed to getting his own way, and when he meets with resistance he's liable to lose his temper. On this occasion, unfortunately, he had a gun in his hand, and it went off. . . .'

This time, the man with the limp was really shattered. With a dazed expression, he stared at Maigret.

'I must ask you to excuse me for a moment. I shan't be long.'

Maigret went through to the Palais de Justice, and made his way up through the maze of corridors, as he had done on the previous Saturday. He knocked at the Examining Magistrate's door, and went in to find him at his desk, immersed in a bulky file. His clerk was in the annexe, carrying on the work of restoring order.

'It's all over!' announced Maigret, collapsing into a chair.

'Has he confessed?'

'Who?'

'Well . . . that fellow Florentin, I presume.'

'He hasn't killed anyone. . . . All the same, I shall require a warrant for his arrest. . . . The charge is demanding money with menaces.'

'And the murderer?'

'He's waiting in my office in company with his lawyer, Maître Bourdon.'

'I can see trouble ahead! He's one of the most. . .'

'Don't worry, you'll find him most accommodating. I wouldn't go so far as to say that it was an accident, but there are a number of extenuating circumstances. . . .'

'Which of them. . . .?'

'Victor Lamotte, the man with the limp, wine-grower of Bordeaux, respected member of the exclusive community of Les Chartrons, where such matters as dignity and rank, not to mention moral rectitude, are not to be trifled with. . . .'

'I'll devote this afternoon to completing my report, and I hope to be able to let you have it by the end of the day. . . . It's almost lunch-time and. . .'

'You're hungry, I expect.'

'Thirsty!' admitted Maigret.

A few minutes later, he was back in his office, where he handed over to Lapointe and Janvier the warrants signed by the Examining Magistrate.

'Take them up to Criminal Records for the usual formalities, and then escort them to the cells.'

Janvier, pointing to the concierge, who had risen to her feet, asked:

'What about her?'

'We'll attend to her later. . . . In the meantime, she'd better go back to the flats. . . . The lodge can't be left unattended for ever.'

She looked at him without expression. Her lips moved, and a little hiss escaped her, as when water is splashed on hot coals, but she did not speak. At last she turned towards the door, and went out.

'I'll see you later, you two, in the Brasserie Dauphine.'

It was only afterwards that he realized how thoughtless it had been of him to toss off this invitation to his men in the presence of those other two, who were about to be deprived of their liberty.

Five minutes later, standing at the bar of the familiar little restaurant, he gave his order:

'A beer. . . . In the tallest glass you can find.'

In thirty-five years, he had not set eyes on a single one of the boys who had been his schoolmates at the Lycée Banville.

And when, at last, he did, of all people it had to be Florentin!

Epalinges, June 24, 1968

MAIGRET AND
THE WINE MERCHANT

★

*Translated from
the French by*
EILEEN ELLENBOGEN

CHAPTER ONE

'YOU KILLED HER in order to steal from her, didn't you?'

'I never meant to kill her. It was only a toy pistol I had. That proves it, surely?'

'Did you know she had a lot of money?'

'I didn't know how much. She'd worked hard all her life, and she was eighty-two or three. I knew she must have a bit put by.'

'How often did you ask her for money?'

'I don't know. Several times. She knew that was why I went to see her. She was my grandmother. She always tipped me five francs. I ask you! What use is five francs to a man out of work?'

Maigret felt weighed down, discouraged, a little sad. This was a commonplace enough crime, it happened almost every week, a lonely old woman, robbed and murdered by a boy not yet twenty. The only difference was that, in this case, Théo Stiernet had killed his own grandmother.

He was taking it all very calmly, quite astonishingly so, in fact, and seemed only too willing to co-operate. He was plump and flabby, with a round face and almost no chin. He had protuberant eyes, and thick lips, so red that, at first glance, Maigret thought he had been using lipstick.

'Five francs! Just like doling out pocket-money to a kid!'

'Was she a widow?'

'Her husband died nearly forty years ago. She had a little draper's shop in the Place Saint-Paul for ages, but a couple of years ago, when she began finding it hard to get about, she gave it up.'

'Have you a father?'

'He's in a nut-house—Bicêtre.'

'Is your mother still alive?'

'I don't live with her, haven't done for years. She's never sober.'

'Any brothers and sisters?'

'One sister. She left home when she was fifteen, and hasn't been heard of since.'

His tone was quite matter-of-fact.

'How did you know your grandmother kept her money in the house?'

'She didn't believe in banks, or the Post Office, either.'

It was nine o'clock at night, just twenty-four hours since the murder had been committed, in an old house in the Rue du Roi-de-Sicile, in which Joséphine Ménard occupied two rooms on the third floor. One of the fourth-floor tenants had met Stiernet on the stairs, on his way out. She knew him well by sight. They had exchanged greetings.

At about half-past nine, Madame Palloc, whose rooms, on the third floor, were opposite those of Madame Ménard, went to call on the old lady, as she often did.

She knocked, but got no answer. She tried the door and, finding it open, went in. Joséphine Ménard was lying dead in a heap on the floor, her skull cracked open, and her face battered to a pulp.

It had not taken them long to track down Théo Stiernet. He was found, at six o'clock the next morning, fast asleep on a bench at the Gare du Nord.

'What did you have to kill her for?'

'I never meant to. She went for me, and I panicked.'

'You threatened her with your toy pistol, I suppose?'

'Yes. She didn't turn a hair. Maybe she could see it was just a toy.

' "Get out!" she said. "It takes more than a guttersnipe like you to scare me!"

'There was a pair of scissors lying on that round table of hers. She grabbed them, and came at me with them.

' "Get out! Get out!" she kept repeating, "or you'll regret it for the rest of your life."

'She was tiny, very frail-looking, but she had a wicked temper.

'She scared the wits out of me, coming at me like that

with the open scissors. She could have blinded me. I looked round for something to defend myself with, and grabbed the first thing I saw, the poker. It was lying beside the stove.'

'How many times did you strike her?'

'I don't know. She wouldn't go down. She just went on standing there, staring at me.'

'Was there blood on her face?'

'Yes, I didn't want to hurt her. I don't know. I just went on hitting her.'

Maigret could almost hear the Public Prosecutor addressing the Court of Assize:

'Thus, the accused Stiernet, with bestial ferocity, struck down his ill-fated victim.'

'When you saw her crumpled on the floor, what then?'

'I just stared at her. I didn't understand. I hadn't meant to kill her. That's how it was, I swear. You must believe me.'

'All the same, it didn't stop you from going through her drawers.'

'That was later. My first thought was to get away. But before I got to the door, I remembered that all the money I had in the world was a franc and a fifty-centime piece. I'd just been turned out of my digs because there was three weeks' rent owing.'

'So you turned back?'

'Yes. The way you put it, you'd think I'd turned the flat inside out. That's not true. I just looked into one or two drawers. In one of them, I found an old purse, and slipped it into my pocket. Then I came across a couple of rings and a cameo brooch in a cardboard box.'

The two rings, the cameo brooch and the shabby purse were lying on Maigret's desk, next to his pipe rack.

'So you didn't find her savings?'

'I didn't look. I couldn't get away fast enough. I couldn't stand the sight of her, lying there. Her eyes seemed to follow me all round the room. On the stairs, on my way out, I ran into Madame Menou. I went into a bar and ordered a brandy. There were sandwiches, ready cut, on the counter. I ate three.'

'Were you hungry?'

'I must have been, I suppose. I ate my sandwiches, had a cup of coffee, and then began wandering the streets. After all that, I was no better off, really, because it turned out that there were only eight francs, twenty-five in the purse.'

'*After all that, I was no better off, really!*'

He had said this as though it were the most natural thing in the world. Maigret, fascinated and horrified, stared at him.

'What made you choose the Gare du Nord?'

'I didn't. I happened to find myself there. It was very cold.'

It was the 15th of December. There was a north wind blowing, creating little eddies among the snowflakes before they settled, like a film of dust, on the pavements.

'Were you thinking of crossing the frontier into Belgium?'

'How could I, with barely five or six francs to my name?'

'What were your plans?'

'First of all, to get some sleep.'

'Did you expect to be arrested?'

'I hadn't thought.'

'What were you thinking about?'

'Nothing.'

He had not found the money, but the police had. It was on top of the mirror-fronted wardrobe, wrapped in brown paper, all twenty-two thousand francs of it.

'What would you have done if you had found the money?'

'I don't know.'

The door of Maigret's office opened, and Lapointe came in.

'I've just had Inspector Fourquet on the phone. He wanted to speak to you, but I told him you were engaged.'

Fourquet was attached to the XVIIth Arrondissement, a wealthy upper-middle-class residential district, where murder was almost unheard of.

'There's been a murder in the Rue Fortuny, a couple of hundred yards from the Parc Monceau. If the papers found on him are anything to go by, the victim is a man of some standing, a wholesale wine merchant in a big way.'

'Anything else known?'

'Apparently he was walking to his car when he was shot. Four shots were fired. There were no witnesses. The street is a cul-de-sac, and it was deserted at the time.'

Catching sight of Stiernet, Maigret gave a little shrug.

'Is Lucas in?'

He went over to the door. Lucas was at his desk.

'Can you spare a minute?'

Stiernet glanced casually from one to the other, his bulging eyes expressing little interest or concern.

'I want you to take over for me. You'd better start again from scratch, and when you've got a signed statement from him, take him down to the cells. I shall want you with me, Lapointe.'

He put on his heavy black overcoat, and wound a navy blue woollen scarf round his neck. Madame Maigret had just finished knitting it for him. He stopped in the doorway to take a last look at the prisoner, then refilled his pipe, lit it, and went off down the corridor.

The night was still young, but there were very few people about, and their faces looked pinched with cold. Even the thickest winter clothing could not keep out the biting north wind. The two men got into one of the little black police cars parked in the forecourt, and drove almost to the other side of Paris in record time.

There were a couple of police constables at the approaches to the Rue Fortuny, diverting traffic and moving on by-standers who had come to stare at the body lying on the pavement. Four or five men were bustling about in the vicinity of the body, Fourquet among them.

He came forward to meet Maigret.

'The Divisional Superintendent has just arrived, with the doctor.'

Maigret shook hands with the superintendent, whom he knew well. He was a man of friendly disposition, and wore his clothes with style.

'Did you know Oscar Chabut?'

'Should I have done?'

'He was a man of some standing, a wholesale wine merchant—Le Vin des Moines, one of the biggest firms in Paris. You must have seen the name on hoardings and delivery vans. And there's a whole fleet of barges and tankers as well.'

159

The man lying on the pavement was heavily built, though not fat. He had the physique of a rugby footballer. The doctor stood up, and dusted the powdery snow from the knees of his trousers.

'He must have died within two or three minutes at most. We'll know more after the autopsy.'

Maigret looked into the staring eyes. They were very light blue, or rather a watery grey. The features were strongly delineated, especially the powerful jaw, which was already beginning to sag.

The van from Criminal Records drew up at the kerb, and the technicians got out and began unloading their equipment, for all the world like a film or television camera crew on location.

'Have you been in touch with the Department of Public Prosecutions?'

'Yes. They're sending over a Deputy and an Examining Magistrate.'

Maigret looked around for Fourquet. He was standing only a few feet away, flapping his long arms and slapping his thighs, in an attempt to keep warm.

'Which is his car?'

There were five or six parked in the street, all expensive-looking. Chabut's was a red Jaguar.

'Have you looked in the glove compartment?'

'Yes. A pair of sun-glasses, a Michelin Guide, two road maps of Provence, and a tin of cough lozenges.'

'He must have been coming out of one of the houses in this street.'

It was not a long street. Maigret, turning round to look at the houses, recognized the one in front of which the body still lay on the pavement. It was built in the style popular in 1900, with fancy stonework, carved with arabesques, surrounding the windows. The front door was of brass-studded oak, with a barred judas window let into it, and Maigret sensed rather than saw that the panel behind the bars had moved.

'Come with me, Lapointe.'

He went up to the door and rang the bell. There was an

appreciable pause before the panel slid back, to reveal an eye and the outline of a woman's shoulder. There was no light in the passage behind her.

'Who's there?'

Maigret recognized the voice. 'Good evening, Blanche.'

'What do you want?'

'Don't you remember me, Chief Superintendent Maigret? It's true it must be all of ten years since we last met.'

Without waiting to be invited in, he opened the door.

'Come on in,' he said to Lapointe. 'You're too young, of course, to have come across Madame Blanche, as she was always known.'

As if familiar with the layout of the house, Maigret switched on the light and made straight for the double doors, which led into a spacious reception room carpeted with overlapping rugs. There were heavy draped curtains over the windows, tapestries on the walls, and multi-coloured cushions everywhere. The room was softly lit by table-lamps with swathed silk shades.

Madame Blanche looked about fifty, though in fact she would never see sixty again. She was small and plump. She was generally considered to be very distinguished-looking. She wore a black silk dress, relieved by several rows of pearls.

'Busy as ever, and still the soul of discretion, I've no doubt.'

When Maigret had first known her, thirty years before, she was still on the streets, round about the Boulevard de la Madeleine, a very pretty girl with gentle manners and a ready, attractive smile which brought dimples into her cheeks.

Later, she had taken over the management of a flat in the Rue Notre-Dame-de-Lorette, where a large number of pretty girls were always to be found.

Since then, she had gone up in the world. She was now the owner of this richly appointed mansion, where luxury accommodation with every comfort, including the best whisky and champagne, was available for couples wishing to meet in discreet surroundings.

Whatever she may have thought of Maigret's appearance on the scene, she was putting a bold face on it.

'How did it happen?' asked the Chief Superintendent.

'Nothing has happened here. I can't tell you what happened out there, though there's been a lot of coming and going, I've noticed.'

'Didn't you hear the shots?'

'Oh! they were shots, were they? I thought it was a car back-firing.'

'Where were you, at the time?'

'To tell you the truth, I was having my evening snack in the kitchen. Just a ham roll. I never eat dinner.'

'Who else was in the house?'

'No one. Why?'

'Who was with Oscar Chabut?'

'Who is Oscar Chabut?'

'You would be well advised to co-operate, otherwise I shall have to ask you to come with me to the Quai des Orfèvres.'

'I don't know the surnames of my clients. They're nearly all people of some standing.'

'And you only open the door to them after you've had a look at them through the judas window?'

'This is a respectable establishment. I don't let in any Tom, Dick or Harry, which is no doubt why I am spared the attentions of the Vice Squad.'

'Were you watching through the judas window when Chabut left?'

'Why should you think that?'

'Lapointe, you'd better take her to the Quai. Maybe she'll have more to say for herself there.'

'I can't leave the house. I'll tell you all I know. I take it that, by Chabut, you mean the client who left about half an hour ago?'

'Was he a regular? Did he come often?'

'From time to time.'

'What do you mean by that? Once a month? Once a week?'

'More like once a week.'

162

'Always with the same companion?'

'Not always, no.'

'What about the one he was with this time? Had you seen her before?'

She hesitated, then said, with a shrug:

'I don't see why I should land myself in trouble for her. She's been here about thirty times in the past year.'

'Did he telephone to say he was coming?'

'That's the usual form.'

'What time did they arrive?'

'About seven.'

'Separately or together?'

'Together. You couldn't miss that red car of his.'

'Did they order anything to drink?'

'I had champagne on ice waiting for them.'

'Where's the woman?'

'But . . . She's gone.'

'You mean she left after Chabut was shot?'

She looked a little uneasy. 'Of course not!'

'Are you saying that she left before him?'

'It's the truth.'

'I'm sorry, Blanche, I don't believe it.'

In the course of his work, he had often had occasion to visit houses of this sort, and he knew the form. He was therefore aware of the fact that, invariably, it was the man who left first, while his companion stayed behind to freshen up and attend to her hair and make-up.

'I want to see the room they used. You stay here, Lapointe, and see that no one leaves the house. Now then, where did you put them?'

'On the first floor. The rose room.'

The walls were panelled with wood, and the staircase, with its thick, pale blue carpet held in place by triangular brass clips, had an elaborately carved balustrade.

'When I saw you arrive . . .'

'So you were watching at the judas window?'

'What did you expect? I was naturally anxious to find out what was going on. As soon as I saw you and recognized you, I knew I was in for trouble.'

'You did know who he was, didn't you? You might as well admit it.'

'Yes.'

'What about his companion?'

'Only her Christian name, honest to God. It's Anne-Marie. I always call her the Grasshopper.'

'Why is that?'

'Because she's very tall and thin, with unusually long arms and legs.'

'Where is she?'

'I told you. She left before him.'

'And I told you I don't believe you.'

She opened a door to reveal a very plushy bedroom. A housemaid was in the process of changing the sheets on the canopied bed. On a pedestal table stood a bottle of champagne and two glasses, one of which was not quite empty, and stained with lipstick.

'See for yourself. . . .'

'I see that she's not here or in the bathroom. So far so good. How many other rooms have you?'

'Eight.'

'Any of them occupied?'

'No. Mostly, my clients come either in the late afternoon, or after dinner. I was expecting one at nine, but he must have seen all those people out there, and . . .'

'Show me the other rooms.'

There were four on the first floor, all furnished more or less in the massive style of the Second Empire, with a good deal of drapery in faded colours.

'As you see, there's no one here.'

'Carry on.'

'Whatever would she be doing up there?'

'I couldn't say, but I want to see for myself.'

The first two rooms on the floor above were, indeed, empty, but, in the third, there was a girl sitting bolt up-right in an over-stuffed chair, upholstered in claret-coloured velvet.

She sprang to her feet. She was tall and thin, with a flat chest and narrow hips.

'Who is this?' Maigret asked.

'She's waiting for the client I was expecting at nine.'

'Do you know her?'

'No.'

The girl looked very young, barely twenty. She shrugged, as though to say, What the hell?

'He's bound to find out sooner or later. He's a policeman, isn't he?'

'Chief Superintendent Maigret.'

'You don't say!'

She looked at him with interest.

'You don't mean to say you're investigating this business yourself?'

'As you see.'

'Is he dead?'

'Yes.'

She turned to Madame Blanche, and said reproachfully:

'Why did you lie to me? You told me that he was only wounded.'

'How was I to know? I didn't go out to look.'

'Who are you, Mademoiselle?'

'My name is Anne-Marie Boutin. I'm his private secretary.'

'Did you often come here with him?'

'Usually about once a week. It was always a Wednesday, because that's the evening when I'm supposed to be at my English class.'

'Come downstairs,' said Maigret, grumpily.

He had had about as much as he could take of pastel colours and soft lighting, in which faces appeared blurred as though seen through a mist.

They were assembled in the drawing-room, but it had not occurred to any of them to sit down. They could hear voices, and footsteps coming and going outside, where the icy north wind was still blowing. Indoors, however, the heat was suffocating, as in a hothouse, and, as in a hothouse, there were gigantic tropical plants everywhere, in ornate Chinese pots.

'What do you know about the murder of your employer?'

'Only what she told me,' replied the Grasshopper, indicating Madame Blanche. 'That someone fired at him and wounded him, and that the concierge next door came running out into the street. She must have telephoned for the police, I suppose, because they were here within a few minutes.'

It was no distance from the Police Station in the Avenue de Villiers.

'Was he killed outright?'

'Yes.'

She did not break down at this, but merely turned a little pale. She appeared more shocked than grieved. She went on, as though scarcely aware of what she was saying:

'I wanted to leave at once, but she wouldn't let me.'

Maigret turned to Madame Blanche.

'Why not?'

'Your men were at the door. She would have walked straight into them. I was hoping to keep her out of it. I didn't want to get involved. I knew it would bring the reporters swarming, and that would almost certainly mean the end of this place.'

'Tell me exactly what you saw. Where was the man when he fired?'

'Facing the door, in the road, between two parked cars.'

'Did you get a good look at him?'

'No. The nearest street lamp is some way off. His face was just a blur.'

'Was he tall?'

'No, below average height, I'd say. He was broadshouldered, though, and wearing a dark coat. He fired three or four times, I think. I wasn't counting. Monsieur Oscar clutched his stomach, swayed a little, and then fell forward.'

Maigret noted that although the girl looked horrified, she did not appear by any means heartbroken.

'Did you love him?'

'I don't know what you mean.'

'How long had you been his mistress?'

She looked a little taken aback.

'I don't think you quite understand. When he wanted me, he would say so, but there was never any question of love. I certainly never thought of him as my lover.'

'What time are you expected home?'

'Between half past nine and ten. My mother will begin to worry if I'm late.'

'Where do you live?'

'Rue Caulaincourt, near the Place Constantin—Pecqueur.'

'Where do you work?'

'Quai de Charenton, out beyond the Bercy warehouses.'

'Will you be there tomorrow?'

'Certainly.'

'It's possible that I may need your help. Lapointe, see her to the Métro, will you. The papers may already have got wind of this business, and I don't want her harassed by reporters.'

He was fidgeting with his pipe, feeling that it would perhaps be inappropriate to smoke in these surroundings. All the same, after some hesitation, he did eventually light up.

Madame Blanche stood calmly watching him, her hands folded on her rounded stomach, with an air of irreproachable rectitude.

'Are you quite sure you didn't recognize the man who fired the shots?'

'I swear I didn't.'

'Did your client ever come here with a married woman?'

'Very likely, I should think.'

'Did he come often?'

'Sometimes two or three times in one week, and then I wouldn't set eyes on him for ten days or a fortnight. But an interval as long as that was unusual.'

'Did anyone ever telephone to make enquiries about him?'

'No.'

The Deputy Public Prosecutor and the Examining Magistrate had gone. The temperature outside had dropped still further. The men from the Forensic Laboratory, having lifted the body of the wine merchant on to a stretcher, were hoisting it into the mortuary van.

The technicians from Criminal Records were loading their gear into their smaller van.

'Did you find anything?'

'The cartridges. All four of them. 6·35 calibre.'

That ruled out a professional gunman. Only an amateur or a woman would use so small a weapon, which could not kill except at very close range.

'No sign of the Press?'

'There were a couple of reporters. They went off in rather a hurry. They were anxious to get their stories in in time for the regional editions.'

Inspector Fourquet stood patiently by, stamping his feet, and holding a handkerchief up to his face, in an attempt to protect his nose from the biting cold.

'Had he been in there?'

'Yes,' said Maigret, grudgingly.

'What will you tell the Press?'

'As little as I can get away with! Have you his wallet and identity papers?'

Fourquet took them from his pocket and handed them over.

'What's his home address?'

'Place des Vosges. I forget the number, but it's on his identity card. Are you going to break the news to his wife?'

'It would be kinder, I think, than leaving her to read the whole lurid tale in the morning papers.'

Maigret could see the entrance to the Malsherbes Métro Station at the junction with the Avenue de Villiers, and Lapointe walking away from it with long, brisk strides.

'Thanks for ringing me, Fourquet. I'm so sorry to have kept you hanging about so long out here. You must be frozen.'

He got into the snug little police car. Lapointe climbed into the driver's seat, and looked enquiringly at the Chief.

'Place des Vosges.'

They drove in silence. Fine, powdery snow was still

falling, and the gilt-tipped railings of the Parc Monceau were covered with a thin film of rime. They drove along the Champs Elysées, and approached the Place des Vosges by way of the Quais. It did not take them long to get there.

The concierge, invisible in the darkened lodge, pressed a time switch, and lights came on everywhere.

'Madame Chabut,' mumbled Maigret, as they went past the lodge.

She did not ask him what his business was. The two men went up to the first floor. On a little brass plate let into the heavy oak door, they read the name Oscar Chabut. It was just half-past ten. Maigret rang the bell. After a brief pause, the door was opened by a girl in a starched cap and apron. She was a pretty girl, dark, with a good figure. Her uniform, a close-fitting black silk dress, suited her admirably. She looked at them enquiringly.

'Madame Chabut. . . .'

'What name, please?'

'Chief Superintendent Maigret, Criminal Investigation Department.'

'Wait here, please.'

Amplified voices could be heard declaiming in one of the rooms, a radio or television play, no doubt. Then the voices were cut off in mid-speech, and a second or two later a woman in an emerald green dressing-gown appeared, looking puzzled. She was a beautiful woman, probably in her late thirties. Maigret was particularly struck by her fine carriage and the grace with which she moved.

'Please come in.'

She ushered them into a very spacious drawing-room. The armchair in which she had been sitting was still drawn up in front of the now blank television screen.

'Please sit down. I hope you haven't come to tell me that my husband has met with an accident.'

'I'm afraid we have, madame.'

'Is he hurt?'

'Worse than that.'

'You mean . . .?'

He nodded.

'Poor Oscar!'

The dead man's secretary had shed no tears when told of his death.

Neither did his wife. She merely looked down-cast and rather sorrowful.

'Was he alone in the car?'

'It wasn't a motor accident. Someone shot him.'

'A woman?'

'No. A man.'

'Poor Oscar!' she repeated. 'Where did it happen?'

And, seeing Maigret's hesitation, she went on:

'You needn't be afraid to tell me. I know what was going on. There hadn't been anything like that between us for years. We were more like good friends than husband and wife. He was rather a pet, really. Only people got the wrong idea because he was always puffing out his chest and banging on the table.'

'Do you know the Rue Fortuny?'

'That's where he nearly always took them. I've even met Madame Blanche, a delightful creature! He was most anxious that I should look the place over. As I told you, we were very good friends. Who was he with?'

'A young girl, his private secretary.'

'The Grasshopper! That was his name for her; now everyone calls her that.'

Lapointe gaped at her, aghast at her cool self-assurance.

'Was he shot in the house?'

'No. It happened outside on the pavement, as your husband was going towards his car.'

'Have you arrested the killer?'

'Unfortunately, there was plenty of time, before the police arrived, for him to get to the Métro at the top of the road, and leap on to any one of a dozen trains. Seeing that you were so fully in your husband's confidence, perhaps you have some inkling as to who might have wanted to kill him?'

'It might have been anyone,' she murmured, smiling disarmingly. 'A jealous husband or lover. Such people do still exist, I believe.'

'Did he ever receive threatening letters?'

'I don't think so. He had affairs with several of my friends, but I really don't see any of their husbands as murderers.

'Don't be misled, Chief Superintendent. My husband wasn't a heartless fiend. He was no coarse brute either, in spite of his looks.

'I daresay it will surprise you to hear me say so, but he was really very shy and insecure, which was why he was always having to bolster up his ego.

'And, you know, there's nothing more reassuring to a man than to know that he can have virtually any woman he wants.'

'Were you always so tolerant?'

'At first he kept things from me. It took me years to find out that he'd been to bed with most of my women friends. It was only after I'd caught him in the act that we had it out once and for all, since when we've been the best of friends.

'You do understand, don't you? In spite of everything, his death is a great loss. We were very fond of one another, and, anyway, old habits die hard.'

'Was he a jealous husband?'

'He allowed me perfect freedom, but I realized that it would be an affront to his manhood to confide in him as he did in me. Where is his body now?'

'At the Forensic Laboratory. I'd be obliged if you could call there sometime tomorrow morning to make a formal identification.'

'Where was he hit?'

'In the chest and stomach.'

'Did he suffer?'

'Death was almost instantaneous.'

'Was the Grasshopper with him when he died?'

'No. He left before she did.'

'So at the end he was quite alone.'

'I'd be grateful if, sometime tomorrow, you would make a list of all your women friends, and of any other women whom you know to have been your husband's mistresses.'

'You're sure it was a man who shot him?'

'If Madame Blanche is to be believed, yes.'

'Was the door left open, then?'

'No. She was watching through the judas window. Thank you for your help, Madame Chabut, and please believe me when I say how sorry I am to have been the bearer of such distressing news. Incidentally, had your husband any relations living in Paris?'

'Only old Désiré, his father. He's seventy-three, but he still has his bistro at the Quai de la Tournelle. It's called *Au Petit Sancerre*. He's a widower. He has a living-in housekeeper, a woman of about fifty.'

Seated in the car, Maigret turned to Lapointe:

'What do you think?'

'She's an odd sort of woman, isn't she? Do you think she was telling the truth?'

'I'm sure of it.'

'She didn't seem much upset.'

'That will come later. It will probably hit her in the night, as she lies alone in her bed. But if anyone sheds any tears, I daresay it will be the maid. There's no doubt in my mind that she was another of his conquests.'

'He sounds like a nut-case to me.'

'I daresay you're right. But there are some like that, who have to keep proving to themselves that they really are men, just as his wife said. The Quai de la Tournelle, I think. . . . It's just possible that the bistro may still be open.'

They arrived just in time to see an old man with white hair pulling down the iron shutter. He was wearing a blue apron of some coarse cotton material. Through the half-open door behind him, they could see the sawdust-covered floor of the bistro, tables, with chairs stacked on them, and the zinc bar on which there were several dirty glasses.

'I'm sorry, gentlemen, we're closed.'

'We just wanted a word with you.'

He frowned.

'You want to talk to me? Who are you, may I ask?'

'Police. Criminal Investigation Department.'

172

'I can't imagine what the Criminal Investigation Department can possibly have to say to me.'

They were now inside the bistro. Désiré Chabut had shut the door. There was a large charcoal stove in one corner, and it was giving out a very good heat.

'It's not to do with you. It's about your son.'

He glowered at them mistrustfully. He looked a regular peasant, with an expression in his eyes that was at once stolid and sly.

'My son? What's he done?'

'He hasn't done anything. He's met with an accident.'

'I've always said he drives too fast. Is he badly hurt?'

'He's dead.'

The old man said not a word, but went behind the bar, poured himself a small glass of marc brandy, and swallowed it down in one gulp.

'Would you like a glass?' he asked.

Maigret nodded, but Lapointe, who loathed marc brandy, refused.

'Where did it happen?'

'It wasn't a motor accident. Your son was shot with an automatic pistol.'

'Who shot him?'

'That's what I'm trying to find out.'

The old man, like the two women before him, showed no outward signs of grief. His furrowed face remained impassive, his eyes hard.

'Have you seen my daughter-in-law?'

'Yes.'

'What did she say?'

'She doesn't know any more than we do.'

'I've had this place for more than fifty years. Follow me.'

He led the way into the kitchen, and switched on the light.

'You see that?'

He pointed to a couple of framed photographs of a little boy of about seven. In one he was carrying a hoop, and in the other, he was dressed up for his First Communion.

'That's him. He was born here, in the room upstairs. He

173

went to the local school, and twice failed his *baccalauréat*. Then he got himself a job with a wine merchant as a door-to-door salesman. His employer was a wine-grower from Mâcon, with a sales branch in Paris. My son became his right-hand man in the end. Success didn't come all that easy to him, you can take my word for it. He worked hard. And when he got married, he barely earned enough to keep a wife.'

'Did he love his wife?'

'Certainly he did. She was his boss's typist. To begin with, they lived in a couple of rented rooms in the Rue Saint-Antoine. They have no children. After a time, in spite of the fact that I did my best to dissuade him, Oscar decided to set up on his own. I was sure he'd come a cropper, but not a bit of it, everything he touched turned to gold. You must have seen his barges on the Seine with *Vin des Moines* on the side in huge letters.

'You must understand that he could never have made such a success of it, if he hadn't been very tough. As his business grew, a great many small businesses were forced into bankruptcy. It was no fault of his, of course, but, all the same, human nature being what it is, he made a lot of enemies.'

'Are you suggesting that he was killed by one of his less fortunate competitors?'

'It seems the most likely explanation, don't you think?'

There was no mention of his son's mistresses, nor of the likelihood of his having been shot by a jealous husband or lover. Quite possibly Désiré knew nothing of these matters.

'Can you think of anyone in particular who might have had a grudge against him?'

'I can't give you their names, but there are such people. It might be worth your while making enquiries at the warehouses at Bercy. My son was generally regarded as a man who would not hesitate to ride rough-shod over anyone who stood in his way.'

'Did he come and see you often?'

'Hardly ever. Latterly we didn't see eye to eye on a number of things.'

'Do you mean you didn't care for his business methods?'

'That, and other things. What does it matter now?'

Suddenly a tear, a single, solitary tear spilled out of the corner of his eye, and ran down his cheek. His hand shook a little, as he raised it to wipe away the tear with his forefinger.

'When can I see him?'

'Tomorrow, if you wish, at the Forensic Laboratory.'

'That's somewhere near the centre of town, across the river, isn't it?'

He refilled the two glasses, and gulped his down. He looked at the Chief Superintendent with glazed eyes. Maigret hurriedly emptied his glass. In the car, a few minutes later, he said:

'I'd be grateful if you'd drive me home. You'd better keep the car for tonight, and drive yourself home in it.'

It was almost midnight when he climbed the stairs to his flat. Before he was half-way up, the door opened, and his wife came out to meet him. He had telephoned her at eight, to say that he would be late. That was before the call from Fourquet, when he had anticipated a protracted session with young Stiernet.

'You must be frozen.'

'I've hardly put my nose out of doors all evening—just getting in and out of the car.'

'You sound as if you've caught cold.'

'My nose isn't running, and I haven't coughed once.'

'Just you w: it until the morning. I'd better get you a hot grog, I think, and you can take a couple of aspirins with it. Has the boy confessed?'

All she knew was that Stiernet had battered his grandmother to death.

'No trouble at all. He didn't even attempt to deny it.'

'Did he do it for money?'

'He was out of work. He'd just been turned out of his digs because he owed three weeks' rent.'

'What's he like? A brute?'

'No. His mental age is about six, I'd say. He doesn't really understand how it happened, and he has no conception of what's in store for him. He answers all the questions put to him to the best of his ability. He's attentive and biddable, like a kid in the class-room.'

'Diminished responsibility, do you think?'

'That's up to the judges. It's no concern of mine, thank Heaven!'

'Will they brief someone good for the defence?'

'A young man, making his first appearance at the Assizes, as usual. He hasn't a penny in the world, except three francs that were found in his pocket. It isn't because of him that I was kept so late. I was called out to another case. A middle-aged man, quite a well-known figure, was shot dead outside one of the most exclusive brothels in Paris.'

'Won't be a moment. I can hear the kettle boiling. Your grog will be ready in a minute.'

While she was in the kitchen, he undressed and got into his pyjamas. Was it too late to smoke one last pipe before getting into bed? he wondered. Needless to say, he decided that it was not. Somehow, though, he did not relish it as much as usual. Could his wife possibly be right? Was he starting a cold?

CHAPTER TWO

WHEN MADAME MAIGRET came into the room with a cup of coffee in her hand and touched him on the shoulder, he was tempted, as he had often been when he was a child, to say that he didn't feel well, and thought he h d better stay warmly tucked up in bed.

His head was throbbing, his sinuses were aching, and his forehead was damp. The window panes were milky white, like frosted glass.

He took a sip or two of coffee, then, with a groan, got out of bed and went to the window. A few early risers, their hands deep in their pockets, were hurrying towards the Métro. He could see them only in shadowy outline in the fog.

It was some time before he felt fully awake. He drank his coffee very slowly, and then lingered in the shower.

It was not until he had finished shaving that his thoughts returned to Chabut.

He was fascinated by the man. Which of the people he had talked to had painted the truest picture of him?

To Madame Blanche, he was just a client, one of her best clients, admittedly, who never failed to order champagne when he was in her house. He needed to splash his money about, to display his wealth.

He must often have reflected: 'I started out as a door-to-door salesman. My father, who can barely read or write, still keeps a bistro on the Quai de la Tournelle.'

And what did the Grasshopper really think of him? She had shed no tears. All the same, Maigret had had the feeling that she was not altogether indifferent to him. She knew that she was not the only woman he took to the plushy little private hotel in the Rue Fortuny, but she had shown no sign of jealousy.

The wine merchant's wife had shown still less. Maigret recalled one or two details that he had not consciously registered at the time. There was, for instance, the life-size portrait in oils over the fireplace in the drawing-room of the flat in the Place des Vosges, a very glossy work, life-like as a photograph. It portrayed Chabut with a clenched fist, as though about to strike a blow, and a challenging expression in his eyes.

'How do you feel?'

'I shall be fine when I've had my second cup of coffee.'

'All the same, you'd better have an aspirin, and keep indoors as much as you can. I'll ring for a taxi.'

The wine-merchant, still a somewhat shadowy figure in his mind, though he was gradually taking on shape and substance, accompanied him all the way to the Quai des Orfèvres. Maigret had the feeling that he had only to get to know Chabut to find his murderer.

The fog was still so thick that Maigret had to switch on the lights in his office. He opened his mail, signed a few inter-departmental minutes, and then, seeing that it was nine o'clock, went off to the daily briefing in the Chief Commissioner's office.

177

When his turn came, he gave a brief summary of the case of Théo Stiernet.

'Is he mentally disturbed, would you say?'

'No doubt his lawyer will plead diminished responsibility, but, in my opinion, it's more a case of an unhappy childhood. The trouble is that he struck her fifteen times, so naturally there will be talk of bestial cruelty, especially as the old woman was his grandmother. He hasn't the faintest conception of what's in store for him. He does his best to answer all questions fully and truthfully, but he can't really see what all the fuss is about.'

'And what about this Rue Fortuny business? There's just a brief mention, I see, in the morning papers.'

'There'll be a great deal more before long, I'm afraid. The victim is a rich man, almost a public figure. You must have seen the *Vin des Moines* advertisements. They're plastered all over the Métro.'

'A *crime passionel*?'

'It's too early to say. If he wanted to make enemies, he certainly went the best way about it. There are a number of possibilities, and at this stage there's nothing to choose between them.'

'Is it true that he was coming out of a brothel?'

'Is that what the papers are saying?'

'No, but I know the Rue Fortuny, and it wasn't difficult to put two and two together.'

Maigret returned to his office, still brooding on the events of the previous night. Jeanne Chabut intrigued him almost as much as her husband. Undoubtedly, his death had been a shock to her, but even she had shed no tears over him.

She was, he would guess, five or six years younger than her husband. She had style. Where had she acquired that air of breeding which showed in her every gesture, in every inflection of her voice?

When they had first known one another, she had been a humble shorthand typist, and he had not yet left the lean years behind him.

For all that Oscar went to the best tailors for his suits, he never lost his coarseness, and remained to the end something of a lout.

His rise had certainly been spectacular, but he had never quite got used to it, and had always felt the need to make a splash.

Apart from the absurdly pretentious portrait, the furniture and decorations of the flat, a harmonious blend of the contemporary and the antique, must, Maigret felt sure, have been chosen by her. The whole atmosphere of the place induced a sense of well-being. About now, she would be getting ready to leave for the Forensic Laboratory, where the autopsy was probably already under way. She would go through the ordeal without flinching. A woman of her fibre would not be got down by the depressing atmosphere of what used to be known as the morgue.

'Are you there, Lapointe?'

'Yes, sir.'

'We're going out.'

He struggled into his heavy overcoat, wound his scarf round his neck, and put on his hat. Before leaving the office, he paused to light his pipe. He and Lapointe got into one of the cars drawn up in the forecourt.

'Where to, sir?'

'Quai de Charenton.'

They drove along the Quai de Bercy, passing warehouse after warehouse set back from the road behind iron railings. Each one bore a famous trade name in giant lettering. Three of the largest buildings were the warehouses of the Vin des Moines enterprises.

Further on, they came to an imposing wharf, where dozens of wine casks were set out in rows, and others were being unloaded from a barge drawn up at the landing stage. More of the Vin des Moines enterprises. More of Oscar Chabut's empire.

The building on the other side of the road was old and shabby, and surrounded by a huge area of featureless concrete. Here, too, there were vast numbers of wine casks. At the far end, open cases of wine in bottles were being loaded on to lorries. A man with a drooping moustache and wearing a blue overall stood nearby, some sort of foreman or supervisor apparently.

'Am I to come in with you?'

'Yes, please.'

'I'll just park the car.'

Even out in the yard there was a pungent winey smell. Maigret made for the nearest door, where an enamel plate invited callers to 'Enter without ringing'. The large tiled entrance hall was also redolent of wine.

On his left was a rather dark room with the door open, in which a girl with a slight squint sat at a telephone switchboard.

'What can I do for you?'

'Is Monsieur Chabut's private secretary in?'

She peered suspiciously at him.

'You mean you want to see her personally?'

'Yes.'

'Do you know her?'

'Yes.'

'Have you heard what's happened?'

'Yes. Tell her Chief Superintendent Maigret is here.'

She gave him a searching look, then turned to young Lapointe, whom she clearly found more interesting.

'Hello! Anne-Marie? There's someone here who says he's Chief Superintendent Maigret. There's another man with him, I don't know his name. They want to see you. Yes. O.K. I'll send them up.'

The staircase was thick with dust, and the walls could have done with a coat of fresh paint. On the stairs, they passed a young man coming down, carrying a bundle of papers. The Grasshopper was waiting for them on the landing. She led them through an open door into an office which, though impressively large, was anything but luxurious.

It was dark and gloomy, and filled, like the courtyard and the rest of the building, with the sour smell of wine. To all appearances, the furniture and decorations had not been changed for fifty years.

'Have you seen her?'

'Who?'

'His wife.'

'Yes. How well do you know her?'

'Sometimes, when he had the 'flu, I went to work at the Place des Vosges. She's a lovely woman, don't you think? And clever too. He set great store by her opinion, and would often ask her advice.'

'This is a very dingy place, isn't it? I'm surprised.'

'Wait till you see the offices in the Avenue de l'Opéra. They're very different. There they've got *Vin des Moines* in lights right across the building, and the offices are light and beautifully furnished, the last word in luxury. They deal with the sales side of the business. There are fifteen thousand outlets at present, and the number is going up every month. They have computers there and are almost entirely automated.'

'And here?'

'These are the original offices. Nothing has changed here, and the provincial dealers like the old-world atmosphere. Chabut looked in every day at the Avenue de l'Opéra, but this is where he really felt at home.'

'Did you go to the Avenue de l'Opéra with him?'

'Occasionally. Not very often. He had another secretary there.'

'Apart from himself, who managed the business?'

'No one, really. He didn't trust anyone. Here, there's Monsieur Leprêtre. He's the head cellarman, in charge of production. Then, there's Monsieur Riolle, who keeps the books. He's only been with us a couple of months. And there are four shorthand typists in the room opposite.'

'Is that all?'

'Except for the switchboard operator, whom you've already seen. And me, of course. It's hard to explain. You could say that this was General Headquarters, with most of the work being delegated to the Avenue de l'Opéra.'

'How much time did he spend there, on average?'

'About an hour a day, sometimes two.'

The old-fashioned roll-top desk was covered in papers.

'How old are the other shorthand typists? Young, like yourself?'

'Do you want to see them?'

'All in good time.'

'One of them, Mademoiselle Berthe, is much older. She's thirty-two, and she's been here longer than the rest of us. The youngest is twenty-one.'

'How did he come to engage you as his private secretary?'

'He was looking for a trainee. I saw the advertisement and applied for the job. That was about a year ago. I was not quite eighteen. I must have seemed a funny little thing to him, I think. At any rate, he asked me whether I had a steady boy-friend.'

'Did you?'

'No. I had only just left secretarial college.'

'When did he start making up to you?'

'He didn't "make up to me", as you put it. The very next day, he called me over, ostensibly to show me some papers, and started to fondle me. He murmured something like "I'll have to work this out".'

'And then?'

'The following week, he took me to the Rue Fortuny.'

'And what about the others? Weren't they jealous?'

'Well, you know, they'd all had their turn.'

'Here?'

'Here or somewhere else. It's hard to explain. He was so open and natural about it, you couldn't hold it against him. I only know of one girl—she came after I did—who walked out on her third day, slamming the door behind her.'

'How many people knew that your day was Wednesday?'

'Everyone, I should think. I always left with him, and drove off in his car. He made no secret of it. Quite the reverse.'

'Who had your job before you came?'

'Madame Chazeau. She's moved to the other office now. She's twenty-six, and divorced.'

'Good-looking?'

'Yes. She has a lovely figure. No one could ever call her a grasshopper.'

'No ill-feeling there?'

'I caught her looking at me with an odd sort of smirk once or twice at the beginning. I daresay she was thinking that I wouldn't last long.'

'Was it all over between them?'

'I don't think so. She sometimes stayed on after office hours, and everyone knew what that meant.'

'Was she at all embittered?'

'I never saw any sign of it. As I said, I rather got the impression that she was laughing at me. I'm quite used to not being taken seriously. Even my mother still treats me like a little girl.'

'You don't think she might have wanted to get her own back on you?'

'She's not that sort. There are other men in her life. She goes out several nights a week, and the next day at work, she can hardly keep her eyes open.'

'What about the third girl?'

'Aline. She's the youngest, except for me. She's twenty-one, very dark, a bit temperamental. She makes a drama of everything. This morning, she fainted, or pretended to, and the next thing, she was howling her eyes out.'

'Was she another of your predecessors?'

'Yes. She was working in one of the big stores, when she saw the advertisement. They all came in answer to an advertisement.'

'Do you think any one of them cared enough to fire a gun at him?'

Madame Blanche, at the judas window, had, so she said, seen the shadowy figure of a man between two parked cars. But might it not just as well have been a woman, a woman wearing trousers? It was dark at the time.

'It wasn't like that,' replied the Grasshopper.

'What about his wife?'

'She wasn't jealous. She did as she pleased. As far as she was concerned, he was just a pleasant companion.'

'Pleasant?'

She thought for a moment.

'When you got to know him, yes. At first sight, he seemed self-important, aggressive. He came the big boss. As far as women were concerned, he was always confident of success. When one got to know him better, one began to suspect that he was more naïve than he looked, and a good deal more vulnerable.

'He often asked, "What do you really think of me?", especially after making love.

'I said, "What should I think of you?"

' "Do you love me? You don't. You might as well admit it."

' "It depends what you mean by love. You make me feel good, if that's what you want to know."

' "What if I were to grow tired of you?"

' "I don't know. I'd just have to put up with it, I suppose."

' "And the other girls across the landing, what do they say?"

' "Nothing. You know them better than I do." '

'Tell me about the men,' said Maigret.

'The men who work here, do you mean? Well, first of all, as I said, there's Monsieur Leprêtre. He used to have a business of his own, but he hadn't got what it takes to make a success of it. He must be nearly sixty by now. He doesn't say much. He's very good at his job, and he gets on with it in his own quiet way.'

'Is he married?'

'Yes. And he has two married children. He lives in a little cottage in Charenton, right at the end of the Quai, and he cycles to work every day.'

Outside the sun, veiled by the fog, filled the sky with a diffused pinkish glow, and vapour rose from the Seine. Lapointe, balancing his pad on his knee, was taking notes.

'When things went wrong for Leprêtre, was Le Vin des Moines already a going concern?'

'I think so, yes.'

'What were his relations with Chabut?'

'His manner was deferential, and yet somehow one felt that he had his pride.'

'Did they ever quarrel?'

'Not in my presence, and as I was nearly always there . . .'

'Am I right in thinking that he strikes you as being very reserved?'

'Reserved, and sad. I don't think I've ever seen him laugh, and besides, he has one of those drooping moustaches that give a man a rather pathetic air.'

'Who else works in this building?'

'The accountant, Jacques Riolle. He's more of a cashier, really. He has his office downstairs. He only deals with some of the smaller accounts—we call them the petty cash transactions. It would take too long to explain all the detailed workings of the business. All the real accountancy work is done at the Avenue de l'Opéra, as well as all the correspondence with wholesalers. Here, our main concern is the buying side of the business. This is where the wine growers from the South come on their periodical visits to Paris.'

'Is Riolle in love with one of you girls?'

'If he is, he doesn't show it. You can judge for yourself. He's about forty, a confirmed bachelor, distinctly stuffy, a bit of an old maid really, timid, scared of his own shadow, always fussing over trifles. He lives in a family boarding house in the Quartier Latin.'

'Anyone else?'

'Not in this building. Out there, in the storage sheds, there are five or six men. I know them by sight and by name, but, for all practical purposes, I have no contact with them whatever. I daresay you must find the whole set-up rather odd, but, if you'd known the boss, you'd have thought it the most natural thing in the world.'

'Will you miss him?'

'I won't deny it. Yes, I will.'

'Did he give you presents?'

'He never gave me money. Once or twice he bought me a scarf that he'd taken a fancy to in a shop window.'

'What will happen to the business now?'

'I don't know who will be taking charge. There is, of course, Monsieur Louceck, at the Avenue de l'Opéra. He's some sort of financial consultant. He and his team are responsible for the preparation and publication of balance sheets and so on. The trouble is he knows nothing about wine.'

'And Monsieur Leprêtre?'

'As I said, he has no head for business.'

'What about Madame Chabut?'

'I presume she'll inherit the lot. I can't say whether she'll step into her husband's shoes. She might well be able to make a go of it. She's certainly a woman who knows what she wants.'

Maigret looked intently at her. He was amazed to find a kid of her age so full of sound common sense, with a shrewd answer to every question. Her directness was very engaging, and he could not help smiling as he watched the gawky movements of her long, thin limbs.

'Last night, I went to the Quai de la Tournelle.'

'To see the old man? Sorry, Monsieur Chabut's father, I should say.'

'How did they get on?'

'From what I gathered, none too well.'

'Why was that?'

'I don't know. I fancy it goes back a long way. In his father's eyes, I think, the son appeared unduly hard and insensitive. He steadfastly refused to accept anything from him, and, if you ask me, he's refused to retire, in spite of his age, just to annoy his son.'

'Did Chabut ever talk about him?'

'Hardly ever.'

'Can you tell me anything more?'

'No.'

'Have you any other lovers?'

'No. He was all I wanted.'

'Will you stay on here?'

'If I'm allowed to.'

'Where is Monsieur Leprêtre's office.'

'On the ground floor, overlooking the forecourt.'

'I'll just look in across the way.'

Here, too, the lights were on. Two of the girls were busy typing, and the third, the oldest, was filing letters.

'Don't let me disturb you. I'm the Chief Superintendent in charge of the case. Later, I daresay, I shall want to have a talk with each of you in turn. In the meantime, I should be glad to know whether any one of you has a possible suspect in mind.'

They exchanged glances, and Mademoiselle Berthe, aged about thirty and rather plump, coloured a little.

'Have you any ideas?' he asked her.

'No. I don't know a thing. I was taken completely by surprise, like everyone else.'

'How did you hear about the murder? From the papers?'

'No. It was when I got here. . . .'

'Had he any enemies, as far as you know?'

Once more they exchanged glances.

'There's no need to feel embarrassed. I already know a good deal about the sort of life he led and, in particular, his relations with women. It could have been a husband or lover, or a jealous woman.'

There was no response. None of them seemed prepared to venture a comment.

'Think it over. Even the most trivial fact may be important.'

He and Lapointe went down the stairs.

On the ground floor, following the Grasshopper's directions, Maigret opened the door of the accountant's office.

'Have you been long with the firm?'

'Five months. Before that, I worked in a shop selling leather goods on the Grands Boulevards.'

'Were you aware of your employer's amorous adventures?'

He flushed, opened his mouth as if to speak, but could find nothing to say.

'Among the people who came here to see him, was there anyone who had reason to hate him?'

'Why should anyone have hated him?'

'He drove a very hard bargain, didn't he?'

'He wasn't exactly soft-hearted.'

No sooner were the words out of his mouth than he was regretting them. He should have known better than to express an opinion.

'Do you know Madame Chabut?'

'Occasionally, she would bring in her personal bills for me to deal with, but usually they came by post. She's a very friendly and unassuming person.'

'Thank you.'

Just one more, the melancholy Monsieur Leprêtre of the drooping moustache. They found him in his office, which was even shabbier and more provincial-looking than the rest of the building. He was sitting at a black-painted table, with a number of wine samples set out in front of him. His eyes, as he looked up at the two men, were full of mistrust.

'I take it you know why we're here?'

He merely nodded. One end of his drooping moustache was longer than the other. He was smoking a meerschaum pipe, filled, if the smell was anything to go by, with a very strong tobacco.

'Someone must have had a very good reason for killing your employer. Have you worked here long?'

'Thirteen years.'

'Did you get on with Monsieur Chabut?'

'I had no complaints.'

'He had the fullest confidence in you, I take it?'

'He had no confidence in anyone but himself.'

'Nevertheless, you were as close to him as anyone, surely?'

Leprêtre looked at him blankly. He was wearing a peculiar little skull-cap, to conceal a bald patch, Maigret supposed. At any rate, he made no attempt to remove it.

'Is there nothing you can tell me?'

'Nothing.'

'Did he ever mention having received threats?'

'No.'

It was useless to persist. Maigret, beckoning Lapointe to follow him, went out of the room.

'Thanks.'

'Don't mention it.'

And Leprêtre got up and shut the door behind them.

It was not until they were in the car that Maigret's cold, which had been incubating since early morning, suddenly burst forth. For several minutes on end he had to keep blowing his nose, so that his face grew flushed, and his eyes watered.

'Sorry about that, laddie,' he murmured to Lapointe. 'It's been coming on since this morning. Avenue de l'Opéra. I forgot to ask the number.'

They had no difficulty in finding the building with the name *Vin des Moines* spread right across it in huge letters, which were lit up at night. It was a massive and imposing edifice, in a row of impressive office blocks, flanked on one side by a foreign bank and on the other by a Trustee Savings Bank.

They went up to the second floor, where they found themselves in a vast, marble-tiled entrance hall with a very high ceiling. Chromium tables were dotted about here and there, with contemporary-style tubular steel chairs set out round them.

Few of them were in use. On the walls were three immense posters, such as are to be found in the Métro, representing a jovial monk, smacking his lips greedily over a glass of wine.

In each poster the wine was a different colour, red, white and rosé.

Behind a glass partition there was a huge office, in which some thirty people, men and women, were at work. Behind them was another glass partition, through which more offices could be seen. It was all very bright, and brilliantly lit, furnished and decorated in the very latest style.

Maigret went up to the reception desk but, before he could state his business, he had to stop and blow his nose. The young receptionist waited, showing no sign of impatience.

'I beg your pardon. I wish to see Monsieur Louceck.'

'What name, please?'

She handed him a pad of slips on which were printed the words: 'Surname and Christian names', and underneath: 'Object of visit'.

He wrote simply: 'Chief Superintendent Maigret.'

She disappeared through a door opposite the first partition, and was away some time. Eventually she returned by way of the front office, and ushered them into a waiting-room, somewhat cosier than the huge entrance hall, but no less stylishly appointed.

'Monsieur Louceck won't keep you a moment. He's on the telephone.'

And, as she had promised, they did not have long to wait. A second girl, wearing spectacles, led them into another spacious office. Here, too, everything was streamlined and contemporary in feeling.

A very small man rose from his chair, and held out his hand.

'Chief Superintendent Maigret?'

'Yes.'

'I am Stéphane Louceck. Do please sit down.'

Maigret introduced his assistant:

'This is Inspector Lapointe.'

'Take a seat, won't you?'

He was very ugly, in a rather repulsive way. His nose was long and bulbous, and streaked with bluish veins, and brown hair sprouted from his ears and nostrils. As to his eyebrows, they were almost an inch wide, and stood out like bristles. His suit needed ironing, and he was wearing a made-up tie that looked as if it was stiffened with whalebone.

'I presume it's about the murder.'

'Needless to say, it is.'

'I was expecting to hear from you before this. I never read the morning papers, my working day starts too early, so the first I knew of it was when Madame Chabut telephoned me.'

'I didn't know of the existence of this office. We went first to the Quai de Charenton. I understand that that's where Oscar Chabut spent most of his time.'

'He called in here every day. He was a man who liked to keep a personal eye on things.'

His face was blank, without expression, and his voice flat and toneless.

'If you don't mind my asking, do you know if he had any enemies?'

'Not that I know of.'

'He was a man of some power and influence. It seems likely that, on his way up, he must have trodden hard on a few toes.'

'I know nothing about that.'

'He had a great liking for women, I understand.'

'His private life was no concern of mine.'

'Which was his office?'

'This one. He shared this desk with me.'

'Did he bring his private secretary with him?'

'No. We have all the staff we need here.'

He did not attempt a smile, nor did he express even the most perfunctory regret at what had happened.

'How long have you been with the firm?'

'I was working for him long before these offices were built.'

'What were you doing before that?'

'I was a financial consultant.'

'I take it you are responsible for the accounts?'

'Among other things.'

'Will you be taking over the business?'

Once more, Maigret blew his nose. He could feel beads of perspiration on his forehead.

'Excuse me.'

'Take your time. I don't quite know how to answer your question. This isn't a public company. It is the personal property of Monsieur Chabut, so that, unless he has left it to someone else in his will, it passes automatically to his wife.'

'Are you on good terms with her?'

'I scarcely know her.'

'Would you describe yourself as Oscar Chabut's right-hand man?'

'I was in charge of sales and of the warehouses. We have more than fifteen thousand retail outlets up and down the country. Here, we have a staff of forty, and we have about twenty inspectors touring the provinces. There is a separate section on the floor above this to deal with Paris and the suburbs. They are also concerned with advertising and exports.'

'How many women on your staff?'

'I beg your pardon?'

'I'm asking how many women and young girls you have on your staff.'

'I don't know.'

'Who engages them?'

'I do.'

'Had Oscar Chabut no say in the matter?'

'Not in this department.'

'Was he particularly attentive to any one of them?'

'Not that I am aware of.'

'Would it be correct to say that the entire responsibility for the sales side of the business rests on your shoulders?'

At this he blinked, but made no reply.

'It se ... :ly, doesn't it, that you will be kept on here, and also invited t. ke charge at the Quai de Charenton?'

He sat motionless and impassive, his expression blank.

'Would any member of your staff have had cause for complaint against your employer?'

'I don't know.'

'I take it you want to see the murderer arrested?'

'Of course.'

'So far, you haven't been much help to me.'

'I'm sorry.'

'What is your opinion of Madame Chabut?'

'She's a very intelligent woman.'

'Do you get on well with her?'

'You've already asked me that, and I've told you that I hardly know her. She scarcely ever set foot in this office, and I never went to the Place des Vosges. I don't go in for dinner parties and nights on the town.'

'Did Chabut go in much for social life?'

'I couldn't say. You'd better ask his wife.'

'Do you know if he left a will?'

'I've no idea.'

Maigret's head was swimming. He realized that he was getting nowhere. Louceck had made up his mind to give nothing away, and he would maintain a stubborn silence to the bitter end.

The Chief Superintendent got up.

'I'd be obliged if you would draw up a list of all your staff, including ages and addresses, and let me have it as soon as possible at the Quai des Orfèvres.'

Louceck, still imperturbable, merely gave a slight nod. He pressed a buzzer, and the door opened to admit a young woman, who promptly showed them out. Before getting back into the car, Maigret went into a bar and had a glass of rum, hoping that it might make him feel better. Lapointe had a fruit juice to keep him company.

'What next?'

'It's nearly midday, too late to call at the Place des Vosges. We'll go back to the office, and then have a bite to eat at the Brasserie Dauphine.'

He went into the telephone box, and dialled number of his flat in the Boulevard Richard-Lenoir.

'Is that you? What's for lunch? No, I shan't be back. Keep it for my dinner tonight. I know I sound a bit hoarse. I've had a streaming nose for the past hour. See you this evening. . . .'

He was not in the best of moods.

'Almost anyone might have had a more or less compelling reason for wishing Chabut dead. But only one gave in to the temptation to shoot him. The others are innocent. All the same, innocent or not, you'd think they were all in a conspiracy to spike our guns, instead of helping us. With one exception, perhaps, the girl they call the Grasshopper. She's a funny kid, but all the same, she seems genuinely anxious to co-operate, and she doesn't weigh every word like the others. How does she strike you?'

'As you say, she's a funny kid. But she's not afraid of looking facts in the face, and she isn't easily taken in.'

The medical report from the Forensic Laboratory was on Maigret's desk. It was more than four pages long, and replete with technical terms. Appended were two diagrams showing the trajectory of the bullets. There were two in the abdomen, one in the chest, and a fourth just below the shoulder-blade.

'No telephone messages?'

He turned to Lucas.

'Have you sent the report to the Public Prosecutor's Office?'

He was referring to the Stiernet case.

'First thing this morning. I've actually been down to see him in the cells.'

'How is he?'

'Giving no trouble. He seems almost serene, really. He doesn't mind being locked up. You'd think he hadn't a care in the world.'

A little while later, Maigret and Lapointe went across the road to the Brasserie Dauphine. At the bar there were two robed barristers, and also three or four inspectors. They were not in Maigret's Division, but they nevertheless greeted him respectfully. He and Lapointe went into the dining-room.

'What's on today?'

'Your favourite, *blanquette de veau*.'

'What's your opinion of Vin des Moines?'

The proprietor shrugged.

'It's no worse than the stuff that used to be sold by the litre in the old days. It's a mixture of wines from the South and from Algeria. Nowadays, people prefer a label on their bottle, and the fancier the name, the better.'

'Do you stock it?'

'Indeed, I don't! What do you say to a drop of Bourgueil? Perfect with the *blanquette*.'

Maigret was fumbling in his pocket for his handkerchief.

'Here we go again! As soon as I come into a warm room it starts.'

'Why don't you go home to bed?'

'What good would that do? It wouldn't stop me worrying about that fellow Chabut. He's certainly making life difficult for us. You'd think he'd done it on purpose.'

'What do you think of his wife?'

'I haven't made up my mind. Yesterday evening, she struck me as very charming and self-possessed, in the circumstances. A bit too self-possessed, maybe. As far as her relations with her husband are concerned, she seems to have been a kind of mother figure, protective and indulgent. Well, we'll see. I may change my mind after I've seen her again. I'm always a bit suspicious of these plaster saints.'

The *blanquette* was tender and beautifully cooked, with a fragrant golden-yellow sauce. They each had a pear, followed by coffee, and, shortly after two, they entered the building in the Place des Vosges. The door was opened by the maid whom they had seen the night before. She left them sitting in the hall, and went to announce them to her mistress.

When she came back, she led them, not into the drawing-room, but into a small sitting-room beyond, where they were almost immediately joined by Jeanne Chabut.

She was wearing a very plain but beautifully cut black dress, with no jewellery of any kind.

'Do sit down, gentlemen. I was there this morning, and, as a result, I can't face the thought of lunch.'

'I presume the body will be brought here?'

'At five this afternoon. The undertaker will be coming to see me first, to decide where to lay him out. It will be in here, I daresay. The drawing-room is too big.'

The little sitting-room, with its huge window, stretching almost from floor to ceiling, was light and colourful, like the rest of the flat, but more distinctively feminine in character.

'Did you choose the furnishings?'

'I've always been interested in interior decorating. I should have liked to have taken it up professionally. My father has a bookshop in the Rue Jacob, not far from the Ecole des Beaux-Arts. That's where all the best antique shops are.'

'What made you take up shorthand-typing?'

'I wanted my independence. I hoped I might be able to go to evening classes after work, but I soon realized that it couldn't be done. And then I met Oscar.'

'Did you become his mistress?'

'From the very first evening. By now, that shouldn't surprise you.'

'Was it he who proposed marriage?'

'Can you see it coming from me? I daresay he was getting fed up with living alone in a miserable little hotel, and cooking his meals on a spirit stove. He was very poor in those days.'

'Did you go on working?'

'For the first two months. After that, he made me give it up. This may surprise you, but he was very jealous.'

'Was he faithful?'

'So I believed.'

Maigret watched her intently. There was something about her that had a false ring, and it made him uneasy. She had a lovely face, but her features were curiously set, almost as though she had undergone plastic surgery.

Her eyes, which were light blue and very large, were unblinking. Had she deliberately cultivated that air of wide-eyed innocence?

His nose was running again. She looked at him in silence, as he dabbed at it with his handkerchief.

'Excuse me.'

'I've given some thought to that list you asked me for, and I've got down all the names I can think of. I didn't like doing it, but I've done it nevertheless.'

She went across to a Louis XV desk, and picked up a sheet of writing paper that was lying there. Her handwriting was large and firm, with no flourishes.

'I have included only those men whose wives I believe to have been on intimate terms with my husband.'

'You're not sure about them?'

'In most cases, no. But, judging from the way he talked of them, and his manner towards them when we entertained them here, I'm pretty sure. It didn't take me long to recognize the signs.'

In a low voice, he began reading out the names.

'Henri Legendre.'

'He's an industrialist. He commutes between Paris and Rouen. Marie-France is his second wife. She's fifteen years younger than he is.'

'Is he jealous?'

'I believe so, but she's one too many for him. They have a place at Maisons-Laffitte, where they have regular week-end house-parties.'

'Have you ever been?'

'Only once, because, as a rule, we had our own week-end house-party at Sully-sur-Loire. We have a summer place at Cannes as well, the two top floors of a new block not far from Palm Beach. We have access to the roof, and I've made a garden up there. . . .'

'Pierre Merlot,' he read.

'A stockbroker. Lucile, his wife, is a little blonde with a pointed nose. She's over forty, but she still affects the urchin look. That must have amused Oscar.'

'Did her husband know?'

'I'm sure he didn't. He's a bridge fiend, and whenever we had people in, he was always one of those shut up in here for a quiet rubber.'

'Did your husband play?'

'No, bridge wasn't his particular game.'

She smiled faintly.

'Jean-Luc Caucasson. He publishes art books. He married a young artist's model. She's pretty foul-mouthed, but good fun all the same.'

'Maître Poupard. Is that the criminal lawyer?'

He was one of the leading lights of the Bar, and his name often appeared in the newspapers. He was married to a very rich American woman.

'Did he suspect nothing?'

'He's often away from home on some case in the provinces. They have a magnificent flat on the Ile-Saint-Louis.'

'Xavier Thorel. The Cabinet Minister?'

'Yes. He's a delightful man, and a dear friend.'

'You make it sound as though he was more your friend than your husband's.'

'I'm very fond of him. As for Rita, she throws herself at every man she meets.'

'Does he know?'

'He's resigned to it. Or rather, he gives as good as he gets.'

More names, Christian names and surnames, an architect, a doctor, a famous dress designer in the Rue François Ier, and Gérard Aubin, partner in the bank of Aubin et Boitel.

'The list could have been much longer, because we have a very wide circle of acquaintances, but I have confined myself to those with whom I felt pretty sure Oscar was on intimate terms.'

Changing the subject abruptly, she asked:

'Have you been to see his father?'

'Yes.'

'What did he say?'

'I got the impression that he wasn't on the best of terms with his son.'

'Only since Oscar started making a lot of money. He wanted his father to give up the bistro, and offered to buy him a nice little estate at Sancerre, not far from where he was born. It was all a misunderstanding. Désiré thought we were trying to get rid of him.'

'What about your own father?'

'He still has his bookshop, and lives with my mother above the shop. She's completely housebound now. She has a weak heart, and has great difficulty in walking.'

The maid knocked at the door and came in.

'The gentleman from the undertaker's is here.'

'Tell him I'll be with him right away.'

And, turning to the two men:

'I'll have to ask you to excuse me. I shall be kept terribly busy for the next few days. Still, if anything new crops up, or if I can be of any further use to you, don't hesitate to let me know.'

She gave them a vague, somewhat mechanical smile and, leading the way with her graceful, fluid walk, showed them to the door.

In the hall, they met the undertaker's man, who, recognizing Maigret, gave a respectful little bow.

The fog, which had almost cleared by lunch time, was now

beginning to thicken once more, and everything in the street looked a little blurred.

As to Maigret, he was blowing his nose again, and muttering heaven knows what imprecations under his breath.

CHAPTER THREE

MAIGRET was never altogether at ease with the aura of opulence generated by some sections of the upper bourgeoisie. It made him feel awkward and out of place. For instance, all the people on the list that Jeanne Chabut had provided belonged more or less to the same set, with its own rules, customs, taboos and private language. They forgathered in restaurants, theatres and nightclubs, spent their week-ends together in country houses, and, in the summer, went off in droves to Cannes or Saint-Tropez.

Oscar Chabut, with his plebeian looks, had elbowed his way ruthlessly into this tight little world, and to prove to himself that he really had arrived, he had found it necessary to go to bed with most of the women in it.

'Where to, sir?'

'Rue Fortuny.'

He was slumped in his seat, with glazed eyes, gloomily watching the streets and boulevards go by. The street lamps were lit, and there were lighted windows in most of the buildings. In addition, lights were strung across the streets, with here and there little fir trees painted gold or silver, and, in the shop windows, glittering Christmas trees.

In spite of the fog, the streets were jammed with sightseers and shoppers, gazing in shop windows and crowding into the stores. He wondered what he should give Madame Maigret for Christmas, but he saw nothing that appealed to him. He blew his nose incessantly, and longed to get home to his bed.

'When we've finished at Rue Fortuny, I'll give you the list, and leave you to find out where they all were round about nine on Wednesday night?'

'Am I to ask them personally?'

'Only if you can't find out any other way. In most cases, I

daresay, you'll be able to get the information from the servants or the chauffeur.'

Poor Lapointe was not exactly overjoyed at the prospect. 'Do you think it's one of them?'

'It could be anyone. Our friend Oscar seems to have gone out of his way to make himself universally detested, at least as far as the men were concerned. You can wait for me in the car. I won't be more than a few minutes.'

He rang the bell of Madame Blanche's house. He had not heard the sound of approaching footsteps, but the judas window opened, and Madame Blanche came to the door, though with obvious reluctance, to let him in.

'What do you want now? This is my busiest time, and I don't want my clients disturbed by policemen trampling all over the house.'

'I want you to take a look at this list of names.'

They were alone in the great drawing-room, lit only by two shaded table lamps. Having looked about for her spectacles, and found them on the grand piano, she glanced through the list.

'What do you want to know?'

'Whether there are any clients of yours on this list.'

'First of all, as I've already told you, I only know my clients by their first names. Surnames are never mentioned here.'

'Knowing you, I haven't the least doubt that you've made it your business to find out all you can about them.'

'People like myself are in a position of trust, in the same way as doctors and lawyers, and I don't see why we shouldn't be entitled to the privilege of professional secrecy, just as they are.'

He listened patiently, then said quietly:

'I'm afraid I shall have to insist on an answer.'

'There are two or three.'

'Who are they?'

'Monsieur Aubin, Gérard Aubin, the banker. He's one of a powerful group of Protestant financiers, and he goes to great lengths to protect his reputation.'

'Does he come often?'

'Two or three times a month.'

'Does he bring his companion with him?'

'No, she always arrives first.'

'Always the same one?'

'Yes.'

'Has he ever run into Chabut in the corridor or on the stairs?'

'I take very good care to see that doesn't happen.'

'He could have seen him entering or leaving the house or recognized his car. What about his wife? Has she ever been here?'

'Yes, with Monsieur Oscar.'

'Who are the others?'

'Marie-France Legendre, the industrialist's wife.'

'Did she come often?'

'Four or five times.'

'Also with Chabut?'

'Yes. I don't know her husband. If he's ever been here, it was under an assumed name. Some prefer it that way. The minister, André Thorel, for instance. He rings me in advance, to give me time to find a young woman for him, preferably a fashion model or a cover girl. He calls himself Monsieur Louis, But as his photograph often appears in the papers, everyone knows who he is.'

'Do any of them come regularly on Wednesdays?'

'No, they haven't any special day.'

'Was Madame Thorel one of Oscar Chabut's mistresses?'

'Rita? She came with him once or twice, but he was by no means the only one. She's a provocative little brunette, and she can't do without men. I don't mean she's a nymphomaniac. It's just that she has to be the centre of attention.'

'Thank you.'

'Will that be all?'

'I don't know, at this stage.'

'Do me a favour, next time you come, give me a ring first. You must understand that if you were seen in this house by the wrong people, it could do me a lot of harm. I'm grateful to you, at any rate, for not having given my name to the reporters.'

Maigret returned to his car. He was not much further forward, but, in the absence of any real lead, he could not afford to leave any stone unturned.

'Where to now, sir?'

'Home.'

His forehead was hot and his eyes smarting, and he was troubled by an ache in his left shoulder.

'Courage, laddie. You've got the list, haven't you? To start with, you'd better go back to the Quai and have a photostat copy made. We don't want to have to bother Jeanne Chabut again.'

Madame Maigret was amazed to see him back so much sooner than expected.

'It looks to me as though you've got a shocking cold. That's why you're home so early, I daresay.'

He was sweating profusely.

'It wouldn't surprise me if I were in for a bout of 'flu. It could hardly have come at a worse time.'

'It's a queer business, isn't it?'

Most of the time, as in this instance, she knew no more about Maigret's cases than she could read in the newspapers or hear on the radio.

'Hang on a minute. I've got to make a phone call.'

He rang the Rue Fortuny and heard Madame Blanche's bland voice on the line.

'Maigret speaking. There's one thing I forgot to ask you, just now. Used Chabut to let you know by telephone when he was coming?'

'Sometimes he did, sometimes not.'

'Did he telephone on Wednesday?'

'No. There wasn't any point. He almost always came on Wednesdays.'

'Who knew that, besides yourself?'

'No one here.'

'What about your maid?'

'She's Spanish—very young. She hardly speaks a word of French, and she can't catch people's names, let alone remember them. . . .'

'Nevertheless, someone must have known, the person who knew roughly what time Chabut would be leaving your house, and was waiting for him outside, in spite of the freezing weather.'

'I'm sorry. I'll have to ring off. There's someone at the front door.'

He undressed, got into his pyjamas and dressing-gown, went back into the sitting-room, and slumped into his leather arm-chair.

'Your shirt is soaked through. You'd better take your temperature.'

She fetched the thermometer from the bathroom, and made him keep it in his mouth for a full five minutes.

'Well?'

'One hundred and two degrees.'

'Why not go straight to bed? Don't you think it would be as well for me to ask Pardon to look in on you?'

'It would be a fine thing, if he were called out every time one of his patients had a mild attack of 'flu!'

He hated bothering the doctor, especially when it was his old friend, Pardon, who seldom managed to get through a meal without interruptions.

'I'll go and turn down the bed.'

'Hold on a minute. Did you keep that *choucroute* for me?'

'You surely don't want it now?'

'Why not?'

'It's so indigestible. You're not well.'

'Warm it up for me all the same, and don't forget the pickled pork.'

It all turned on one crucial point. Someone had known that Chabut would be in the Rue Fortuny that Wednesday evening. It was unlikely that the murderer had followed him. In the first place, it was no easy matter to follow anyone in Paris, in particular if he was in a car. In the second place, it had been seven o'clock or thereabouts when the wine merchant had arrived, in company with the Grasshopper.

Was it conceivable that the murderer should have hung about for the best part of two hours in freezing weather, and that no one should have noticed him? And another thing, he had obviously not come by car, since, as soon as he had fired the shots, he had rushed off to the Malesherbes Métro station.

His head was fairly spinning. He really must pull himself together and think.

'What will you drink?'

'Beer, of course. What else would go with *choucroute*?'

Much as he had been looking forward to the *choucroute*, when it came to it, he could manage no more than a mouthful or two, and he quickly pushed his plate aside. It was unheard of for him to go to bed at half-past six in the evening. All the same, he did so. Madame Maigret brought him two aspirins.

'What else can I give you? Last time, I seem to remember —it must have been about three years ago—Pardon gave you a bottle of something that did you a lot of good.'

'I don't remember.'

'Seriously, don't you think I should give him a ring?'

'No. Draw the curtains and put out the light.'

Within ten minutes, he was perspiring freely. His thoughts began to drift and, in a little while, he fell asleep.

But it was to be a long night. Several times he woke, with his nasal passages blocked, gasping for breath. It was not easy to get back to sleep. He lay, for a while, in a semi-conscious doze and, in this state, kept imagining he heard his wife's voice.

Then he saw her, standing beside the bed, with a pair of clean pyjamas over her arm.

'You'll have to change. You're sopping wet. I wonder if I shouldn't change the sheets as well.'

He let her get on with it, only dimly conscious of what was happening. Later, he found himself inside a church, which reminded him, on a much larger scale, of Madame Blanche's drawing-room. All down the centre aisle there were couples, seemingly queuing up to get married. Someone was seated at a piano, but the music that filled the church was that of an organ.

There was something he had to do, but he could not remember what it was, and, out of the corner of his eye, he could see Oscar Chabut sneering at him. As each couple filed past him, he hailed the woman by her Christian name.

At last, half awake, Maigret saw the grey light of morning creeping into the bedroom, and caught the smell of coffee coming from the kitchen.

'Are you awake?'

He was no longer sweating. He felt drained and languid, but otherwise quite comfortable.

'Is my coffee ready?'

He could not remember when he had last enjoyed a cup of coffee so much. He drank in little sips, savouring it.

'Hand me my pipe and tobacco pouch, there's a dear. What's the weather like?'

'A bit misty, but not nearly as bad as yesterday. I think the sun will be out shortly.'

Not often, but once or twice in his childhood, he had made himself ill because he had not managed to finish his homework. Had this cold of his been just such a psychological indisposition? Surely not, since he had actually run a temperature.

Before giving him his pipe, Madame Maigret handed him the thermometer. Obediently, he slid it under his tongue.

'Ninety-eight. Below normal.'

'No wonder, considering the way you've been perspiring.'

He smoked his pipe, and drank another cup of coffee.

'You'll give yourself at least one day's rest, I hope!'

He did not reply immediately. He had not made up his mind. He felt very comfortable, tucked up in his warm bed, especially now that he no longer had a headache. Lapointe was hard at work, checking the alibis of all the men on the list.

The case was hanging fire. It was disheartening, the more so because he somehow felt himself to blame. The key to the mystery was within his grasp, if only he could put his hand on it.

'Anything new in the papers?'

'They say you're on the track of someone.'

'Which is exactly the opposite of what I told them!'

By nine o'clock he had drunk three large cups of coffee, and the air in the bedroom was blue with the fumes of his pipe.

'What do you think you're doing?'

'I'm getting up.'

'You're not going out, are you?'

'Yes.'

Knowing that it would be useless, she did not protest.

'Would you like me to ring the Quai and ask them to send an inspector with a car?'

'Good idea. Lapointe won't be there. See if Janvier is available. No, on second thoughts, he's on another case. But Lucas could probably manage it.'

He did not feel quite so well, out of bed. His head was

swimming a little, and when he shaved, his hand shook, and he gave himself a slight cut.

'You'll be in to lunch, I hope? It won't do anyone any good to have you seriously ill.'

She was right, of course, but he could not help himself. His wife wound his thick scarf round his neck, and stood on the landing, watching him as he went down the stairs.

'Good morning, Lucas. The Chief hasn't been asking for me, has he?'

'I told him you weren't feeling too good last night.'

'Anything new?'

'Lapointe was out all evening with his list, and he was off again first thing this morning. Where would you like me to take you?'

'Quai de Charenton.'

He was already beginning to feel at home there. He went straight upstairs, followed by Lucas who, not having been there before, was looking about him at the dingy walls. He knocked at the door, and went in, to find the Grasshopper at her desk, typing.

'It's me again. This is Inspector Lucas, my oldest colleague.'

'You look tired.'

'I am. I have several important questions, one in particular, to ask you.'

He sat down in Chabut's chair, behind the roll-top desk.

'Who knew that your employer was always to be found in the Rue Fortuny on Wednesdays?'

'Among the people here, do you mean?'

'Here, or elsewhere.'

'Everyone here knew. Oscar was nothing if not indiscreet. The minute he made a new conquest, he had to let everyone know.'

'Used you to leave the office at the same time as he did?'

'Yes, and I drove off in the car with him. It was all perfectly obvious.'

'And this took place every Wednesday, more or less?'

'More or less, yes.'

'Did Monsieur Louceck know?'

'I couldn't say. He scarcely ever came here. The boss was

there every day, in the Avenue de l'Opéra, and he usually stayed for an hour or two.'

'Can you give me some idea of his usual timetable?'

'Well, it varied, of course, but let's take an average day. He would leave home at about nine in the morning, driving the Jaguar. He had a chauffeur, to drive the Mercedes, but that was mostly for his wife's use. He usually called in first at the Quai de Bercy, just to keep an eye on things. That's where the wines are blended and bottled. . . .'

'Who's in charge there?'

'Nominally, Monsieur Leprêtre. He goes there from time to time, but there is also a sort of assistant manager on the spot. He comes from Sète originally, I believe.'

'Does he ever come here?'

'Very rarely.'

'Does he know of your relations with your employer?'

'I daresay he's heard the gossip.'

'Has he ever shown any particular interest in you?'

'I doubt if he's even noticed me.'

'I see. Well, go on.'

'Monsieur Chabut would get here at about ten, and go through his mail. If he had any engagements fixed for that day, I reminded him of them. Usually, one or two wholesalers from the South would call in to see him, during the course of the morning.'

'What was his attitude to you, during working hours?'

'It varied. Sometimes, he'd scarcely notice I was there. At other times he'd say: "Come here," and hitch up my skirt, and make love to me on the edge of the desk. He never bothered to lock the door.'

'Were you ever caught in the act?'

'A couple of times, by one of the shorthand typists, and once by Monsieur Leprêtre. It was no surprise to the girls, they'd had the same experience themselves.'

'What time did he leave?'

'If he was lunching at home, about midday. If he had a lunch appointment in town, as he often did, he would leave at about half-past twelve.

'Where do you have lunch?'

'Not two hundred yards from here, on the Quai. There's a little restaurant where the food isn't at all bad.'

'What about the afternoon?'

Lucas, worthy soul that he was, was listening to all this in amazement, and looking the Grasshopper up and down, as though he couldn't make her out at all.

'Almost every day, he went on to the Avenue de l'Opéra, where he generally stayed until about four. He shared an office with Monsieur Louceck.'

'Did he carry on with the girls there, too?'

'I don't think so. It's a different world. The atmosphere isn't the same at all. Besides, I suspect he wouldn't have had the nerve, not with Monsieur Louceck around. Strange as it may seem, he was a bit scared of him, I think. Well, perhaps scared is too strong a word. At any rate, he treated him differently from the others, and, as far as I know, he never raised his voice to him.'

'So he'd be back here soon after four?'

'Between four and half-past. He would usually spend some time with Monsieur Leprêtre, and occasionally he would go down to the wharf to watch a barge being unloaded. Then he'd come up here, ring for a shorthand-typist, and dictate letters.'

'Wasn't that your job?'

'No. I only dealt with his personal correspondence. What he really needed was someone about the office, someone who didn't matter, with whom he could think aloud. That was my job. It wouldn't have made any real difference if I'd done no work at all.'

'What time did he leave?'

'Six, as a rule, except when he felt like staying on with me, or one of the other girls.'

'Did he never spend a whole evening with you?'

'Only on Wednesdays, till about nine.'

'Did you always stay behind at Madame Blanche's?'

'No, sometimes we left together, and he drove me home to the Rue Caulincourt. He always dropped me about a hundred yards from my front door. Last Wednesday, he was in a hurry, so I said not to wait for me.'

'I'd be glad if you'd give it a little more thought. Try and

207

think of anyone else who might have known about your visits to the Rue Fortuny.'

He blew his nose, and put on his hat. Madame Maigret had been right. The sun had come out, and was casting glittering reflections on the Seine.

'Thanks, Mademoiselle. Come on, Lucas.'

As the car was turning into the forecourt of Police Head-quarters, Maigret caught a glimpse of a man standing near the parapet of the Quai. It was no more than a glimpse, and the Chief Superintendent thought nothing of it at the time, especially as, almost at once, the man made off towards the Place Dauphine, limping a little.

But some time later he said to Lucas:

'Did you spot him?'

'Who?'

'The man in the gaberdine raincoat. He was across the road, watching the entrance and looking up at the windows. As we drove past, he looked me straight in the eye. I'm sure he recognized me.'

'A tramp?'

'No, he was clean-shaven and decently dressed, though I should scarcely have thought this was the weather for a gaberdine coat.'

When he got to his office, Maigret still had the unknown man on his mind. Mechanically, he crossed to the window and looked out. Needless to say, he was no longer there, on the Quai.

He tried to recall what it was about the man that had struck him so forcibly. Perhaps it was the intensity of his gaze, he thought. There had been something pathetic about him, as though he were faced with a grave problem, or in the throes of some deep personal unhappiness.

Maigret could almost have believed that he had seen a direct appeal for help in his eyes.

He shrugged, filled his pipe, and sat down at his desk. Every now and again, for no apparent reason, he broke out in a sweat, and had to mop his face with his handkerchief.

He had promised Madame Maigret that he would be home

to lunch, but had forgotten to ask her what they would be having. He always liked to know before he went out in the morning. It gave him something to look forward to.

The telephone rang. He picked up the receiver.

'I have a call for you, sir, but the caller refuses to state his name or business. Do you wish to speak to him, all the same?'

'Put him through. Hello! . . .'

'Chief Superintendent Maigret?' the caller asked, in a somewhat muffled voice.

'Speaking.'

'I have just one thing to say: Don't lose any sleep over the wine merchant. He was a lousy swine.'

'Did you know him well?' Maigret asked, but the caller had already rung off. Slowly, Maigret replaced the receiver, and remained gazing thoughtfully at the instrument. This, perhaps, was what he had been waiting for since the start of the case: a real lead at last.

Admittedly, he had learnt nothing from the caller, except that someone, somewhere in this business—the murderer, more likely than not—was one of those people who could not endure being completely ignored. Such people usually wrote anonymous letters, or telephoned. They were not necessarily all madmen or cranks.

He had encountered this sort of thing once or twice before. In one case, the guilty man had given him no peace until he had arrested him.

With an aching head, he opened his mail, signed a number of reports, and dealt with various administrative matters, which always seemed to him to take up just as much of his time as the actual conduct of an investigation.

At midday, he left the office. He walked as far as the entrance to the Palais de Justice, then, after a moment's hesitation, went into the café on the corner. His mouth felt dry, and he needed a drink. Having had a glass of rum the night before, he decided to order the same again. Actually, he ordered two. They were very small glasses.

He went home in a taxi, and, rather slowly, climbed the stairs. He had barely reached the landing when his wife opened the door and, taking a good look at him, enquired:

'How are you feeling?'

'Better. Except that, every now and then, I break out in a sweat. What's for lunch?'

He removed his coat, hat and scarf, and went into the living-room.

'Calves' liver *à la bourgeoise*.'

It was one of his favourite dishes. He sat down in his arm-chair, and glanced absent-mindedly through the newspapers.

Could it be that the mysterious caller was the same man whom he had noticed a short while before on the Quai, opposite the entrance to Police Headquarters?

He would have to wait for him to telephone again. He might even ring him here at home. His flat in the Boulevard Richard-Lenoir was always being mentioned in the papers. Besides, every taxi-driver in Paris knew his address.

'What's on your mind?' asked Madame Maigret, as she was laying the table.

'I caught a glimpse of a man earlier on today. Our eyes met, and I had the feeling that he was trying to convey some sort of message to me.'

'With a look?'

'Why not? Not long afterwards, a man telephoned me just to tell me that Chabut was a lousy swine. Those were his exact words. I don't know if it was the same man. He hung up on me before I had a chance to find out.'

'Are you hoping he'll ring again?'

'Yes. They nearly always do. They get a kick out of playing with fire. Unless, of course, it's just some unfortunate crank, who knows no more about the case than he's read in the news-papers. I've had a few of those, too, in my time.'

'You don't want the television on, do you?'

They ate almost in silence. Maigret's mind, needless to say, had reverted to the case and the people involved.

'Have you had enough? If so, we can have the rest cold as a first course tomorrow.'

If anything, he preferred calves' liver cold, after it had stood for a day. For dessert, he cracked a few walnuts and almonds, and ate them with a couple of figs. He had only had two glasses of claret with his meal. All the same, he felt drowsy. He got up from the table, and slumped down in his armchair by the window.

He closed his eyes, and dozed for some considerable time on the brink of sleep. He could feel himself drifting into sleep. It was a pleasant sensation, and he had no wish to dispel it.

And there, before his eyes, was the man whom he had seen on the Quai, the man with a slight limp. Was it in his left foot or his right? Half asleep as he was, the question assumed an importance that he would have been hard put to it to justify if he had been fully awake.

Madame Maigret cleared the table, going back and forth to the kitchen without a sound. Had he not felt a slight draught from time to time, he would not have known she was there.

Gradually, he ceased to be aware of his surroundings. His mouth, though he did not know it, had fallen open, and he was snoring gently. He woke with a sudden start, surprised to find that he was in his own armchair. He glanced up at the clock. It was five past three. He looked about for his wife. A slight swishing sound from the kitchen told him that she was in there, ironing.

'Did you have a good sleep?'

'Marvellous. I could have slept all day.'

'Won't you take your temperature?'

'If you want me to.'

This time it was a hundred.

'Do you have to go back to the office?'

'I'm afraid so, yes.'

'You'd better have an aspirin first.'

Obediently, he took one, then, to get rid of the taste, he poured himself a small tot of sloe gin from the bottle his sister-in-law had sent them from Alsace.

'I'll ring for a taxi right away.'

Although the sky was clear and blue, rather pale blue, and the sun was shining, it was still very cold.

'Shall I turn the heater on, sir? You look as if you have a cold. My wife and kids are all down with 'flu. When one gets it, we all get it. It will be my turn next, I daresay.'

'Thanks, but I'm better off without the heater. I keep breaking out in a sweat as it is.'

'You too? I've been soaked through three or four times today already.'

The stairs seemed steeper than usual, and it was a relief, when he finally reached his office, to sit down at his desk. He rang and asked for Lucas.

'Nothing new?'

'Nothing at all, Chief.'

'No anonymous phone calls?'

'No. Lapointe has just got back. He's waiting to see you, I think.'

'Send him in.'

He took a pipe from the rack on his desk, the smallest one, and filled it slowly.

'Were you able to get all the information we needed?'

'More or less, yes. Luck was on my side.'

'Sit down. Let's see the list.'

'You won't be able to read my notes. If you don't mind, I'll read them out to you, and later I'll let you have a full report. To start with the Minister, Xavier Thorel, I didn't have to ask any questions. I found out from Thursday's papers that he was representing the Government that night at the world première of a film about the Resistance.'

'With his wife?'

'Yes, Rita was there too, and their eighteen-year-old son.'

'Go on.'

'It struck me that there might be others on the list, who had also attended the première, but who weren't important enough to get their names in the papers. And, in fact, one of them was, a Dr Rioux, who lives in the Place des Vosges, only a couple of doors away from the Chabuts.'

'How did you find out?'

'Simple. I asked the concierge. Perhaps not the most up-to-date method of gathering information, but still the best. It seems that Madame Chabut is Dr Rioux's patient.'

'Has she had much illness?'

'Well, at any rate, she sends for him fairly often, it seems. He's rather a fat man, with a few sparse brown hairs, that he brushes carefully over his bald patch. His wife is a big horsey red-head, not at all Oscar Chabut's type, I'd guess.'

'That's two of them. Go on.'

'Henri Legendre, the industrialist, was in Rouen, where he has a pied-à-terre. He usually spends one or two nights a week there. I got all this from his chauffeur, who mistook me for an insurance tout.'

'What about his wife?'

'She's been in bed for a week with 'flu. I couldn't get anything definite on the stockbroker, Pierre Marlot. He's said to have been dining out with his wife Lucile, which apparently he often does. He's said to be something of a gourmet, so I shall do the rounds of the best restaurants as soon as I can. That should produce something.'

'What about Caucasson, the art publisher?'

'He was at the cinema in the Champs-Elysées, same as the Minister.'

'And Maître Poupard?'

'He was one of dozens being entertained to dinner by the American Ambassador in the Avenue Gabriel.'

'What about Madame Poupard?'

'She was there, too. Then there's a Madame Japy, Estelle Japy, widowed or divorced. She lives alone in the Boulevard Haussmann. Apparently, she was Chabut's mistress for years. To find out about her, I had to make up to her maid. She hasn't seen Chabut for months, and I gather he treated her very shabbily. On Wednesday, she was alone for dinner, and spent the rest of the evening looking at television.'

Maigret's telephone rang. He lifted the receiver.

'A personal call for you sir. I think it's the same man who rang this morning.'

'Put him through.'

There was a long silence, during which he could hear breathing on the line.

At last the man spoke:

'Are you there?'

'Yes, I'm listening.'

'It's only to tell you again that he was a lousy swine. Never lose sight of that.'

'Hold on a minute.'

But the man had already rung off.

'He could be the murderer, but he could just as well be a practical joker. As long as he keeps hanging up on me, I've no way of finding out. There's no means of tracing him either. We can only hope that he'll drop his guard and say too much, or do something silly.'

'What did he say?'

'The same as he said this morning, that Chabut was a lousy swine.'

No doubt there were a great many people in Chabut's circle, who shared this view. He had done everything possible to get himself disliked, if not hated, both in his pursuit of women and in his conduct towards his staff.

It almost looked as if he had deliberately set out to provoke animosity. Yet, until last Wednesday, no one, as far as was known, had ever attempted to put him in his place. Had he ever had his face slapped? If so, he had kept it very dark. Had anyone ever, in a fit of jealousy, punched him on the jaw?

He had been overweeningly arrogant, and so sure of himself that he had not shrunk from tempting providence over and over again.

But in the end, someone, a man according to Madame Blanche, had had enough, and had lain in wait for him outside the house in the Rue Fortuny. This man must have had an even more compelling reason than the rest for hating him, since he had been prepared to risk his liberty, if not his life, by killing him.

Was it among Chabut's friends that this man was to be found? The results of Lapointe's enquiries had been, on the whole, disappointing. Matrimonial infidelity scarcely ever ended in murder nowadays, especially in the circles in which Chabut moved.

Was the murderer one of the employees at the Quai de Charenton? Or at the Avenue de l'Opéra?

And was he or was he not the nameless man who had twice telephoned the Chief Superintendent, in order to unburden himself?

'Have you been through the whole list with me?'

'Just a couple more names: Philippe Borderel and his mistress. He's a theatre critic on one of the leading dailies. He was at a dress rehearsal at the Théâtre de la Michodière. Then there's Trouard, the architect. He was dining at Lipp's with a client, name unknown.'

How many more people, not on the list, had good cause to bear a grudge against the wine merchant? The only way to find out was to interview scores of men and women, one by one, face to face. And that, needless to say, was just not on, which was why Maigret set so much store by the unknown man who had telephoned him, and who might or might not be the same man whom he had seen standing near the parapet that morning.

'When is the funeral, do you know?'

'No. The undertaker's men had just arrived as I was leaving Madame Chabut. The body should have been taken to the Place des Vosges late yesterday afternoon. Come to think of it, perhaps we might go along there and have a look.'

A few minutes later, they were in the car, on their way to the Place des Vosges. The door to the first-floor flat was open. They went in, and were at once assailed by a strong smell of chrysanthemums and candlegrease.

Oscar Chabut was lying in an open coffin, with the lid beside it. Kneeling on a prie-dieu was an elderly woman dressed in deep mourning, and a youngish couple stood near by, looking at the dead man, whose face was illuminated by the flickering candles.

Who was the old woman in mourning? Jeanne Chabut's mother? It was certainly possible, indeed probable. The young couple seemed very ill at ease. The man took his companion by the elbow and, after they had both crossed themselves, hustled her out.

Maigret, in accordance with custom, took the little sprig of rosemary from the bowl of holy water, and made a sign of the cross with it over the coffin. Lapointe followed suit with such fervour that Maigret could not help smiling to himself.

Even in death, Oscar Chabut was impressive. Coarse-featured though he was, his face was strong and endowed with a strange kind of beauty.

As the two men were leaving, they came face to face with Madame Chabut in the hall.

'Were you wanting to see me?'

'No. We came to pay our last respects to your husband.'

'You'd think he was alive, wouldn't you? They've done a marvellous job on him. You've seen him now, exactly as he was in life, except, alas, for the expression in his eyes.' Like an automaton, she led them across the hall to the front door.

Abruptly, Maigret murmured:

'There's something I should like to ask you, Madame.'

She looked at him with interest.

'I'm listening.'

'Do you really want your husband's murderer found?'

It was so unexpected that, for a moment, she could not get her breath.

'Why ever should I want that man, of all men, to go free?'

'I don't know. If he's found, there will be a trial, a sensational trial, with full coverage by the press, radio and television. What's more, a great many public figures will be called as witnesses. Your husband's employees will also have to give evidence. Some of them, at least, will tell the truth. Maybe some of your husband's friends will, too.'

'I see what you mean,' she murmured thoughtfully, as though she were weighing up the pros and cons.

After a brief pause, she added:

'There'll be an almighty scandal!'

'You haven't answered my question.'

'To be honest, I don't care one way or the other. I'm not out for revenge. I daresay the man who killed him believed he had good cause for what he did. Maybe he really had. What good would it do anyone to lock him up for ten years, or even for the rest of his life?'

'In other words, if you had some inkling of who he was, you'd keep it to yourself?'

'As I have no such inkling, that's a hypothetical question. If I had, it would be my duty to tell you, wouldn't it? And I believe I should do so, however unwillingly.'

'Who is going to take over your husband's business? Louceck?'

'That man frightens me. He's a cold-blooded fish, and I can't bear to feel his eyes on me.'

'Still, your husband seems to have trusted him.'

'Louceck coined money for him. He's very shrewd. He knows every law on the Statute Book, and how to get round it. To begin with, he was merely my husband's tax consultant, but he gradually worked his way up, until he was his right-hand man.'

'Who founded Vin des Moines?'

'My husband. The business was run entirely from the Quai de Charenton in those days. It was Louceck who advised Oscar to open an office in the Avenue de l'Opéra and to set up more warehouses in the provinces, so as to increase the retail outlets.'

'In your husband's opinion, was he honest?'

'Oscar needed him. And he was able to stand up for himself.'

'You haven't answered my question. Will he be running the business?'

'He'll carry on as he is, no doubt, at least for a time, but he won't rise any higher.'

'Who will be the boss?'

'I will.'

She said this quite simply, as though anything else was inconceivable.

'I've always been a businesswoman at heart. My husband often turned to me for advice.'

'Will you have your office in the Avenue de l'Opéra?'

'Yes, but I won't share it with Louceck, as Oscar did. There's plenty of space.'

'And will you supervise the warehouses, and the cellars and offices at the Quai de Charenton?'

'Why shouldn't I?'

'Are you thinking of making any staff changes?'

'I don't see why I should. Because nearly all the girls there have been to bed with my husband, do you mean? If I were to let that worry me, I shouldn't have a single woman friend left, except those who were past it.'

They were interrupted by the arrival of a young woman, a vivacious little doll, who rushed up to the lady of the house, flung her arms round her, and exclaimed:

'You poor darling!'

On the way downstairs, Maigret, pausing to mop his face with a handkerchief, mumbled:

'That's a very strange woman.'

A few steps lower down, he added:

'Either I'm much mistaken, or we're nowhere near the end of this case.'

To be fair, he reflected, Jeanne Chabut was at least to be commended for her frankness.

CHAPTER FOUR

AT ABOUT FIVE O'CLOCK, there was a discreet knock on Maigret's office door. Without waiting for an answer, Joseph, an old man, the oldest of the departmental messengers, came in and handed a printed slip to the Chief Superintendent.

Name: Jean-Luc Caucasson.

Object of Visit: The Chabut Case.

'Where have you put him?'

'In the aquarium.'

This was the name jocularly given to one of the waiting-rooms, which was walled with glass on three sides, and where there were always one or two people waiting to be seen.

'Leave him to stew for a few minutes, then bring him in.'

Maigret blew his nose vigorously, went over to the window, and stood looking out for a little while. Then he opened the cupboard where he always kept a bottle of liqueur brandy, and poured himself a nip.

He was still a little light-headed, and he had an uncomfortable feeling of stuffiness, as though he were breathing through cotton wool.

He was standing beside his desk, lighting his pipe, when Joseph announced Monsieur Caucasson.

Caucasson did not appear unduly overawed by the atmosphere of the Quai des Orfèvres. He came forward with hand outstretched.

'Have I the honour of addressing Chief Superintendent Maigret?'

By way of reply, Maigret mumbled, 'Please take a seat,' retreated behind his desk, and sat down.

'You are a publisher of art books, I believe?'

'That is so. I also have a shop in the Rue Saint-André-des-Arts. Perhaps you know it?'

Maigret did not reply, but subjected his visitor to a thoughtful scrutiny. He was a fine-looking man, tall and spare, with a thick crop of well-brushed grey hair. His suit and overcoat were also grey. He wore a slight, self-satisfied smile, which Maigret took to be his habitual expression. He had the look of a pedigree animal, an Afghan hound, perhaps.

'Please forgive me for taking up your time like this, especially as it's more in my interests than yours. Oscar Chabut was a friend of mine. . . .'

'I know. I also know that last Wednesday night you attended the world première of a film about the Resistance. The film didn't start until half-past nine, leaving you ample time to get from the Rue Fortuny to the Champs-Elysées.'

'You mean I'm on your list of suspects?'

'Everyone who knew Chabut is more or less suspect, until I have evidence to the contrary. Do you know Madame Blanche?'

He hesitated, but only for an instant.

'Yes. I've been there once or twice.'

'Who with?'

'With Jeanne Chabut. She knew her husband went there regularly, and she wanted to see for herself what sort of place it was.'

'Are you Madame Chabut's lover?'

'I was. I have no reason to suppose that I was the only one.'

'When was this?'

'The last time we met by arrangement was about six months ago.'

'Used you to go and see her at the Place des Vosges?'

'Yes, when her husband was on one of his trips to the south. Almost once a week, in fact.'

'Is this what you came to see me about?'

'No. You asked me a question, and I've answered it to the best of my ability. What I really came about was the letters. I suppose you've found them?'

Maigret, still watching him closely, frowned.

'What letters?'

219

'Private letters, addressed to Oscar. Naturally, I don't mean his business correspondence. I felt sure he must have kept them somewhere, either in his flat or at the Quai de Charenton.'

'And you feel that you have a claim on these letters?'

'Meg, that's my wife. . . . Meg, as I say, is a compulsive letter writer, and she has a habit of saying whatever comes into her head. . . .'

'In other words, you want to get back her letters?'

'She had an affair with Oscar. It lasted quite a long time. I caught them together. He seemed very much put out at the time.'

'Was he in love with her?'

'He's never been in love in his life. She was just another scalp to add to his collection.'

'Are you jealous?'

'I've got used to it by now.'

'Has your wife had other lovers?'

'There's no point in denying it.'

'So your wife was Chabut's mistress, and you were Madame Chabut's lover? Is that a fair way of putting it, would you say?'

There was a hint of restrained irony in Maigret's voice, but the art publisher apparently failed to notice it.

'Did you write any letters yourself?'

'Three or four.'

'To Madame Chabut?'

'No. To Oscar.'

'To protest about his relations with Meg?'

'No.'

He was coming to the awkward bit now, and had assumed an air of studied negligence.

'You don't know much about the art publishing business, I daresay. It caters for a very small public, and production costs are extremely high. It sometimes takes years to recover the capital outlay.'

'And, for that reason, backers are essential.'

Maigret, the underlying note of irony much sharper now, asked with apparent artlessness:

'Was Monsieur Chabut one of your backers?'

'He was a very rich man. He was making money hand over fist. It occurred to me that he might be willing to help. . . .'

'So you wrote to him?'

'Yes.'

'In spite of the fact that he was your wife's lover?'

'That had nothing to do with it.'

'Was this after you had caught them together?'

'I don't remember the exact dates, but I think so, yes.'

Maigret tilted his chair on to its back legs, and pressed down the ash in his pipe with his thumb.

'Were you and Jeanne Chabut already lovers?'

'I knew you wouldn't understand. You still cling to the good old-fashioned middle-class virtues, which simply have no meaning in our world. Wife-swopping is nothing to us. It's happening all the time.'

'I understand perfectly. What you're trying to say is that you approached Oscar Chabut because he was a rich man, and for no other reason?'

'That's it exactly.'

'Just as you would approach an industrialist or a banker with whom you were not personally acquainted?'

'If I found myself in difficulties, yes.'

'But, in this case, you weren't in difficulties, were you?'

'I was considering publication of a major work on some aspects of Asiatic art.'

'Did you say anything in the letters that you have since had reason to regret?'

He was growing more and more uneasy, and yet managing, somehow, to keep his dignity.

'Let's say that they could be open to misinterpretation.'

'In other words, if they got into the wrong hands, if they were read by anyone who didn't share your own broad-minded outlook, they might seem to smack of blackmail? Is that it?'

'More or less.'

'Did you press very hard?'

'I wrote three or four letters.'

'All on the same subject, and within a short space of time?'

'I was anxious to get the book launched as soon as possible.

I already had the text, by a very distinguished authority on the subject.'

'Did he pay up?'

Caucasson shook his head.

'No.'

'Were you very disappointed?'

'Yes. I'd expected better of him. I didn't really know him.'

'He was a hard man, wasn't he?'

'Hard, and very scathing at times.'

'Did he reply by letter?'

'He didn't even bother. One evening, when we were having cocktails at his flat with about thirty other people, I tackled him, hoping to get an answer there and then.'

'And did you?'

'I did, a very brusque one. At the top of his voice, to make sure that others beside myself should hear him, he said:

' "It may interest you to know that Meg doesn't mean a damn thing to me, and as for your goings-on with my wife, I couldn't care less. So I'd be obliged if you'd stop pestering me for money." '

He had looked rather pale when he came into the room, but now he was flushed, and his long, well-manicured hands shook.

'As you see, I'm being perfectly frank with you. I could have kept my mouth shut, and waited to see how things developed.'

'Waited to see whether I would find the letters, you mean?'

'They might be found by anyone.'

'Have you seen him since?'

'Twice. It didn't stop him inviting Meg and me to his parties.'

'And you went?' murmured Maigret, in mock admiration. 'So you believe in forgiving those who trespass against you?'

'What else could I do? He was a brute, and, at the same time, you could no more resist him than the forces of nature. There must be others who have been humiliated by him, even among our own friends. He couldn't help himself. He had to feel his own power. He didn't ask to be liked.'

'I take it you're asking me to return these letters to you?'

'I'd rather they were destroyed.'

'Your wife's as well as yours, I presume?'

'If I know Meg, she will have struck an exaggerated note of passionate eroticism. As to my own letters, as I told you, they're open to misinterpretation.'

'I'll see what I can do for you.'

'You have found the letters, then?'

Instead of replying, he got up and went to the door, to indicate that the interview was at an end.

'Incidentally, do you happen to own a 6.35 automatic pistol?'

'I keep an automatic in my shop. It's been there, in the same drawer, for years. I don't even know the calibre. I don't much care for firearms.'

'Thank you. By the way, did you know about your friend Chabut's regular weekly visits to the Rue Fortuny?'

'Yes. Jeanne and I would occasionally take advantage of them to arrange an assignation of our own.'

'Tha will be all for the present. If I need to see you again, I'll be in touch.'

At last, Caucasson left, stumbling against the doorpost as he went. Maigret stood watching him until he reached the head of the stairs, then returned to his desk, and asked to be put through to the flat in the Place des Vosges. This took some time, as the line was continuously engaged.

'Madame Chabut? Chief Superintendent Maigret speaking. I'm sorry to trouble you again, but I've just had a visitor, and there are one or two questions I want to ask you about him.'

'I'd be glad if you'd keep it short. I'm terribly busy. At any rate, the funeral arrangements are completed at last. It's to be tomorrow morning, and it will be strictly private.'

'Will there be a religious service?'

'Just a short memorial prayer. I haven't let anyone know except a couple of very close friends, and one or two members of my husband's staff.'

'Including Monsieur Louceck?'

'I couldn't very well leave him out.'

'What about Monsieur Leprêtre?'

'Him, of course. And Oscar's private secretary as well, that gangling kid they call the Grasshopper. I've ordered three cars to drive us straight to Ivry Cemetery.'

'Do you happen to know where your husband kept his personal letters?'

There was an appreciable pause.

'Believe it or not, I've never given it a thought! I'm just trying to think. He got very few letters addressed to him here at the flat. Most of his mail went to the Quai de Charenton. Have you any particular letters in mind?'

'Letters from friends, men and women.'

'If he kept them, they must be in his personal safe.'

'Where is that?'

'In the drawing-room, behind his portrait.'

'Have you got the key?'

'It was one of your staff, I think, who brought back the clothes he was wearing on Wednesday. That was yesterday. There was a bunch of keys in one of the pockets. I noticed a safe key among them, but I thought nothing of it at the time.'

'I won't take up any more of your time today, but after the funeral . . .'

'It will be all right if you ring me tomorrow afternoon.'

'Meanwhile, I must ask you to be sure and destroy nothing, not even the smallest scrap of paper.'

Would her curiosity get the better of her? he wondered. If so, she would probably lose no time in opening the safe and reading those precious letters.

Next, he telephoned the Grasshopper.

'How are things at your end?'

'Fine! What did you expect?'

'I've just heard that you've been invited to the funeral.'

'Yes, I had a phone call. I wasn't expecting it, I must say. I rather got the impression she didn't like me.'

'Tell me, is there, by any chance, a safe anywhere in your building?'

'Yes, on the ground floor, in the accountant's office.'

'Who has the key?'

'The accountant, of course. I daresay Oscar had a duplicate.'

'Do you happen to know if he kept any personal papers— letters, for instance—in the safe?'

'I don't think so. As a rule, when he'd read his personal

letters, he either tore them up into little bits, or stuffed them into his pocket.'

'All the same, I'd be glad if you'd ask the accountant, and let me know what he says. I'll hold on.'

He took advantage of the interval to re-light his pipe, which had gone out. At the other end of the line, he could hear receding footsteps and the opening and shutting of a door, then, a few minutes later, the door opening again, followed by approaching footsteps.

'Are you still there?'

'Yes.'

'It's as I thought. There's nothing in the safe but papers relating to the business, and a certain amount of cash. The accountant isn't even sure that it was the boss who had the spare key. It's more likely to be Monsieur Leprêtre, he thinks.'

'Thanks.'

'Will you be going to the funeral?'

'I don't think so. For one thing, I haven't been invited.'

'A church service is open to all.'

He put down the receiver. He still had a bit of a headache, but he had recovered a little from his earlier gloom. He got up and went next door into the Inspectors' Duty Room. Lapointe was typing out his report. He only used two fingers, but could type faster than most trained secretaries.

'I've had a visitor,' murmured Maigret, 'the art publisher.'

'What did he want?'

'To get back some letters. It's unforgivable of me not to have thought of Oscar Chabut's private correspondence. There are sure to be some very revealing letters. Caucasson's are a case in point. He wrote demanding money. . . .'

'Because the wine merchant was having an affair with his wife?'

'Caucasson caught them in the act. Admittedly, he was having an affair with Jeanne Chabut at the same time. . . . But that's just one example. I have a feeling that, when we get our hands on all the letters he kept, we shall find others.'

'Where are they?'

'Seemingly, in a safe behind our friend's portrait in the drawing-room of the flat.'

'Has his wife read them?'

'Apparently it didn't occur to her to look in the safe. She came upon the key by accident, in one of the pockets of the suit Chabut was wearing on Wednesday.'

'Have you told her about them?'

'Yes, and I'm quite sure she'll have read them before the day is out. The funeral is tomorrow. There is to be a memorial prayer in the Church of Saint Paul. She's invited so few people that only three cars will be needed to take them to Ivry Cemetery.'

'Are you going?'

'No.'

What would be the use? Whoever he was, the wine merchant's murderer was unlikely to give himself away by behaving in a conspicuous manner at a funeral.

'I think you're on the mend, sir. You're not blowing your nose so often.'

'Don't talk too soon. Wait and see how I am tomorrow.'

It was half-past five.

'There's nothing to keep me here till six. I think I'd be better off at home.'

'Goodnight, sir.'

'Goodnight, lads.'

And Maigret, pipe clenched between his teeth, and shoulders hunched, turned and walked out of the room. He was still feeling a little weak at the knees.

He slept heavily. If he had had any dreams that night, he had forgotten them by the morning. The wind must have changed during the night and, with it, the weather. It was much less cold. Rain was falling in a steady downpour, and the windows were streaked with it.

'Aren't you going to take your temperature?'

'No, I can tell it's normal.'

He was feeling better. He drank two cups of coffee with relish, and, once again, Madame Maigret rang for a taxi.

'Don't forget your umbrella.'

When he got to his office, he glanced quickly through the pile of mail on his desk. This was a long-established habit of his. He liked to see if there were any envelopes addressed in a hand he recognized, a letter from a friend, perhaps, or one containing some information that he was waiting for.

Today, there was an envelope addressed in block capitals, and marked 'Personal' in the top left-hand corner. The word 'Personal' was underlined three times.

'*Chief Superintendent Maigret,*
Officer In Charge of Criminal Investigations,
38, Quai des Orfèvres.'

He opened this letter first. It contained two sheets of paper of the kind normally to be found in cafés and brasseries. The headings had been cut off. The sheets were covered with very neat handwriting, with regular spacing between the words, suggesting that the writer had an orderly mind, and was a stickler for detail.

'*I trust that this letter will not be held up in your outer office, and that it will receive your personal attention.*

I have already spoken to you twice on the telephone, but, on each occasion, I felt obliged to ring off somewhat abruptly for fear that you should be able to trace the call. Although I am assured that this is impossible with an automatic exchange, I was unwilling to take the risk.

I was surprised to find no reference in the newspapers to the personal character of Oscar Chabut. Is it possible that there is not one among all those interviewed by the press who was prepared to speak out and expose him for what he was?

Instead, he is described as a man of vision, adventurous and resilient, who fought his way to the top, and, by his own efforts, created one of the greatest wine industries in the country.

Surely you must see that this is a disastrous state of affairs! The man was a lousy swine. I have already told you so, and I make no apology for repeating it. He was ready to sacrifice everyone and every-thing to his overweening ambition and delusions of grandeur. In fact, I do not think it would be going too far to say that, on some subjects at least, he was a madman.

For it is hard to believe that a man who was perfectly sane could have behaved as he did. Take his attitude to women, for instance. What he wanted, above all, was to debase and defile them. His desire to possess every woman he met was really a desire to reduce them all to the same level, and thereby assert his own superiority. And this was why he was always boasting of his conquests, without any regard for the reputations of the women concerned.

And what of the husbands? Is it possible that they were ignorant of what was going on? I do not believe it. They too were under his domination, preferring to remain silent rather than incur his open contempt.

He felt the need to reduce everyone else in power and stature, in order to enhance his own. Do you follow me?

I sometimes find myself thinking of him in the present tense, as if he were still alive, even now that he has, at long last, got his just deserts. No one will mourn his passing, not even his nearest and dearest, not even his father, who, for years, has refused to see him.

There is not a word of all this in the newspapers, so that if, in the course of time, you are able to apprehend the man who shot him and, in so doing, put paid to his crimes, he will be an object of loathing to the whole world.

I felt I had to make contact with you. I watched you going into the house in the Place des Vosges with another man, whom I took to be one of your inspectors. I caught sight of you also at the Quai de Charenton where, it may interest you to know, things are not quite what they seem. Everything that man touched is contaminated in one way or another.

You are seeking the murderer, are you not? Well, that is your job, and I do not hold it against you. But, if there were any justice in the world, you would be seeking him, not to condemn him, but to congratulate him.

The man, I repeat, was a rotten, lousy swine, wicked and vicious to the core.

I conclude, Chief Superintendent, with my respectful good wishes, and my humble apologies for omitting to append my signature to this communication.'

There was, nevertheless, appended to the letter, an illegible scrawl.

Slowly, sentence by sentence, Maigret re-read the letter. He had, in the course of his career, received hundreds of anonymous letters, and he had learned to recognize those that deserved to be taken seriously.

In spite of the intemperate language, the accusations in this particular letter were not without foundation, and the portrait of the wine merchant drawn by its author was a fair likeness of the original.

Was this the work of the murderer himself? Was he one of the many victims of Oscar Chabut's lust for power? If so, was he one of the husbands whose wives Chabut had appropriated and then rejected, as was his wont, or was he one of those who had suffered from his harsh business methods?

In spite of himself, Maigret found that he was identifying the writer of the letter with the limping man who had waited for him across the road from Police Headquarters and then hurried off towards the Place Dauphine. He was nothing much to look at, yet, in spite of the fact that his clothes looked as though they had been slept in, he was obviously no tramp. Paris was full of such men, men who fitted in nowhere. Some went inexorably from bad to worse, until they touched rock bottom, others committed suicide.

But a few gritted their teeth and hung on, and eventually surfaced again, especially if someone happened to be standing by to give them a helping hand.

In his heart of hearts, Maigret would have liked to hold out a helping hand to this man. In spite of his pathological hatred of Chabut, which appeared by now to be the sole object of his existence. Maigret did not see him as a madman.

Was it he who had murdered the wine merchant? It was certainly possible. He could picture him waiting in the shadows his fingers gripping the ice-cold butt of the pistol.

As he had promised himself that he would, he fired one, two, three, four shots and then made off, limping, towards the Métro.

Where had he gone from there? Where did he live? Perhaps he had made for the bright lights of the Grands Boulevards, and gone into a bistro for warmth and a private celebration.

The murder of Chabut was not unpremeditated. The man who had perpetrated it had been planning it for a very long time and, no doubt, deferring it, until some final outrage had at last goaded him into action.

And now his enemy was dead, and, very possibly, the murderer was discovering that life had suddenly lost all meaning for him. The victim had once again stolen the limelight. His name was on everybody's lips, he was spoken of with admiration, almost as a man of genius. No one had given a thought to the man who had shot him, nor to his reasons for doing so.

So he had telephoned Maigret. Then he had written to him. And he would write again, driven, though he did not know it, by the need to reveal himself, and bring about his own arrest.

The bell was ringing. It was time for Maigret to go to the Chief Commissioner's office for the daily briefing.

'Anything new on the shooting in the Rue Fortuny?'

'Nothing definite. But I think I'm on the verge of a breakthrough.'

'Does that mean there is a scandal in the offing?'

Maigret frowned. He had not told the Chief the details of Chabut's personal life, and there had been no mention of it in the papers. Why then should he be worrying at this stage about the possibility of a scandal?

Was it that the Chief Commissioner was personally acquainted with the wine merchant, or that Chabut was well-known in the circles in which the Chief Commissioner moved? If so, he must certainly know that Chabut had a great many enemies, all of whom had a good reason to wish him dead.

Evasively, he replied:

'I can't put a name to the killer yet.'

'Be that as it may, you would be well advised to say as little as possible to the Press.'

Shortly after this, he went through the rest of his mail, and dictated a few replies to a shorthand typist. His back was aching, and he was still feeling a little below par, but at least his nose had stopped running.

Lapointe came in just before noon.

'I hope you won't hold it against me, sir, but I just couldn't resist it. I know I'm not supposed to do things off my own bat, but I just had to go to that funeral. There were about twenty people there in all, and the only representative of the staff was Monsieur Louceck.'

'No one else that you recognized?'

'As we came out of the church, there was a man standing on the pavement opposite, looking at me. I tried to get to him, but by the time I had threaded my way through the traffic, he had disappeared.'

'You don't say! Here, read this.'

He held out the anonymous letter. Every now and then, as he read it, the Inspector smiled to himself.

'The same man, wouldn't you say?'

'Remember, he saw me in the Place des Vosges, at the Quai de Charenton, and, I'm pretty sure, going in through the door of this building. He must have been expecting to see me again this morning at the funeral.'

'And he would have seen us together, and so recognized me.'

'I think it would be a good idea to have someone watching the flats in the Place des Vosges this afternoon. I shall probably be calling on Madame Chabut myself, later. Tell him to ignore me. The important thing is for him to keep his eyes skinned for anyone loitering near the flats. Up to now, our friend has shown himself to be a past master in the art of vanishing.'

'Shall I go myself?'

'If you like. You do have the advantage of knowing him by sight.'

He went home to lunch, which he ate with relish, and afterwards had forty winks in his armchair. When he got back to the Quai des Orfèvres, he put a call through to Jeanne Chabut's number, and asked to speak to her. He was kept waiting some time.

'I'm sorry to bother you so soon after the funeral, but I must admit I'm anxious to have a look at your husband's personal letters as soon as possible. I have a feeling I shall learn a lot from them.'

'Do you want to come here this afternoon?'

'If it's at all possible.'

'I've got someone coming at five. I can't get out of that, I'm afraid. Could you possibly come right away?'

'I'll be with you in a few minutes.'

Lapointe was already there, watching the flats. Maigret got Torrence to drive him to the Place des Vosges, and then sent him back to the Quai des Orfèvres. The black draperies, embroidered with silver tears, no longer adorned the front door, and the little sitting-room, where the body had lain, was back to normal. Only the scent of chrysanthemums persisted.

She was wearing the same black dress as on the previous day, but she had added a clip of coloured stones, which made it look less severe. She was as neat as a new pin, and completely self-assured.

'I suggest we use my sitting-room. The drawing-room is far too big for just the two of us.'

'Have you opened the safe?'

'I must confess I have.'

'How did you get it open? Did you know the combination?'

'Of course not. But I realized that my husband probably kept it somewhere on his person, so I went through his wallet. Inside his driving licence, I found a slip of paper with a string of figures, so I tried them out on the safe, and they worked.'

On top of a Louis XV chest, there was a rather bulky parcel, clumsily tied with string.

'I'd better tell you right away that I haven't read all of them. It would have taken all night. I was surprised to find how many he'd kept. I even found my old love letters, written before we were married.'

'I think I'd better work backwards. I'm more likely to find a clue to the murderer in the later letters.'

'Sit down, won't you?'

To his astonishment, she put on a pair of spectacles. They transformed her. He could see now why she had always wanted to go into business. Here, he realized, was a woman with nerves of steel and a will of iron. Once she made up her mind to a thing, she would never g ve up.

'These are all short notes—A¹ ! here's one signed "Rita". I don't know which Rita that would be. . . . It just says: "*I shall be free tomorrow at three. Usual place? Love and kisses, Rita.*"

'Not much given to sentimental outpouring, is she? I must say, I don't care for her stationery. I think scented notepaper is in pretty poor taste, don't you?'

'Is it dated?'

'No, but it was in a bundle with a lot of letters, all of recent date.'

'Did you come across any from Jean-Luc Caucasson?'

'So you know about him! Has he been to see you?'

'He's extremely anxious about those letters of his.'

It was still raining, and the tall windows were spattered with zigzag streaks. The flat was very quiet and restful. Between them lay a pile of letters, several hundreds of them, the abstract and brief chronicle of a man's life.

'Here's one. Shall I read it to you?'

'I'd rather read it myself, if you don't mind.'

'Do smoke your pipe, if you want to. It won't worry me in the least.'

'*My dear Oscar,*

For a long time, I could not bring myself to write to you on this subject but, on reflection, we are such old friends that I feel I may venture to do so.

It is, as you can imagine, extremely distasteful to me to raise the subject of money, especially knowing what a brilliant businessman you are as compared with myself, who, alas, have no head for figures!

Art publishing is in a world of its own, unlike any other. One is always on the look-out for the work that will bring one financial reward as well as critical acclaim. Sometimes, one has to wait a long time for it and, when one does eventually discover it, one may find oneself without the resources needed to publish it.

This is precisely the position in which I now find myself. Business in the shop is very sluggish at present, and it is more than a year since I brought out my last book, and, as luck would have it, just when things are at their lowest ebb, I have the opportunity of publishing a work of exceptional merit entitled "Aspects of Asiatic Art". I am confident that this is a great book, and that it will have the success it deserves. In fact, I am virtually certain of being able to sell the rights in the United States for a sum which would cover the production costs many times over.

But publication would entail an initial outlay of two hundred thousand francs, of which I cannot produce a centime myself. Admittedly there is Meg's little nest-egg, but that does not amount to more than ten thousand francs or so.

Can you see your way to lending me this money? It will seem a trifling sum to you, I know. This is the first time I have ever asked for money in this way, and I confess I find it extremely embarrassing.

Before I finally made up my mind to write to you, I consulted Meg,

233

and she said she felt sure that you were too good a friend to both of us to refuse to help.

I will be glad to come and see you at home or at either of your offices, whichever suits you best. Just ring me or drop me a line to say where and when, and I shall be there. I shall be only too willing to put my signature to whatever written undertakings you may require of me.'

'Sickening, isn't it?'

Seeing that she had just lit a cigarette, Maigret ventured to light his pipe.

'Did you notice the reference to Meg? The second letter is much shorter.'

Both letters were handwritten. He had small, neat hand-writing, but it was a little shaky here and there, indicating nervous tension.

'*My dear friend,*

I am surprised that you have not yet found time to reply to my letter. It took a lot of courage to write to you in the first place. I would not have opened my heart to you as I did, if I had not had the fullest confidence in you.

The situation has deteriorated somewhat since I last wrote. A number of heavy bills will shortly be falling due, and, unless I can meet them, I may be forced to leave the country.

Meg, who knows just how things stand, is very much upset. Indeed, it is she who has urged me to write to you again.

I trust I shall soon be vindicated in my belief that friendship is not just an empty word to you.

I am relying on you, as, I am sure I need not tell you, you can rely on me.

                         Yours. . .'

'I don't know how that strikes you, but it reads like a veiled threat to me.'

'Yes,' growled Maigret, 'and not all that veiled, either.'

'Wait till you see what Meg has to say!'

He picked up one of the letters at random.

'*My dearest darling,*

It seems an eternity since I saw you last, though, in fact, it's barely a week. It was so good to be in your arms and feel the beating of your heart. I feel so safe when I'm with you!

I dropped you a note the day before yesterday saying I wanted to see you. I was at the usual place at the time I mentioned, but you never came, and Madame Blanche said you hadn't telephoned.

I'm worried. I know how busy you are, and how important your work is, and I realize I'm not the only one. I'm not jealous, and I never will be, so long as you don't drop me altogether. I need you. I long for you to crush me in your arms until it hurts. I long even for the smell of you.

Write soon. I don't expect a long letter, just the date and time of our next meeting.

Jean-Luc has a lot of worries at the moment. He's got some book or other in mind which, according to him, is going to bring us fame and fortune. What a will-o'-the-wisp he is, compared with a real man like you!

I long to kiss every part of you.

Your very own
Meg.'

'There are lots more in the same vein. Some of them are pretty hot stuff.'

'When was the last one written?'

'Before we went on holiday.'

'Where did you go?'

'To our place in Cannes. Oscar had to fly back to Paris a couple of times. Some of our friends were there at the same time, but not the Caucassons. I seem to remember they have a little cottage, somewhere in Brittany, in one of those villages where all the artists forgather.'

'Are there any other begging letters?'

'I haven't nearly finished reading them yet. But there is one, a note from Estelle Japy. She's a widow, an enterprising soul, as you will see. Oscar and she were pretty thick for a time.'

'*My dear friend,*

I enclose a bill which, I regret to say, I am unable to meet. I look forward to seeing you in the near future.

Yours,
Estelle.'

'Is the bill enclosed with the letter?'

'I didn't see it. I've no idea what it was for, or for how much. A piece of jewellery, maybe, or a fur coat? She was in church this morning, but she didn't come on to the cemetery.'

'Would you mind if I took these letters home? Or if you'd rather, I could look in on Sunday, and finish reading them.'

'I hate to refuse you anything, but to tell you the truth, I don't want to part with them, even temporarily.

'Come whenever you like, tomorrow if you wish, and I'll leave you on your own to read them in peace. There are a couple more I think you should see before you go. There's this one from Robert Trouard, the architect, asking my husband to put up the capital for the building of luxury flats.'

'Did he ever invest in any project of that sort?'

'Never, as far as I know.'

'What about Trouard's wife?'

'Needless to say, she was another of them. Only in her case I don't think her husband knew.

'Now this one, you must see. There are six sizzling pages of it. The name of the lady in question is Wanda—she's a new one on me. Not only does she feel it incumbent upon her to describe in the minutest detail exactly what they did at their last meeting, but she goes on, by a dazzling feat of the imagination, to predict just what they will do the next time. I think she must be a Russian or a Pole. I fancy Oscar must have had his work cut out, getting her out of his hair.

'Here's another interesting one, from Marie-France, Henri Legendre's wife.'

She held out a sheet of pale blue writing paper. The ink used was of a somewhat darker blue.

'*Darling old horror,*

I ought to hate you, and I will too, if you don't come to me and say you're sorry very soon. I've just heard the most hair-raising tales about you. I won't say who told me, only that it was one of your other conquests. Anyway, you may not even remember her. I don't see how you can remember them all.

What really riles me is that you should have spoken of me in the way you did at the top of your voice at a cocktail party in the hearing of at least half-a-dozen people. Remember? Someone mentioned my name, and you said: "It's such a pity she's got sagging breasts." Well, I always knew you were a low-down skunk. Now I have proof of it, but I somehow don't seem to be able to face life without you.

Your move.'

'Of course it's all much more fun if you happen to know the people concerned, the lovely Madame Legendre, for instance. I always see her in my mind's eye, sweeping into a drawing-room on her husband's arm, with a perfect cascade of diamonds glittering on her bosom.

'And now I really will have to ask you to go. I'm expecting Gérard any minute. Gérard Aubin, the banker, you know. I need his advice on one or two matters. He's someone I can really trust.

'If you'd care to come back tomorrow afternoon . . .'

'I don't think that will be necessary.'

'No, of course, you're entitled to spend Sunday with your family.'

It would have surprised her to learn that the Maigrets would probably do nothing more exciting than they usually did on Sundays, which was to spend the afternoon in a local cinema, and then walk home afterwards arm in arm.

Outside in the square, Maigret spotted Lapointe.

'You were right, sir, but he was one too many for me. That man is as slippery as an eel. I waited as close to the house as I dared, over there by the railings of the square garden. The garden was almost deserted, because of the rain, but, after I'd been there about half an hour, I noticed a man sitting on a bench on the far side. I'm almost sure I recognized him. He was wearing a shabby brown hat, and a raincoat over a rather dark suit.

'I went into the garden and began to walk towards him, but I hadn't gone ten paces when he got up, made off in the direction of the Rue de Birague, and vanished.

'I broke into a run, much to the astonishment of two old ladies who were sitting chatting under one umbrella. I ran as far as the Rue Saint-Antoine, but there was no sign of our friend. One almost has the feeling that he's trailing you, to reassure himself that you haven't slackened off on the job!'

'He probably knows more about the case than I do. If only we could make him talk! Did you come by car?'

'No, by bus.'

'We'll go back by bus, then.'

They set off, Maigret with his hands deep in his pockets.

CHAPTER FIVE

THEY DID NOT, after all, go to the cinema, as Maigret had planned. The day started with a heavy downpour of rain. It beat down upon the almost deserted pavements of the Boulevard Richard-Lenoir. By ten o'clock in the morning, the wind had risen and was blowing in fitful gusts. There were very few people about, only one or two intrepid, black-clad men and women with umbrellas, hugging the walls of the buildings for shelter, on their way to or from Mass.

It was about ten o'clock by the time the Chief Superintendent started to get dressed, which was most unusual for him. Up to this time, he had sat about in his pyjamas and dressing-gown, doing nothing in particular.

His temperature was up again. It was nothing much, just over a hundred, but enough to make him feel rather limp and listless. Madame Maigret naturally took advantage of this to make a bit of a fuss of him, and every time she did some little thing for him, he scowled with feigned displeasure.

'What are we having for lunch?'

'Roast beef, with braised celery and mashed potatoes.'

The Sunday joint. It reminded him of his childhood, except that, in those days, he had liked his meat well-done. There were several little things that day that brought back memories of his childhood.

Safe and warm together in the flat, they watched the rain beating down. Just before lunch, Maigret murmured a little hesitantly, 'I feel like an aperitif, a small glass of sloe gin, I think.'

She did not attempt to dissuade him. He went across to the sideboard and opened the drinks cupboard. As well as the sloe gin, there was a bottle of raspberry liqueur, both from his sister-in-law in Alsace. The raspberry liqueur won. It was deliciously fragrant, and it needed only a sip for the flavour to linger on the palate for as long as half an hour.

'Won't you have a drop?'

'No. You know very well it sends me to sleep.'

Appetizing smells were coming from the kitchen, though his nostrils were a little less sensitive than usual, on account of his cold. He glanced through one or two weeklies, which he never had time to read except on Sundays.

'It's interesting, you know, in some walks of life, the normal rules of decent conduct seem to have vanished altogether. . . .'

She did not need to ask what he was referring to. He was still, in spite of everything, in spite of himself, absorbed in the Chabut case, and, at intervals through the day, he reverted to it.

'When you have a hundred or more people, all with more or less sound reasons for wishing a man dead . . .'

He was haunted by the thought of the little man with the limp, who was so skilful at getting lost in a crowd, and who always seemed to be lurking in wait for Maigret, wherever he went. Who was he?

He took his afternoon nap in his armchair. He woke to find his wife busy with some sewing. She never could bear to sit doing nothing.

'I slept longer than I intended.'

'It will do you good.'

'I do hope it turns out not to be 'flu after all.'

He went across to switch on the television. It was showing a Western, and he quite enjoyed watching it. Needless to say, there was a villain, and Maigret could not help thinking that, in some respects, he was not unlike Chabut. Like Chabut, he was always having to prove his strength to himself and other people and, to this end, he bullied and humiliated them.

When the film was over, he murmured, recalling his tête-à-tête with Madame Chabut on the previous day in her little sitting-room in the Place des Vosges:

'A strange woman, that.'

'Who will be running the business now?'

'She will.'

'What does she know about it?'

'Very little. But she'll soon grasp it, and I'm pretty sure she'll make a success of it. I bet you anything you like that, within a year, Monsieur Louceck will find himself out of a job.'

He was in the middle of reading an article on deep-sea exploration, when he suddenly had a thought. What was it the Grasshopper had said on the subject of the accountant? That

239

he was a newcomer, who had been there only a matter of months. What had happened to his predecessor? Had he left of his own accord, or been sacked?

He must find out right away. Trembling with excitement, he looked up the girl's number in the telephone book. He held on for some time, but there was no reply. No doubt, the Grasshopper and her mother were at the cinema, or out visiting. He tried again at half-past seven, but there was still no reply.

'Do you think she knows something?'

'I daresay she didn't attach any importance to it, and that's why she didn't think it worth mentioning. Besides, there's probably nothing to it, but I'm so much at sea at the moment. . . .'

In spite of everything, it had been an enjoyable day. They had cold meat and cheese for dinner, and, by ten o'clock, had already retired to bed.

Next morning, instead of going straight to the Quai des Orfèvres, Maigret rang Lapointe and asked him to come and pick him up in a car.

'I hope you had a restful day, sir.'

'I hardly moved from my armchair the whole day. As a result, I'm feeling a bit stiff. Quai de Charenton, laddie!'

The staff were at their posts, but there was no sense of urgency. In fact, there was almost nothing doing, except at the far end of the yard, where men, their heads covered in sacks to protect them from the rain, were rolling barrels from one place to another.

'While you're waiting, you might as well go and have a chat with the accountant.'

He went up the stairs, knocked at the door, and was greeted by the Grasshopper with a broad smile. She looked, as usual, as though she found life something of a joke.

'You didn't go to the funeral, after all," he remarked.

'The staff were requested not to do so.'

'By whom?'

'Monsieur Louceck. He sent round a memo.'

'It struck me yesterday that there was something I'd forgotten to ask you. Am I right in thinking that, when I was asking you about the accountant, you said that he was new to the job?'

'He's only been here since the first of July. It's odd you should mention it now.'

'Why?'

'Because I was thinking about it only yesterday in the cinema, and I intended to tell you when I saw you next. It's about the former accountant, Gilbert Pigou. He left the firm in June, towards the end of June, if I remember right, and that's why I didn't think to mention him to you.'

Maigret was sitting in Oscar Chabut's revolving chair, opposite the Grasshopper, who had her legs crossed, so that her mini-skirt had ridden more than half-way up her thighs.

'Did he leave of his own free will?'

'No.'

'What sort of man was he?'

'Completely colourless. One scarcely noticed him. You've been into the accounts office downstairs, overlooking the courtyard. We call it the accounts office, though, in fact, all the real accounting is done at the Avenue de l'Opéra. They never get their hands on any of the big stuff down there.'

'Was he married?'

'Yes, I think so. I'm sure he was. I remember, he telephoned one day to say he wouldn't be in because his wife was having an emergency operation. Acute appendicitis, I think it was.

'He hardly ever opened his mouth, and he seemed to shrink when one looked at him. I think people scared him.'

'Was he good at his job?'

'It's all pure routine. It doesn't require any initiative.'

'Did he seem particularly interested in you, or in any of the other typists?'

'He was much too timid for anything of that sort. He was brought in fifteen years ago or so, when the business was just beginning to expand. He was rather a pathetic soul, really.'

'Why do you say that?'

'I was thinking of his last interview with the boss. I'd have given anything not to have been there. I've never felt more miserable in my life. It was ten o'clock in the morning. Oscar had just arrived, having first called in at the Avenue de l'Opéra. I can see him still, rubbing his hands, and telling me to ring down and summon Pigou.

'He seemed to be full of gleeful anticipation, and it worried me.

'"Sit down, Monsieur Pigou. Move your chair a little to the left, the light's better there. I can't stand talking to someone whose face is just a shadowy blur. How are you?"

'"Very well, thank you."

'"And your wife?"

'"She's well."

'"Is she still selling shirts in that shop in the Rue Saint-Honoré? It was the Rue Saint-Honoré, wasn't it?"'

The Grasshopper interrupted herself to remark:

'He had an extraordinary memory for detail. He had total recall about people. He'd never met Madame Pigou, yet he hadn't forgotten that she sold shirts in the Rue Saint-Honoré.

'"My wife no longer goes out to work."

'"I'm sorry to hear it."

'The accountant gaped at him, not knowing what to think. Then, as cool as you please, Chabut said:

'"You are dismissed, Monsieur Pigou. After today, you will never again set foot in this building. As I have no intention of giving you a reference, I fancy it will be some little time before you find other employment."

'He was thoroughly enjoying his little game of cat and mouse. I couldn't bear it.

'Pigou sat on the edge of his chair. He seemed bewildered, not knowing what to do, not knowing where to put his hands. I could feel waves of misery coming from him, so much so that it wouldn't have surprised me if he'd burst into tears.

'"Understand this, Monsieur Pigou, there's no future in being dishonest unless you can manage it with some degree of skill, and carry it off with something of an air."

'The accountant was still wrestling with himself, trying to make up his mind what to do. Then, suddenly, he raised his hand, and opened his mouth as if to speak.

'"Here. Take this, I have a copy. It's a detailed record of the sums of money you have stolen from me in the past three years."

'"For fifteen years . . ."

'"You've been in my employ. Correct. I wonder why you

let all those years go by before you started putting your hand in the till?"

'Pigou was deathly pale, and there were tears rolling down his cheeks. He began scrambling to his feet, but Chabut barked at him:

'"Stay where you are. I can't endure having people stand when I'm talking to them. In three years, as you will see if you look at the statement I have just handed you, you have robbed me of three thousand, eight hundred and forty-five francs. A few francs at a time. To begin with, fifty francs, more or less regularly, once a month. Then seventy-five. And, on one occasion, a much larger sum: five hundred francs."

'"That was at Christmas."

'"What of it?"

'"Ostensibly it was my Christmas bonus."

'"I don't follow you."

'"My wife had given up work by then. Her health isn't too good."

'"Are you saying that you stole money from me on account of your wife?"

'"It's the truth. She never stopped nagging me. She said I had no ambition, and that my employers exploited me and paid me less than I was worth."

'"You don't say!"

'"She would keep on at me, about asking for a rise."

'"And you hadn't the guts."

'"What would have been the use?"

'"You've got something there. Men like you are two a penny. You have no qualifications, and no initiative. Why should anyone pay you more?"

'Pigou sat motionless, staring down at the desk in front of him.

'"I told Liliane I'd asked for a rise, and that you'd agreed to an increase of fifty francs a month."

'"'Well', she said. 'Your boss hasn't exactly gone overboard, but it'll do for a start.'"'

Once again the Grasshopper interrupted herself.

'I was finding it more and more painful to watch. The clearer it became that the accountant was quite unable to

243

defend himself, the more the boss's eyes sparkled with jubilation.

'"It went up to a hundred francs a month a year ago. And last Christmas, I was supposed to have given you a bonus of five hundred francs. In other words, as far as your wife was concerned, you had made yourself quite indispensable to me. Is that it?"

'"I'm sorry. . ."

'"Too late, Monsieur Pigou. As far as I'm concerned, you no longer exist. It is not beyond the bounds of possibility that, one day, Monsieur Louceck may decide to help himself to my money. I don't trust him any more than I do anyone else. He may even have done so already, but, if he has, he's at least been clever enough to prevent anyone from finding out. And he certainly isn't the man to indulge in petty pilfering, just to impress his wife. If he ever cheats me, it will be on the grand scale, and, in consequence, I shall take off my hat to him.

'"You see, Monsieur Pigou, you're nothing but a shabby little nonentity. You always have been and you always will be. A constipated little nonentity. Come over here, if you please."

'As Chabut rose to his feet, I could scarcely prevent myself from crying out:

'"No!"

'Pigou came forward, his arm half-raised to protect his face, but Oscar was too quick for him. He slapped him hard on the cheek.

'"That's for trying to make a fool of me. I could turn you over to the police, but I don't choose to. You will now about face, and walk out of this room for the last time. Get your things together, Monsieur Pigou, and go. You're fit for nothing but the scrap heap and, what is worse, you're a fool."'

The Grasshopper fell silent.

'Did he go?'

'What else could he do? He even forgot to take his fountain pen. It's still in his desk. He never came back for it.'

'Was that the last you heard of him?'

'For several months, yes.'

'Did his wife never telephone?'

'Not till the end of September or early October. Then she came herself.'

'Did she see Chabut?'

'She was waiting for him when he got in. She wanted to know whether her husband was still working here.

'"Didn't he tell you he'd left us in June?"

'"No. He still went out every morning at the same time, and came back as usual in the evening. And at the end of the month, as usual, he handed over his salary. We didn't have a summer holiday this year, on account of pressure of work, he said:

'"'I'll make it up to you in the winter. I've always had a hankering after winter sports.'"

'"Didn't that surprise you?"

'"Well, you know, I never paid much attention to what he said."

'She was much prettier than I'd have expected, with a trim little figure. And she was nicely dressed too.

'"I was hoping you might be able to give me news of my husband. He walked out two months ago, and I haven't set eyes on him since."

'"Why didn't you come sooner?"

'"I was sure he'd be back, sooner or later. . . ."

'She was taking it all very casually. She had large, rather vacant, dark brown eyes.

'"But now, I've no money left, so. . ."

'At this point, Chabut came in. He looked her up and down, then turned to me:

'"Who is she?"

'"Madame Pigou," I said. I had no choice.

'"What does she want?"

'"Her husband has disappeared. She thought he was still working here."

'"Good Lord!"

'"For some time after he left, he gave her the equivalent of his salary at the end of each month."

'He turned and looked her full in the face.

'"Didn't you notice anything wrong? I don't know where your husband got the money, but it can't have been easy.

Didn't you know he was a thief, a miserable little thief, who wanted to make you believe he'd had a rise in salary? If he's stopped coming home to you, it must be because he's finally gone under."

'"What do you mean?"

'"A man can keep himself going somehow for a month or two, but after that, he's bound to go under, with no hope of ever surfacing again."

'"Leave us for a while, will you, Anne-Marie."

'I knew what that meant. It made me sick. I went down into the courtyard to get a breath of air, and, half an hour later, I saw her come out. She turned her head away as she went past, but I had time to see that she had lipstick smeared all over her cheek.'

Maigret was silent. Slowly and deliberately, he filled his pipe and lit it. Then, in a very low voice, he said:

'My dear, do you mind if I ask you a personal question, though it's no concern of mine, I know.'

She looked at him a little uneasily.

'Knowing him as you did, how could you remain on intimate terms with him?'

She tried at first to shrug it off.

'Well, if it hadn't been him, it would have been someone else. . . . I had to have someone. . . .'

But then her expression changed. Gravely, she said:

'The man I knew was quite different. With me, he didn't feel the need to bully and show off. On the contrary, he let me see how vulnerable he was. He said once:

'"Maybe it's because you're of no account, just a nice kid, and, besides, I know you'd never take advantage of me."

'He was terribly afraid of dying. It was almost as though he had a presentiment. . . .

'"So help me, God, sooner or later one of those swine is bound to turn on me. . . ."

'I said: "Why do you go out of your way to make people hate you?"

'"Because I can't make them love me. On the whole I prefer hatred to indifference."'

246

As she told him this, she became quite agitated. In a calmer voice, she concluded:

'Well, there it is. I heard no more of Pigou. I don't know what became of him. It never occurred to me to mention him to you. It seemed like ancient history really. It was only yesterday, in the cinema, that I suddenly remembered that slap in the face.'

A few minutes later, Maigret went down the stairs, knocked on the door of the accounts office, and went in. Lapointe was there, talking to a nondescript young man in a dark, ill-fitting suit.

'This is Monsieur Jacques Riolle, sir.'

'We have already met.'

'So you have. I'd forgotten.'

Riolle, somewhat in awe of the Chief Superintendent, had risen to his feet. His office was the darkest and dingiest in the whole building, and, for some obscure reason, it smelt even more strongly of wine. There were rows of green files on shelves, reminding Maigret of a lawyer's office in the provinces. Between the two windows stood an enormous, old-fashioned safe, which dominated the room. The furniture must have been a job lot, picked up in some auction. There were inkstains everywhere, and the desk, which had probably once been in a schoolroom, was defaced with carved initials.

Riolle, intimidated in the great man's presence, shifted his weight from one foot to the other, and Maigret had the feeling that here was another, younger Gilbert Pigou.

'Are you ready, Lapointe?'

'I was only waiting for you, sir.'

They took their leave of the young man, and went out to the little black car.

As they were getting in, Lapointe said, with a sigh:

'I thought you were never coming. It was heavy going, trying to make conversation with that young man. I've seldom met anyone so dull. It was really depressing.

'All the same, I did get him to talk in the end. He's not a qualified accountant, but he goes to night school and expects to complete the course in two years. He's engaged to a girl in his home town. He's from Nevers. He can't marry on his present salary, but he's hoping it won't be too long before he gets a rise, which will enable him to set up house. . . .'

'Is she still in Nevers?'

'Yes. She lives with her parents, and works in a haberdasher's. He goes home once a month to see her.'

Lapointe was well on his way back to the Quai des Orfèvres before Maigret noticed.

'We won't be going back to the Quai just yet. First, I want you to take me to 57B Rue Froidevaux.'

They drove along the Boulevard Saint-Michel, and then turned right towards the Cemetery of Montparnasse.

'Did young Riolle say if he'd ever met his predecessor?'

'No. He applied for the job in answer to an advertisement. He was interviewed by Chabut himself.'

'Determined to make sure for himself that the applicant was a nonentity!'

'What do you mean?'

'With the exception of Louceck, all his employees were ineffectual and submissive. He liked to be surrounded by people he could despise. Come to think of it, he despised all his associates, men and women, at home and at work. I'm convinced that he went to bed with all those women only in order to show that he was master and, to some extent, to defile them. . . .'

'This is it, sir.'

'I think it would be better if you didn't come in with me. I'm going to see Madame Pigou. Two of us together would give the game away, and might scare her off. Wait for me in that little bar over there.'

He pushed open the door of the lodge.

'Which is Madame Pigou's flat, please?'

'Fourth floor, on the left.'

'Is she at home?'

'She should be. I haven't seen her go out.'

There was no lift, so he had to walk up the four flights of stairs, stopping from time to time to get his breath back. The house was clean and in good repair, and the staircase less dark than it might have been. There was a radio blaring in one of the first-floor flats. On the second floor, a small boy of four or five was sitting on the top step, playing with a model car.

When he got to the fourth floor, Maigret knocked at the door of the flat, as there appeared to be no bell. He waited for quite a time, and then knocked again, fervently hoping that he would not have to climb all those stairs again later.

He listened with his ear against the door, but could hear no sound from within. Nevertheless, he knocked yet again, this time so sharply that the door quivered on its hinges, and was at last rewarded by the sound of approaching footsteps, or rather, the slither of feet encased in bedroom slippers.

'Who's there?'

'Is Madame Pigou at home?'

'One moment.'

He waited for over a minute before the door was finally opened, and a young woman, holding her dressing-gown together to prevent it from falling open, stood there looking enquiringly at him.

'What have you got to sell?'

'I'm not a salesman. I would like a word with you, that's all. I'm Chief Superintendent Maigret of the Criminal Investigation Department.'

She hesitated, then stood aside to let him in.

'Come in. I was resting. I haven't been too well lately.'

On her way into the living-room, she hastily shut the bedroom door, but not before Maigret had caught a glimpse of the rumpled bed.

'Do sit down,' she said, pointing to a chair.

The window looked out on to the cemetery, with its alleys of tall trees. The furniture was of the sort to be found in any of the big stores in the Boulevard Barbès, and usually described in the catalogues as 'rustic'.

There was a divan with records strewn all over it and, next to it, a record-player on a pedestal table. Apparently Liliane was in the habit of reclining on the divan and listening to music. On the floor was an ashtray, overflowing with cigarette ends.

'Is it about my husband?'

'Yes and no. Have you any news of him?'

'Still not a word. I called at his place of work, only to discover that he hadn't set foot there for six months.'

'How long ago did he leave you?'

'Two months ago. It was at the end of September, the day when he should have given me his pay.'

She was perched on the arm of a chair, and every now and then her dressing-gown fell open to reveal a sugar pink slip underneath. It did not seem to worry her. No doubt she lived in a dressing-gown, except when she went out.

'Have you been married long?'

'Eight years. He just happened one day to come into the shop where I worked, to buy a tie. He took ages choosing it. He seemed very much smitten. That evening when I left work, he followed me. And the same thing happened the next day and the next. For four or five days he followed me, not having the courage even to speak to me.'

'Was he living in this flat then?'

'No. He had a furnished room in the Quartier Latin. He hadn't known me three weeks before he proposed to me. I wasn't too keen. He was a nice enough boy, but nothing to write home about.'

'You weren't in love with him, then?'

She blew out a cloud of cigarette smoke, and looked at him.

'Is there any such thing as love? I'm none too sure myself.'

'Just one question, Madame Pigou, is your husband slightly lame?'

'Yes. He was knocked over by a car, and broke his knee-cap. Ever since, he's had a slight limp in the left leg, especially when he walks fast.'

'How long ago was the accident?'

'It was before I knew him.'

'How long have you known him?'

'Eight years. An engagement, if you can call it that, which lasted a month, followed by eight years of wedded bliss!'

'Did you go on working after you were married?'

'For three years. But it was an impossible situation. Before I left home in the morning I had to get breakfast, wash up, and clean the flat. We used to meet for lunch in some restaurant, and in the evening I had to do the shopping, cook dinner, and get through the rest of the household chores. It was no life.'

He looked at the narrow divan, littered with gramophone records and magazines, and at the overflowing ashtray. Her favourite resting-place, no doubt. Very possibly she had been asleep on the divan when he had disturbed her with his insistent knocking.

Did she have lovers? He was pretty sure she did, partly, no doubt, because she had nothing better to do, and partly as a means of escape.

At present she was looking rather sulky, and this, he suspected, was her habitual expression.

'You suspected nothing until your husband disappeared?'

'No. I don't know whether he got another job, but, as far as his comings and goings went, he kept to his normal working hours.'

'And at the end of the month, he gave you the usual sum?'

'Yes. I allowed him forty francs a month for cigarettes and fares.'

'When he didn't come home, weren't you worried?'

'Not all that much. I'm not the worrying kind. I did ring his office. Some man answered. I asked to speak to my husband.

'"He's not here," he said.

'"Do you know when he'll be back?"

'"I can't tell you," he said, "I haven't seen him for a long time."

'And he hung up on me. It was then that I began to be a little worried. I went to the police station to see if they could tell me anything. I thought he might have been involved in an accident.'

Clearly, she had not troubled her head very much about it.

'Do you know where he is?' she asked.

'No. That is what I came to ask you. Have you no idea where he might have gone?'

'Not to his father, at any rate. He's lived in the same flat in the Rue d'Alésia for nearly fifty years. That's where Gilbert was born. In fact, he's spent almost the whole of his life in this district. His mother is dead. His father was a cashier in a branch office of the Crédit Lyonnais. He's retired now.'

'Did he get on well with his father?'

'Until we were married. His father couldn't stand me, or so I believe. Gilbert, naturally, stood up for me, so relations have been rather strained in the past few years.'

'Have you informed his father of his disappearance?'

'There was no point. They only met once a year, on New Year's Day. We used to pay a formal call together, and were treated to a glass of port and a biscuit. He fusses over that flat like a proper old maid.'

'How do you think your husband managed to give you the equivalent of his salary for three months after he left his job?'

'He must have got another job.'

'Had you no savings?'

'Only debts! The refrigerator isn't fully paid off yet, and we had a dish-washer on order for last September, but I managed to cancel that just in time.'

'Did he have any personal possessions of value?'

'Of course not! Even the rings he gave me are just cheap rubbish. By the way, you haven't told me yet why you are so interested in him.'

'He was dismissed at the end of June, because his employer found out that he had been milking the till—not very skilfully, I'm afraid—for the past three years.'

'Was he keeping a mistress?'

'No. He only took very small sums, fifty francs a month to begin with.'

'So that's where he got his so-called rise!'

'Just so. You kept telling him that he ought to tackle Monsieur Chabut, and as he hadn't the courage to do so, and knew besides that it would do no good, he decided to cook the books instead. From fifty francs it crept up to a hundred. and then, last Christmas. . . .'

'The five-hundred-franc bonus!'

She shrugged.

'The idiot! A fat lot of good it did him. I hope, for his sake, that he's found another job.'

'I doubt it.'

'Why?'

'Because I happen to have seen him hanging about in the

street at various times of the day, when offices and shops are open.'

'What has he done? You must want him for something.'

'Oscar Chabut was killed last Wednesday by a man who was lying in wait for him outside a brothel in the Rue Fortuny. Did your husband have a gun?'

'A small black automatic, given to him by a friend when he was doing his military service.'

'Is it still here?'

She got up and shuffled off into the bedroom. He could hear her opening and shutting drawers.

'I can't find it. He must have taken it with him. As far as I know, he's never used it, and I don't know that he ever had ammunition for it. I've never seen any.'

She lit another cigarette and, this time, sat not on the arm but in the chair.

'Do you really think he had it in him to kill his boss?'

'Chabut treated him abominably, and on one occasion slapped his face.'

'I know him. At least I've met him. What you say doesn't surprise me. He was a hulking great brute.'

'Didn't he tell you what had happened?'

'No, he just said he was glad to be rid of my husband, and that it was good riddance for me too.'

'Did he give you money?'

'Why do you ask that?'

'Because it would be in character. It's not hard to imagine how the interview went.'

'You must have a very vivid imagination!'

'No, I just happen to know how he treated women.'

'Do you mean, he treated them all alike?'

'Yes. Did you arrange to meet again?'

'He took my telephone number.'

'But he never rang you?'

'No.'

'You haven't answered my question. Did he give you money?'

'He handed me a thousand-franc note.'

'And how have you managed since?'

253

'As best I can. I've answered a few advertisements, but so far without success.'

Maigret got up. He was aching all over, and his forehead was bathed in perspiration.

'Thank you for your co-operation.'

'Look, you say you've seen him several times. Surely, then, you ought to have no difficulty in finding him?'

'Provided I see him again, and he doesn't vanish into thin air, as, up to now, he's always managed to do.'

'How was he looking?'

'Exhausted, as if he'd slept rough the night before. Has he no friends in Paris?'

'Not that I know of. The only people we ever saw were a school friend of mine, Nadine, and the man she lives with. He's a musician. They sometimes came and spent the evening with us. We'd have a couple of bottles of wine, and Nadine's friend would entertain us on the electric guitar.'

Probably she had slept with the musician and, no doubt, others as well.

'Au revoir, Madame.'

'Au revoir, Chief Superintendent. If you have any news, I'd be most grateful if you'd let me know. After all, he is my husband. If he really has killed someone, I'd sooner know about it. I take it it constitutes grounds for divorce?'

'I believe so.'

He made a note of the address of Pigou's father, who lived in the Rue d'Alésia, and went into the little bar, where he found Lapointe reading the afternoon paper.

'Well, sir?'

'She's a proper little bitch. I've never come across a more unsavoury crowd than have turned up in this case! Waiter, a glass of rum!'

'Does she know anything that might be of help to us?'

'No. She's never cared tuppence for him. She gave up work at the very first opportunity, and, as far as I can see, she lies sprawled on a divan from morning to night, playing gramophone records, reading magazines, and smoking like a chimney. I bet there's nothing she doesn't know about the private lives of the film stars. She wasn't bothered when her husband disappeared, and when I told her it was possible he had killed a man, her only reaction was to ask me whether that constituted grounds for divorce.'

'What do we do next?'

'Take me to the Rue d'Alésia. I want a few words with the father.'

'Her father?'

'No, his. He's a retired cashier, used to be with the Crédit Lyonnais. He and his son fell out over the marriage.'

The father's flat was a good deal cosier than the son's, and, to Maigret's great relief, there was a lift. He rang the bell, and almost at once the door was opened.

'Yes?'

'Monsieur Pigou?'

'I am Monsieur Pigou, what do you want?'

'May I come in?'

'Are you selling encyclopaedias? If so, you're the fifth this week.'

'I'm Chief Superintendent Maigret of the Criminal Investigation Department.'

The flat smelt of furniture polish, and there was not a speck of dust anywhere. Everything was scrupulously neat and tidy.

'Please sit down.'

They were in a small sitting-room, that looked as if it was scarcely ever used. The curtains were partly drawn, and Pigou went over to open them.

'You're not the bearer of bad news, I hope?'

'As far as I know there's nothing wrong with your son. I just wanted to ask you when you saw him last.'

'That's easy. It was on New Year's Day.'

He smiled a little bitterly.

'I was foolish enough to warn him against that girl he was absolutely set on marrying. The minute I saw her, I knew she wouldn't do for him. He got on his high horse, and called me a selfish old man, and a good deal more besides. Before that, he always came to see me once a week, but after his marriage he stopped coming, and I only saw him once a year. He called on me with his wife every year on New Year's Day, a very formal visit. He came out of a sense of duty, I suppose.'

'Did you bear him any resentment?'

'No. He's completely under her thumb. It's not his fault.'

'Has he ever asked you for money?'

'You obviously don't know him. He's much too proud.'

'Not even in the last few months?'

'What's happened to him?'

'He lost his job in June, and for three months after that he went out in the morning and came back at night, just as though he were still working at the Quai de Charenton. What's more, at the end of each month, he gave his wife the equivalent of his earnings.'

'He must have found another job.'

'That's not so easy for a man of forty-five with no qualifications.'

'Maybe. All the same . . .'

'He must have got the money somewhere. At the end of September, he disappeared.'

'You mean his wife hasn't seen him since?'

'That's right. And someone, not yet identified, shot his former employer, Oscar Chabut, in the street. He put four bullets into him.'

'And you think . . . ?'

'I don't know, Monsieur Pigou. That's what I'm trying to find out. I came to see you in the hope that you might be able to help me.'

'I know less than you do. His wife didn't even go to the bother of letting me know. Do you think that he's done something to be ashamed of, and that's why he's gone into hiding?'

'It's possible. I've seen a man two or three times in the last few days whom I believe to be your son. I have also had two anonymous telephone calls, and a letter written in block capitals which I have every reason to think came from him.'

'You didn't tell him . . . ?'

'Tell him what? If he's the man who shot his former employer, then he's playing with fire, almost as if he wanted to get himself arrested. It's more common than you'd think. He has no home and no money. He knows he's bound to be caught sooner or later. He's not ashamed of what he's done.

On the contrary, he's more likely to be congratulating himself. Chabut was a despicable character.

'I'll keep you informed, Monsieur Pigou. Meanwhile, if you hear anything, I'd be grateful if you'd give me a ring.'

'As I said, it's most unlikely that he'll come to me.'

'Thank you for your help.'

'Was he any help?' Lapointe asked.

'Even less than the wife. He didn't even know his son had disappeared. He's a dapper little man. I liked him a lot. He spends all his time polishing the floors and the furniture, and he keeps the flat as neat as a new pin. He doesn't have a television set or a radio, at least I saw no signs of them.

'Back to the Quai, now. It's time we got to the bottom of this business.

Within the hour, Maigret and five of his inspectors were assembled in his office for a final briefing.

CHAPTER SIX

'SIT DOWN, ALL OF YOU. Needless to say, you're welcome to smoke if you want to.'

Maigret hims lf proceeded to light up and, puffing at his pipe, he looked thoughtfully at each of them in turn.

'You all know the main facts. Ever since I started making enquiries into the death of Oscar Chabut, as a result of shots fired when he was leaving a house in the Rue Fortuny, a man has been keeping a close watch on my movements. He's no fool, and he has more than once anticipated my next move. What's more, he's a remarkably slippery customer. I've been close to him once or twice, but he's always managed to slip away and melt into the crowd.'

It was already dusk, but it had not yet occurred to anyone to switch on the lights, so that the whole room was in shadow. With so many people in the office—two extra chairs had had to be brought in from next door—it was stiflingly hot.

'I have no evidence that this man is the murderer, only a strong feeling, reinforced by his persistently behaving as if he were guilty.

'This afternoon, I discovered his identity and learned something of his history. At first sight it seems almost beyond belief.

'The man in question was an employee of the wine merchant, ostensibly an accountant, but in fact just an underpaid book-keeper, a nonentity. He has been married eight years. His wife, who was a shop-girl when he met her, gave up her job as soon as she decently could, and never stopped reproaching him for not bringing home more money. Make a note of her name and address, Loutrie, I'll explain why, later. Liliane Pigou, 57B Rue Froidevaux. It's opposite the Montparnasse Cemetery. She spends most of the day half-naked, lying on a divan, listening to gramophone records, smoking like a chimney, and reading magazines and strip cartoons.

'I've called you together this evening, because I feel that the time has come to bring him in, whatever the cost. The likelihood is that he's got a gun, but I don't think he'll attempt to use it.

'I want you, Janvier, to pick six men to patrol the Quai des Orfèvres in pairs on a twenty-four-hour rota. As well as telephoning me twice and writing me a longish letter, the man has been keeping a watch on me here from across the road. I caught sight of him once, but, unfortunately, he slipped away before I could catch up with him.'

The bluish twilight was beginning to deepen. Maigret switched on his green-shaded desk lamp, but not the overhead light, thus illuminating the faces of the men, while leaving the rest of the room in shadow.

'Here's his description. Take it down, all of you: Below average height, say about five-foot-five. Plumpish though not fat, and very full in the face. He wears a dark brown suit and a crumpled raincoat. He smokes cigarettes. Finally, he has a slight limp. His kneecap was injured in an accident some years ago, and as a result his left foot turns over a little as he walks.'

'Dark hair?' asked Loutrie.

'Brown hair and eyes, yes, and rather thick lips. Although he's shabby and obviously at the end of his tether, you wouldn't mistake him for a tramp.

'The reason I want two men on a twenty-four-hour watch is that he's so remarkably good at vanishing.

'Is that clear, Janvier?'

'Yes, sir.'

Maigret turned to fat Loutrie, who was smoking his pipe in little puffs.

'What I've just said to Janvier applies to you, too. I'm not asking any of you to go on watch yourselves, just to make sure that your men are in position, and that they are relieved at regular intervals.'

'I'll see to that.'

'Now you, Torrence. You'll need a team of six, like the others. The stakes are high. I can't risk letting him slip through our fingers again. Your men are to cover the Chabuts' place in the Place des Vosges. Madame Chabut is a beautiful woman of about forty. She's extremely elegant, and gets her clothes from the top fashion houses. She has a Mercedes and a chauffeur. It's just possible that she may decide to go out in her husband's car, so you'd better also be looking out for a red Jaguar convertible.'

They exchanged glances, like a class of schoolchildren.

'And you, Lucas. You're to cover the Quai de Charenton. Today being Saturday, the offices and warehouses will probably be deserted this afternoon, and tomorrow as well. There may be watchmen or caretakers on duty. I don't know.'

'I see, Chief.'

'I think that covers all the places where he's most likely to turn up. Usually he keeps watch from a little way off. He seems to be obsessed with finding out what we're up to. Sometimes he's close on our heels, and at others he's one jump ahead.

'I can't help wondering whether he hasn't a kind of unconscious longing to get caught.'

'What about me?' asked Lapointe.

'I want you here on call, ready to come and fetch me and drive me anywhere, at any time of the day or night. It will also be your job to take any messages that may come in, and keep me informed by telephone.'

Under the impression that he had finished, they half-rose from their chairs, but Maigret motioned them to remain seated.

'There's one very puzzling thing. This man lost his job at the end of June. It appears that he had no savings, at least not

259

to his wife's knowledge, and remember, he was in the habit of handing over his pay-packet to her every month. He got no salary for June, as his employer refused to pay him, on the grounds that he had a right to retain the money in part compensation for the thefts. Nevertheless, on June 30th, the man went home, and handed his wife the equivalent of a month's salary.

'From then until the end of September, he continued to leave home at the usual time every morning, and to return at the usual time in the evening. All this time, of course, his wife had no idea that he was no longer working at the Quai de Charenton.

'I presume he tried to get another job, but failed to do so.

'In September, he vanished. It was then, I think, that he decided to give up the struggle, and, from what I've seen of him, he hasn't slept many nights in a bed since.

'But he had to have some money, if only a few francs to buy food. Now if there's one place that seems to have an irresistible fascination for down-and-outs, it's Les Halles. I wonder where they'll all go in a few months' time, when the market is transferred to Rungis.'

The telephone rang.

'Hello! Chief Superintendent Maigret? It's that man again. The one who always asks to speak to you personally.'

'Put him through.'

Looking up, he said to his men:

'It's him! Hello! Yes, I'm listening. . . .'

'You've been to see my wife. I thought you would. You were with her a long time, and your assistant waited for you in a bar near by. Is she terribly angry with me?'

'Not in the least, as far as I could tell.'

'Is she very unhappy?'

'That isn't how she struck me.'

'Did she say anything about money?'

'No.'

'I can't think how she manages.'

'She went to see Chabut some weeks ago, and he gave her a thousand francs.'

The man at the other end sniggered.

'What did my father say?'

It was staggering. He was aware of Maigret's every move. Yet he had no car, and was certainly in no position to take taxis. Apparently, he had managed to limp all over Paris without being seen, and when anyone did catch sight of him, he vanished as if by magic.

'He didn't say very much. I gather he doesn't terribly care for your wife.'

'What you mean to say is that he detests her. It was on account of her that we quarrelled. I had to choose between him and her. . . .'

In Maigret's opinion, he had backed the wrong horse.

'Why not come and see me here, at the Quai des Orfèvres, for a chat? If you didn't kill Chabut, you'll be free to come and go as you please. If you did kill him, than I can recommend a good lawyer, who will at least make a plea in mitigation, even if he doesn't manage to get you acquitted. Hello! Hello! . . .'

Gilbert Pigou had rung off.

'You heard that? He already knows I've been to his flat to see his wife, and that afterwards I called on his father.'

It was a kind of game, and up to now Pigou had won all along the line. And yet he wasn't particularly bright. Quite the reverse, in fact.

'Where was I? Oh, yes. Les Halles. In the whole of Paris, it's the one place where a man on the run is most likely to fetch up. By tonight, I want twelve men going through the whole area with a fine-tooth comb. They can get help if they need it from our colleagues in the First Arrondissement, who know the district inside out.'

Of course, it was always possible that all this elaborate planning would lead to nothing. There was no harm in hoping, but, on present showing, it was unlikely that Pigou would fall an easy victim to Maigret's schemes. As like as not, he was at this very moment looking up at the lights in Maigret's windows from across the road.

'Well, lads, that's the lot.'

They all got up, like schoolboys, and were making for the door, when Maigret spoke again.

'One very important point. I don't want any of your men

carrying guns. And the same goes for you. Whatever happens, whatever the cost, I don't want him shot at.'

'What if he shoots first?' grumbled fat Loutrie.

'I said "whatever the cost". Anyway, he won't shoot. I want him brought in sound in wind and limb.'

It was half-past five. Maigret had done all he could. Now, he could only wait. He was tired, and had still not quite recovered from his bout of 'flu.

'Hang on a minute, Lapointe. What do you think of my strategy?'

'It might work.'

Clearly, the Inspector was none too hopeful.

'If you want my honest opinion, either he'll fall into our clutches by sheer accident—and that may not be for days or weeks—or he'll go on eluding us until he decides to give himself up.'

'I'm inclined to agree with you. All the same, I had to do something. I'll be glad if you'd drive me home. I'm longing to get into my slippers and toast my toes by the fire. Or rather, to tell you the truth, I'm longing to get to bed.'

He was very flushed, and his throat was sore. Perhaps this was not 'flu at all, but tonsillitis?

As they drove out of the forecourt, Maigret looked about him with interest, but there was no sign of the shabby figure of the man who was so much on his mind.

'Stop at the Brasserie Dauphine.'

He had a nasty taste in his mouth, and a sudden craving for a glass of very cold beer. It couldn't wait till he got home.

'What will you have?'

'Same as you, a beer. It was very stuffy in your office.'

Thirstily, Maigret gulped down two glasses of beer, then wiped his mouth, and lit his pipe. The Chatelet was ablaze with Christmas decorations and lights strung across the street. From one of the big stores, loud-speakers were relaying seasonal music.

When they reached the Boulevard Richard-Lenoir, Maigret once more looked searchingly up and down the street, in the hope of seeing Pigou, but there was no one about who was even remotely like him.

'Good night, laddie.'

'I hope you'll be feeling better tomorrow, sir.'

He took the stairs slowly, but was nevertheless out of breath when he reached the top. Madame Maigret was waiting for him on the landing. She could see at a glance that he was no better, and that it was beginning to get him down.

'Hurry up and come in out of the cold.'

He was not cold. On the contrary, he was much too hot, and bathed in perspiration. He took off his heavy overcoat and his scarf, loosened his tie, and, with a sigh, slumped into his armchair.

'I've got the beginnings of a sore throat.'

She was not unduly worried; an attack of 'flu, lasting a week or two, was more or less an annual occurrence with him. He was inclined to forget this, and could never quite shake off his dread of being permanently handicapped by illness.

'Any phone calls?'

'Should there have been?'

'I was half expecting one. He rang me up at the Quai earlier on, and he must know my home address. He's extremely restless at the moment, and feels under some sort of compulsion to keep in touch with me.'

This was not the first case of its kind that he had come across. Years ago, there had been a murderer who had written him a letter several pages long, every day for a month. Each had been written in a different brasserie but, in that instance, the man had not cut off the heading. The only hope of catching him would have been to put a watch on every brasserie and café in Paris, and there were simply not enough men available.

One morning, on his way to his office, Maigret had noticed an elderly little man sitting patiently in the glass-walled waiting-room generally referred to as the aquarium.

It was the man he had been looking for.

'What's for dinner?'

'*Raie au beurre noir*. I hope it's not too rich for you.'

'There's nothing wrong with my stomach.'

'What about asking Pardon to look in on you?'

'Leave the poor man alone. He's got enough to do, caring for people who are really ill.'

'Would you like your dinner in bed?'

'What! And have the sheets soaked through in an hour?'

He did, however, agree to get undressed. Comfortable in pyjamas, dressing-gown and slippers, he settled down with the newspaper, but his mind was not on it. His thoughts kept returning to Pigou, keeper-of-the-petty-cash turned thief, on account of his wife, who had taunted him with being frightened of his boss. And he had been frightened of him, far too frightened to ask for a rise.

Where was he at this moment? Had he any money left at all? If so, how and where had he got it?

Then there was Chabut, arrogant, irresistibly impelled to shower contempt on others and make himself universally detested. In business, he had been insolently triumphant, yet he had remained as vulnerable as in the days when he had tramped from door to door in the hope of securing an order for a case of wine.

He was not the first man, in Maigret's experience, whom insecurity had driven to mete out punishment to all those within his orbit.

'Dinner is ready.'

He was not hungry. All the same, he ate what was put before him. He had some difficulty in swallowing his food. By tomorrow, he would probably have lost his voice.

By now, the men from the Quai des Orfèvres would all be at the posts assigned to them by Maigret. At the last minute, he had been tempted to add:

'And you'd better set a watch on my flat in the Boulevard Richard-Lenoir as well.'

But some obscure feeling, of decency perhaps, had deterred him.

It was almost as though he were afraid of something. He got up from the table and went across to the window. It was not raining, but a strong east wind was blowing, which meant that colder weather was on the way. He saw a pair of lovers go by, arm in arm, stopping every few yards to kiss.

Two policemen on motor-cycles, wearing capes, went past the window, presumably on routine patrol. There were lights in most of the windows across the street, and, behind the net curtains, shadowy figures could be seen, in one case, an entire family sitting at a round table.

'Do you want to look at television?'

'No.'

There was nothing he really wanted to do except grumble, as was his wont when he was not feeling well, or when a case had dragged on too long.

He was determined not to go to bed before his usual time, and settled down once more to try and read the paper. But half an hour later he was back at the window, peering into the street, in the hope of catching sight of a figure which, although he had only once caught a glimpse of it, was beginning to seem familiar to him.

The boulevard was deserted, except for a passing taxi.

'Do you think he'll come here?'

'How should I know?'

'Are you expecting fresh developments?'

'That's always a possibility. I may get a phone call from Lapointe.'

'Is he on duty?'

'He'll be on all night, to take any messages that may come in.'

'Do you think your man is beginning to crack?'

'No. He hasn't lost his nerve yet. He doesn't seem to realize the predicament he's in. All his life, he's been the underdog. He's never known what it means to hold his head high. And now, all of a sudden, he feels, in an odd sort of way, free. The entire police force is looking for him, and he has managed to elude us all. That's quite a feather in his cap, don't you see? For the first time in his life he's important, he matters.'

'And he'll feel even more important when he stands his trial.'

'That's just it, and he can't make up his mind whether to give himself up, or to carry on with his little game of cat and mouse.'

He returned to his newspaper. His pipe was alight and, although he was not enjoying it, he went on smoking as a matter of principle. He too was unwilling to surrender. He was not going to allow the 'flu to get the better of him. His eyelids were inflamed and his eyes smarting, but he was determined to keep them open.

At half-past nine, he got up from his chair and returned to the window. On the pavement opposite stood a man gazing upwards, apparently at the windows of the flat.

Madame Maigret was sitting at the dining-table. She looked up to speak, but was silenced by what she saw. Her husband's broad back was turned towards her. He was tense and motionless, and looked, somehow, larger than life.

There was something mysterious, almost awe-inspiring, in his sudden stillness.

Maigret watched the man, scarcely daring to breathe, lest he should frighten him off, and the man looked back at him, although he could probably see nothing but a bulky shadow behind the muslin curtains.

Once, at Meung-sur-Loire, while he was lounging in a deck-chair, Maigret had seen a squirrel drop from the plane tree at the bottom of the garden.

For a time, the squirrel had remained motionless under the tree, and Maigret had seen the rise and fall of its silky breast fur in time to the beating of its heart. Then, with extreme caution, it had inched forward, and stopped again.

Maigret had watched it, scarcely daring to breathe, and the little russet creature had stared back at the man as though fascinated, yet with every muscle taut, ready for instant flight.

It had been like a slow-motion film interspersed with stills. The squirrel, growing bolder, had reduced the distance between them by a yard or more. For a further ten minutes, it had continued to advance cautiously, until there was barely a yard between it and Maigret's hand hanging over the side of the chair.

Had the squirrel wanted to be stroked? Not then, at any rate. Its bright glance travelled from the hand to the face, and back again. Then, in a couple of bounds, it was back in the tree.

Maigret recalled the incident as he stood gazing fixedly at the shadowy figure of the man across the street. Gilbert Pigou, like the squirrel, seemed fascinated by the Chief Superintendent, whom he had, in a sense, been stalking for days.

But like the squirrel, he was tense and ready to take flight at the slightest alarm. The Chief Superintendent knew that it would be useless for him to dress and go downstairs. By the time he got outside, there would be no one in sight. It would be equally useless to alert the nearest police station.

Was he trying to pluck up the courage to cross the road and come into the house? It was not all that unlikely. He had no friends, no one whom he could trust.

He had made up his mind to act, and he had done so. He had killed Oscar Chabut. Afterwards, he had fled. Why? An instinctive reaction, no doubt. What would he do next? Keep on the run?

As with the squirrel, it went on for all of ten minutes. At last the man took a step forward, but immediately regretting it, or so it seemed, turned on his heel and, with one last backward glance at Maigret's window, made off in the direction of the Rue du Chemin-Vert.

The bulky frame of the Chief Superintendent relaxed. He remained for a moment at the window, as though to recover himself, then went across to the sideboard to fetch his pipe.

'Was it him?'

'Yes.'

'Did he mean to come and see you, do you think?'

'He was tempted. I think he's afraid I'll be a disappointment. Men of his sort are terribly sensitive. They long to talk, to make themselves understood, and yet they don't really believe there is anybody capable of understanding them.'

'What will he do now?'

'Walk, I should think, but God knows where to. He'll walk on and on, alone with his thoughts, and muttering aloud to himself, I shouldn't wonder.'

He scarcely had time to sit down in his chair when the telephone rang. He picked up the receiver.

'Yes?'

'Chief Superintendent Maigret?'

'That's right, laddie.'

He had recognized Lapointe's voice.

'We're getting results already, sir, thanks to the efforts of colleagues in the First Arrondissement, in particular Inspector

Leboeuf, who knows Les Halles like the back of his hand. Until about a fortnight ago, Pigou had a room, if you can call it that, in the Rue de la Grande-Truanderie.'

Maigret knew the street. There, at night, one had the illusion that the days of the King's Evil had returned. It swarmed with the dregs of humanity, in search of some stinking bistro, where they could get a bowl of soup or a glass of red wine. Many spent the night there, dozing in a chair or propped up against a wall. There were almost as many women as men, and they were by no means the least drunken and filthy.

It really was a human sewer, fouler even than the darkest places under the bridges. In the old, cobbled roadway, outside the rooming houses, lingered still more women, most of them ageing and hideous, waiting for the men to come out.

'He was staying at the Hotel du Cygne. Three francs a day for an iron bedstead with a straw mattress. No running water. Toilets in the back yard.'

'I know it.'

'Apparently he spent most of the night unloading fruit and vegetables from the lorries. He didn't get in till morning and slept half the day.'

'When did he leave the hotel?'

'The owner says he hasn't seen him for a fortnight. Needless to say, he lost no time in letting the room to someone else.'

'Are they still searching the district?'

'Yes. There are about fifteen men on the job. The chaps in the First Arrondissement can't think why we haven't laid on a full-scale raid, such as they carry out from time to time.'

'That's the last thing we want! I hope you told them not to do anything rash.'

'I did, sir.'

'No news from the others?'

'Not a word.'

'Pigou was here, in the Boulevard Richard-Lenoir, just a few minutes ago.'

'You mean you saw him?'

'From my window. He was on the pavement, just across the road.'

'Didn't you go out to him?'

'No.'

'Is he still there?'

'No, but he may come back. If so, he'll probably hang about for a while trying to make up his mind, and then, quite possibly, make off again.'

'Have you any fresh instructions for me?'

'No. Good night, laddie.'

'Good night, sir.'

Maigret's head was aching. Before returning to his armchair, he poured himself a small glass of sloe gin.

'Won't it make you perspire?'

'Well, you always say grog is the best cure for 'flu. Incidentally, though, Pardon doesn't agree with you.'

'It's time we had them to dinner. We haven't seen them for over a month.'

'Let me get shot of this business first. Lapointe had some news. We now know where Pigou was living until recently. It's a crummy joint in Les Halles with the charmingly poetic name of Hotel du Cygne. He may have been there for months.'

'Isn't he there any longer?'

'He left a fortnight ago.'

Maigret was determined not to go to bed before what he considered to be a reasonable hour, and, in his book, that meant not before ten.

He made yet another attempt to read the paper, but kept darting surreptitious glances at the clock. He did manage to take in the first few lines on the front page, but after that, the words no longer made any sense to him.

'You're dead tired.'

'We'll go to bed in ten minutes.'

'You'd better take your temperature.'

'If you say so.'

She went to fetch the thermometer. Obediently, he put it in his mouth, and kept it there for five minutes.

'A hundred and one.'

'If you've still got a temperature tomorrow, I'm sending for Pardon, whether you like it or not.'

'Tomorrow's Sunday.'

'Sunday or no, Pardon won't mind.'

Madame Maigret went into the bedroom to undress. She went on talking to him with the door open.

'Your throat is raw. I don't like it at all. I'm going to paint it in a minute.'

'You know it makes me sick.'

'You won't feel a thing. You said you were going to be sick last time, and you weren't.'

She returned armed with a bottle of viscous liquid, the main ingredient of which was blue methylene, and a paint brush. It was an old-fashioned remedy, but Madame Maigret still believed in it, after more than twenty years.

'Open wide.'

He could not resist one last look out of the window, before closing the shutters and going to bed.

There was no one standing on the pavement across the way. The wind had almost reached gale force, and eddies of dust were rising all down the central section of the dual carriageway.

He fell into a deep, feverish sleep from which it took him a long time to wake. He felt the touch of living flesh on his arm, insistently. His first reaction was to recoil from it.

It was a human hand, and it seemed to be trying to communicate some sort of message to him. Once more, he pushed it away, and turned over on his side.

'Maigret. . . .'

It was his wife's voice, but so soft as to be barely audible.

'He's out there on the landing. So far, he hasn't plucked up the courage to ring the bell, but he's tapped on the door once or twice, very gently. Can you hear me?'

'What's that?'

He stretched out his hand, switched on the bedside lamp, and looked about him in bewilderment. He had been dreaming. He had already forgotten his dream, but he still had the feeling of having come back from a long way off, from another world.

'What did you say?'

'He's here. He keeps tapping on the door, very gently.'

He got out of bed, and put on his dressing-gown, which was lying on a chair.

'What time is it?'

'Half-past two.'

His pipe lay half-full on the bedside table. He re-lit it.

'You don't think there's any danger he might . . . ?'

He switched on the living-room light on his way to the front door, and stood absolutely still for a moment before opening it.

The light on the stairs, which was operated by a time switch, had long since gone out, and the man stepped out of darkness into the patch of light streaming from the doorway. He seemed at a loss for words. No doubt he had a long speech prepared, but, on seeing Maigret within arm's length of him, wearing a dressing-gown and with his hair all over the place, he was so overwhelmed that he could do no more than stammer:

'I'm afraid I've come at an inconvenient time. . . .'

'Come in, Pigou.'

It was still not too late for him to bolt down the stairs and escape, for he was a good deal younger and more agile than the Chief Superintendent. Once he had crossed the threshold, it would be too late, and Maigret, as he had done with the squirrel, was careful to remain absolutely still.

Probably, the man hesitated for no more than a few seconds, but it seemed much longer. Then he took a step forward. For a moment, Maigret considered locking the door and pocketing the key, but finally, with a little shrug, he decided against it.

'You must be cold.'

'It's not exactly warm outside. There's a biting wind.'

'Here, sit down. You'd better keep your raincoat on until you've warmed up a bit.'

He went over to the bedroom, where his wife was getting dressed, and called through the door:

'Make us a couple of grogs, will you?'

Then, feeling as though a great weight had been taken off his shoulders, he sat down opposite his visitor. It was the first time he had seen him at close quarters. Seldom, if ever, had he been so eager to learn more about anyone than about this man.

What surprised him most was that Pigou looked so young. His round, rather chubby face was immature, almost child-like.

'How old are you?'

'Forty-four.'

'You don't look it.'

'Did you order the grog especially for me?'

'For me too. I've got 'flu, and possibly tonsillitis as well. It will do me good.'

'I don't drink as a rule, except for a glass of wine with my meals. I daresay you've noticed how dirty I am. I haven't been able to keep my things clean for a very long time, and it's a whole week since I washed in hot water—that was at the public baths in the Rue Saint-Martin.'

As they talked, they were keeping a close watch on one another.

'I've been expecting you for some little time.'

'You saw me, then?'

'Not only that, but I could sense your uncertainty. You took a step forward, and then turned on your heel and made off towards the Rue du Chemin-Vert.'

'I saw you at the window, but, as I wasn't standing under a lamp, I wasn't sure whether you could see me.'

At the sound of approaching footsteps he started, just as the squirrel would have done. It was Madame Maigret with their drinks. Considerately, she avoided looking at him.

'Do you like it sweet?'

'Yes, please.'

'Lemon?'

Having added the sugar and lemon, she put the glass down on the table in front of him. Then she served her husband.

'If you need anything, just give me a shout.'

Later they might want more grog. Who could tell?

It was obvious that Pigou had been brought up to mind his manners, and that correct behaviour was important to him. Holding his glass in his hand, he waited for the Chief Superintendent to drink before taking a sip himself.

'It's scalding hot, but it does one good, don't you think?'

'At any rate, it will warm you up. Now perhaps you'd like to take off your coat.'

He did so. His suit, which was quite well cut, was very creased and badly stained. There was a long streak of white paint on the jacket.

Suddenly they were tongue-tied. Both knew that, when

they spoke again, it would be to discuss matters of grave import, and, for quite different reasons, neither was eager to start the ball rolling.

The silence continued for a long time, as they both sipped their grog. Then Maigret got up to refill his pipe.

'Do you smoke?'

'I'm out of cigarettes.'

There was a packet in the sideboard drawer. Maigret offered it to his visitor. Pigou looked uneasily at Maigret, and could scarcely believe his eyes when his host lit a match and held it out to him.

When they were once more seated opposite one another, Pigou said:

'I must, first of all, apologize for bursting in on you like this, and in the middle of the night too! . . . I hadn't the courage to go to the Quai des Orfèvres. . . . And I just couldn't go on alone, walking all over Paris for ever.'

There was not so much as a flicker of his eyes that Maigret was not acutely aware of. Here, in the intimacy of his own home, with a glass of grog in his hand, he looked like a benign uncle, to whom one could safely confide one's most intimate secrets.

CHAPTER SEVEN

'WHAT's your opinion of me?'

These were almost the first words he had spoken, and it was clear that it was a question of crucial significance to him. No doubt, he had spent the greater part of his life searching people's faces to find out what they thought of him.

What could one say?

'I don't know very much about you yet,' murmured Maigret, with a smile.

'You're very kind. Do you always treat criminals so considerately?'

'I can be very rough at times.'

'Who with?'

'Men like Oscar Chabut, for instance.'

Suddenly, Pigou's eyes lit up. At last he had found a friend.

'I admit I stole a little money, but it was nothing to him, hardly as much as he would hand out in tips in a month. But if anyone was a thief, he was. He robbed me of my manhood, and my self-respect. He degraded me to the point where I was almost ashamed to be alive.'

'What finally induced you to put your hand in the till?'

'I'll have to tell you the lot, I suppose.'

'Why else should you have come here?'

'You've seen my wife. What did you make of her?'

'I know very little about her.

'I fancy she looked upon marriage as a way out of having to earn a living. What surprises me is that she went on working for three years.'

'Two and a half years.'

'What she most wanted was to queen it in a cosy little home of her own. Some women are like that.'

'You realized that, did you?'

'It was pretty obvious.'

'I often had to do the housework myself, when I got home in the evening. If she'd had her way, we would have eaten out every night, to spare her the trouble of cooking a meal. I don't think she can help it. It's something to do with her metabolism. Her sisters are the same.'

'Do they live in Paris?'

'One is in Algiers. She's married to an engineer, who works for a petroleum company. The other lives in Marseilles, and has three children.'

'Why didn't you have children?'

'I wanted to, but Liliane wouldn't hear of it.'

'I see.'

'She has another sister, and a brother who . . .'

With a shake of the head, he pulled himself up.

'But it's no good going on about them. Don't think I want to blame anyone but myself. . . .'

He took a gulp of rum, and lit another cigarette.

'I'm keeping you up. . . . It's so late. . . .'

'Go on. Chabut humiliated you, and so did your wife.'

'How did you know?'

'She was always complaining that you didn't earn enough to live on, wasn't she?'

'She kept saying she couldn't think why she married me. And then she would sigh and say:

'"Am I to live my whole life in two rooms with no domestic help, not even a daily?"'

He was looking not at Maigret but at a patch of carpet. It was almost as though he were talking to himself.

'Was she unfaithful to you?'

'Yes, before we had been married a year. I didn't find out until two or three years later. One day, I left the office early to go to the dentist, and I saw her with a man, near the Madeleine. She was clinging to his arm, and then I saw them go into a hotel together.'

'Did you say anything to her?'

'Yes, but, according to her, it was all my fault. I couldn't give her the kind of life a girl has a right to expect. In the evenings, I was always half asleep, and it was all she could do to drag me out to a cinema, that sort of thing. And besides, I was no good in bed. . . .'

He flushed as he spoke. This last insult must have wounded him more keenly than any other.

'Three years ago—it was on her birthday—I took some money out of the petty cash. It was just enough to pay for a decent dinner, and I took her to a restaurant on the Grands Boulevards.

'I told her I was expecting a rise very soon.

'"And about time, too," she said. "Your boss should be ashamed of himself, paying you such a miserable pittance. If I ever see him, I'll tell him a thing or two."'

'You only took small sums?'

'Yes. To begin with I told her I'd had a rise of fifty francs a month. It wasn't long before she was complaining that that wasn't enough, so I raised it, so to speak, to a hundred francs.'

'Weren't you afraid of being found out?'

'It had almost become a habit. No one ever checked my books. And besides, considering the enormous turnover of the business, it all amounted to so very little!'

'On one occasion, you took a five-hundred-franc note.'

'That was at Christmas time. I pretended I'd had a bonus. I almost came to believe it myself. It made me feel less of a worm, somehow.

'I've never had a very high opinion of myself, you see. My father wanted me to follow in his footsteps and take a job with the Crédit Lyonnais, but I couldn't face the thought of competing with people much more capable than I was. I was happy in my little office at the Quai de Charenton, where I was virtually my own master.'

'How did Chabut find out?'

'He didn't. It was Monsieur Louceck. He did very occasionally look in to see what I was up to. This time, he must have noticed something amiss, but he didn't say a word to me. You'd have thought he'd have asked for an explanation, wouldn't you? But no, he behaved as though nothing was wrong, and went straight off and told Monsieur Chabut.'

'This was in June, wasn't it?'

'Yes, the end of June, the twenty-eighth, to be exact. Shall I ever forget it! He sent word that he wanted to see me in his office. His secretary was there, but he didn't send her out of the room. I didn't mind, because, to tell you the truth, it never entered my head that I'd been found out.'

'He told you to sit down.'

'Yes. How did you know?'

'The Grasshopper, Anne-Marie, I mean, told me the whole story. After the first few minutes, she felt as uncomfortable as you did.'

'It made it worse for me, being trampled on like that in front of a woman. He said the most humiliating and wounding things. Looking back, I'd much rather he'd handed me over to the police.

'I honestly believe he enjoyed every minute of it. Each time I thought he'd finished, he came back with something worse. Do you know, he even taunted me because I took so little?

'He claimed he would have had some respect for a real thief, but not for a petty pilferer like me.'

He stopped for a moment to get his breath back. He had been speaking with some vehemence, and his face was scarlet with emotion. He took another sip of rum. Maigret did so too.

'When he said: "Come here!" I hadn't the least idea of what he intended to do, but I was frightened all the same. He slapped me full in the face with tremendous force, I could feel the imprint of his hand for quite a while after.

'No one had ever raised a finger to me before. Even when I was a kid my parents never smacked me, I just stood there swaying, stunned. He said something like: "Now get out."

'I can't remember whether it was then or earlier that he told me he wouldn't give me a reference, and that he'd see to it that no reputable firm would give me a job.'

'He felt humiliated as well,' murmured Maigret, very gently.

Pigou's head jerked up, and he gaped at Maigret in astonishment.

'Didn't he actually say that no one could make a fool of him with impunity?'

'You're right, he did. It never occurred to me that that was what was at the back of everything he did. Do you think he was really riled?'

'More than that. He was a strong man, or thought he was, and he had succeeded in everything he had ever undertaken. Don't forget that he started as a door-to-door salesman.

'As far as he was concerned, you hardly existed. You were little more than part of the furnishings of an office on the ground floor, where he practically never set foot. He probably thought that it was an act of charity to keep you on at all.'

'That would be like him, yes.'

'He was in need of reassurance, just as you were, and that's why he wanted to possess every woman who came his way.'

Gilbert Pigou raised his eyebrows. Suddenly, he felt uneasy.

'Are you saying that he was to be pitied?'

'All of us are to be pitied, to a greater or lesser extent. I'm just trying to see things as they are. It's not my business to apportion blame. You left the Quai de Charenton. Where did you go from there?'

'It was eleven o'clock in the morning. I'd never been out at that time. It was a very hot day. I walked past the Bercy warehouses, in the shade of the plane trees, and then went into a bistro somewhere near the Pont d'Austerlitz. I had two or three brandies, I think. I don't remember very clearly.'

'Did you have lunch with your wife?'

'She'd stopped meeting me for lunch, ages before that. I walked for miles, and drank a great deal, and then, because my shirt was sticking to me, I went into a cinema to cool down. Do you remember last June? It was a scorcher.'

Clearly, he was anxious to tell the whole story, in the minutest detail. He desperately needed to get it off his chest. Maigret was a sympathetic listener. He was attentive to every word, and obviously interested. Pigou felt he owed it to him to leave nothing out.

'When you got home in the evening, didn't your wife notice you'd been drinking?'

'I told her that my colleagues had treated me to an aperitif to celebrate my promotion and transfer to the Avenue de l'Opéra.'

Far from smiling at his naïvety, Maigret looked very grave.

'How did you manage, two days later, to give your wife the equivalent of a month's salary?'

'I had nothing saved up. She allowed me just forty francs a month for cigarettes and fares. I had to find some sort of job. I lay awake all night thinking about it. When I left in the morning, I told her I wouldn't be home to dinner, because I'd have to spend most of the evening getting things straight in my new office.

'I had forgotten, the previous day, to hand in the key of the safe before leaving. I knew there would be an unusually large sum of money in the safe, as the next day was pay day.

'From time to time over the years, I had to go back to the office at night, to finish some urgent job or other. On those occasions, I would take the front door key home with me.

'Once I forgot it. I circled the building, trying to find a way in, when I remembered that the back door, which had warped, didn't close properly, and could be prised open with a pen-knife.'

'Wasn't there a night watchman?'

'No. I waited till it was dark, and crept into the courtyard. The little door opened, as I had hoped it would. I went into what used to be my office, opened the safe, and grabbed a bundle of notes. I didn't even wait to count them.'

'Was it a large sum?'

'More than I earned in three months. That evening I hid the money on top of the wardrobe, keeping back just the equivalent of a month's salary. I left home at the usual time. I just couldn't bring myself to tell Liliane that I'd got the sack.'

'Why did it matter to you so much what she thought of you?'

'Because there was no one else. For years, she, and she alone, had witnessed my life and actions. She was critical, of course, but, in a way, I think she trusted me.

'I went out every day to look for another job. I thought, at first, it would be easy. I read the small ads, and applied in person for whatever was going. Sometimes there were queues of people waiting, nearly all of them old and hopeless. I felt really sorry for them.

'I was asked questions, starting with my age. Usually, when I told them I was forty-four, that was the end of it.

'"Thirty is the upper age-limit. This is a job for a young man."

'I thought of myself as a young man. I felt young. As the days went by, I became more and more discouraged. After a fortnight, I realized I couldn't be choosey. By then, I'd have been quite contented as an office boy or a shop assistant.

'At best, they took my name and address, and said: "You'll be hearing from us."

'Those who thought I might be suitable asked me about my last job. Naturally, in view of Chabut's threats, I dared not tell them.

'I said: "I've done a bit of everything. I've been abroad a good deal."

'As I don't speak anything but French, I had to pretend I'd worked in Belgium and Switzerland.

'Then they asked for my references. I said I'd send them.

'Needless to say, those people never heard from me again.

'The end of July was even worse. Offices were closed down, and managerial staff on holiday. I took home my salary, as usual, or rather I got the necessary amount from the bundle on top of the wardrobe.

'"You haven't been yourself lately," my wife said. "Is the work more tiring in your new office?"

' "It's just that it takes a little time to get used to. I'm having to learn to work with computers. All the sales side of the business is dealt with at the Avenue de l'Opéra, and there are more than fifteen thousand retail outlets. It's a great responsibility."

' "When do you get your holiday?"

' "I won't be able to manage a holiday this summer. Maybe at Christmas. I've always thought a winter holiday in the snow would be fun. You could go away, though. Why not go home to your family for three or four weeks?" '

Did he himself recognize the pathos, indeed the tragedy, of what he was saying?

'She went away for a month. She spent a fortnight with her parents in Aix-en-Provence—her father is in practice there as an architect, then went on for another fortnight to stay with one of her sisters, the one with three children, who had rented a house at Bandol for the summer.

'I felt utterly lost, all on my own in Paris. I went on going to the Rue Réaumur to see what jobs were available, and applying for any I thought might do, but with no more success than before.

'I was beginning to realize that Chabut had been right. I would never get another job of any kind.

'I began to haunt the Place des Vosges, where he lived, not with anything particular in mind, but just in the hope of seeing him, but he, like so many others, was away on holiday, probably in Cannes, where they have a flat.'

'What were your feelings towards him?'

'I hated him with my whole being. It seemed so cruelly unjust that he should be basking in the sun, while I was looking for work, almost alone, as it seemed to me, in Paris.

'There was still enough money on top of the wardrobe for me to give my wife the equivalent of another month's salary, and still have a little over for myself.

'And after that? What was there left to do but confess the truth to my wife? I was certain she'd leave me. She's not the sort who would stay with a man who was no longer able to support her.'

'Did you still care for her?'

'I think so. I don't know.'

'And now?'

'She's become a stranger to me. It happened gradually, I think, but now I can't imagine why what she thought or didn't think should have mattered so much to me.'

'When did you see her for the last time?'

'She got back from the south at the end of August. I gave her my so-called salary. I stayed on another three weeks with her, although I knew that this time I wouldn't be able to give her anything at the end of the month.

'I decided one morning to go and not come back. I took nothing with me except the few hundred francs that were left.'

'Did you go straight to the Rue de la Grande-Truanderie?'

'So you know about that? No. I took a room in a cheap but respectable hotel near the Bastille, where there was no risk of running into my wife.'

'Was that when you started following Oscar Chabut?'

'I knew where he was likely to be at most times of the day, so I hung around the Quai de Charenton, the Avenue de l'Opéra and the Place des Vosges. I also knew that, almost every Wednesday, he went with his secretary to the Rue Fortuny.'

'What had you in mind, all this time?'

'Nothing. He was the man who had turned my life upside down, robbed me of my self-respect, and deprived me of all hope.'

'Were you armed?'

Pigou put his hand in his trouser pocket, and drew out a small, bluish, automatic pistol. He got up and laid it on the table in front of Maigret.

'I took it with me in case I should decide to kill myself.'

'Were you ever tempted to do so?'

'Often, especially at night, but I was too scared. I've always been afraid of violence, of physical pain. Chabut may have been right. Perhaps I am a coward.'

'I must interrupt you for a moment to make a telephone call. You'll see why, shortly.'

He dialled the number of the Quai des Orfèvres.

'Put me through to Inspector Lapointe, please, miss.'

Pigou opened his mouth as if to speak, but he said nothing. Madame Maigret was busy in the kitchen preparing fresh grog.

CHAPTER EIGHT

'IS THAT YOU?' asked Maigret.

'Why aren't you in bed, sir? You don't sound as if you've just woken up. There's no further news.'

'I know.'

'How can you know? Where are you speaking from?'

'From home.'

'It's three o'clock in the morning!'

'You can call off the search. Everyone can go home.'

'Have you found him?'

'He's here, opposite me. We've been having a quiet chat.'

'Did he come of his own free will?'

'Can you see me chasing him all along the Boulevard Richard-Lenoir?'

'How does he seem?'

'Fine.'

'Will you be wanting me?'

'Not immediately. But don't leave the office. Call in the patrols and let Janvier, Lucas, Torrence and Loutrie know. I'll ring you back later.'

He hung up, and waited in silence while Madame Maigret cleared away the empty glasses, and handed them full ones.

'I forgot to say, Pigou, that although we are together like this, here in my flat and not at the Quai des Orfèvres, I am still a police officer, and I reserve the right to make what use I think fit of anything you may tell me.'

'I quite understand.'

'Do you know a good lawyer?'

'I don't know any lawyers, good or bad.'

'You'll need one tomorrow, when you appear before the Examining Magistrate. I'll give you a list of names.'

'Thank you.'

Following the telephone call, there was a slight chill in the air. Both men felt a sense of strain.

'Your very good health.'

'The same to you.'

And, making a jest of it, he added:

'I daresay it will be a long time before I see another glass of grog. I'm in for a very stiff sentence, aren't I?'

'Why should you think that?'

'First of all, because he was a man of wealth and influence. And secondly, because I've no excuse to offer.'

'When did you first get the idea of killing him?'

'I don't know. First of all I had to give up my room near the Bastille, and that's when I moved to the Rue de la Grande-Truanderie. Things were very tough after that. I spent most of the night unloading vegetables in Les Halles, and didn't get to bed until the early hours of the morning. I used to cry myself to sleep. The smell was nauseating. Even the noises were sickening. I felt as if I had been exiled from the civilized world to a kind of limbo, unlike anything I had ever known.

'I still spent my days lurking in the vicinity of the Place des Vosges, the Quai de Charenton, and the Place de l'Opéra. Once or twice, I even spied on Liliane, hiding in the shadow of the trees in Montparnasse Cemetery.

'More and more often, whenever I caught sight of Chabut, I found that I was muttering to myself:

'"I'll kill him!"

'It was no more than an empty threat. I had no real intention of killing him. I was standing on the side-lines, so to speak, watching him live his life. I observed his big red car, his self-satisfied face, his beautifully cut, freshly pressed clothes.

'In contrast, I was going rapidly downhill. I had left the Rue Froidevaux, taking only the suit I was wearing. By now it was terribly creased and covered in stains. My raincoat was far too thin to keep out the cold, but I couldn't afford to buy an overcoat, not even a second-hand one.

'As it happens, I was watching the Quai de Charenton offices from a distance when Liliane went there. Presumably, she had gone first to the Avenue de l'Opéra, as I'd told her I had been transferred there.

'She was in there a long time. At one point, I saw Anne-

Marie come out into the yard for a breath of air, and I guessed what had happened.

'I wasn't jealous. It was just one more slap in the face. The way that man behaved, you'd have thought he owned the earth. Once more, I found myself muttering:

'"I'll kill him!"'

'I moved off, dragging my foot. The last thing I wanted was to be seen by my wife.'

'When did you first go to the Rue Fortuny?'

'About the end of November. By that time, I couldn't even afford a Métro ticket.'

He gave a bitter little laugh.

'It's an odd sensation, you know, not having any money in one's pocket, and knowing that never again will one be able to live like a normal human being. Most of the people one meets in Les Halles are old, but there are a few young ones, and they all have the same lost look. I have it too, haven't I?'

'No.'

'I should have, because there's no difference now between them and me. What I brooded over most was that slap in the face. He ought not to have hit me. I might have got over the things he said, wounding and humiliating though they were. But he slapped me as he would a naughty child.'

'Last Wednesday when you went to the Rue Fortuny, did you know that it was to be for the last time?'

'I wouldn't have come here, if I hadn't made up my mind to tell you everything. I didn't know I was going to kill him. That's the truth, I swear it. Believe me, I wouldn't lie to you, of all people.'

'What was your state of mind?'

'I felt I was reaching the end of my tether. I couldn't sink any lower. Sooner or later, I was bound to be picked up in a police raid, if I wasn't carried off to hospital first, suffering from exhaustion and starvation. Something was bound to happen soon.'

'What, for instance?'

'I thought of paying him back in kind. I imagined him coming out of that house with Anne-Marie. I would go up to him and raise my hand. . . .'

He shook his head.

'But, of course, it was out of the question, really. He was so much stronger than I was. I waited there till nine o'clock. I saw the light go on in the hall. He came out alone. The gun was in my pocket, but it didn't take a second to whip it out.

'I didn't really take aim. I just fired again and again, three or four times, I think, I can't remember now.'

'Four.'

'I had no thought of running away, at first. I meant to stay there and wait for the police. But then I began to think what they might do to me. I was afraid of being knocked about. So I started running towards the Métro in the Avenue de Villiers. No one gave chase. Almost before I knew it, I was back in Les Halles, and signing on as a vegetable porter. I couldn't face a whole night alone in that room.

'Well, there you are, Chief Superintendent, that's the whole story.'

'What prompted you to telephone me?'

'I don't know. I felt so isolated. I didn't think anyone would ever understand. I'd often read pieces about you in the paper. I'd always wanted to meet you, and, by that time, I'd almost made up my mind to put a bullet through my brain.

'I longed to talk to someone just once, before I died. But I was frightened the whole time, not of you, but of your men.'

'My inspectors don't knock people about.'

'I've heard it said that they do.'

'People say all sorts of things, Pigou. Have a cigarette. You're not still frightened, are you?'

'No, I telephoned you a second time, and then, almost immediately afterwards, I wrote you a letter from a café in the Boulevard du Palais. I felt very close to you. I would have liked to follow you about the streets, but you were always in a car. I had the same problem with Chabut.

'So I had to try and put myself in your place, guess where you were likely to go next, and get there before you.

'That's how I came to be waiting for you, when you went to the Quai de Charenton. I was certain that Anne-Marie would tell you about me. In fact, I can't imagine why she didn't that very first day.

'But then, the scene with Chabut took place in June, and I suppose it seemed like ancient history to her.

'I saw you in the Place des Vosges too.'

'And at the Quai des Orfèvres.'

'Yes. I didn't see any point in keeping out of sight, as, by then, it seemed inevitable that I should be caught. It wouldn't have been long before I was arrested, would it?'

'If you had stayed in Les Halles, you would almost certainly have been found and arrested tonight. By ten o'clock, it was known that you had a room in the Hotel du Cygne. From there, it was just a matter of searching all the neighbouring bistros to find you. Had you taken to drinking?'

'No.'

Most men, in similar circumstances, would have drowned their sorrows in drink.

'I intended originally to go to the Quai des Orfèvres, and ask to be taken to you. But then I thought they'd probably turn me over to just any inspector who happened to be on duty, and I probably shouldn't be allowed near you. So I came to the Boulevard Richard-Lenoir.'

'I saw you.'

'I saw you, too. I meant to come up to your flat. You were standing there in your dressing-gown, framed in the window with the light behind you. You looked enormous. All of a sudden, I took fright, and made off as fast I could. I wandered about the district for hours. I came back at least five times, but by then the lights were out in your flat.'

'Excuse me a minute.'

He dialled the number of the Quai des Orfèvres.

'Put me through to Lapointe, please. Hello! Have you sent all the men home? Is there anyone there with you?'

'Lucas is on night duty, and Janvier has just got in.'

'I want you and Janvier here as soon as possible with a car.'

'Will they take me away?' Pigou asked, when Maigret had replaced the receiver.

'I'm afraid so.'

'I quite understand. All the same, I'm nervous. It's like going to the dentist.'

He had killed a man. He had come to Maigret of his own

286

free will. Even so, it was fear that was uppermost in his mind. Fear of being beaten up and ill-treated.

He had almost forgotten that he was a murderer.

Maigret was reminded of the boy, Stiernet, who had done his grandmother to death by hitting her repeatedly with a poker, and who had as good as said:

'I didn't mean to do it.'

He subjected Pigou to a long, hard stare, as though trying to see into his innermost being. The accountant looked back at him uneasily.

'Is there anything else you want to ask me?' he said.

'I don't think so. No.'

What was the use of asking him if he was sorry for what he had done in the Rue Fortuny? Was Stiernet sorry for what he had done?

No doubt, the question would be put to him at the Assizes, and, if he answered it truthfully, there would be a murmur of disapproval in the body of the court.

There was a long silence, while Maigret drank the remains of his grog. Then they heard a car draw up, followed by the opening and shutting of a door.

He refilled and lit his pipe, more to keep himself in countenance than because he felt like smoking. Footsteps sounded on the stairs. He went to open the door. The two inspectors peered into the living-room with frank curiosity. A cloud of bluish smoke drifted across the ceiling light.

'This is Gilbert Pigou. We have had a long talk. Tomorrow, we will proceed to the official interrogation.'

The accountant looked at the two inspectors. Their appearance reassured him a little. They did not look the sort of men who would beat anyone up.

'Take him to the Quai, and see that he gets a few hours' sleep. I'll be in myself round about midday.'

Lapointe made a sign to him. He was so tired and bemused that he did not, at first, understand it. Once more Lapointe pointed to the handcuffs, as if to say:

'Shall I put them on?'

Maigret turned to Pigou.

'It's not that we don't trust you,' he murmured, 'but we

have to comply with the regulations. They will be removed as soon as you get to the Quai des Orfèvres.'

On the landing, Pigou stopped and took one last look at Maigret. The very sight of the Chief Superintendent seemed to give him courage. There were tears in his eyes.

But were they not simply tears of self-pity?

Epalinges, September 29, 1969.